HI

A Novel of Suspense

by

THOMAS HALL

PUBLISHED
BY
BRIGHTON PUBLISHING LLC
501 W. RAY ROAD
SUITE 4
CHANDLER, AZ 85225

HIDDEN

A Novel of Suspense

BY

Thomas Hall

Published
By
Brighton Publishing LLC
501 W. Ray Road
Suite 4
Chandler, AZ 85225
www.BrightonPublishing.com

Copyright © 2012

ISBN 13: 978-1-62183-129-7

ISBN 10: 1-62183-129-9

Printed in the United States of America

First Edition

Cover Design: Tom Rodriguez

DEDICATION

To friends who have left us too soon.

John Dunne, Jim Pryal, and Karl Smith

PROLOGUE

April-Present Day

STANFIELD, MASSACHUSETTS

It had been nearly two weeks since the dream had invaded Jonathan's sleep. And with the wishful thinking born of desperation, he had dared to believe it was gone for good. But as he started to drift off on this particular night, he could sense its return. It hovered around his subconscious like some sort of poltergeist waiting to unleash itself. But unlike a poltergeist, it wasn't supernatural; it was all too real, and it was back with a vengeance.

He willed himself to wake up, a futile gesture that had never worked in the past, and didn't this time. He tried to force his mind to construct some sort of mental barrier to prevent the dream from insinuating itself into his sleep. If he had been fully awake, he would have realized how foolish that effort was. Dreams can't be contained by imaginary images; they *are* imaginary images. A dam made out of mud can't prevent silt from seeping through. A shroud made out of smoke can't keep noxious vapors at bay.

But when the mind knows nothing but desperation, it resorts to foolish things. And Jonathan Allen was most assuredly desperate. He knew that once the dream gained a foothold, it would transform itself, as it always did. And for the entirety of his sleep, it would seem as real as his own flesh and blood.

The dream first began visiting Jonathan about six months ago, shortly after his wife was killed. And although most of the core aspects of the dream never changed, over the past several months a number of variations had appeared. Without question, the version he was experiencing tonight was the worst. It always left him eviscerated, as if the parts of him that could still engender hope or happiness were being physically ripped from his body.

The dream always started out innocently enough: *Jonathan and his wife, Cindy, are sitting on a beach blanket by a lake, laughing and joking about something or other. Cindy then decides to go for a swim. Jonathan stays on the blanket, preferring to read.*

After several minutes, and without warning, the sky turns the color of putty. It's as if God has taken a paintbrush and in a single stroke obliterated the blue overhead. Even more startling is the condition of the lake: There are rolling waves and whitecaps heading toward Cindy.

Jonathan calls to her with fear in his voice, but she dismisses him. "If it starts thundering and lightning, I'll come in."

"Please, Cindy. It doesn't look safe."

Cindy shakes her head. "You're such a worrywart."

"But the waves. Why are there waves?"

"I don't know, but it's fun. It feels like a Jacuzzi."

"Something's not right. Please."

Cindy slaps at the water. "All right, all right." And she starts to swim back in. But with each stroke, she seems to go backwards. Something is pulling her farther and farther out, despite the fact that she's an accomplished swimmer.

At first, Jonathan thinks she's joking. "Stop it, Cindy, this isn't funny."

"I don't know what's happening! There's some kind of undertow."

Jonathan moves closer to the water, and Cindy finally begins to make some progress. Initially, they are separated by twenty feet, then ten, then three. He grabs for her hands, but he can only touch her fingertips, and each time she slips away.

In some versions of the dream, Jonathan calls out for someone to help, but there's nobody around. But in this variation, their six-year-old son, Eric, is on the beach. "Eric, help us! Help us!"

Eric is building sand castles. He seems to hear his father, because he looks up briefly. But then he returns to the sand castles.

Jonathan tries again. "It's important, son. Please!" This time Eric stares directly at his father, but still doesn't move.

Three more times Jonathan is able to touch Cindy's hand, but each time he's unable to hold on to her. He yells his son's name again, but Eric ignores him. As Cindy starts to slip below the surface, Jonathan looks back toward the shore. Eric finally looks up and sees what's happening. He remains frozen in place, and then screams in horror.

Jonathan awoke covered in sweat. His heart was racing, and he had trouble catching his breath. In a flash of misguided emotion, his eyes darted to the other side of the bed, but of course Cindy wasn't there. That's when he knew for certain that the dream had returned. The renewed reality of her death caused his stomach to churn and his throat to constrict.

For the briefest of moments, he considered himself fortunate. After all, it had been two weeks since he'd had the dream, two weeks of relative peace. But it had also been two weeks during which the outcome of the dream couldn't change. Jonathan wasn't delusional. He knew that even if the ending of the dream was altered, Cindy would still be dead. But for some reason, he was sure that if he could somehow manage to save her in the dream, it would allow him to move on with *his* life.

He took a deep breath and repeated the regimen he always followed when his son was part of the dream. He went to Eric's room and stood in the doorway. As Jonathan watched his son sleep, he tried for the hundredth time to make sense of what was happening.

Other than the fact that Cindy had died, nothing in the dream had actually occurred. There was no lake, no drowning. Jonathan hadn't even been present when Cindy was killed. Initially, the police assumed that she was the victim of a hit-and-run driver while she was jogging in a nature preserve a short distance from their home. But the autopsy results suggested that she may have been beaten before she was run over.

Jonathan had been questioned extensively in the first few days following Cindy's death. But nothing was uncovered to suggest he was involved in any way—He was at his law office at the time of the killing; there was no damage to his car; there was no large insurance policy; and from all accounts he and his wife had enjoyed a very good marriage. Without any obvious motive, the police began to look elsewhere.

One promising lead that they pursued came from a man who was walking his dog near the nature preserve. He claimed to have seen a silver, late-model luxury car—"Infiniti, Lexus, something like that"— with Rhode Island plates speeding away around the time Cindy was killed. But nothing came of the lead, and eventually Cindy's death became a cold case.

Jonathan began seeing a therapist a few weeks after his wife was killed. He had never liked the idea of sharing his innermost feelings with anyone; he had reserved that for Cindy. But she was gone, and he was a total wreck. Initially, the therapy didn't go well, but gradually a level of trust was formed, and he began to make progress. Unfortunately, during the months that it took for that to happen, the quality of Jonathan's life had further deteriorated. He had cut way back on his law practice. He had neglected himself, but more disturbingly, he had neglected his son—not social-services-intervention type of neglect. But other than providing for his son's basic needs, Jonathan hadn't been there for him.

Jonathan had heard it described in adult relationships as being "emotionally unavailable." He had always considered that description to be pretentious psychobabble. But when Eric's school suggested that he have an evaluation to try to discover what could be done to help him cope with the loss of his mother—Eric had become extremely withdrawn and rarely spoke—then the description made perfect sense.

Jonathan realized that he couldn't just snap his fingers and be ready to live again. But he also realized that, for the sake of his son, he had to start taking some baby steps to begin to reconstruct his life. He also thought there might be an additional benefit: Maybe those steps would make the dream disappear.

As it turned out, it did—Jonathan had the dream only once more. Of course, he had no way of knowing after that last time, it was gone for good. He just accepted each day without it as a gift.

But if he had been given a choice, he might have opted to continue to have the dream, rather than experience the unspeakable horror that filled the void left by its departure—especially since this new nightmare was always with him, even in the daylight.

CHAPTER ONE

Ten Months Earlier—June 30

PROVIDENCE, RHODE ISLAND

Tony Sarno stood across the street from Lucy's Bar and Grill in an older section of the city. In actuality, the name of the bar was Lucky's. But a few years back, the "k" in the bright green neon sign above the door had burned out—not unlike most of the regulars who inhabited the place. None of them cared that the sign now read Lucy's. Most of them hadn't even noticed.

Although Tony had quit school in the ninth grade and hadn't paid much attention when he was there, the irony of the bar's actual name wasn't lost on him—*Yeah, like the low-lifes and hookers inside sure are lucky.* But what was lost on him was the hypocrisy inherent in the fact that he was about to join them. If it had been brought to his attention, he would have dismissed it—*I'm not like those losers. I just do business with them.*

Despite his lack of a formal education, Tony was quite intelligent, at least when it came to the latest technology. Computers had always made much more sense to him than people. He understood them intuitively, as if circuitry were part of his DNA. Plus, computers didn't disappoint you the way people did. Computers were consistent. They didn't promise something and then not deliver. They weren't nice to you one day and then pretend you didn't exist the next.

Tony continued to peer across the street, an uneasiness preventing him from taking the few steps required to enter the bar. He had the feeling that someone was watching him. That was why he had circled around, and eventually parked his car a few blocks away, and why he wasn't already in the bar having a drink.

He surveyed the dirt and gravel parking lot. None of the cars was newer than six years old, another reason he hadn't wanted to park his new Lexus there. His eyes traveled up and down the street, but he saw nothing out of the ordinary. Still, he didn't move. He trusted his instincts, and they were telling him something wasn't right.

1

He focused briefly on the entrance to the bar, and then raised his eyes to take in the three floors above it. Technically, those three floors comprised the Regal Hotel and Apartments. If the exterior of Lucky's could be described as dilapidated, the exterior of the Regal would have required major renovations to reach that threshold.

Until ten years ago, it had been known as the Regal Hotel. But then the new owner had decided to create twelve apartments from the twenty-four hotel rooms on the top two floors, adding modern kitchens and high-end decorations. He left the twelve hotel rooms on the first floor pretty much as they were when the Regal was built in the late 1940s.

The dichotomy was purposeful. All of the apartments were designed for "working girls." They could live there and conduct business there. It gave new meaning to the phrase "working out of your home." By keeping the exterior of the building an eyesore, there was little chance that anyone would stumble across the hotel and actually want to stay there. On occasion, the hotel did have individuals spend a night or two. But none of them would fall into the category of upstanding citizens who might be inclined to question all the comings and goings.

Despite numerous attempts by media investigative teams to discover the true identity of the Regal's owner, they were unsuccessful. There was little doubt that he was "connected;" anybody running the kind of operation the authorities suspected was going on there would have to be. Of course, being "connected" in this day and age was quite different from what it had been thirty or forty years ago. Now, it might mean Asians, or Russians, or even more likely, some multi-ethnic conglomeration.

And what made things even more difficult for law enforcement was that, unlike the old days of organized crime, twenty-first century criminals weren't "organized" in the same way. There was no hierarchy; it wasn't possible to pull at one errant thread and expect the whole sweater to unravel. This new breed simply agreed to divide the city and divide the types of illegal activities they wanted to be involved with. After that, they rarely crossed paths. They had learned from the mistakes of their forefathers in crime; power struggles were bad for business.

And while law enforcement personnel hadn't been able to discover who owned the Regal either, what the owner had been able to pull off was acknowledged as quite impressive. That acknowledgement occurred only behind closed doors, however.

During the late 1970s, the prostitution problem in Rhode Island cities had reached epidemic proportions. Streetwalkers seemed to inhabit every corner. A few years later, the state legislature finally decided to do something about it. A new law was passed that was intended to be much tougher than anything previously on the books. Much to the legislature's chagrin, however, it didn't work out that way. In their rush to strengthen the law addressing street corner solicitation, the lawmakers actually gave tacit *approval* to prostitution—as long as it was conducted indoors.

Initially, the future owner of the Regal made sure all of his girls plied their trade indoors. And then ten years ago, shortly after he acquired the Regal, he converted the top two floors into apartments for his best "talent." It became the East Coast version of Nevada, and many wealthy high rollers took advantage of the services. Rhode Island might be small, but Boston is only forty miles from Providence. Business was booming.

Finally, a year ago, the legislature got around to closing the loophole in the law. Initially, that didn't deter the Regal's owner from keeping his girls working out of their apartments. After all, it was still difficult to make solicitation charges stick when the women were "performing" in their own homes. However, the new law did deter many of the wealthy Johns from continuing to partake. It forced the owner to scale back. A number of the apartments were now vacant. With the substantial loss in revenue, the owner realized it was time to expand into other business ventures. That's when Tony Sarno was brought on board.

Tony was recruited by a man called Runner—no actual first name, and no last name. Runner served as the intermediary between Tony and his employer. And despite the fact that Tony never met or talked directly to the man in charge, it didn't require a high school diploma to figure out the type of person he was working for, and therefore, how careful he had to be.

Whether that knowledge was fueling his paranoia tonight, Tony didn't know. Nevertheless, he had remained in the same position for nearly ten minutes. He still had some trepidation as he continued to look around, but nothing struck him as out of place. He did another survey of the street, eventually focusing on the hotel's entrance. He rarely used that door, even if one of the apartments was his ultimate destination. Instead, he preferred to go into Lucky's, have a couple of drinks, and then use the concealed stairway in the back that led to the third floor of the hotel. Most times when he concluded his business, however, he would exit through the rear door of the Regal, especially if he had a "package" that

3

he didn't want to carry through Lucky's.

Eventually, with one more perusal of the street, Tony crossed over to the bar. He ordered a beer, chatted with the bartender, and as casually as possible surveyed the darkened corners of Lucky's. He was still early for his appointment, so he ordered another beer, and then moved to a table so he could watch the door. After another fifteen minutes, he got up and headed into the back toward the men's room. He stopped outside a door labeled "Storage," punched in a code on the keypad, and quickly went inside.

Once inside, he went to another door on the left, opened it and started the climb to the third floor. When he reached the top of the stairs, he opened the door a crack, saw nobody in the hallway, exited, and quietly closed the door behind him. The door had a sign on it that read "Electrical Room," but of course, it was no such thing. The sign on the door, however, as well as the keypad on the outside, prevented anyone from thinking otherwise.

Tony walked slowly down the hallway toward room thirty-one. The young woman who lived and "worked" there had affixed a two-sided door decoration just above the peephole. On one side was a bucolic summer scene, depicting a meadow filled with lavender. The other side had a pineapple on it with the word "Welcome" superimposed. If the summer scene was displayed, it was a signal that the woman had a customer. Tony was a little surprised, but then realized that he was still quite early. Plus, this was an unusual time for him to come, anyway. It just happened that he had the night off from his real job and had decided to conduct some business while he had the opportunity.

Tony had no way of knowing how long the customer was going to be, and he would just as soon not be seen hanging around. So he decided to go back to the "Electrical Room" and wait until he heard some noise in the hallway, signaling that the customer was leaving.

As he walked back in the other direction, he took out his cell phone to check his e-mail. He opened his everyday account, bypassing his other protected accounts, and started to scroll through the list. As his search was about halfway completed, he heard the "ding" of the elevator a few yards behind him. He rushed to try to punch in the code on the keypad, but as he did, he dropped his phone. Realizing he didn't have enough time to retrieve it and open the door, he moved in the other direction toward the actual interior staircase.

Before he got there, the elevator door opened and two uniformed

4

police officers stepped out. At the same time, the door to apartment thirty-one opened, and a man appeared. He called to the two officers, "In here. Take her into custody." The man then saw Tony. "Who's that guy?"

The older and heavier of the two policemen responded, "Don't know, detective."

"Well, take him in, too. I don't think he's here to deliver Girl Scout cookies. Any luck on the other floor?"

"Yeah," replied the officer. "We got two more lovelies going downtown."

The detective looked annoyed. "All right. I was hoping for more, but okay."

Tony listened to this exchange, but decided to keep his mouth shut. It wasn't possible to pick up his phone without being seen, so he tried to kick it against the wall where it would be less noticeable. But the younger cop saw what he was doing. "Hey, move away from the wall, and keep your hands where I can see them."

As the younger cop approached, he started the verbal routine. "Now, put your hands behind your back. You're under arrest for solicitation. You have the right to remain silent…"

Although he had done plenty of illegal things, Tony had never been convicted of anything as an adult. But he had been arrested a number of times, so he was well aware of the remainder of the cop's recitation. When the cop finished, he asked Tony, "Is that your phone?"

Tony wasn't sure which answer would cause him the least amount of trouble. He certainly wasn't worried about the solicitation charges; he couldn't imagine that they would hold up. But what about his phone? He was reasonably sure that anything in his protected accounts was sufficiently encrypted. But just before the elevator had opened, had he imagined it, or was there something in his everyday account that shouldn't have been there?

The cop interrupted Tony's thoughts. "Why don't I just take it, and we'll figure it out later? Seeing that it wasn't in your possession, we can pretty much do whatever we want with it."

Tony spent the night in jail. It was easy for the police to jam up almost anybody for one night—delay booking, lose paperwork, wait for shifts to change. In his case, Tony figured the police were more pissed off than anything else. They had evidently set up a sting and had only brought in three women—no Johns, unless you counted Tony. And while the police suspected Tony was about to engage the services of a prostitute, they probably weren't going to be able to prove it. Tony understood that he was bearing the brunt of their frustration. He could live with that. He just hoped his night in jail had nothing to do with his cell phone.

A part of Tony was actually pleased that the police thought he was going to visit a high-priced hooker. It painted him as a player, someone who could afford the best. But more importantly, if they thought he was visiting one of the girls, they wouldn't be looking at the real reason he had been there.

In reality, however, Tony wasn't allowed anywhere near the "merchandise" in the Regal. Word had been passed to him through Runner: "Don't go mixing business with pleasure. It's a dangerous combination." Tony resented his employer's edict, but also understood the implied threat. So instead, he began visiting the less "talented" girls in his employer's stable. Tony evidently had misunderstood that the edict included those girls as well. Any girl who worked for Tony's employer was off-limits. Tony suspected that the only reason he was still walking around without a limp, or still walking around at all, was because Runner hadn't made the parameters of the edict clear. It was an honest mistake— "honest" being an adjective rarely used in describing anything having to do with his employer's enterprises. Regardless, Tony wondered whether Runner had paid a price for his lack of clarity. Tony had no idea what that might have been, and certainly didn't ask.

Tony's employer didn't quite have a monopoly on the prostitution trade in Providence, but it was close. Tony was therefore relegated to visiting hookers who were very low on the food chain—crack heads or worse. Over the last several months, his resentment had grown more pronounced, and there was no one to take it out on but the girls. He started getting rough with them, leaving bruises and bloody lips. He hated them for what they were, and he hated that he kept going back to them. He tried to stop, but his physical desires outweighed any rational assessment of what was happening. He told himself that if he had been allowed to go to any of the girls at the Regal, or got a girlfriend, things would be different. Neither was true. And somewhere inside himself, Tony knew that. What he didn't know was that he had started a downward spiral, and it wasn't about to let up anytime soon.

Shortly after Tony was brought to the police station, he had decided that the less he said the better. He didn't want to take the chance that he might inadvertently disclose something he shouldn't. When the detective questioned him, Tony gave his answers in a clipped and non-committal manner, as if he were of very limited intelligence.

After about a half hour of questioning Tony finally asked, "Aren't I supposed to have one of those lawyers, like on TV?"

The detective responded sarcastically, "You don't have your own lawyer, Tony? That's hard to believe."

Tony pretended not to understand the sarcasm. "No, I don't. But aren't you guys supposed to give me one?"

The detective's eyes narrowed. "You mean a public defender?" he asked.

"I guess." Tony replied innocently.

"Yeah, we'll get right on that." The detective glanced at his watch. "Uh, oh, it looks like it's too late. You'll have to wait until the morning."

Tony knew that wasn't true, but he stayed in character. "So, I have to stay here tonight?"

The detective feigned shock. "What's the matter, you don't like us?"

Tony paused before he replied, "I don't think I want to talk anymore."

"Anymore?" the detective countered. "You've barely said two words to us, like what you were doing at the Regal."

"I did tell you that," Tony replied. I was visiting a friend."

"But you can't remember her name?" the detective pressed. "Did you pay this friend to have sex with you?"

Tony shook his head. "No, I told you that. I don't want to tell you her name because I don't want her to get in trouble."

The detective came right back at him. "Why would she get in trouble if she hasn't done anything wrong?"

Tony slipped out of character and changed his tone slightly. "I'm in trouble, and I didn't do anything wrong."

The detective stared at Tony, trying to decide if he was being played or not. Eventually, he said, "Okay, hotshot, we'll leave it at that. You'll get your lawyer in the morning."

To confuse the detective even further, Tony said, "Thank you, detective. I appreciate that."

In truth, Tony wasn't eligible for a public defender. He had more money stashed away than the detective made in two or three years. But that money was hidden. Even the Lexus wasn't listed in Tony's name. With his computer skills, it only took a few keystrokes to make it appear that he was leasing the car. Of course, in reality, the leasing company didn't exist. Tony had paid cash for the Lexus.

Tony was confident that no matter how inept the public defender might be, the solicitation charges would be dropped. It was a bit of a gamble, but if he were to hire his own attorney, it might raise some red flags about his finances, and he didn't want that.

CHAPTER TWO

The public defender arrived at a little after nine the next morning. He looked about twelve, but was actually twenty-six; five years younger than Tony.

"Hi, I'm Aaron Phillips. Sorry I'm late. I stopped to check where you were on the arraignment list. The hearings start at ten, but you're last on the list, so I'm not sure when they'll get to you. It's kind of odd that you're last. The women who were brought in with you are up first."

Tony shrugged. "Doesn't matter."

"So, Mr. Sarno, I read the charges and your statement, as brief as it was. But could you tell me in your own words what happened?"

Tony was about to suggest that the lawyer call him by his first name, but then realized that he liked the show of respect, so he didn't correct him. Tony went through the events of the previous night, leaving out how he had entered the Regal and his real reason for being there. The public defender didn't ask, assuming that it was for the same reason that the police believed it to be. Tony debated whether to mention his cell phone, but decided against it.

After he finished, the lawyer asked again, "And you never went into any of the apartments? Never had any money visible? Never even came in contact with any of the women there?"

Tony nodded. "That's right."

"This is ridiculous. Why the hell did they even arrest you?"

Tony's voice suddenly took on a harsher tone. "Because they're fucking morons," he retorted.

This was the first time that the public defender had seen anything resembling anger from his client. The lawyer noted that Tony spoke with a detachment that suggested he was angry at the whole world, not necessarily at the police who had arrested him. In some ways, the lawyer found that more disturbing than if Tony had slammed his fist into the table.

9

He stared briefly at Tony. Since he still wasn't sure what he was dealing with, he threw out an innocuous caution. "That may be true, but I would advise against saying that in court."

Tony's expression didn't change. "Yeah, I know. Not a problem."

Aaron Phillips looked down at his paperwork. "We've got some time before the hearing. I should get some information from you in case this goes forward."

Tony looked surprised. "I thought you said this whole thing was bogus."

"It is," replied Phillips. "But it's still somewhat unusual for the judge to dismiss a case outright at an arraignment."

Tony didn't like what he was hearing, but he stifled his anger. "What kind of information do you need?"

"I need to be able to show that you're not a flight risk; that you'll show up for court when you're supposed to, information like that."

"Okay," Tony sighed impatiently. "What do you want to know?"

Phillips took out a pen and got ready to write. "Where do you live?"

"I have an apartment in Cranston."

"How long have you lived there?" Phillips asked.

"Five years."

The lawyer nodded as he took notes. "That's good. Do you have a job?"

"Yeah, I work at the Stateline Mall."

"In Massachusetts, right? Just over the border in Stanfield?"

Tony nodded.

"How long have you worked there?"

Tony thought. "Two and half, three years."

"And what do you do there?" Phillips persisted.

"I'm the night watchman."

Phillips looked up. "But you didn't work last night."

"No," Tony replied. "I had the night off."

The question and answer routine went on for another twenty minutes, and then it was time to go across the street to the courthouse. By the time they finally got to Tony's case, the courtroom was nearly empty. Other than the assistant district attorney, Tony, and his lawyer, there were only a couple of other onlookers.

After the charges were read and Tony pleaded not guilty, the ADA gave a somewhat grandiose speech that lasted much longer than the occasion called for, periodically glancing at the rear doors of the courtroom, obviously expecting someone to walk through them. The judge recognized that something was going on, but was not sure what. He interrupted her ramblings. "Is there a reason that we're being treated to this lecture on the evils of prostitution? This is about to challenge the record for the longest arraignment I've ever presided over. Could we move it along, Ms. Lopez?"

"Sorry, Your Honor. I just thought you should be aware of the efforts being made by the police to put a dent in the prostitution problem by arresting the Johns as well as the women involved."

"Yes. I got that the first three times you said it." Just as the judge finished speaking, the rear courtroom doors opened and a young man headed for the ADA and handed her a folder. The judge then continued. "I trust that what's in that folder was the reason for your delaying tactics, Ms. Lopez. Can we get on with it now?"

The ADA faltered. "I wouldn't call it delaying ..." she began.

"Ms. Lopez, you're trying my patience. I'm going to hear from Mr. Phillips now. If you have anything else to say, you'll have to wait for him to finish."

The public defender stood up and addressed the judge. "Thank you, Your Honor. I'm a little confused. I have no idea why my client was even arrested. He was not in the company of another person. He did not exchange money with anybody. He was walking in a hallway when he was put in handcuffs. Last time I checked, none of that is illegal."

"I tend to agree." The judge turned slightly in his chair to face the ADA. "Ms. Lopez, perhaps you can shed some light on that."

The ADA appeared to be considering something, and couldn't decide how to proceed. The judge prompted her. "Ms. Lopez, I'm waiting."

After another moment she finally responded, "Information just came to us that Mr. Sarno placed a phone call to one of the women who was also arrested just a few hours before he was taken into custody."

The public defender interjected. "That's not illegal, either."

"He's correct, Ms. Lopez," the judge acknowledged wearily. "Anything else to add?"

The ADA could sense that the judge was about to dismiss the case, and she couldn't blame him. Although she really wasn't ready to move on the other situation, she decided she didn't have a choice. "I think the people would like to add to the charges."

The judge said, "You think, or you do?"

"We do, Your Honor. We'd like to add the charge of possession of child pornography."

The judge's eyebrows shot up as he looked over at Tony and then back to the ADA. "Are these new charges related to the original solicitation charge?"

The ADA replied, a little defensively, "To some degree, yes; the images were found on Mr. Sarno's phone when he was arrested."

"You're kidding, right, Ms. Lopez?" The judge paused. "That's not how these things work, and you know it. Let's try to do this by the book, shall we?"

"Yes, Your Honor."

While this exchange was transpiring, Tony stood mute, although his stomach started to clench. Aaron Phillips turned briefly to look at Tony, and then turned back to the judge. "Your Honor."

The judge held up his hand. "No need, counselor. I'm going to do your work for you." He addressed the ADA again. "This is a little unorthodox, Ms. Lopez, but I'd like to know what your intentions are before we proceed any further."

Lopez feigned confusion. "I'm not sure I understand," she replied.

"I think you do, but I'll state it another way. What are you trying to accomplish here?" The judge paused. "Think carefully before you answer. I won't look favorably upon any deception."

The ADA gathered herself and decided to go with the truth. It was obvious that the judge was not going to accept anything else. "We just discovered some disturbing images on Mr. Sarno's phone, and intend to file charges against him for the possession of child pornography."

"And you thought it was okay to just slip that charge in during an arraignment for a totally separate charge?"

"We only just found the images."

"So what?" said the judge. "That doesn't allow you to deny Mr. Sarno due process. This arraignment hearing is for the charge of solicitation, and unless additional charges are related to the original, you can't add them on. We're not having a two-for-one special today. Are you telling me you weren't aware of the law in that regard?"

The ADA remained silent for a moment, and then said, "I believed there was a link, because the images on his cell phone were present when Mr. Sarno was arrested on the other charge."

It was obvious from the judge's expression that he wasn't buying that explanation for a minute, but he also wasn't going to let Tony skate on a possible felony. "Okay, here's what's going to happen. I'm going to dismiss the solicitation charge against Mr. Sarno and release him. But before I do, I want to make it clear that if he's taken into custody again sometime today, and charged with another crime, the arraignment hearing will be held tomorrow morning at ten o'clock. I don't want any stalling tactics. We're coming up against the Fourth of July weekend, and I'm not going to have Mr. Sarno's rights trampled on for the next several days. Do we understand each other, Ms. Lopez?"

"Yes, Your Honor."

"Good," the judge responded. "Because if you try to do anything differently from the way I've outlined it, you'll be in contempt." He turned toward Tony. "Mr. Sarno, the charges against you for solicitation are dismissed. You're free to go."

As the judge started to rise, Tony's lawyer spoke up. "Your Honor, if I may?"

The judge straightened for a moment, but then sat back down. "Go ahead," he sighed.

"First of all, on behalf of my client, thank you." The judge nodded as the public defender continued. "I'm not sure what the assistant district attorney's intentions are, but I wanted to advise the court that this afternoon a number of us from the regional office have a pre-trial hearing, which will undoubtedly continue into tomorrow. I'm not sure who would be able to represent Mr. Sarno, should new charges be filed."

The judge frowned. "You're telling me there's no one available?"

13

"As you probably know, Your Honor, with the re-organization, there are only five public defenders currently working in our office. That will change in a few days, once the new fiscal year begins. But right now …" Phillips' voice trailed off.

The judge looked none too pleased. "I've ordered Ms. Lopez to be here tomorrow morning if she files any new charges. I'm ordering that someone from the Office of the Public Defender be available to meet and represent Mr. Sarno within an hour of any new charges being filed. What's good for the goose is good for the gander. Got it?"

Phillips nodded. "Yes, Your Honor."

The judge softened his tone slightly. "I know you're not in charge, but make sure my message gets to your boss. Is there anything else?"

Phillips shook his head slightly. "No, Your Honor."

While this exchange was going on, Tony was only half listening. Inside he was seething—that stupid bastard, Gleeson. *I told him over and over again to send the pictures to the protected e-mail account. There's no way the police could have gotten into that account. He had to have sent them to the regular one. That must have been what I thought I saw just before I dropped the phone. Now I'm fucked!*

Tony was still lost in thought and didn't hear his lawyer speaking to him until he repeated his words.

"We dodged a bullet with the solicitation complaint, but it sounds like they're going to come after you on these new charges. I'll walk out with you in case they're waiting for you." He paused. "What's the story on your phone?"

"I dropped it."

Phillips' expression remained neutral. "It could be tricky, then. Even if you're in possession of it, and it's in plain sight, the police might have been able to look at it. But if it wasn't in your possession, they've got a lot more latitude."

Tony wasn't about to share too much more information with this guy. He'd probably never even see him again. But he did throw out an idea that he'd been thinking about since he realized what Gleeson had done. "I never opened any e-mail that had child pornography on it. And even if I did, how am I supposed to control what somebody sends me?"

Phillips stared at Tony, not necessarily believing that he was innocent, but acknowledging to himself that Tony had made a valid point. "If you get arrested, make sure you tell your new lawyer what you just said to me. That's certainly something to work with."

The public defender opened the back door of the courtroom and peeked out. There was no one in the corridor. He held the door for Tony and said, "So far, so good."

But after about fifty feet, two uniformed policemen came out of a side office with the ADA and stood in front of Tony. The taller of the cops said, "Anthony Sarno, place your hands behind your back. You're under arrest for possession of child pornography. You have the right to remain silent …"

While the cop continued the Miranda warning, Aaron Phillips spoke to his client. "Just go quietly, and don't say anything. Somebody will be there within the hour. I'll make sure of it."

Tony nodded, barely containing his anger. Both cops sensed that Tony could explode at any moment. They were right, but once again, his anger wasn't directed at them.

God damn Gleeson! He's a dead man. And then his emotions shifted; his anger gave way to something else. I've got to contact Runner, so he can get the word out to the boss that this wasn't my fault.

In legal circles, the Rhode Island Public Defender office (RIPD) was considered among the most progressive in the country.

In medical parlance, its approach would be termed holistic. A number of years ago, those in charge of the office recognized that, for many of their clients, simply providing legal representation wasn't enough. With that in mind, they began hiring social workers, investigators, and community outreach personnel to assist those they represented, especially if their legal entanglements were alcohol-or drug-related.

One additional component of these progressive efforts was the recruitment of newly certified members of the Rhode Island Bar to volunteer to take on a few cases a year. This volunteer program helped prevent the RIPD office from becoming overwhelmed. It also gave new lawyers some experience, while providing a built-in support system. One other benefit was that a number of these lawyers—after volunteering with the RIPD—decided that's where they wanted to start their careers.

The typical demographics of those who volunteered didn't apply to Jerry Hanson, other than he was a newly certified member of the Rhode Island Bar. He was thirty-six, and had practiced law for eleven years in a one-man office, exclusively in Massachusetts. But at the beginning of the year, with the proximity of his office to the Rhode Island border, he decided to try to expand his potential client base by seeking admittance to the Rhode Island Bar.

It was a relatively easy process, since he was already a practicing lawyer in Massachusetts: sit for an essay exam in February, pay $500, and then wait for the results. Jerry received notification in April that he had passed, and everything was in order. Included with the letter welcoming him to the Rhode Island legal community was a form asking if he wanted to participate in the RIPD volunteer program.

He was reluctant at first, but then figured, why not? It would instantly raise his profile in Rhode Island, and it might result in some business, especially from those who were found to be ineligible for a public defender.

Jerry hadn't thought about the volunteer program for months. So when the paralegal from the RIPD office called, it took Jerry a moment to put it into context.

After the young woman again identified herself, and repeated where she was from, it finally started to register. "Mr. Hanson, as I said I'm from the East Providence Public Defender's office. I was asked to contact you because you're on our list of volunteers. I'm aware that this is short notice, but we're in need of your services as soon as possible. There was a bit of a snafu in court this morning, and the judge ordered representation for one of our clients within an hour of his arrest. Everyone in this office, as well as the Providence office, is tied up with other matters. And frankly, even though you're in Massachusetts, you're closer than anyone else."

Jerry's initial reaction was that he didn't want any part of this. He didn't like the idea that he would be taking on a case that he knew nothing about. In private practice, he could pick and choose whether he wanted to represent someone. This was different—a pig in a poke. But he also knew it wouldn't look good if he asked questions, didn't like what he heard, and then tried to weasel out of it. Plus, the truth was, he didn't have any cases pressing at the moment. With some serious reservations he eventually said, "I'll have to juggle some things around, but yeah, I can do it."

The young woman sounded relieved. "That's great. Thank you so much."

After Jerry got all the pertinent information, he asked the question he had wanted to ask initially. "What are the charges?"

"We don't have anything in writing yet, but my understanding is that there was an initial charge for solicitation, but that was dropped. I believe the new charges are for possession of child pornography."

Jerry closed his eyes and didn't speak for a moment. All he could think of was that this was exactly the kind of case he avoided in his private practice—defending scum bags. He had no illusions that all of his clients were innocent, but when it came to charges like child pornography or worse, he just wouldn't take them on. He finally found his voice, trying hard at keeping his disappointment from coming across. "Okay, I think I have everything I need. I'll be leaving shortly."

The woman thanked him and added, "You have our number, if you need anything else. Goodbye."

Jerry's tried not to allow his displeasure to come through. "Bye."

Shortly after Jerry put down the phone and prepared to head to Providence, his regret at saying 'yes' began to intensify. This had the potential to be a nightmare. What if it went to trial? That could tie him up for months. He thought he remembered a provision in the volunteer program that compensated the volunteering attorney for extended service. But he was sure any compensation would be minimal. And in reality, his discomfort wasn't about the money; it was about the person he might be representing and what he had done.

As a defense attorney, he had taken an oath to provide the best defense possible for his clients. And for the most part, he bought into that. It was the only way for the legal system to work properly. And overall, he accepted the fact that sometimes guilty individuals got off on technicalities. And you didn't throw out the whole system because it wasn't perfect.

But he had no idea how he'd react if he had to defend someone he knew was guilty, not of something like public intoxication, or even solicitation, but anything involving the exploitation of children.

Evidently, he said to himself, *I may be about to find out.*

He arrived at the East Providence police station about fifteen minutes after he left his office. He was brought to an interrogation room where Tony was being questioned. Before Jerry went into the room, he asked, "Does this room have a two-way mirror?"

The officer responded, "Yes."

Jerry stepped back. "I'd like to talk with my client someplace that doesn't," he said.

The officer gave Jerry a look that suggested he couldn't understand how defense attorneys did what they did. Jerry assessed the officer's expression, and thought to himself, *Welcome to the club.*

There was a hint of sarcasm in the officer's voice when he replied, "I'll see what I can do."

A few minutes later, a different officer asked Jerry to follow him down a short corridor. He then showed him into a small room with a table and a couple of chairs. "We'll bring your client here in a moment."

"Thank you."

Five minutes later, Tony Sarno was ushered into the small room. Jerry Hanson considered himself an astute judge of character. He was usually able to take the measure of a person almost immediately. As soon as he saw Tony, his stomach dropped, and once again he wondered what he had gotten himself into.

CHAPTER THREE

Jerry continued to assess his new client as he sat across from him in the small interrogation room. Tony returned the stare. Most disturbing to Jerry was what he thought he saw behind Tony's eyes. It was something that he had seen before in other clients, something that made them potentially explosive or unstable, or both. There had only been a few of those situations, but they were memorable for all the wrong reasons.

What was especially frightening about what seemed to be behind Tony's eyes was that it didn't appear to be fully formed yet. It was as if it were waiting for some additional sense of being wronged, legitimate or not, and then it would manifest itself in some violent outburst, like an overworked steam pipe gasket.

Jerry finally spoke in the calmest voice he could conjure up. "Hello, Mr. Sarno, I'm Jerry Hanson."

Before he could continue, Tony interrupted. "Are you the public defender?"

"No, not exactly. Actually, I'm in private practice, but …"

Tony interrupted again. "I can't afford my own attorney."

"This won't cost you anything," Jerry assured him. "I'm part of a volunteer program sponsored by the Public Defender's office."

Tony took a moment to process this, and as he was doing so, the rage Jerry had sensed a moment ago seemed to lessen slightly. "Okay." A pause. He liked the idea that he had a private attorney. It showed respect. "You can call me Tony."

The attempt at familiarity made Jerry cringe. "All right …Tony. I'll tell you what I know so far, and you can tell me if it's correct."

Tony nodded. "Okay."

"You're being charged with possession of child pornography because of images found on your cell phone."

"That's right, except they told me the pictures were attached to an e-mail sent to me. They weren't actually on my phone."

Jerry looked up from the papers he was holding. "That's a very good distinction," he responded. "You seem to know your way around this kind of technology."

Tony's voice had a sense of pride in it when he responded. "Yeah, I do all right with it."

Jerry decided to ask a question that cut to the chase, although it was dangerously close to the question that he never asked his clients: "Did you do it?" Instead, he asked, "How did those pictures get on your e-mail account?"

Tony's shrug was almost imperceptible. He then gave a response that didn't actually answer the question, but was technically the truth. "I never asked anyone to send pictures to that e-mail account." He was careful to glide over the word 'that,' so it could easily have been heard as 'the.' And while Tony was aware that any conversation he had with his lawyer was privileged, he decided not to tell him anything incriminating. He was prepared, however, to bend the truth into any contorted state that didn't reflect badly on him.

As Jerry was listening, he again thought he perceived Tony's anger slip a notch. But with that as his focus, he missed the nuances in Tony's response. Before Jerry could follow up with another question, Tony said, "I get twenty or thirty e-mails a day. A lot of people have my address. Just from work alone, there are fifty or sixty."

"What do you mean?"

"I'm a night watchman at the Stateline Mall."

Jerry scribbled some notes. "Right."

Tony continued. "Well, sometimes, if one of the stores is getting a shipment after hours or someone forgets something, they e-mail me and I open up the store for them. All the store managers have my e-mail address."

Jerry felt as if he was not getting the whole story, but Tony was making a plausible case for the pictures having been sent accidentally, or without him requesting them. Tony saw the initial skepticism in Jerry's expression and said, "Can I show you something? Do you have your phone on you?"

Jerry hesitated. "Yeah, why?"

"I can show you that there's nothing like those pictures in my e-mail history."

Jerry wondered if it was okay to hand over his phone to his client. While he was wrestling with that decision he said, "The history only goes back a month or so, doesn't it?"

That note of pride returned to Tony's voice. "You can go back further, if you know how to do it."

Jerry shook his head. "That could help your case, but I'm sure the police are going to say it doesn't matter. It's what they found now."

At the mention of the police, Jerry sensed another shift in Tony's demeanor. It didn't appear to be anger, more like contempt.

"I understand that," he retorted. "But like I told the other lawyer, how am I supposed to control what people send me?"

Jerry didn't say anything, so Tony continued. "Can I at least show you what I'm talking about? You can even check out the pictures that I was sent. I haven't seen them, and I don't want to."

This last comment surprised Jerry. If Tony really got his jollies from looking at child porn, wouldn't he want to see to see the pictures, even on the pretense of viewing what he got arrested for?

As he was mulling that over, another idea popped into Jerry's head. "You can use my phone in a minute. But I need to ask you a question first. I have no doubt that the police are going to be able to get a search warrant for your home computer, and maybe for your whole apartment as well. And what about work; do you have a computer at work?"

"Yeah, I do." Tony knew where this was going, but he had always been very careful with anything that could possibly trip him up—Gleeson notwithstanding. And that hadn't been his fault, anyway. "They won't find anything, because there's nothing there. Never was. They can check the history on both computers and they won't find a thing."

"You're sure?" Jerry asked the question knowing full well it might upset Tony. But that wasn't the case. Instead, Jerry detected a smugness emanating from Tony that he was not sure how to interpret.

Was it possible that this guy was telling the truth? When he first laid eyes on him, he wouldn't have believed it. But maybe he was pissed off for a reason. Plus, the sickos who looked at child porn always had a stash someplace. They never took just one peek and then chucked the pictures out. So either this guy was telling the truth, or something else was going on. But he had no idea what that might be.

Tony seemed to read Jerry's mind about a possible stash. "And they won't find anything hidden in my apartment either."

Jerry said the only thing he could. "Okay, this is all good."

Tony was very pleased with himself. He had manipulated the truth, and his new lawyer seemed to be buying it. In addition, the guy appeared to be more than competent. Tony started to entertain the notion that he might walk away from this. Of course, even if he did, he'd have a lot of cleaning up to do—first with Runner and their employer, and then with Gleeson. But that one he was looking forward to.

He mentally patted himself on the back for devising the plan to get the night watchman's job, with all the perks it afforded him. One of the anchor stores at the Stateline Mall was The Computer Supermarket. Even if someone had seen him in there at three o'clock in the morning, it wouldn't have seemed suspicious. After all, he was the night watchman. But Tony covered himself even further. He had made a deal with the computer store's manager which allowed Tony to go into the store a couple of nights a week, clean up the demo computers, and make sure nothing was amiss—no charge.

Of course, the manager had no idea that Tony was transmitting child pornography to various addresses in the United States, as well as around the world. The recipients of these transmissions paid quite handsomely for their Internet purchases; all of it done electronically to protected accounts that Tony's employer owned.

Tony had thought through all of this very carefully. Even if something went wrong on the recipient's end, where the images were received, Tony had made it nearly impossible to determine where the images had originated. And if somehow, someone did, it would turn out to be a demo computer that thousands of people had used. Tony even altered the times when the images were sent, from AM to PM, when the store was always open.

Another perk of the night watchman's job was the presence of a Massachusetts Registry of Motor Vehicles office in the mall. Even though Tony didn't live in Massachusetts, it was relatively easy for him to use the Massachusetts' RMV computers to access the Rhode Island RMV, hence the fact that the title to Tony's Lexus was in the name of a rental company that didn't exist.

Access to RMV records also afforded him another benefit: he could find out the address of anyone who had a car. He didn't know where Gleeson lived, but he did know he owned a car. When Tony's current situation sorted itself out, he'd be paying Gleeson a visit.

Jerry and Tony talked for a few more minutes, and then Tony again raised the issue of using Jerry's phone. "I really think you should look at the e-mail account."

Jerry reluctantly agreed. "I guess there's no harm." With that, he reached into his briefcase, took out his phone, and handed it to Tony.

Tony's fingers flew over the device in a blur. After less than thirty seconds, he returned it to Jerry and said, "There are thirty-three e-mails, but only four have attachments. I know who three of them are, so it's got to be the one I highlighted. You can open it, and then I'll show you the history. That address won't be there."

"You don't want to open it?"

Tony paused. "No. I want to be able to tell the judge that I've never seen the pictures."

Jerry began to feel as if he'd underestimated Tony in any number of ways. But he'd been taken in before. He promised himself that he wouldn't let that happen this time.

He stared down at his phone. As a lawyer, he had an obligation to look at the attached pictures. But he hesitated, knowing that he'd undoubtedly be totally disgusted at what he was about to see.

After a moment he lightly touched the screen, and the first image popped up. He suspected that in the world of child pornography the photo of the young boy was considered tame—no posing, nobody else in the picture—but for Jerry, he had all he could do not to be physically ill. He could feel the bile rise in his throat, forcing him to take a breath and look away. What he really wanted to do, however, was to delete the attachment, and send it off into cyberspace.

He took another moment to calm himself, and then opened the second attachment. This time it was a little girl. And while no one else was in the photo, the youngster was posed provocatively—if that description could even be applied to a child. He quickly closed both attachments, and pushed the phone across the table, as if touching it any further would contaminate him.

Jerry's thoughts turned to a number of cases he had taken on in the past that had left him feeling in need of a shower after each contact with those clients. But there had been relatively few of those situations, and none of them involved kids. The perversions adults perpetrated on each other were bad enough. But these pictures, especially the second one—this was beyond sick.

Tony had been watching Jerry's reaction the whole time, imagining the very internal conversation Jerry was having with himself. Tony searched for something to say to put himself in the best light possible. "From the way you reacted, I guess they're pretty bad."

Jerry searched for some degree of sincerity in Tony's facial expression, but found none. He then forced himself to speak without emotion. "It really doesn't matter what I think. But I'd say the pictures certainly qualify as child pornography. Whether the police can tie you to them, however, is the real question."

Tony reached for the phone, thumbed on a few icons, and found the account history. He then handed it back to Jerry, who began scrolling through over a hundred e-mails. He failed to find anything that stood out. "It's definitely a plus that there's nothing incriminating in the history, but it doesn't negate the charges."

"I know. But what about when they don't find anything on my computer, or in my apartment?"

"Again, that's all in your favor, no question. But I doubt it's going to be enough to get the charges dropped. My best guess is that the DA's office is still going to try to go forward." He paused. "It's also good news that the arraignment hearing is tomorrow. There's not enough time to dig up anything else." As soon as the words left his mouth, Jerry regretted them, but it was too late.

A flash of anger showed on Tony's face. "I told you, there's nothing to dig up!" he snapped.

Jerry scrambled to pacify his client. "I'm sorry. What I meant was that the judge probably will be inclined to go easy on you in terms of bail, since the only evidence they have are the pictures." As the images he had seen a few minutes before returned to his mind's eye, Jerry's entire body shuddered.

Before either of them could say anything further, there was a knock on the door. Jerry said, "Yes?"

The door opened and the officer who had shown Jerry into the interrogation room was standing there. He took a few steps into the room and placed some folded papers on the table. "That's a search warrant."

"That was fast," said Jerry.

"It's the same judge who did the hearing this morning," the officer informed him. "He likes to move things along."

Jerry glanced through the papers. "I'd like to read this and then talk with my client before anything happens."

The officer looked at his watch. "I'd say you've got about ten minutes, maybe less, before we head to Cranston."

Technically, the police didn't have to give him any time, so Jerry didn't complain. "I'll finish up with my client, and be right out."

The cop left without another word. Jerry waited for the door to close, and then said, "Let me take a quick look at this, and then we'll talk." It took less than a minute. "It's pretty standard—your apartment, your computer. It doesn't mention your computer at work, though. They probably figured that other people have access to it."

"I'm really the only one who uses it. The other guy who fills in for me wouldn't even know how to turn it on. But like I said, it doesn't matter."

Jerry did his own manipulation of the truth. "I believe you." And he did, as far as there being nothing in the apartment or on the computers. But as far as Tony being innocent, he wasn't so sure about that.

Jerry shifted gears slightly. "I think it would be best if I were in the apartment when they did the search. I'll need your permission to get your keys, so the police don't have to break the locks."

Tony felt his anger start to flare again, but he didn't say anything. Jerry extracted a piece of paper from his briefcase, wrote a few lines, and then had Tony sign it. "I'll be back as soon as I can." Tony nodded.

Jerry knew that if the officer at the "cage" where Tony's personal effects were being held wanted to, he could delay the keys being turned over for quite a while. But he didn't, and Jerry was on his way to Tony's apartment within ten minutes of exiting the interrogation room. The police who would be conducting the search followed five minutes later.

Jerry entered Tony's address into his GPS. It indicated that the ride would take about fifteen minutes. It wasn't much, but at least it provided some time for him to think.

I wish I could figure out what the hell is going on. The guy is much brighter than I thought – the way he retrieved everything on my phone, and I'm sure he's just as good with computers. But he didn't have access to a computer after he was arrested, so he couldn't have erased anything. But something's not right. He should have been acting differently, if he really didn't do anything wrong.

Maybe he's a sociopath. It would make sense. When he gets angry, it's almost for the wrong reason, or directed at the wrong people. It's as if he's incapable of showing how he feels about anything, except when he gets angry. Anger seems to be his default setting.

I know the solicitation charges were dropped, but it seems pretty obvious why he was at the hotel. Is it possible for a guy who uses prostitutes to also be a pedophile? I don't know. On the other hand, I believe him that the police won't find anything.

Is it because this guy creeps me out that I don't believe he's leveling with me? And those pictures—God! But he didn't even look at them. I don't know what to think.

For just a moment, his thoughts returned to the first time he had seen Tony, and what his initial reaction had been. But then, the same mitigating possibilities he had thought of earlier forced their way into his brain. It became an endless loop pushing him one way and then coming full circle in the other direction.

Just before he pulled into Tony's apartment complex, Jerry came to the realization that since he couldn't figure out all the intricacies of what was happening, he didn't have a choice. He was a defense attorney; it was his job to offer the best defense possible. And that's what he was going to do. If the prosecution couldn't convince the judge to move the case forward, then so be it.

He knew that this approach would allow him to proceed on autopilot, not having to consider the ultimate question of guilt or innocence. And maybe he wouldn't do anything differently, even if he had additional damaging information. But no matter how things played out, he knew there were a number of sleepless nights in his future.

CHAPTER FOUR

The police spent a little over an hour in Tony's apartment. They removed his computer and three boxes of papers, mainly financial records. As Jerry had suspected, and Tony had assured him, there was no "aha" moment like on TV, when some incriminating evidence turns up in plain sight for the police to find.

After the police left, Jerry drove back to the station to talk to Tony as he had promised. Once again, the time in the car afforded him the opportunity to try to figure out what was going on, but no new insights came to him.

When he arrived back at the police station, he was shown to the same interrogation room he had been in before. He waited less than five minutes for Tony to be brought in. "Just like you said, they didn't find anything, although they did take your computer and a few boxes of papers."

Tony put on a worried look. "I get that back, right? I can't afford a new computer." Of course that statement was untrue, but he figured that's what someone making a night watchman's salary would say.

"Yeah, you will," Jerry assured him. "But when, and in what condition, is another story."

Tony appeared angry, at least on the surface. But Jerry felt as if it were forced; certainly it seemed much different from the anger Tony had displayed before.

Tony asked, "What happens now?"

"You'll be arraigned tomorrow morning. Honestly, I don't think they have much of a case, but the judge has already dismissed one set of charges. I doubt he'll do it again."

"Then what?" Tony asked.

"I'll ask for your release, pending trial. Most likely it'll be personal recognizance, but there might be a small amount of bail. I could ask for a preliminary hearing, but that'll just delay things, and I don't think that's a good idea."

"So, you think there's definitely going to be a trial?"

"I'd say there's about an eighty percent chance," Jerry replied. "As I told you before, they don't have a lot. But it's hard to imagine the judge ruling that it's not enough to go to trial, especially if he gets a look at the pictures."

"How come it doesn't matter that I've never seen them?"

Jerry shrugged. "Technically, it only matters that they were in your possession."

Tony's anger, which had seemed forced before, was now all too real. "That's bullshit!" he protested.

Jerry tried to sound sympathetic. "I don't necessarily disagree, but that's how the system works."

They talked for a few more minutes, and then Jerry drove back to his office in Massachusetts. He called the RIPD's regional office and told them the status of the case. He then cleaned up a few things and headed home. Whatever preparation he had to do for the hearing in the morning, he could do just as easily from there.

Tony's case was first up on the docket. The judge arrived on the dot of ten o'clock, and got right to it. After the assistant district attorney introduced the charges, it was Jerry's turn to speak. "Jerry Hanson for the defense, Your Honor."

"Good morning, Mr. Hanson. Are you new with the Public Defender's office?"

"No, Your Honor. I'm part of the volunteer program for attorneys recently admitted to the Rhode Island Bar."

"Are you new to the profession, or just new to Rhode Island?"

"I've practiced in Massachusetts for the past eleven years."

"Well, I commend you for volunteering, and welcome to Rhode Island."

This is good, thought Jerry. *I don't know if it's going to help the case any, but it can't hurt.* "Thank you, Your Honor."

The judge nodded before speaking. "How do you plead, Mr. Sarno?"

There was some defiance evident in Tony's voice when he responded. "Not guilty."

"So noted. Am I correct in assuming, Mr. Hanson, that your client is not interested in a preliminary hearing?"

"That's correct," Jerry replied.

"Okay," the judge nodded. "Then you may proceed."

Jerry gathered himself before he spoke. He had done this a hundred times before, but for some reason he was more nervous than usual. "While Ms. Lopez is technically correct that pictures of a questionable nature were found attached to an e-mail in my client's account, there is no evidence that he requested them, or even knew that they were there."

The judge turned toward the ADA. "What do you say to that, Ms. Lopez?"

"First of all, common sense should tell us that people who traffic in child pornography don't accidentally send out pictures unsolicited. And secondly, for the purposes of this hearing, it doesn't matter. Mr. Sarno was in possession of child pornography. At trial, his attorney can argue how the pictures got there. But certainly there's enough to go forward at this time."

There wasn't much Jerry could say. The ADA was right; any argument he put forth now was more appropriate at trial, not at an arraignment hearing. But he gave it a shot, nonetheless. "Your Honor, it doesn't seem fair that my client should have to face a trial for something completely out of his control. Anybody could have sent those pictures. And it's not as if Mr. Sarno's e-mail address is something obscure." Jerry paused briefly, and then tried one more argument. "Besides, my client didn't have the phone in his possession when he was arrested."

The ADA spoke up before the judge had a chance to say anything. "That's because he dropped it, and tried to kick it out of sight. Why would he do that if he wasn't trying to hide what he knew was on it?"

Jerry started to object, but the judge spoke before he had a chance. "We're getting a little far afield here, people." He paused. "I hear what you're saying, Mr. Hanson, but I have to agree with Ms. Lopez's initial point. The main issue here is whether there's sufficient evidence to suggest a crime may have been committed. And I believe there is. Therefore, I'm going to rule that the case should go to trial."

The ADA spoke again. "Thank you, Your Honor. The people request $25,000 in cash bail." The judge looked surprised, but didn't say anything. He just nodded at Jerry, who said, "That's way over the top, Your Honor. These are the first charges filed against Mr. Sarno in years."

The ADA interrupted. "Other than solicitation, you mean."

The judge intervened. "Play nice, Ms. Lopez. Those charges were dropped. They're not relevant here. You may continue, Mr. Hanson." After a brief pause the judge said, "On second thought, I don't need to hear anymore. I'm releasing Mr. Sarno on personal recognizance."

The ADA reacted. "Your Honor, these are serious charges."

"I agree. But that's all they are—charges. I don't see Mr. Sarno as a flight risk. He's got a steady job…"

"What about an ankle monitor?"

"What for? Knowing Mr. Sarno's whereabouts every minute is irrelevant to the crime he's charged with. Anything else?"

"No, Your Honor."

"Okay then, Mr. Sarno, you're free to go. A trial date will be set for Superior Court, probably in four to six weeks."

Tony remained motionless. Jerry said, "Thank you, Your Honor."

Outside the courtroom, Jerry expected Tony to offer his hand and thank him. Neither happened. Jerry shrugged it off and said, "You can get your personal effects across the street. I'll wait for you, if you'd like. And then I can give you a ride someplace."

"No," Tony shook his head. "I'll be all right."

"Are you sure?" Jerry asked.

"Yeah," Tony said.

"Okay then," Jerry took out his car keys. "I'll be in touch." He paused. "I'm sure I don't need to remind you, but it would probably be best to keep your nose clean."

"Not a problem," Tony replied. Then, almost as an afterthought, he said, "Thanks." He still didn't offer his hand.

As Jerry was walking away, he thought—*What a weird guy. I'll be glad when I'm done with this case and I don't have to deal with him anymore.*

For some reason, something the ADA said came into his head. She had mentioned the phrase 'traffic in child pornography.' *Was that what was going on here? That would explain why Tony didn't care about seeing the pictures, or why the police didn't find anything at his house. But, if he really was distributing child porn, why were the pictures so easy to find? The guy's a computer whiz. He would have been more careful than that.* The trafficking idea made sense on one level, but there were still a lot of things that didn't fit. Jerry wasn't sure he was seeing anything clearly. *And what if he is distributing child porn? Is that better or worse than collecting it? It's probably worse. So if that's what he's doing, it's my job to get him off, and allow him to keep doing it. Great!*

That night Tony went to work as usual. He was a little worried that the mall manager, his immediate boss, might have heard about his court appearance and would decide to suspend him, or worse. But that never happened.

He waited until three-thirty in the morning and then entered the computer store. He sat at one of the demo computers, accessed his e-mail, and began to search for the attachment from Gleeson. When he couldn't easily locate it, he reasoned that the police must have deleted it. He was confident that he could have retrieved the pictures if he really wanted to. *But why tempt fate?* he thought. *"I'm not going to send them out anyway—too much of a risk."*

He next used one of his encrypted accounts to send an e-mail to Runner, suggesting a late night meeting at the mall the next day. Immediately after sending the e-mail, he "cleaned" the computer, eliminating any trace that he had been there, and then went back to his office. Before heading out again, he accessed the centralized surveillance system and disabled the cameras in the two areas he was going to visit.

His first stop was the RMV. Within two minutes of sitting at one of the computers, he had Gleeson's address in Massachusetts. Just thinking about Gleeson pushed his anger to the boiling point. But he was able to dial it back, reminding himself that he had better not go near Gleeson until after his meeting with Runner. It was possible that their employer might have some objection to Tony teaching Gleeson a lesson. But he certainly hoped not.

A few minutes later, he was inside one of the phone stores in the mall. Since the police had kept his phone, he needed a new one. But he thought it was too risky to have it registered in his own name. So he selected a basic model with Internet access, made it appear that it had been legitimately purchased earlier in the day, and then entered all of Gleeson's information into a contract form on the computer. Besides not being traceable to him, the fake contract also had another benefit: In case he was told not to mess up Gleeson physically, Tony might be able to cause him a great deal of pain electronically.

Shortly before midnight on the following day, Runner showed up at one of the rear doors to the mall. Usually, Tony wasn't nervous around Runner; he considered them to be on equal footing. But tonight was different. Tonight he had to try to explain what had gone wrong, and why he wasn't to blame.

Tony vowed to himself to be straightforward. If it appeared that he was making excuses, he would look guilty. But he didn't want to be on the defensive, either; it would make him look weak. He had to walk a fine line; the way Runner conveyed Tony's explanation to the big boss would make all the difference.

As Tony secured the outside door, Runner noticed a couple of old chairs in the hallway that led into the mall. Instead of heading to Tony's office, Runner grabbed one, sat down, and motioned for Tony to do the same. Tony couldn't tell whether Runner was angry or not. Nothing in his posture or facial expression gave anything away. Not even the first words he spoke provided an answer. "So what happened?"

Tony tried to keep his voice steady. "I'm not sure how much you already know ..." he began.

"I got a text from a couple of the girls at the Regal," Runner paused, and a touch of anger entered his voice. "And that's problem number one. What the hell were you doing there? You've been warned about that."

Tony hadn't expected the question. And despite his intention to avoid being defensive, he knew it was evident in his voice. "I wasn't there for what you think. That's the truth. I had to give Chandra her cut."

Runner's eyes narrowed. "What are you talking about?"

"Chandra gets a cut for arranging things with the other girls whose kids I use in the pictures," Tony told him.

Runner stared at him, obviously trying to assess whether he was getting the true story. "Do you always go to her apartment to give her the money?"

"Yeah," Tony replied. "But usually during the day, when fewer people are around. But I had the night off, so I figured I'd take care of it then."

Some impatience crept into Runner's voice. "So what happened? You didn't see the cops before you went up?"

Tony decided not to mention the misgivings he'd had that night before he went into the bar. "No. I just went through Lucky's, same as always." He spent the next few minutes explaining about his initial arrest, dropping his phone, the first hearing, and then the second set of charges.

Runner cut in. "We knew about most of that already. The boss wants to know how the police got a hold of the pictures."

"The guy who takes them for me screwed up. He sent them to my regular e-mail, not the protected one."

Now Runner showed some anger. "Why the hell did he do that?"

"I don't know," Tony said. "I didn't want to contact him until I talked to you and found out what the boss wants me to do."

"What's the guy's name again?" Runner asked.

"Gleeson."

Runner frowned. "He's the same guy you always use?"

"Yeah, right from when we started," Tony nodded.

Runner was quiet for a few moments. "I want to hear the whole story from the beginning, and then we'll decide what's going to happen. And it better be the truth, Tony; I'm going to check."

"You want me to start from when I first picked up the kids?" Tony asked.

"Everything."

"Okay," Tony began. "I think it was last Thursday. Chandra left word at Lucky's that two of the girls at the Regal wanted to make some extra money, and I could pick up their kids around three in the afternoon."

Runner broke in. "You've used these kids before?"

Tony nodded. "A few months ago. There are around fifteen girls that work for the boss whose kids I use. I mix it up month to month."

"All right," Runner said. "Go ahead."

"Anyway, I got the kids, a boy and a girl, at Chandra's place. Sometimes I have to use chloroform, but not with these two. They kind of know me, so I didn't have any trouble walking them out. Gleeson uses an old storefront a few miles from here that he rents. He takes the pictures. I sit out front in case anybody shows up. He gives the kids candy and stuff. It takes maybe a half hour, usually."

Runner interrupted again. "And nothing was different this time? You didn't tell him to do anything different?"

"No. It's always the same."

"So then why did he send the pictures to the other account?" Runner sounded annoyed.

Tony shrugged his shoulders. "I told you—I have no idea."

"I'm sure I don't have to tell you, the boss is pissed," Runner told him.

"I understand, but it's not my fault."

Runner stared at Tony for a moment before he spoke. "Maybe."

Tony didn't like the remark, but he kept his mouth shut, as Runner continued. "This is going to cost the boss a shitload of money. Our best customer is a local guy who's willing to pay a bundle if the kids are from around here. He figures he might run into them someplace or something. He's a sick bastard, but he pays real well. But now we've got to shut the whole thing down."

Tony was surprised. He expected things to be put on hold, but it sounded more permanent than that. And if it were shut down, it meant that he was expendable. Tony searched for the right thing to say. Eventually he offered, "I understand that things are hot right now. But once this blows over, there's no reason we can't start up again."

Runner snorted. "You're kidding me, right?"

Tony felt things slipping away. "I mean, I'll have to get a new guy to take the pictures, but this can still work."

Runner shook his head. "You think you're going to be able to do that from a jail cell?"

"My lawyer says they have no case." This was a total

exaggeration, but Tony felt he had to make the situation look better than it was.

Runner was unimpressed. "All lawyers say that."

Tony was beginning to fear the worst about his expendability. It might not be just the child pornography enterprise that disappeared. "Tell the boss that, obviously, I'll do whatever he wants. But he should know that none of this can be traced to him."

"What about the photo guy, Gleeson?" Runner asked. "How much does he know?"

"He doesn't even know about you, never mind the boss,"

Runner studied Tony again. "Let me ask you something else. The police have these pictures, right?" Tony nodded. "Is there any chance somebody could recognize the kids?"

Tony had hoped Runner wouldn't ask this question. He considered lying, but remembered Runner's admonition about checking the truth of what Tony told him. "I guess it's possible, but I doubt it."

Runner shook his head in disgust. "This just keeps on getting better and better. Why do you doubt it?"

"I altered the faces on all the other pictures that Gleeson took. Obviously, I didn't get a chance to do it to the ones the police have. But none of the other photos look like these kids. Plus, they're not in school yet. That means it won't do any good for the police to show the photos to anybody in the schools. They won't recognize them."

That seemed to satisfy Runner, somewhat. "Tell me again what you're planning to do with Gleeson."

"I told you. I was waiting until after I met with you," Tony responded.

"The boss doesn't like loose ends." Runner said. "Do what you want, but keep the boss out of it, understand? Although if I were you, I wouldn't do anything that would bring more attention to myself."

Tony could feel himself relax. It sounded like there were no plans to take this whole mess out on him. "Yes, absolutely."

"Okay." Runner paused. "I don't want you to contact me again until after the trial is over. If you beat this, I guess it's possible that the boss might want to start it up again. It made him a lot of money, but he doesn't like it when people get sloppy."

Tony responded without thinking how defensive it sounded. "I wasn't sloppy."

"Well, the guy you hired was," Runner countered. "That's on you."

Tony didn't want to be shut off like that, but he was reluctant to say anything.

As Runner stood up to leave, he repeated what he had said before. "Remember. I don't want to hear from you."

Tony knew he had pushed things more than he should have, but the words escaped from his mouth before he could stop himself. "I understand. But what about Gleeson?"

"What about him?"

"Once I find out what happened, don't you want to know?"

"He fucked up, and maybe you did too," Runner said flatly. "That's all I need to know."

This was a step backward. Tony knew he should have left it alone, but he tried to fix it. "I just thought the boss would want me to confirm that nothing else happened."

"Are you telling me there might be more?"

"No, no "I just want him to know that everything's been taken care of."

Runner thought for a moment. "When are you seeing Gleeson?"

"Tomorrow," Tony said.

"I'll contact you tomorrow night. And there better not be any more fucking surprises."

CHAPTER FIVE

Tony planned to show up at Gleeson's apartment around five in the afternoon. He had briefly considered calling ahead to make sure he was home, but decided he didn't want to give him the opportunity to concoct some story about what had happened. Tony preferred to catch him off guard; it was more likely he'd get the truth that way. If it turned out that Gleeson wasn't home, he'd just wait.

But as soon as Tony turned the corner onto Gleeson's street, he saw his car out in front of a small two-family house. Tony drove half a block past and walked back. There was a separate bell for the ground floor apartment, but Tony knocked instead.

About thirty seconds later, the door opened and Gleeson appeared. He took a moment to process Tony's presence. "Tony, what are you doing here?" A pause. "How do you even know where I live?"

Tony outwardly appeared calm, although he was seething on the inside. His rage had grown more and more intense from the moment he had gotten into the car, as he thought about the trouble Gleeson had caused for him. "Let's go inside."

"Uh, yeah, sure," Gleeson faltered.

Gleeson let Tony in and turned his back to shut the door. As he turned around, Tony was already midway through his windup. He hit Gleeson with everything he had right in the stomach. He really wanted to punch him in the face, but he knew he might hurt his own hand if he did that. A stomach hit wouldn't do as much damage, but it would still put Gleeson out of commission for a while, and would certainly get his attention.

Gleeson doubled over and expelled a sound like a wounded animal. He grabbed his mid-section and fought to remain upright. His eyes bugged out of his head as he fought for air. Tony was prepared to hit him again, but realized it wasn't necessary. Instead, he calmly crossed over the small living room and sat down on the couch, waiting for Gleeson to recover.

After a minute, Gleeson went down on all fours. After another minute, he was finally able to lift his head and try to talk. He knew he looked like a fool, but he also knew it would be difficult for Tony to punch him again if he remained in that position, so he stayed where he was. The words he spoke came out haltingly. "What, what … was that for?"

Tony leaned forward. "For screwing me."

Gleeson appeared surprised. "What … do you mean?"

"The e-mail. What the fuck do you think I mean?"

Since Tony hadn't moved from his seat on the couch, Gleeson thought it might be safe to stand up. But he kept his distance.

Despite his disorientation from the punch, things started to fall into place. He realized that Tony must be talking about the e-mail he had sent to the regular account. "I didn't have a choice. I got a virus or something on my computer and it wiped out all my contacts. The only address I could find for you was for that account. I figured it would be okay to use it just this once."

Tony's first inclination was to punch him again. But the mention of the virus negated that, only because the way Tony was wired, anything having to do with computers tended to trump everything else. Tony said, "Show me."

Gleeson tentatively moved closer and pointed. "It's in there."

He tried to steer clear of Tony, but the rooms were small. As they passed through the dining area, Tony's anger flared again. He slapped Gleeson across the face with his open palm, and then again with a backhand. Another punch would have hurt much more, but the slaps were more humiliating, as if Gleeson were a child, or one of the prostitutes Tony pushed around.

Gleeson put his hands up to defend himself, but Tony was done, at least for the time being. "I got arrested because of you, and it's not over yet."

Gleeson struggled to come up with the words that might pacify Tony, but he couldn't. So he simply apologized. "I'm sorry, Tony. I didn't know what else to do."

"You could have waited."

Gleeson responded before he thought about what he was going to say. "You said that you wanted the pictures as soon as possible."

Tony slapped him again. "So it's my fault?"

Gleeson didn't answer. Tony started walking away. "Where's the computer?"

Gleeson pointed to a small alcove off the kitchen.

Tony moved the mouse and the screen came to life. Gleeson was already logged in, so there was no need to ask for the password. For the next few minutes, neither of them spoke. Finally, Tony got up, moved toward Gleeson, and looked him in the eye. "It's a good thing you didn't lie to me. That's the only reason you're still in one piece."

Gleeson went pale, but kept quiet. Tony got in his face again. "Because of what you did, the whole operation has to shut down. And if you think I'm upset, you should see my boss."

Tony's last remark surprised Gleeson. He had assumed Tony was doing all of this on his own. The thought of somebody else, possibly even more violent, paying him a visit almost caused him to vomit.

Tony continued. "I might go to prison because of you."

Gleeson thought for sure he was about to be hit again, but Tony made no move to do that. Instead, he spoke more calmly than at any time since Gleeson had opened the door to let him in. "Okay, here's what's going to happen. You're going to disappear."

Gleeson's heart sank. Did Tony mean what he thought he did?

Tony read his mind, and actually smiled. "Not like that, although I considered it. And I'm sure my boss has too. No, you've got two weeks to move. I want you out of here, out of New England. I don't want to ever see you again. And if you're not gone in two weeks, I'm going to reconsider option one."

With that, Tony headed toward the front door and said, "Have a nice day."

After the door closed, Gleeson rubbed his face and stomach, took three or four deep breaths, and went over and locked the door. He wished he had never laid eyes on Tony Sarno. He had thought about breaking ties with him before. But nothing had ever come of it, mainly because of what he had seen in Tony's eyes—flashes of the same rage he had seen today. He told himself that maybe this was for the best. But regardless, there was no way he was going to defy Tony.

On the ride back to his apartment, Tony started to reflect on what had just occurred with Gleeson. Tony had no regrets. Of course, he rarely did. If his actions brought him pleasure, made him money, or enhanced his reputation, that was all that mattered. He did acknowledge to himself that he had exaggerated the likelihood of his boss coming after Gleeson. But it had made Gleeson more afraid while at the same time bolstering Tony's status. All in all, a good move.

Tony's thoughts then shifted to the previous night and his conversation with Runner.

I think I handled it okay. But how is Runner going to present it to the boss? That's what I don't know. Maybe I can figure that out when Runner contacts me later. But what if he doesn't? That might tell me something, too. Maybe I should try to contact the boss and talk to him directly. At least then I'd be sure he heard my side of the story. Plus, I could tell him about my new idea. Maybe that's the way to go. After all, it's possible Runner is still pissed at me about the mix-up with the prostitutes. He could be telling the boss anything. But even if I wanted to contact the boss, how could I? Maybe the place where Runner first talked to me.

With that last thought, Tony's mind traveled back fifteen years to the circumstances that had led him to where he was now:

Right after he quit high school, his father told him he had to get a job if he expected to still live at home. With Tony's gift for understanding everything electronic and mechanical, he quickly found employment in a small fix-it shop. He stayed there for four years, until he came home one day and found two policemen at the door. He assumed that they were there to arrest him for some break-ins he had committed. But that was not the case. They were there to inform him that his parents had been killed in a car accident. (He remembered feeling relief that it wasn't about the break-ins.)

Tony didn't shed a tear. Not when he got the news, not at the wake, not at the funeral. In fact, the last time he remembered crying was when he was around six and he had broken his arm. But that was because of physical pain. He didn't feel emotional pain.

In their will, his parents left him the house and two small insurance policies. He stopped working, bummed around for a while, and then signed up for a couple of computer courses at the local community college. He was a natural and probably could have taught the second course better than the instructor.

Eventually, money started to become an issue, especially with the upkeep on the house. So he sold it, and moved into an apartment closer to Providence, because there was a lot more action of all kinds in a large city.

For the next few years, he worked at a number of jobs. And then someone he met at a nightclub suggested he go talk to the manager of an upscale auto repair shop. Once the manager saw what Tony could do with a computer, he was hired on the spot. It wasn't much of a challenge for Tony to double-bill insurance companies or pad repair costs, especially on the luxury cars that were the shop's specialty. Money became less of a problem. And then Runner recruited him, and the problem disappeared entirely.

As he finished that thought, Tony pulled into a parking space in front of his apartment. He exited the Lexus, walked to the front door of the building, got his keys out, and opened up his apartment door. Subconsciously, he acknowledged that if he really needed to talk to the boss directly, he could probably figure out how to contact him by going to the repair shop. Somebody there would probably know something.

Nevertheless, he felt a wave of relief wash over him when he checked his e-mail account on his phone and found a message from Runner giving him a number to call. "Hey, Runner. It's me."

Runner got right to the point. "Yeah. So the boss wants to know what happened with Gleeson."

Tony told him the whole story, exaggerating much of it to make himself look good. He also emphasized the fact that Gleeson didn't know anything about Runner or the boss. Runner listened without commenting.

When Tony finished, Runner said, "That it?"

Tony wasn't ready to end the call. "That's it about Gleeson. But there's something else I wanted the boss to know."

Runner grunted. "I'm not sure the boss is real interested in anything you have to say right now."

Tony didn't like the implication, but he forced himself not to allow his concern to come through in his voice. "I figured out a way to start up with the photos again with absolutely no risk at all."

"Haven't we already had this fucking conversation?"

Tony persisted. "Just listen, all right?"

Runner paused before responding. "You got one minute."

It only took Tony forty-five seconds. He would have preferred to elaborate, but decided not to push it. "What do you think?"

"I'll pass it along."

The tone of Runner's voice said much more than his words. So much so that Tony felt reasonably sure Runner had been impressed with the idea, and would advise the boss to seriously consider it.

Runner spoke again. "Remember, no more contact."

Tony didn't have a chance to respond before Runner hung up.

During the next several weeks, Tony kept a low profile. He stayed away from Lucky's, away from the Regal, even away from the prostitutes he was "allowed" to frequent. This display of willpower had its consequences, however. His built-up anger, fueled by his physical frustration, threatened to reach the breaking point a number of times.

One night around nine-thirty, shortly before he had to be at work, Tony took a ride to Gleeson's apartment. He hadn't communicated with Gleeson since the day he had told him to disappear. There was little doubt in Tony's mind that Gleeson was gone, but part of him hoped that he wasn't. The thought of beating Gleeson within an inch of his life got his adrenaline pumping and his pulse racing.

But when he got to Gleeson's, there were no lights on in the first floor apartment, and Gleeson's car was nowhere in sight. It was possible that he was just out, but Tony didn't think that was likely. Gleeson was gone. Tony felt a sense of pride because he had been able to intimidate Gleeson into leaving. On the other hand, he would have enjoyed using his fists on somebody right then.

Partly through happenstance and partly because of Tony's emotional state, that opportunity presented itself a few minutes later as he drove to the mall. On a side street several blocks from Gleeson's, Tony came upon a nondescript older car going about twenty-five miles an hour. From Tony's perspective the driver looked to be a man in his forties or fifties. It also appeared from the speed he was going and his frequent glances to both sides of the street that he was looking for an address.

Tony slowed down and settled in behind the car. They traveled together for less than half a block. And although Tony had at least two opportunities to take a turn to bypass the slower driver, he stayed on the car's bumper. He began flashing his high beams, all the while shouting, "Get a fucking GPS!"

Although the driver probably didn't hear Tony, he obviously must have seen the high beams, because he signaled and attempted to pull over to the curb. But there were cars parked on both sides of the street, and there wasn't enough room for another car to get by. Tony didn't even make the attempt. He just leaned on his horn as the car in front of him traveled another hundred yards. The driver finally found an empty spot and pulled over. As Tony went by, he lowered his window and shouted, "Get out of the way, you fucking moron!"

There were a couple of empty parking spaces about twenty yards in front of Tony. He debated for just a moment, and then aimed the nose of the Lexus into one of the spots as he screeched to a halt. He got out of his car and headed toward the other driver. Midway there, he remembered what his lawyer had said about staying out of trouble, but he couldn't seem to help himself. Both his hands were balled into fists as he kept moving forward. He finally stopped five feet from the front bumper. He paused for a moment, glanced at the license plate, gave the guy the finger, and then reluctantly headed back to the Lexus and sped away.

Later that night, he made a visit to the RMV. He typed in the license plate number he had memorized, and all the pertinent information popped up on the screen. Initially, Tony thought about paying the guy a visit, but once again was able to hold himself back. Instead, he decided there was another, less risky way to get back at the driver. He deleted the excise tax that the guy had paid on his car for the past three years. That would automatically trigger notification to the town clerk where he lived. And then the guy would be threatened with having his license suspended. It wasn't as satisfying as punching the guy's lights out, but it would have to do.

After Tony left the RMV and took another few moments to calm down, he headed for the photography studio on the second floor of the mall. Initially, there wasn't much to see. But that was okay; he mainly wanted to get the lay of the land. He attempted to access one of the computers, but for some reason he was having more difficulty than he had anticipated. He was about to give up when he noticed exactly what he needed right there in plain sight—pictures and names of all the employees of First Class Photo posted on the wall.

Tony moved closer and focused his attention on the picture of a young man in his late twenties named Josh Raybeck. Tony considered going back to the RMV and seeing what information he could dig up on Josh, but then decided that there would be plenty of time for that. Tony couldn't put his new idea into motion until after the trial was over, anyway. Those thoughts reminded him of how little patience he had left. He had called his lawyer three times in the past week, but there had been nothing to report.

A few days later however, Tony and Jerry received notification that the trial date had been set for the first week in August, less than three weeks from now. Tony went to Jerry's office on the last Monday in July.

"Hi, Tony," the attorney greeted him. "How have you been?"

"Okay," said Tony.

"Anything going on that I should know about?"

"No. I've just been going to work and staying home."

"That's good. I'm glad to hear it." Jerry opened a folder in front of him. "I wanted to let you know what to expect, and what I'm going to be doing."

Tony didn't say anything, so Jerry continued. "Before the trial even starts, I'm going to attempt to get the pictures suppressed. That's really their whole case. I'm intending to argue that even though it was your phone, it wasn't in your possession. But frankly, that's not our strongest argument. Our strongest argument is that you were unaware that the pictures were even there; you didn't request them, and you didn't open the attachment."

Tony perked up, realizing that the argument just described by Jerry, was, in essence, his idea. "That's because of what I said, right?"

"Yes, for the most part." Jerry paused. "But you have to understand, any chance of this motion being successful probably depends on who we get as a judge. Some judges give a lot of leeway to the prosecution. If we get one of those, then it's going to be much more difficult to get the pictures thrown out."

Tony hadn't thought that much about the notion that he very well could be headed to prison. That wasn't his style. He was impatient for it to be over, but he didn't dwell on the possible outcome. However, Jerry's last remark struck a chord. "I still can't believe this. Don't those people get all sorts of shit in their e-mail accounts, too?"

Jerry stared at his client but didn't respond. While there was some anger behind Tony's outburst, it appeared to Jerry that he was more frustrated than angry. Jerry was somewhat relieved. Frustration would play much better in the courtroom than anger, especially given the level of rage he believed Tony was capable of.

They talked for another fifteen minutes, and then Jerry said, "We haven't really discussed it, but without question, we should opt for a bench trial. That's where the judge decides the case. I don't think you want a jury trial."

Tony's belligerence gave way to concern. "I thought you said that sometimes judges give the other side leeway."

"I did; that's true," Jerry acknowledged. "But I still think the bench trial is the best option." He paused to make sure his next statement appeared as non-judgmental as possible. "If those pictures are admitted, and a jury sees them, they're going to want to punish somebody."

Somewhat to Jerry's surprise, Tony didn't react, other than to nod his head in understanding.

On the Thursday before the trial was scheduled to begin, Jerry found out that Tony's case would be heard before Judge Alexander Titus. That was not good news. Being new to the Rhode Island court system, Jerry didn't know any of the judges. When he made inquiries about Judge Titus, he was told that he had a nickname: "Judge Tight Ass." And evidently, the nickname had been legitimately earned.

Jerry called Tony to give him the bad news. After a few moments of back and forth, Jerry said, "But despite his reputation, most of the lawyers I spoke with said that he was tough, but fair. So I still think we should go with the bench trial."

With some reluctance in his voice Tony said, "All right."

However, the next morning Tony called back to say he had changed his mind. He wanted a jury trial. After an initial pause, Jerry said, "Obviously, it's your call, Tony. But I think it's a mistake. I realize Titus is not the kind of judge we were hoping to get, but still …"

"No. I've made up my mind. I want a jury trial."

Jerry could hear the finality in Tony's voice. "Okay. As I said, it's your call. I'll notify the court."

Naturally, Jerry had assumed that Tony's change of heart was because they had drawn Judge Titus. But that had nothing to do with it.

Tony had received an e-mail from Runner, the first contact in several weeks. The e-mail gave Tony a phone number to call. When he did, the only words spoken were, "The boss says get a jury trial." And then the line went dead.

CHAPTER SIX

Despite the way he had presented it to his lawyer, Tony had major doubts as to whether a jury trial was the right way to go. *I'm not sure I trust Runner. This whole thing could be a set-up to make sure I'm out of the picture. But on the other hand, why would Runner do that? And would he risk going behind the boss' back? Could the boss want me to get convicted? Or maybe the boss wants me to have a jury trial because he can fix it somehow.*

Tony's mind went through a number of additional scenarios until he tired of the process. Eventually, he settled on the probability that the boss liked his new idea and was planning on making sure that Tony was acquitted. It was the only thing that made sense to him. Of course, there was no real evidence that the boss was going to do anything of the kind. But Tony's arrogance and inflated sense of importance served to solidify his belief.

On Monday morning Tony and Jerry arrived at the courthouse simultaneously around eight-thirty. They found a small conference room where they talked for a few minutes before the nine o'clock court appearance.

"As I mentioned, Tony, the judge will be hearing pre-trial motions this morning. It's also possible that the cops who arrested you might testify. But no matter what's said in there, try not to react," Jerry cautioned his client.

"This is when you're going to get the pictures thrown out, right?"

"I'm going to try," said Jerry. "But you shouldn't get your hopes up."

"When will we know— right away?"

Jerry shook his head. "I doubt it. Probably not until tomorrow."

"What happens then?" Tony asked.

"Well," Jerry replied, "I have to be prepared to go forward, no matter what. So, I think tomorrow will probably be jury selection."

"Am I supposed to be part of that?"

The attorney shook his head. "You're not required to be." In truth, Jerry didn't want Tony anywhere near the jury selection. He was too unpredictable.

But Tony persisted. "I think I want to be there."

Jerry's stomach knotted. "Why don't we see how the motions go, and then we can talk about it?"

It was obvious that Tony wasn't thrilled with that response, but he let it go. A few minutes later they headed for Judge Titus' courtroom. The proceedings began at ten past nine. It took five minutes for introductions and paperwork, and then the judge indicated he would entertain pre-trial motions.

Jerry had decided to put forth two. In essence, they were the same arguments that he had outlined for Tony a few days previously, although at that time, he had presented a far rosier scenario than he had come to believe was likely. The problem, as he saw it now, was that in the first motion he had to argue that the evidence was obtained illegally. But there was little question that that was a bogus claim. He realized that, in his desire to end his association with Tony as quickly as possible, he had allowed his thinking to become clouded.

And as far as the second motion was concerned, if he had been honest with himself, he would have acknowledged from the beginning that the argument belonged at trial, not as a motion at pre-trial. The judge was not going to suppress the pictures just because Tony hadn't seen them. The assistant district attorney would simply point out that the only reason Tony hadn't looked at them was because he was arrested before he had the chance. And more importantly, since the pictures were part of an e-mail sent to Tony's account, there was a strong case to be made that that constituted possession.

There was one related motion Jerry had considered—a motion to exclude the photos because they were inflammatory and would prejudice the jury by their very nature. But Jerry was reluctant to offer it on top of the other two motions. Jerry was afraid that it would make him appear desperate, as if he were trying every possible maneuver to disguise the real facts of the case. This was something he suspected would not sit well with Judge Titus. And even though it was a jury trial, it was still important that the judge view Jerry in a positive light. On the other hand, if the actual photos were excluded, and the jury never saw them, it would certainly help the case.

In the end Jerry decided, if need be, he would wait until the trial to raise an objection to the photos being admitted. Although it was a bit unusual, it was permissible. He still hadn't convinced himself that this was the best course of action, but he went forward with just the two motions.

While Jerry was speaking, Judge Titus attempted to appear impartial. To the inexperienced eye, he gave away very little as to how he might rule. Jerry noticed the occasional raised eyebrow and knew it was not going in his favor. He started to second-guess himself and considered making another motion to exclude the photos. But ultimately, he didn't.

Judge Titus then indicated that he would consider the motions overnight and rule the next morning. Once again, Jerry had the feeling that the overnight consideration was just an empty gesture; the judge had already made up his mind. But in all honesty, Jerry couldn't fault him for that. When the judge spoke again, any realistic chance that Jerry's thinking was in error went out the window.

"Regardless of my rulings tomorrow, I want both sides to be prepared to go forward with jury selection. Obviously, it's still possible that a trial could be avoided, but I want both parties ready to proceed, no matter what. Is that understood?"

Jerry and the ADA responded simultaneously. "Yes, Your Honor."

"Good. I also want to remind both parties that should there be a trial, it will be recorded, not for media broadcast, but simply as an additional means of memorializing the proceedings. It probably goes without saying, but jury selection will not be recorded."

Somewhat to Jerry's surprise, Tony had remained relatively calm during the entire pre-trial process. Still, Jerry had major reservations about him being present when the jury was selected. But he knew he had to approach the subject carefully. Ironically, the first thing Tony said after they left the courtroom was about that very topic. "How come you don't want me there when you pick the jury?"

"I didn't say that," Jerry replied.

"But that's what you think, right?"

Jerry had been provided an opening. He wasn't about to let it close

49

without making his strongest argument. "It's probably best that the jury see you for the first time at trial. If, for some reason, they form a negative opinion of you because of your body language or your reaction to something being said then it might carry over to the trial."

Jerry paused, realizing that the corollary to the argument he had just given was also true. He didn't know if Tony would pick up on that, but he decided to take a slightly different tack anyway. "Jury selection can take several hours. It's easy for anybody to get bored or have their mind wander. And some of the potential jurors could easily misinterpret that. I don't think we should take that chance."

Tony didn't like the way Jerry had just spoken to him—as if he wouldn't know how to act in that situation. He'd been fooling people his whole life. He'd know what to do. And then he thought back to Runner's message about getting a jury trial. If the boss was truly going to help him, it would have to be after the jury was selected. Tony didn't think there was any way the boss could fix who was put on the jury. Or could he?

It was also possible, thought Tony, that when the jury was being selected, someone would give him a signal. So maybe he should be there. But then how would he recognize it? He was torn. But then he thought about sitting in the courtroom for another three hours without being able to talk and defend himself. He didn't like the prospect of that.

And there was something else. If anything went wrong, and he wasn't there, it would be his lawyer's fault. That last thought was enough to change his original idea on the matter. "Okay, if that's what you think." Tony paused a moment and then added, "It didn't go too well in there, did it?"

"About what I expected. But who knows, we might get a surprise tomorrow." Despite the fact that Jerry spoke these last words with as much conviction as he could muster, Tony saw right through it. They said 'goodbye,' and parted ways outside the courthouse.

On the ride back to his office, Jerry reconstructed the morning's events in his head. It had, in fact, gone almost exactly the way he had come to believe it would. There was, however, one positive development that he had taken from the morning: He had been able to put aside the way he felt about Tony, and argue that he was innocent. Jerry wondered if a jury would be able to make a similar distinction.

～

The next morning, Jerry used the half-hour before Judge Titus was scheduled to rule to prepare Tony for a less-than-favorable outcome. "I know I might have made it seem like we could win at least one of these motions, but I'm afraid I'm a lot less confident than I was. But regardless, I still think we have a strong defense, especially with the fact that you never opened the attachment, and you never saw the photos." Jerry recognized that Tony's ego often needed stroking, so he added, "That was a great move on your part not to look at the pictures when you had the chance."

Tony didn't exactly beam, but it was obvious that he was pleased. "Thanks," he responded.

Jerry continued "I also wanted to remind you, just like yesterday, it would be best if you didn't show any reaction. I know it might be difficult, but we don't want to antagonize the judge. If you think something needs to be said, whisper it to me, and let me say it."

They talked for a few more minutes, and then walked down the corridor to the courtroom, arriving about ten minutes early. The ADA was already there. She and Jerry exchanged "hellos," and then went about their business. Judge Titus entered the courtroom at precisely nine o'clock. After the bailiff made the standard announcements, the judge began. And although Jerry wouldn't have been able to come up with the exact wording the judge used, he could have predicted the essence of what he had to say.

On the first motion, the judge declared that there was no merit to Jerry's argument that the phone was obtained illegally, and therefore should be suppressed. "The phone was not in the defendant's possession, but rather on the floor in plain sight. Therefore, the defendant could have no expectation of privacy. Accordingly, anything on the phone may be used as evidence.

"As far as the second motion is concerned, that also is denied. I'm aware that my ruling on the first motion might appear to be contradictory to the denial of the second motion *vis-à-vis* the concept of possession, so let me elaborate. Besides holding something or having it on your person, possession can also mean that you own it, or it belongs to you. And there's no doubt in my mind that the phone belongs to Mr. Sarno, and therefore meets one of the criteria of possession. And secondly, as I believe you are probably aware, Mr. Hanson, the argument that your client had no knowledge of what was on his phone is more appropriately brought up at trial."

This last statement brought a small reaction from Tony. "But I didn't know they were there!" he insisted.

The judge obviously heard Tony's remark, but since it wasn't overly loud or disruptive, he ignored it. However, the judge did look toward Jerry, and asked, "Is there anything else, Mr. Hanson?"

Jerry almost said 'yes,' but caught himself. While the judge had not been particularly harsh in his pronouncements, Jerry felt certain another motion to suppress the photos because they were too graphic would be denied as well. Pursuing this particular avenue would be like using the challenge flag in the NFL. If you knew you were going to lose, it made no sense to waste the time-out. "No, Your Honor."

"All right then. We'll start picking a jury at one o'clock this afternoon."

The jury selection process, known in legal terms as *voir dire*, took almost two hours. Although it wasn't overly complicated or contentious, it did require Jerry's full concentration. If Tony had been there, Jerry was convinced that he wouldn't have been able to focus properly. He was very thankful that he had prevailed, and Tony had stayed away.

Jerry didn't have quite the same degree of luck in getting all he wanted during jury selection, however. As he had suspected would be the case, he and the ADA were at odds over one particular demographic pertaining to the jury pool. The ADA wanted as many jurors as possible who had children—and grandchildren were even better. Jerry, on the other hand, wanted as many jurors as possible without children. When the dust settled, the final makeup was split down the middle: six with kids, six without. Jerry was philosophical about the result. After all, he reasoned, he only needed one juror to get Tony acquitted.

Shortly after three o'clock the judge thanked the jurors for their willingness to serve, and thanked the attorneys for their professionalism. He closed the proceedings by saying, "Okay, we'll see everybody tomorrow morning, nine o'clock sharp."

But that was not to be.

CHAPTER SEVEN

A s soon as Jerry left the courthouse, he called Tony to let him know what had transpired. They arranged to meet later that night to go over Tony's testimony. Jerry wasn't sure that they'd get to Tony tomorrow but he wanted him to be prepared, just in case. There were three points that Jerry was planning to elicit from Tony that constituted the linchpin of the defense's argument.

First, Tony had never requested that the photos be sent to his e-mail account. Second, Tony had never seen the photos in question. And third, the police had seized Tony's computer, but had not found anything incriminating on it. Jerry was convinced that points two and three were true. As to the first point, he had his doubts, but he was now long past trying to sort out what was really going on. For good or bad, he was totally committed to defending his client. And while Jerry felt that the basic facts of Tony's testimony would be convincing, that alone might not be enough. The manner in which Tony conducted himself on the witness stand was probably just as important, if the jury was going to believe he was telling the truth. That was why the preparation was so critical.

The next morning, Jerry and Tony entered the courtroom fifteen minutes early. Ms. Lopez, the ADA who had been assigned to Tony's case from the beginning, was already there. If the two attorneys had looked toward the judge's bench, they would have noticed that the name plate read William A. Lancaster, not Alexander Titus.

A few minutes before nine o'clock, Judge Lancaster entered the courtroom from behind the bench. Both Jerry and the ADA glanced up and did a double-take. As the bailiff asked everyone to rise, their expressions turned into looks of puzzlement and curiosity. A moment later the judge said, "Please be seated." He paused. "I know you were expecting Judge Titus this morning, but I'll be filling in for him instead. I don't have all the details, but evidently there was a robbery at his home late last night, and he sustained injuries. We don't know the extent of those injuries, but he's still in the hospital."

For the briefest of moments, Jerry glanced at Tony, wondering if he could have had anything to do with the attack on Judge Titus. But then he dismissed it as improbable. There was no logical reason for Tony to do that, he thought. He also recognized that Tony's actions were very often more grounded in emotion than logic. Still, it seemed like a stretch.

Jerry's attention was forced back to the bench as Judge Lancaster continued. "When I found out from the clerk what had happened, I volunteered to step in. I've reviewed the files and feel confident that I'm up to speed. Therefore, there doesn't seem to be any valid reason to postpone the trial. But before we get started, I wanted to give both parties an opportunity to voice any concerns they may have." He turned toward the ADA. "Ms. Lopez?"

It was quite obvious to Jerry that the ADA was very disturbed by this development. Whether it was simply concern for Judge Titus' well-being, or more realistically, concern that Judge Lancaster would not look upon the case with the same mindset, he couldn't tell.

The ADA didn't answer immediately, which produced a slight smile on Judge Lancaster's face. Jerry thought the judge appeared to be enjoying the ADA's discomfort. And from her body language, Jerry could sense that the ADA wanted to object. But he also recognized her dilemma: on what grounds could she do that? The trial hadn't even started yet.

Jerry watched the looks between the judge and the ADA go back and forth like some invisible ball in a tennis match. Eventually, Jerry concluded that there must be some history between the two of them, either professional or personal. Regardless, it seemed obvious that there was no love lost there.

The judge waited another ten seconds and then said, "Did you want to say something, Ms. Lopez?"

"Uh, no, Your Honor," she replied.

"Good. How about you? It's Mr. Hanson, correct?"

"Yes, Your Honor, it is," said Jerry.

"Anything you want to say? Any additional motions you would like to make before I bring the jury in, and we get started?"

Jerry considered for a moment whether he should make the additional motion to exclude the photos. Now, with a new judge, Jerry's concern about how the shotgun approach to filing motions would be perceived was no longer an issue. He continued to look at Judge Lancaster, and thought he saw an expression of encouragement. However, at the last moment Jerry decided not to offer the new motion. "Not at this time, Your Honor."

The judge nodded and said, "Okay." He extended the first syllable so that his response suggested he was surprised by Jerry's inaction. While this exchange was going on, the ADA was shaking her head and rolling her eyes. "Then let's bring in the jury," the judge continued.

Once the jury was seated and received instructions from the judge, it was the ADA's turn. She gave a brief opening statement that was more matter-of-fact than theatric, which Jerry couldn't help but believe was a result of the change in judges. Jerry decided to follow suit, keeping his remarks brief and to the point.

After the opening remarks were concluded, the two arresting officers were called to testify in succession. Both of them stayed on script. And although they appeared to state the facts about what happened accurately, in Jerry's view their testimony seemed overly rehearsed and not particularly effective.

Next up was the computer tech expert who had uncovered the photos attached to the e-mail. The ADA asked him about his background and experience. As she started to introduce the photos into evidence, Jerry stood up and made a motion. "Your Honor, I move that the photos in question be excluded."

Before he could finish, he was interrupted by the ADA. "Your Honor, we already have a ruling on that motion."

The judge used his gavel. "One at a time, one at a time. Ms. Lopez, before you object, you should allow Mr. Hanson to finish. I suspect he wasn't going to repeat the motion he already filed. But even if he were, I have the right to reconsider the original one."

Jerry's mouth flew open. It remained agape for another few seconds until he finally realized how he must look, and closed it. Jerry was stunned. The judge had gone way beyond where he should have in chastising the ADA. Jerry considered trying to revisit the original motion to exclude the photos, but went with the new one instead. "Thank you, Your Honor. I would like to move that …"

This time the judge interrupted. "Hold on a minute, counselor. Would the two parties approach for a side bar, please?"

This request again surprised Jerry, but it was welcome news. It meant that the jury wouldn't hear the basis for his motion—to exclude the photos because of their inflammatory nature due to how graphic they were. Jerry knew that just hearing words like "graphic" or "explicit" in conjunction with child pornography could trigger jurors' imaginations. And it was possible that whatever they imagined would be just as bad as the actual photos, or worse. But now it appeared that Jerry wouldn't have to worry about that. And it was sounding more and more like the jury wouldn't see the photos, either.

When Jerry and the ADA arrived for the side bar, the judge covered his microphone and told Jerry to restate the motion in its entirety. When he finished, the judge said, "Now I'll hear from you on the matter, Ms. Lopez."

Jerry could see the contempt in the ADA's eyes as she spoke, but initially she didn't let it affect her response. "The introduction of these photos is critical to the people's case. The jury needs to see what was on Mr. Sarno's phone."

The judge looked almost disinterested. It was obvious that the ADA's words were having no effect. This time, as she spoke, her frustration spilled over. "Have you even seen the photos?" she snapped.

Judge Lancaster appeared taken aback. "I don't like your tone, Ms. Lopez. And you will address me as 'Your Honor.' " He paused, all the time staring at the ADA. " And yes, I told you. I saw them last night."

The ADA refused to back down, as her voice became louder. She pointed toward Tony. "And you think predators like him should get a pass? Those pictures are disgusting."

It was obvious to Jerry that the interaction between the ADA and the judge had now become more personal than legal. Judge Lancaster was visibly fuming as he removed his hand from the microphone and threw his arms in the air. "That's exactly the point that Mr. Hanson was trying to make. Viewing those photos could easily prejudice the jury. You want it in legal terms, Ms. Lopez? The photos have no probative value." And then he added, "You're just looking to sensationalize this. Some people would find *that* disgusting."

If the jury hadn't been able to hear the ADA's outburst, there was little doubt that they had heard the judge's comments, loud and clear.

For the next ten seconds, the courtroom was silent. Then the judge said, "Go back to your respective tables."

Jerry knew what he had to do, but he waited a moment to allow everything to calm down. "Your Honor, may I be heard?"

"Yes, Mr. Hanson."

Jerry spoke quietly, as if what he was saying was being offered with reluctance. "I move for a mistrial."

The ADA reacted immediately, but was much more subdued than she had been. "There's no need for that, Your Honor."

Judge Lancaster had also regained some of his composure. "Let me hear what else Mr. Hanson has to say."

Jerry kept his tone professional. "Thank you, Your Honor. It would appear that regardless of your ruling on the admissibility of certain potential evidence, the jury has heard it described in exactly the inflammatory terms that was the basis for the motion to exclude."

The judge appeared ready to respond, but instead turned to the ADA. "Ms. Lopez, I'd like your input on this."

"I believe it would be more than sufficient to instruct the jury to disregard anything they might have heard. They're intelligent enough to do that."

Not to be outdone, Jerry followed up with the flattery. "I agree that the jury is intelligent. But no matter how intelligent they are, it's unrealistic to expect them to ignore what just happened. We can't un-ring the bell, Your Honor." Jerry wanted to add—*My client shouldn't be made to suffer the consequences, especially since you were one of the bell ringers*—but he didn't.

The courtroom became quiet again. The judge looked at the ADA and then at Jerry, obviously weighing what to do. He then turned slightly and addressed the jury. "You have just witnessed an unusual and unfortunate occurrence. Before I make a ruling, I would like a show of hands to indicate whether you heard the exchange between me and Ms. Lopez. A show of hands please."

None of the jurors hesitated. All twelve raised their hands.

The judge nodded, almost to himself. "I don't see any choice. I'm declaring a mistrial." He then shifted his attention to the ADA. "You can re-file if you'd like, Ms. Lopez." Another shift. "You are free to go, Mr. Sarno. Jury members, thank you, you're dismissed."

Jerry shook his head in disbelief, and thought to himself—*What the hell just happened?* He looked over at Tony, who appeared to have been watching everything as if it were a reality show, rather than his life. Jerry stole a glance at the ADA, who finished throwing her papers into her briefcase, brushed past him, and exited the courtroom as quickly as possible.

Outside on the courthouse steps, Jerry and Tony spoke. "That's the craziest thing I've ever been associated with, Tony. But it all worked out in the end."

"So you think it's really over?" Tony asked.

"Well, you heard the judge. They can re-file." Jerry paused. "When things calm down a little, I'll call the DA's office and try to find out what they're intending to do. But honestly, I'd be surprised if they re-file. I think they were pushing it to begin with, and they knew it." Another pause. "My suggestion is to just get on with your life, and try not to think about it."

Tony said, "Okay," and this time extended his hand, although it seemed to Jerry like it was an effort.

"Well, good luck," Jerry said.

"Yeah, you too."

As Jerry walked toward his car, he reflected on how bizarre this case had been, especially regarding his client. But he decided it was too soon to start analyzing everything that had occurred. He wouldn't think about it for the next several days. Maybe the additional time would provide him with some perspective to make sense of things.

Tony, on the other hand, was more of an in-the-moment kind of person. As he drove away from the courthouse, he had no intention of looking back, literally or figuratively. Instead, he was already thinking about his new plan to get back in business. But before he did anything, he wanted to talk with Runner, so he could try to determine whether Runner had been telling him the truth. The thought that Runner might have been playing with his life moved Tony's anger into the red zone.

Tony called the number Runner had given him a few weeks earlier. Runner answered on the second ring. "Tonight, eleven o'clock at the mall." Tony hadn't been able to say a word. But he took the fact that Runner was willing to meet with him as a good sign. It diffused some of his anger, but he still wanted answers.

~

Runner showed up a few minutes past eleven. "The boss says to tell you congratulations." A slight pause. "He wants to know when you can start up again."

"A couple of weeks, probably," Tony told him. "I have to get a guy to replace Gleeson."

"Yeah, I heard he took off."

Tony wondered how Runner would know that, but obviously he did. "Right."

"So does this new guy have a name?" Runner asked.

"I haven't finalized anything yet," Tony responded.

"Okay, but the boss wants you to get right on it," Runner said. "So when you get the name, he wants to know. And another thing, no prostitutes. Not the boss', not anyone else's. They're cracking down. They'll be looking for you. And besides, you don't need their kids for your new plan anyway, right?" he smiled. "Of course that could make it tough on you, not being able to get your ashes hauled. Looks like your right hand might be your new best friend."

Tony was pissed at what he had just been told, but he was more focused on getting the answers he wanted. He took a chance and eased into it. "Obviously, you heard what happened with the trial. How come the boss wanted me to have a jury trial?"

"What do you care?" Runner retorted. "You got off."

"Yeah," returned Tony. "But it could have gone another way."

Runner was unapologetic. "The boss had it covered."

"What do you mean?" Tony pressed. "If it had gone to the jury, he would have been able to fix it?"

Runner stared at him. "What it means is that no matter what, he had it covered. Now, drop it!"

Tony took Runner's advice, at least for the time being. An hour later he was sitting at the RMV computer getting information about Josh Raybeck.

CHAPTER EIGHT

The Following May

STANFIELD, MASSACHUSETTS

Jonathan Allen glanced over at the clock next to his bed. The green LED numbers read nine forty-five. He looked up from the clock toward the window, trying to determine whether the rain had let up since he had driven Eric to school. It didn't appear so. The start of the month had been especially cool. That, coupled with forty-eight hours of precipitation, had made the last two days feel more like March than May.

In actuality, Jonathan had already resigned himself to the fact that it was going to remain gloomy for the rest of the day, and he was going to indulge himself—which was precisely why he had flopped back on his bed shortly after he had returned from dropping Eric off. He had intended to put his head on the pillow for only a few moments, but it was now forty-five minutes later. He hadn't really slept; he had just closed his eyes and let his mind go wherever it wanted. If this had been a number of months ago, especially right after Cindy's death, going back to bed until noon or later would have been the norm. But now, even a forty-five minute catnap was the exception. Jonathan felt as if he had finally broken the cycle of self-pity that had fed off his sadness and anger, and had left him incapable of living his life.

He was certain that part of the reason for this change in behavior was because the dream that had been plaguing him since October had stopped invading his sleep as often. The nightmare had visited only twice in April, and only one of those times had it been the version that truly horrified him.

He also acknowledged that even if the diminished frequency of the dream had helped him make changes, there was something else: Jonathan had started to be a parent again. He had come to the realization that, while he had lost his wife, Eric had lost his mother. As devastating as Jonathan's loss had been, his son's was ten times worse. Maybe "selfish" was too strong a word, but that's what Jonathan believed he had become. And now, from what the school personnel were telling him—never mind his own realization—he knew that he had to do everything possible to rescue his son from the abyss he had fallen into. Jonathan had been there, and he knew it all too well.

Another thought started to enter Jonathan's brain, but before it could form itself into anything substantive, the phone rang. It was the landline, not his cell phone. He picked up and said, "Hello."

No one responded, and then a recorded message came on – "This is the Stanfield Elementary School. Your child ... Eric Allen ... is listed as absent today. Please call to confirm the reason for the absence. If you have already called to report the absence, thank you, and have a nice day. The phone number for ..."

Jonathan caught the implication of the message midway through, but listened for a few more moments before he sat up. The fact that he had heard this same message a number of times before, and they had all been mistakes, lessened his immediate anxiety. He used the phone's callback feature to make certain it was simply an error—that Eric was right where he was supposed to be, right where Jonathan had dropped him off. But before the call kicked in, he realized it would just reconnect him to the automated number, not the school office.

Why hadn't he listened to the rest of the message? *What the hell is the school's number, anyway?* he thought. Maybe it's on that school magnet we have on the refrigerator. He hurried to the kitchen, found the magnet and pulled it off, causing one of Eric's papers to flutter to the floor. He punched in the school's number on the wall phone and waited. After the second ring he was connected, but it was three push-button commands later before he reached anyone.

"Stanfield Elementary School. This is the school secretary, Mrs. Brewer. How can I help you?"

For some reason, Jonathan was relieved it was Mrs. Brewer. He had met her a few times, although he wouldn't have been able to come up with her name if she hadn't just told him who she was. "Hi, Mrs. Brewer. It's Jonathan Allen, Eric's father." He waited a moment for her to process the information.

"Oh, yes, Mr. Allen." she said. "What can I do for you?"

"I just got a call that Eric is absent, but I dropped him off this morning, probably an hour ago," he told her.

Mrs. Brewer's tone was light. "You're the third parent who's called. It's probably just a clerical error. The other two were. Things have been a little hectic this morning. The fire alarm went off before school even started. Some students were in the school already having breakfast, and some were still coming in. It was ..."

Jonathan cut her off. "Could you please check on him?"

If Mrs. Brewer was offended by Jonathan's curtness, she didn't let it enter her voice. "Uh, of course. Do you want to hold, or should I call you back?"

"I'll hold," Jonathan told her.

"Okay, I'll be right back."

Nearly five minutes went by. Jonathan's sense that this was just a mistake began to waver, and his emotions threatened to spill over the brink. But he forced himself to pull back from the edge. *It's got to be a clerical error, just like Mrs. Brewer said.* And then she came back on the line.

"Mr. Allen, I'm sorry. Eric's class has library second block today. So when I called down to his classroom, there was no answer. I tried the library, but the class is either on the way there or they might be in the reading room. I'll send someone up there, and call you back. But I'm sure it's nothing."

Jonathan didn't hesitate. "I'm going to come to the school right now. Call me on my cell if you find out anything." He gave her the number.

"Okay, Mr. Allen, but I'm not sure it's necessary ..." Mrs. Brewer stopped talking when she realized there was nobody on the other end.

Jonathan jumped in the car and sped toward the school, still trying to keep his emotions in check. Then he replayed the morning in his mind, searching for anything out of the ordinary.

Eric had been quiet, as usual. He didn't want breakfast, claiming he preferred to eat at school. Again, that wasn't unusual. When that particular ritual had started, Jonathan had hoped it was because Eric was meeting classmates or friends. But he suspected it was really because Eric didn't want to spend any additional time with his father. He wondered if it were possible for a six-year-old to feel resentment.

Jonathan's mind moved forward to when he had dropped Eric off. He was the fourth or fifth car in the parent drop-off lane. When their car had reached the front of the line, Eric got out and headed off to the school entrance. Jonathan had called after him to put up his hood because of the rain, but Eric didn't respond. Whether he hadn't heard him, or chose to ignore the suggestion, like a typical six-year-old, he wasn't sure. Then he remembered watching Eric just before he reached for the school door, but couldn't recall whether he saw him go in or not. This morning seemed the same as every other morning. Usually Jonathan waited until he saw the door close behind Eric. But had he done that this morning? He simply didn't know.

His thoughts shifted again. Why had he given in to Eric always wanting to be early to school? If he had arrived when most of the other kids arrived, probably none of this would be happening. Of course, that was assuming that this was just a mix-up—which was all Jonathan would allow himself to seriously consider at the moment.

His mind then moved back to why he had given in to Eric. Actually, he thought, I do know why: Cindy. From the time Eric could understand the rudiments of speech, Cindy had talked to him as if he were an adult. She would say, "You have to eat your vegetables, Honey." And even if Eric didn't ask 'why,' she would say, "Because they're good for you, and they'll make you healthy and strong." And later, as he got older, and did ask why, she repeated the same answer. She never said to him "Because I say so," or "Because there are starving children in the world." Jonathan remembered her voice when she explained her reasoning to him. "I want Eric to eat his vegetables because it makes sense to him, not because I can bully him into it, or make him feel guilty."

Jonathan remembered having trouble believing that Eric could understand any of that, certainly not when he was two years old. But Cindy's voice had such a combination of love and trust and quiet authority, that to this day, Eric always ate his vegetables. Of course, so did Jonathan. He smiled at the memory.

And as far as being on time to school, that was all Cindy as well. She had told Eric that being late was disrespectful. Again, it was almost impossible for Jonathan to imagine that a young toddler heading off to preschool had any notion of what respect was. But even now, at age six, Eric hated to be late for anything, even more so than his mother had.

Jonathan recalled telling Cindy, "He's such a fanatic about this; you've created a monster, you know?" But in truth, Eric was as wonderful a little boy as any parent could have hoped for - at least until Cindy was taken from them.

Jonathan's mind jumped again, trying to make sense of what he had just been thinking. Maybe eating all his vegetables and being early to school were simply Eric's way of honoring his mother, remembering what she had taught him, a way of holding on to her somehow. Maybe it didn't have anything to do with resentment.

As his mind started to transition back to the present, Jonathan briefly marveled at the human brain's capacity to hold certain thoughts at bay, until you were ready or forced to confront them. In this moment when the worst fear imaginable was facing him, he had thoughts of vegetables and being on time. *But maybe thinking normal thoughts in the midst of potential horror was what enables us to keep going.*

As if to disprove his theory, at that precise moment all of Jonathan's philosophical thoughts left him; and all he could think of was Eric. This had to be mistake. But what if it isn't? Could Eric have run away? That idea hadn't even crossed his mind until now. Was that possible?

That thought was interrupted by the chirp of his cell phone. He picked it up off the passenger seat, glanced at the school's number on the screen, and pushed to connect. "Did you find him?"

No immediate response, and then Mrs. Brewer said, "I'm sorry, Mr. Allen, he's not with his class. His teacher said she hasn't seen him at all today."

"Oh my God, no" said Jonathan. A split second delay. "I'm almost at the school. Call the police as soon as I hang up."

The secretary sounded flustered. "I'll have to tell the principal, and then she …"

"Just do it, damn it! I'll take responsibility."

He broke the connection, threw the phone back down on the passenger seat, and sped up. He slammed his hands against the steering wheel, and then his emotions went over the brink.

Less than five minutes had elapsed from the moment Jonathan disconnected the call until he pulled into the school's parking lot. The closest spot to the entrance was labeled "handicapped." Jonathan didn't give the sign a second thought as he steered the car between the blue lines and screeched to a halt. He threw open the car door and ran to the school's main entrance. He yanked on the door, but it was locked.

As he tried again, he could see a man approaching through the narrow panel of safety glass in the door. Jonathan released the handle and waited for the man to arrive. But instead of pushing down on the release bar to let Jonathan in, the man peered back at Jonathan and said, "I'm sorry, sir, we're in lockdown. Nobody can come in or out."

"You have to let me in; I'm the one whose son is missing." As Jonathan spoke the words out loud, their meaning brought home the devastating reality of what was happening. And whatever slim hope he had been harboring that this was simply a mistake began to disappear completely.

The man's voice became more sympathetic. "You're Eric's father?"

"Yes," Jonathan answered.

"I'm one of the guidance counselors here. I've just started testing Eric." The man paused. "I'm sorry Mr. Allen, but the police ordered the lockdown. The principal sent a few of us to guard the doors until they get here."

Jonathan was about to protest when he heard sirens approaching. As anxious as he was, he made himself step back from the door and wait. An unmarked car, followed immediately by three cruisers, pulled to within twenty yards of the school's entrance. The first person out was from the unmarked car, and he was in plain clothes. He headed straight toward Jonathan. "Who are you?"

"Jonathan Allen. My son, Eric, is the one who's missing."

"Have you been inside the school?"

"No, no. I just got here. They said I had to wait for you."

By this time, the cruisers had emptied, and six additional uniformed officers had rushed to the entrance. After seeing the cops exit their cars, the guidance counselor pushed open the door he had been guarding.

The man in plain clothes grasped the handle and opened the door wider as he motioned to the other cops. "Okay, let's go." He then looked over toward Jonathan. "You can come, too." After he thanked the guidance counselor for letting them in, he added, "Can you stay here and make sure no one goes in or out?" It was more a command than a question.

Once inside, he continued to give orders to the uniformed officers. "You go ahead to the main office. I'll be right there." He then stopped moving and signaled Jonathan to do the same.

The man then held out his hand. "I'm Detective Munoz, Mr. Allen. I'm going to want to talk with you in a few minutes. But first, I want to organize a search of the building. Let's hope your son is just hiding somewhere."

As Munoz paused, Jonathan got the sense that the detective was assessing Jonathan's body language to determine if Jonathan thought that was likely. Then after a moment passed, Munoz continued. "I know you want to be doing something, but right now I'm going to find someplace for you to wait until I'm finished. And then we'll talk. Can you do that?"

The detective's take-charge, no-nonsense manner was so reassuring that, despite Jonathan's overwhelming fear and anxiety, he responded calmly. "Yes." But then he added imploringly. "Please find him."

They went to the main office where Munoz spoke to the "crisis team" that had assembled there at the principal's directive. The detective's bearing had the same effect on the school personnel that it had had on Jonathan. They moved without hesitation as he instructed them to show the police officers around the school and assist them in searching for Eric.

Munoz addressed the principal next. "Can we talk in your office?"

"Certainly."

The detective then turned back to Jonathan. "I'm going to speak with the principal for a few minutes. I'll be with you as soon as I can." He looked around the main office briefly and noticed an empty conference room across from the principal's office. "You can wait in there." When Jonathan didn't immediately move, Munoz went over to him and spoke quietly. "I can't pretend to imagine what you're going through. But you need to trust that I know what I'm doing." Jonathan recognized that this wasn't some sort of bravado; this was a confident man doing his job.

The detective continued. "Right now, the principal and the people she's spoken to have more information than anyone else. That's why I'm talking to her first. Okay?"

Jonathan nodded, as Munoz placed a hand on his shoulder. Jonathan then headed toward the conference room as the detective and the principal went into her office.

Jonathan felt that the only thing that had kept him from falling apart at that moment was Detective Munoz's behavior; he seemed to know exactly the right thing to say and do. If this horror had any chance of ending well, thought Jonathan, it would be because of Munoz. *He must be new. I don't remember him being in the department when they investigated Cindy's death. I wonder where he came from. And what's he doing in Stanfield? I guess it doesn't matter; I should just be grateful he's here.*

A flood of emotions began to overtake him. Jonathan covered his face with his hands and stayed like that for a full minute. And even though he had closed his eyes, when he removed his hands they were wet with tears.

He blinked back some additional tears that threatened to spill over. When he was able to focus again, he realized that the principal's office was directly across from where he was sitting. And although Jonathan was able to see into the office, Munoz's back was to him, and the principal was out of his sight line. There was no way for Jonathan to even get a sense of what was being said, or how they were interacting.

After about five minutes, Munoz got up out of his chair and picked up the phone on the principal's desk. He appeared very animated. Another minute went by, and then he seemed to end the call and push some buttons to make another. He spoke briefly and then appeared to be on hold, as he moved the receiver away from his mouth, and presumably started talking to the principal. After another minute, he returned to speaking on the phone. He finally hung up a few minutes later.

After he hung up, Munoz remained in the principal's office for an additional five minutes, at various times pointing to something out of Jonathan's sight. And once, Munoz got out of his seat and walked in the direction where he had been pointing. When he returned to the principal's desk area, he appeared to offer his hand to shake, and then left the office and headed toward Jonathan.

The silent movie that had been playing for Jonathan as he observed all the activity in the principal's office had barely managed to keep his worst fears from entering his consciousness. Thirty seconds later, Munoz was sitting across from him. "Thanks for your patience, Mr. Allen."

Jonathan was only able to nod, not trusting his voice just yet.

Munoz spoke again. "When I'm conducting an investigation,

especially one like this, I can't waste time worrying about people's feelings, or about second-guessing anyone. Time is critical here, so I'm just going to ask what I need to ask. If you take offense, I can't help that. Understand?"

Munoz's directness caught Jonathan off-guard, which he realized might have been the point. But for some reason it also provided the impetus he needed to attempt to speak. "Okay. Go ahead."

"Did you drop off your son this morning?" the detective asked.

"Yes, of course," Jonathan affirmed.

Munoz watched his face. "The principal tells me that no one remembers seeing him, or you, for that matter."

Under normal circumstances that statement would have upset Jonathan. But in this instance, it didn't. "I did drop him off," he insisted. "I don't know why no one saw him."

Munoz' expression didn't change. "Did you watch Eric go into the school?"

Jonathan hesitated, but he had promised himself that he wasn't going to lie, no matter what. He had to trust someone if he hoped to get his son back. And if he were caught in a lie, no one would believe anything else he said. "I'm not sure. I usually do, but this morning, I just don't remember."

"Okay," the detective responded. Jonathan expected some kind of follow-up, but Munoz quickly moved on. "Is it possible that Eric ran away?"

Again, Jonathan hesitated, but more because something inside him didn't want to acknowledge that possibility, despite the fact that it was far preferable to the alternatives. In the end, he told the truth. "Yes, it's possible. But honestly, I don't think so."

Munoz stared at Jonathan for a moment before he spoke. "Why not? The principal told me your wife passed away at the beginning of the school year. That's got to be devastating for a little boy. The principal said that Eric's been different since then—'distant.' That was her word, not mine. Your son's got every reason to be unhappy. Sometimes unhappy kids run away."

At the mention of Cindy's death and Eric's difficulties, tears started to form in Jonathan's eyes again. But he was able to compose himself enough to say, "If he was going to run away, I think he would have done it right after his mother died, or even a month ago, but not now." He paused. "I was a wreck after my wife died. I didn't handle it very well, especially with Eric. But I've started to pull myself together. Things between Eric and me are the best they've been in months." The tears came again, as Jonathan struggled to continue. "He's just not that kind of a kid."

Before Munoz could ask another question, there was a knock on the door, and a uniformed cop came in. "The tech guy is here, Detective."

"Thanks," Munoz said. "Would you please ask the principal to show him where he needs to go?"

The short exchange between the two policemen allowed Jonathan to gather himself. But before he could say anything, Munoz jumped in and moved the conversation in a totally different direction. "So we're clear, I believe you when you say you dropped off your son. And although we haven't quite finished the search, I don't think he's hiding in the building. Of course, I've been wrong before, but I don't think I am this time. I do think it's possible he ran away, however." Munoz held up his hands as if he were going to physically ward off any additional objections from Jonathan. "I say that only because Eric might have had an unexpected situation present itself when the fire alarm went off. I think it's possible that once he went outside, maybe he decided not to go back in. I've already called to have some additional cruisers patrol the area, especially near your house. When six-year-olds run away, they tend not to go very far."

But before Jonathan could take any solace in the possible scenario Munoz had outlined, the detective backtracked somewhat. "There's something that's got me concerned about that likelihood, however. The alarm was pulled. It wasn't an accident." He expanded his explanation. "There's what's called an 'annunciator box' in the principal's office. It shows which alarm has been pulled, so that when the fire department shows up to reset it, they know exactly where the box is located."

Jonathan wasn't quite following where this was headed, and his expression must have conveyed that, because Munoz tried to spell things out more clearly. "Let me go back, so you know what I'm thinking. The school was supposed to get surveillance cameras this year, but they were cut out of the budget. So we don't have any video to show us who pulled the alarm. The principal told me that the alarm that was pulled is in a corridor that is rarely used by students or staff. It mainly contains storage areas and things like that. As soon as I found all this out, I called for a tech person to come and take fingerprints off the alarm. We might not be able to identify who pulled it, but we should be able to tell whether it was a student or an adult. I also called the fire department and spoke to the fireman who reset the alarm. He was wearing gloves, he told me. So his prints won't be there."

Jonathan had tuned in to some of what Munoz was saying, but still hadn't completely figured out the detective's thought process, and where he expected it to take him. Before Jonathan could ask for clarification, the tech person returned and knocked on the door. This time Munoz stepped outside of the conference room. He and the tech person talked quietly for about thirty seconds, and then Jonathan heard Munoz raise his voice. "Damn it!" He then thanked the tech guy, and came back into the room.

"What's the matter?" asked Jonathan.

"He dusted for prints, but there weren't any," Munoz shook his head. "It was wiped clean."

"What does that mean?"

Munoz took in a deep breath as if he were about to dive under water. "No kid is going to wipe down the alarm. This was an adult. And I don't think it was a staff member. This was somebody from the outside."

The unthinkable then started to register with Jonathan. "Are you saying what I think you're saying?"

"I hope I'm wrong, but all this seems to have a purpose to it: Select a time of day when there's almost no supervision. Pull an alarm and wipe it clean. You've got fire engines coming and going; it's totally chaotic. Plus, it's raining; people pay less attention to their surroundings when it's raining."

Munoz continued laying out his argument, but Jonathan had stopped listening. His hand went up to his mouth, and the words "Oh, my God" were muffled.

But the next words that came out of his mouth were not.

CHAPTER NINE

"Are you telling me you think somebody kidnapped my son?" Jonathan gave an anguished cry.

Munoz didn't answer right away; he just stared at Jonathan across the table. Eventually, he said, "I pray to God I'm wrong. But everything is starting to point to that."

Jonathan jumped to his feet, knocking over the chair he had been sitting on. He didn't attempt to pick it up. Instead, he intertwined his hands behind his head and moved his elbows toward each other, blocking his ears, as if that would prevent Munoz's words from getting through. He then started to hyperventilate, making it difficult to talk. When he calmed down somewhat, he asked, "How can this be happening? Who would do this? He's just a little boy, for God's sake!"

Munoz let Jonathan vent, knowing that there was nothing he could possibly say that would make any difference. Another minute passed, and Jonathan's arms dropped, making him look more defeated than anything else. As he tried to come to grips with the escalating horror, another thought entered his mind. "I don't have any money. What kind of ransom could they expect to get?"

Munoz wished that he didn't have to answer that question. It was just going to add to Jonathan's terror. "Most abductions don't involve a ransom."

The implications of what Munoz was saying hit Jonathan like a knife stabbing him in the midsection. All of his focus then shifted to Eric. "He must be so scared." Jonathan broke down completely, as the next words he spoke struggled to emerge. "You've got to find him!"

Munoz decided to allow Jonathan's emotions to run their course before he spoke again. In his experience, that was the best thing to do at this point. Then, after Jonathan had calmed down, Munoz would explain what he was going to do next, involving Jonathan as much as possible. That way, Jonathan would feel as if he were doing something, and it might help distract him, however briefly.

71

Munoz made eye contact. "I'm going to wait a few more minutes for the search to be completed, and then I'll contact the sector cars to see if they've come up with anything. We'll also canvass the neighborhood around the school to see if anybody might have seen something. After that, I'll contact all the media outlets. I'm going to ask them to report a missing child, no other details except his name, a description, and where Eric was last seen. I'll need a recent photo for the canvass and for TV. Do you have one?"

Again, Munoz's take-charge attitude pulled Jonathan back into the moment. "Let me think. He didn't have one taken for school this year; that was right after Cindy was killed. I think we have one that was taken last summer, maybe. Is that okay?"

That was almost a year ago, thought Munoz. But he wasn't about to point that out to Jonathan. However old it was, it would have to do. "That'll be fine. I'm going to have one of the officers drive you home to pick it up. We'll make copies and show it around. We can also scan it into the computer and transmit it to the TV stations in time for the noon news."

Jonathan started to speak, but Munoz anticipated the question. "By doing it this way, we're covering all bases. If Eric did run away, every cop will have his picture as they patrol the area. If it's ... something else, his picture on the news might trigger someone's memory." He paused. "We probably need to hold off before we issue an Amber Alert; we're not supposed to do that until we're certain it's an abduction. Plus, if we wait to do that until after the noon news, we'll get twice the coverage."

Jonathan nodded in appreciation, as Munoz spoke again. "There's one more thing. If nothing substantial breaks by this afternoon, I'm going to make a preliminary call to the FBI."

This last piece of information threatened to send Jonathan off the deep end. Up until now, at times everything seemed surreal, as if it were outside of him, not something he was really a part of. But the mention of the FBI changed all that. There was no escaping it—Eric was missing, probably kidnapped, and the FBI was being called in.

Logically, Jonathan knew that this last piece of information should be greeted as good news. But it didn't feel like that. It felt as if his personal fear and pain and the task of finding Eric was being passed off to people he didn't know. Jonathan had just met Munoz, but he trusted him implicitly.

Again, Munoz seemed to read Jonathan's mind, no doubt from the skepticism clearly visible on his face. "The FBI has a lot of resources we don't have." He paused. "They'll coordinate everything with us. It's what we need to do."

Jonathan believed the part about the resources, but he had his doubts about the coordination part. Munoz had been less than convincing when he had made that point. And if coordination were a problem, wasn't it possible that calling in the FBI would slow everything down? But Jonathan didn't raise any objections. He had placed his faith in Munoz, and besides, he didn't have the emotional energy or wherewithal to question the decision.

Munoz waited a moment to see if Jonathan was going to say anything. When he didn't, Munoz rose out of his chair and said, "Okay, Mr. Allen, let's find one of the officers to drive you home so you can get that picture. Then he'll drive you back to the station; I'd like to talk with you some more, just to make sure we haven't missed anything."

Jonathan remained numb. He quietly answered, "Okay."

As they left the conference room, four of the uniforms had returned to the main office. Munoz caught the eye of one of them. "Anything?"

The tallest of the cops responded, "No. And I radioed the other two. They're almost finished; there's no sign of the boy."

Munoz turned to the principal. "As soon as we leave, you can call off the lockdown. If the media contacts you, refer them to me. Thanks for your cooperation. And if you or any of your staff think of anything else, please call me."

As he headed for his unmarked car, Munoz arranged for Jonathan to get a ride in one of the cruisers. Then, on the drive back to the station, Munoz called the sector cars, but they had nothing to report. Five minutes later he was at the station house. He went into his office and closed the door.

From his bottom drawer he dug out material about the FBI unit that specialized in crimes against children. He wanted to re-familiarize himself with the protocols of the Child Abduction Rapid Deployment (CARD) teams before he placed the phone call. Less than ten minutes later, he was on the line with the FBI field office in Boston.

Munoz explained the situation, emphasizing that it was impossible to completely rule out the runaway scenario, but that all his instincts and

73

experience had led him to believe it was an abduction. He also indicated that he was intending to release a photo to the media and then issue an Amber Alert.

Munoz thought for sure he was going to receive some pushback, but the special agent he was speaking with encouraged him to go ahead. "I would agree with everything you're going to do. And as far as our involvement is concerned, even though there are still some questions, I think it's warranted. We should be able to get a team together in the next few hours. We'll be there sometime this afternoon." There was a pause on the line. "And Detective Munoz, you did the right thing. As you know, time is critical in these situations. Sometimes it's literally the difference between life and death. Call me at this number if anything develops before we get there; they'll patch you through."

As soon as Munoz hung up, he noticed that the chief of police was now back in his office; he hadn't been there when Munoz had returned from the school. Munoz walked over, knocked on the door jamb, and was waved in. "I wanted to give you an update on the missing Allen boy."

The chief said, "Yeah, thanks. How's that going?"

The detective outlined what was transpiring, including his plans for notifying the media, issuing the Amber Alert, and his call to the FBI. Since Munoz had joined the department six months ago, the chief had given him carte blanche in every situation, and this case was no different. The chief knew how lucky the town was to have landed Munoz—a ten-year, decorated veteran of the Boston Police Department. And Munoz had never disappointed him.

Shortly after Munoz finished briefing the chief, Jonathan arrived with an envelope in his hand. Munoz invited him into his office and told him about the call to the FBI. It was obvious to Munoz that Jonathan had been crying, but his outward demeanor was eerily subdued. Munoz had seen this before. It appeared that Jonathan had resigned himself to the worst and had started to give up.

It was hard for the detective to blame him—first his wife, and now possibly his son. People had only so much fight in them. As he looked at Jonathan, he wanted desperately to tell him that they were going to find Eric. But he had vowed long ago, when he became a detective, that he would never promise something he wasn't sure he could deliver. Instead, he offered, "The FBI will be here this afternoon. Having them involved so early is a real plus." He paused, hoping to see some positive reaction from Jonathan. When none came, he continued, "It's also possible that showing Eric's picture on the news, as well as the Amber Alert, may produce something."

Jonathan nodded, but didn't say anything.

Munoz held out his hand. "May I see the photo? I'd like to get copies made as soon as possible."

Jonathan removed it from the envelope and handed it over. He then spoke for the first time, but his voice carried no emotion. "I couldn't find anything more recent than this. I think it was taken last summer, but there's no date on it."

Munoz took the photo and looked at the blond-haired, blue-eyed little boy. He was struck by how handsome the boy was. But it was more than that. Eric had a self-assuredness that radiated from his smile and lit up the whole photograph. Munoz wanted to comment on the photo, but he was reluctant to do so. Once again, his experience told him that saying anything, even something complimentary, would ironically make Jonathan feel worse. So he settled on a benign response. "This will do fine. I'll be right back."

As Munoz was heading out of his office, he glanced at the photo again, and had the same reaction as when he first saw it. He turned it over. In the upper left corner he saw the words "Eric—age 5" written with precise penmanship. *Undoubtedly by Eric's mother*, thought Munoz.

And at the bottom, slightly off-center, he saw a stamped imprint that read:

First Class Photo

Josh Raybeck

Munoz waited while the IT specialist scanned Eric Allen's photo into the computer and then printed out multiple copies. On the way back to his office, he gave copies of the photo to the two-man teams who were heading out to begin canvassing. Once Munoz returned to his office, he handed the original photo back to Jonathan and placed the remaining copies in the case file. He and Jonathan continued to talk for a few more minutes, the detective trying to prompt Eric's father into recalling anything else about the morning that he hadn't thought of. Unfortunately, nothing else came to Jonathan's mind.

Eventually Munoz said, "I think the best place for you to be right now, Mr. Allen, is at home. I know that might be difficult, but there isn't anything more you can do here." To further bolster his argument, Munoz added, "While it's probably a long shot, maybe Eric will show up at your house. Somebody needs to be there. It's also possible that one of your neighbors might have seen him, and once his picture is on TV, they might try to contact you."

The detective could see in Jonathan's expression that he didn't want to go anywhere. He wanted to stay right where he was. But in spite of those obvious feelings, Jonathan responded, "If you think it's best, okay."

"I do. I'll have one of the officers drive you back to your car; then he'll follow you home. I'm also going to have him park outside your house, in case anything develops."

Jonathan looked more intently at Munoz. "Shouldn't he come inside, in case there's a ransom call?"

Munoz couldn't bring himself to tell Jonathan that there was virtually no chance of that happening. So he avoided a direct answer. "If you'd be more comfortable with him inside, that's fine. Just let him know."

Jonathan didn't pursue the ransom call possibility any further, so Munoz moved on. "I'm going to contact the radio and TV stations in Boston and Providence shortly." He paused. "Do you have caller ID?"

Jonathan nodded. "Yes."

"Of course, you can do what you want," said the detective. "But if I were you, I'd screen my calls and avoid talking to the media. There may come a time when we'll want you to go on TV, but not yet."

Jonathan shook his head. "I'm not sure I'd know what to say to them anyway. I don't think I could hold myself together."

Munoz didn't know how to respond. Another moment passed, and then he offered, "When the time comes—if it comes—I'm sure you'll do fine."

Jonathan smiled weakly. "Thanks."

"Come on. I'll find somebody to drive you to your car."

As they left the office, Jonathan asked, "Have you decided to put out the Amber Alert?"

"Yes, probably around one o'clock," answered the detective. "As I mentioned, by doing it then, the TV stations will break in to their regular shows, so we'll get additional coverage."

"Then you must be pretty sure that Eric was kidnapped."

Munoz turned and looked directly at Jonathan. "I am."

"But you don't think it was done for a ransom, do you?"

The detective replied quietly, "No."

Jonathan fought to stay in control. He didn't say another word, even when Munoz introduced him to one of the uniformed cops, and they left the station together.

Over the next several hours, Munoz systematically went about completing all the tasks he had outlined for Jonathan, and a critical one that he had not—he generated a list of all known sex offenders living within a twenty-mile radius of Stanfield. Since that area included a relatively large city, Providence, the numbers were almost staggering: one hundred and fifty-seven.

Even when Munoz pared the list down by only including Level Three offenders, it was still eighty-eight. The number of man hours required to interview even eighty-eight people would take a week. In child abduction cases, that was an eternity. The chances of finding a kidnapped child unharmed once the investigation went beyond forty-eight hours were close to zero. Plus, the Sex Offender Registry only included individuals who had been convicted of a crime. There were plenty of predators out there who had avoided being caught, or had somehow beaten the justice system.

With all that in mind, suddenly the prospect of finding the handsome little boy whose photo had filled the TV screen a couple of hours ago seemed out of reach.

Munoz had always performed his job with a quiet confidence. But the thought of what was at stake and the lack of any solid leads threatened to chip away at that. He closed his eyes for a moment, trying to clear his mind of all the negative thoughts. When he opened them again, he glanced at the clock; it read two twenty. He wondered when the FBI team was going to show up; he hoped it was soon.

Forty-five minutes later, Munoz saw a tall man who appeared to be in his late forties being shown into the chief's office. After ten minutes, the chief brought the man over to Munoz. "Hello, Detective

Munoz, I'm Special Agent Walker. We spoke on the phone."

Munoz got up from behind his desk and offered his hand. "Good to meet you. I'm glad you're here."

The chief spoke up. "As I mentioned, Agent Walker, you should coordinate everything with Detective Munoz. If either of you need anything from me, just let me know." He turned to Munoz. "Make sure you keep me in the loop, Dave."

After the chief left, Agent Walker said, "Your first name's Dave?"

Munoz nodded. "Right."

"Mine's Craig. I prefer first names, if you don't mind."

"Not at all." Munoz paused and looked over Walker's shoulder.

The agent picked up on it. "The rest of the team's not here yet. I figured I would come ahead and get some more preliminary information before they arrive."

"Do you want to use one of the conference rooms?" Munoz asked him.

"No, this is fine."

Munoz had a question in his voice. "I guess I meant when the team arrives, and you take over the case."

The agent smiled. "We're not taking over the case. We're going to work this together."

Walker saw the look of surprise on Munoz's face and said, "I know that's not how we're usually portrayed on TV— we're the big bad FBI who comes in and pushes the local guys out of the way." He paused. "When we talked on the phone, you said you were on the job in Boston for a few years. Is that what you experienced there?"

"Most of the abduction cases I worked were domestic situations, parent against parent. So I was only involved in a couple where the FBI was called in. But, yeah … honestly, that's almost exactly what happened."

"Well, that's not how the teams I head up do it." A pause. "The first commander I ever worked under used to say, 'You can get a lot more accomplished if you don't care who gets the credit for it.' I've never forgotten that."

Munoz nodded, obviously pleased, as Walker continued. "Now

that we've gotten that out of the way, why don't you bring me up to speed? Start at the beginning, if you don't mind, Dave. I want to get a sense about how everything's developed."

Munoz described arriving at the school, seeing Jonathan Allen, talking to the principal and then to Jonathan, ordering the fingerprint check on the fire alarm, and finally having the other officers search the building. At that point Walker asked, "Any chance the father's involved?"

"I don't see it, Craig. He seems too broken up. I know sometimes people can fool you, but it's also more than that. Every question I asked him, his answers were straightforward. There were never any signs of deception. Plus, if he did something to his own kid, why the fire alarm?"

"Yeah, I agree. That doesn't make any sense. Where's the father now?"

"I sent him home, but I've got a cruiser stationed there."

"That's good." Walker was obviously considering something before he spoke again. "From what you've told me, I assume you've also ruled out a kidnapping for ransom?"

"Jonathan Allen doesn't have a whole lot of money; we checked. If this were about money, I think whoever did it would have picked somebody else."

Walker nodded, and then moved on. "I saw that you've got the boy's picture on TV, and then I heard the Amber Alert over the police radio. Anything else you're doing?"

"I've got four officers canvassing the neighborhood around the school." Munoz then extracted some papers from the case file and pushed them across the desk. "And then there's this."

CHAPTER TEN

Walker read the bold heading on the top of the cover page—Sex Offender Registry. He then fanned through the copies, focusing on the last page. "A hundred and fifty-seven, huh? How large an area?"

"Twenty-mile radius," said Munoz.

"It could be worse," Walker replied. "It could include Boston."

Munoz reached for the list. "If we just go with the Level Threes, it's down to eighty-eight."

Walker nodded. "A little more manageable. Okay, let's start with those."

"That's what I was thinking, but how do we do that?" asked Munoz. "We can't possibly interview all of them. It would take weeks."

Walker elaborated. "One of the shortcuts we've used in the past is to find out how many of these guys are on probation or out on parole. Then we can contact their probation officers and have them call the parolees' jobs to see if they showed up for work this morning. It should cut down the numbers."

Munoz was impressed, but he didn't say anything. It was obvious to him that Walker didn't need to have his ego stroked. In fact, Munoz thought he might consider it unprofessional. Instead, he offered, "I can have one of our guy's cross-check the computer records against the list to find out who's on parole."

"That'd be good. Once we have the list, we need to move on it right away. We should call the P.O.'s at home, if need be. The numbers will be in the system." Walker glanced at his watch. "It may be too late for them to reach the parolees' job sites this afternoon. But if we have everything else in place, they can start first thing in the morning." Another pause. "We should also set up a hotline. We'll probably have to sift through a lot of bogus calls. But you never know; we might get lucky."

"Okay," replied Munoz. "I'll get somebody on that as well. After the hotline is set up, I'll contact the media and have them broadcast the number."

"Good. While you take care of that, I think I'm going to go meet up with the rest of the team. They should be arriving at the motel where we're staying shortly. How about we see you back here between four-thirty and five?"

"Sure." Munoz waited a moment before he spoke again. "Is there anything else you think I should be doing? I've put some ideas together, but nothing real specific. Frankly, I wasn't sure how involved I'd be once you guys showed up."

A slight smile formed on Walker's face. "Your instincts are good, Dave. I told you, we'll figure this out together. I'm going to need your input."

Munoz wasn't sure that was true, but he was flattered just the same. He started to say something, but Walker interrupted. "Actually, there is one more thing you can do. I think it's helpful if everyone working on this has his own copy of the case file." Walker picked up his copy off the desk. "I'm going to take mine with me now. Can you have someone make copies for the other guys on our team?"

Munoz reached into his bottom drawer, extracted additional files, and handed them to Walker. "Already done. Also, the officers who are conducting the canvass have copies, too."

"I like how you think, Dave." Walker rose to leave. He shook hands with Munoz and said, "We need to find this little boy and nail the bastard who took him."

It was the first sign of emotion that Munoz had seen from Walker. He wondered briefly if Walker's relatively stoic persona was typical. He finally decided that it had to be. Walker had told him that he'd worked over a hundred abduction cases. Anyone who'd worked that many, and didn't distance themselves emotionally, would have burned out by now. Munoz had worked less than a tenth of that number, and it had taken its toll. It always did, when little kids were involved. He remembered feeling relief right after he left Boston, believing that he might never have to deal with one of these cases again. But now, six months later, here he was.

His thoughts were interrupted by the return of the officers who had been canvassing. They didn't have any good news. Their shift was almost over, so he told them to go home and to be ready to start fresh in the morning with the FBI team. Exactly what that meant, however, he didn't know.

Munoz then went to help set up the hotline and contact the media so they could broadcast the number. Next, he told one of the officers that had just come on duty what he wanted done with the Sex Offender Registry.

Returning to his office, he opened the case file and looked through it again. After a few minutes, his mind returned to the conversation with Craig Walker about figuring out what to do next. He wondered if Walker was serious about wanting his input. Munoz decided that he would try to come up with some ideas, just in case.

Shortly before five o'clock, Walker and the rest of the CARD team arrived at the station house. Introductions were made all around, and then the group proceeded to a conference room, where Walker asked Munoz to review the case file.

Since the team had it in front of them, Munoz just offered a summary, highlighting the things he felt were most important. After another ten minutes, Walker indicated to his team that he wanted them to stay in the conference room and brainstorm. He then turned to Munoz. "Dave, let's go back to your office."

Once again, Munoz was surprised. But he also knew that Walker had done this so many times before that there was no reason to question it. Back in Munoz's office, Walker spoke first. "Good job on the briefing. Where are we on the hotline and cross-checking the sex offender list?"

"The hotline's up and running, and one of the guys who just came on duty is working on the registry list," Munoz told him. "He'll start calling the probation officers as soon as it's complete."

"Okay, good," Walker responded. "So, did you think about what I said? Any thoughts on how we should proceed from here?"

Munoz hesitated. "Actually, I do. It's mainly what I thought the Stanfield officers should be concentrating on. I wasn't sure about your team."

"That's all right," Walker encouraged. "Let's hear it."

"Okay," Munoz began. "Even though we've already canvassed the school neighborhood, I think we should do it again. But we should do it tomorrow morning, just around the same time the Allen boy disappeared. It's more likely that the people who will be home tomorrow morning at nine o'clock were also home this morning at that time."

"Excellent. I agree," Walker nodded. "One suggestion though, let's pair up each of the Stanfield officers with an FBI team member. Your guys know the area, and our guys provide a little more weight to the situation. And thinking along the same lines, why don't you and I go back to the school? We should get there early, when the parents are dropping their kids off. They may have seen something they're not even aware of."

"I hadn't thought of that."

"It's okay. You're doing great."

Munoz didn't say anything for a moment, and then, "Can I ask you something, Craig?" He didn't wait for an answer. "How come you're involving me like this? I don't have anywhere near the experience that you do."

Walker smiled. "I learned early on that I don't have a monopoly on good ideas. Sure, there are routines and protocols that we follow, but each location has a different feel to it, a different dynamic. You'd be amazed at how many times a local cop has come up with an idea we didn't think of. Okay, so what else have you got?"

Munoz outlined his ideas for monitoring the hotline and contacting the probation officers. Walker concurred, and then made another suggestion. "I think one of our team members should alternate with the guys who are staying with Mr. Allen. I don't think we need to tap his phone though, since we're not expecting a ransom call, right?"

"No, we're not. But I think Jonathan Allen wants to hold on to that idea, even though I told him there was very little chance."

"Is he holding on to it because he believes it might be true?" Walker asked. "Or is it because he's not ready to face the alternative?"

"The second one," Munoz acknowledged

"Well then, let's make sure the people monitoring him stay inside the house. We can tell Mr. Allen it's in case there's a ransom call. It'll make him feel better, and it doesn't hurt anyone."

"I think he'd appreciate that."

Walker shifted gears. "There's another thing I wanted to ask you about. I saw in the notes that the boy's mother was killed last year. Do you have more information on that?"

"She was killed in October," Munoz told him. "I didn't start here until November, so almost everything I know about it came from the case file, although I did ask around."

"Was the father a suspect?"

"In the beginning, yes. You know, you always look at the spouse. But there was nothing to link him to it."

Walker wasn't satisfied. "It's still seems a little suspicious, don't you think? Especially since they never found out who did it."

"I guess," Munoz agreed. "But honestly, I have trouble believing he was involved in either one."

"Okay. It's probably not relevant anyway." Walker paused and looked at the notes he'd been making. "Here's what I'm thinking about logistics for tonight. I'm going to have our team work in four-hour shifts. Obviously, if anything breaks, everybody can be here in minutes; we're only a few miles away. What about your guys?"

"We have a regular night shift."

"That should be fine." Walker paused. "If we were anticipating a ransom demand, I might handle it differently. But in the absence of that likelihood, this seems to make the most sense. Other than monitoring the hotline and reviewing what we already know, there's not a whole lot we can be doing. It's a pretty helpless feeling."

"Which shift are you taking?" asked Munoz

"I don't need a lot of sleep. I'll grab three or four hours, and then head back here."

"I'll do the same then."

"Good." Walker glanced at his notes a second time. "Let's go see how the brainstorming is coming along in the other room."

The brainstorming session lasted for an additional hour. There were a few minor changes to the plans that Munoz and Walker had come up with earlier. But all in all, everyone was pleased with the direction the investigation would be taking the next day.

Ten miles away, just over the Massachusetts border in Rhode Island, a little boy was trying to wake up.

Eric struggled to keep his eyes open. He was so sleepy. He blinked

four or five times, and then rolled over. This isn't my bed, he thought.

He forced his eyes open, but couldn't see very much. It was dark, except for the light from a small lamp. He touched the blanket covering him. But it wasn't a blanket; it was a sleeping bag. It was much bigger than the Transformers sleeping bag that his mommy had bought for him. That thought triggered something inside him. He opened his eyes wide, and called out, "Mommy, Mommy!" Once again, "Mommy!" And then he remembered.

He closed his eyes again, not because he was tired, although he was, but because he didn't want to cry. He lay there for a few minutes, sniffling and wiping his nose. He then noticed that his mouth tasted funny. But he didn't remember eating anything. And his stomach felt funny too, like he was going to throw up.

Finally, he opened his eyes, and kept them open. He was too scared to get up, so he stayed where he was and looked around. After a minute, he began to see things better. He was in a room. But not like in a house, someplace else. He looked straight ahead, and then side-to-side. It was a funny kind of room; it didn't have any windows. But there were lots of shelves, just like in the garage at his house. Then he saw his jacket on a shelf next to the lamp, and he started to remember.

He was at school and the fire alarm rang. He went outside because that's what you're supposed to do when there's a fire alarm. He put up his hood because it was raining, even though he hadn't done it when his daddy had told him to.

Ironically, the memory brought him back to the present, and he called out, "Daddy!" Again, "Daddy!" A third time, even louder, "Daddy!" Then he started to cry.

After a few minutes, he thought about the fire alarm again and about going outside. He remembered that someone called his name; someone said, "Eric." He turned to see who it was, but the side of his hood was in the way. Then he felt something on his mouth. He couldn't remember anything after that.

He started to cry again, much harder than before. His eyes became sore and red. Between sobs, he called out again, "Daddy, Daddy." But the words barely escaped his lips.

And then he heard a noise. It came from in back of him. He turned toward it. It looked like some kind of door was there. Then the noise moved closer. Someone was coming in.

CHAPTER ELEVEN

Not surprisingly, when Munoz finally arrived home and tried to go to sleep, it eluded him. His brain wouldn't shut down, as theories and strategies about the case pin-balled through it. Twice, he got out of bed and switched on the computer, aimlessly Googling words and phrases, as if somehow those searches would help him develop a lead. But of course it was a futile gesture, primarily borne out of his need to be doing something.

Munoz finally got up for good around five thirty, showered, made some coffee, and turned on the TV. One of the national morning programs was hyping a reality show that aired on the same network. But at five minutes before the hour, they shifted to local news, and Eric Allen's photo appeared in the corner of the screen. The anchorwoman parroted the standard line that all police departments issued to the media—still investigating, no suspects at this time, the police are pursuing a number of leads. *And what leads would those be?* thought Munoz.

He decided to leave the house before six twenty-five so he wouldn't be tempted to watch the local news again. As he walked to his car in the driveway, he noted that the rain had finally stopped after two full days. He wondered what part the weather had played in Eric's disappearance and, to a greater extent, how much it had served to stymie the development of any leads. Munoz had said it himself—"People pay less attention to their surroundings when it's raining."

He pulled into the police station parking lot shortly before seven. Once inside, he touched base with the FBI agents who were there, as well as the Stanfield night shift, but there was little to report. A couple of calls had come in on the hotline, but nothing significant.

By seven fifteen, Munoz was in his office. And once again, because he needed to be doing something, he opened the case file, searching for anything he might have missed. But it proved to be as fruitless as his online search several hours before. After a few more moments, he resigned himself to the reality that this morning's efforts— re-canvassing the neighborhood, talking to the parents in the drop-off

86

lane, and working the sex offender list—constituted the best hope of generating a meaningful lead.

Walker and the rest of his team showed up at seven thirty. The other Stanfield officers who were going to partner with the FBI agents were already there, even though their shift didn't start until eight. Nobody was worried about putting in overtime, paid or not. They just wanted to do whatever they could to bring Eric Allen home safely.

Everyone gathered in the conference room, where the pairings of the three Stanfield officers and three of the FBI agents was finalized, and they were given their assignments. A fourth FBI agent was assigned to relieve the Stanfield officer who was at the Allen house. Munoz spoke to him before he left. "Tell Mr. Allen that I'll be there later this morning to give him an update. I'm planning on calling him myself, but in case I get tied up, I don't want him to think I forgot."

The agent nodded. "Sure thing, Detective."

Two of the paired teams were scheduled to start the re-canvass at eight thirty, a reasonable hour when most people would be up. The other team involved in contacting the probation officers would begin at nine. But Walker and Munoz decided to be in place at the school by eight, just in case some of the parents were particularly early.

On the short ride over to the school, they finalized the logistics of their plan: They would station themselves on the driver's side of the drop-off lane and take turns asking the parents if they had seen anything yesterday morning. If the answer was yes, Walker or Munoz would instruct the driver to pull up to a coned-off area so a more extensive conversation could take place.

As they expected, there were only a handful of students being dropped off between eight and eight-fifteen, and none of those parents had seen anything the previous day. The number of cars picked up substantially over the next several minutes, and by eight forty-five there was a backup.

Five minutes later, Munoz approached a mid-sized SUV. The driver lowered her window, as she must have seen the drivers in front of her do. Munoz showed his badge and said, "Good morning. I'm Detective Munoz with the Stanfield police. We're investigating the disappearance of Eric Allen, and we were wondering if you may have seen something when you dropped off your child yesterday."

The woman's eyes were wide. "Oh my God, isn't this awful? I

can't believe it."

Almost every parent Munoz had spoken with had the same reaction. After the first few conversations, he settled on a response that conveyed his empathy, but also made it clear that he was looking for their assistance. "You're right; it is horrible," he agreed. "But if you saw anything, you may be able to help. Did you?"

"Well, I didn't hear the fire alarm, so I must already have left by then," she told him. "But before that, I'm quite sure I saw the little boy who's missing."

It might not be much, thought Munoz, but it was the first time anybody had indicated that they'd seen Eric at the school. "Ma'am, would you mind pulling up to that area up there? I'd like to ask you some additional questions."

"Of course, anything I can do to help."

By the time Munoz had walked up to the coned-off area, the woman had exited her car. She offered her hand and said, "I'm Barbara Atwood."

"Detective Munoz."

"Yes," she said. "What else would you like to know?"

"What time were you here yesterday?"

"Just about this time," the woman replied. "I try to drop off my daughter the same time each day. She does better with routine."

"And what did you see?" he asked her.

"Well, I don't know the Allen boy. I think they said on TV that he's in first grade, and my daughter, Sofia, is in third. So there'd be no reason for them to know each other."

Munoz was getting a bit impatient, but he didn't let it show, and the Atwood woman finally got to the point.

"I think it was the car right in front of mine, although it could have been two cars in front. Anyway, I saw this young boy start to get out of the car. I wasn't paying that much attention, just waiting for the line to move. But then I noticed his blond hair. It especially stood out because almost all the other kids were wearing hats or had their hoods up."

"So, you're sure it was the Allen boy, Eric?"

"Yes, especially after I saw his picture on TV. I mean, in the picture his hair was much shorter than it is now. But you couldn't mistake the color; it's so light. I even mentioned it to my husband last night at dinner." She paused. "Did I do something wrong by not calling the hotline? I didn't call because they said on TV that he had disappeared from the school. So I figured you already knew that he had been here."

Munoz shook his head. "No, no; you didn't do anything wrong. Did you by any chance see him go into the school?"

"Yes, actually I did. I'm not sure why, but I watched him the whole time. In fact, I remember the person behind me honking because I hadn't moved up." Munoz asked for the woman's address and phone number, and handed her one of his cards. "Please call me if you remember anything else. And thank you; you've been very helpful."

"You're welcome," She responded, then paused. "Do you have any idea what happened to him?"

Munoz gave her the standard response. "We're still investigating."

"I hope you find him soon," she told him. "A lot of the kids, and their parents, for that matter, are really nervous about this. I mean, you think when they're at school, they're safe."

There was nothing Munoz could say to that. He just nodded and thanked her again.

Walker and Munoz continued to talk to parents for the next forty-five minutes. Ten additional drivers were asked follow-up questions, two of whom also thought they may have seen Eric enter the school, but they were far less certain than Barbara Atwood. And no one indicated that they had seen Eric outside after the fire alarm went off. But that was not surprising, given that most of the parents described the scene outside the school as chaotic.

Before heading over to talk with Jonathan Allen, Walker and Munoz went into the school and spoke briefly with the principal, hoping that some new information might have come to light. But it hadn't. And while it was quite obvious that the principal's main concern was Eric, she was also dismayed because at least thirty parents had decided to keep their children home in light of what had happened. The principal repeated the same sentence a number of times—"This is such a nightmare."

Walker asked if he and Munoz could use a conference room for a half hour or so. The principal found them one and they sat down to talk. Walker opened up the discussion. "I thought we should compare notes, especially before we go see Mr. Allen. So what's your take on this morning?"

Munoz looked disappointed. "I'm not sure we made a lot of headway. We've got one witness who says she saw Eric get dropped off and go into the school, and two more who think they might have. That's certainly sufficient to back up the father's story. But I never really doubted that he was telling the truth anyway. And we didn't get much from the people who were there yesterday morning right after the alarm went off. In fact, most of the ones I talked with said that a lot of the parents told their kids to get back in the car because it was raining. So it's not surprising that nobody noticed one kid leaving, either by himself or with someone. Although it is interesting that Mrs. Atwood said Eric stood out because of his hair. I wonder why nobody else noticed him." He paused. "Of course, maybe when he went back out, he put his hood up."

Walker agreed. "No way to tell. I hate to say it, but I think we've gotten everything we're going to get from interviewing the parents. But what you said about that witness, Mrs. Atwood, that gives me an idea. I know there are no surveillance cameras here at the school, but what about nearby, at intersections, or town offices, anything like that? I know the odds aren't great, but it's possible whoever took Eric might have driven past one of them. And maybe with his blond hair, he might be visible in the car. Of course that's assuming a whole lot. But right now, we don't have very much else. I hope the other teams are faring better than we are."

"Yeah, me too. I think the surveillance camera idea is worth a shot, Craig, although off the top of my head, I can't recall too many places that have them." Munoz paused, obviously remembering something. "Of course, the Stateline Mall is not far from here. They must have them. Plus, a lot of people use the road in back of the mall as a shortcut to get to I-95."

Walker stood up. "That sounds like a good place to start. Let's go see Mr. Allen, touch base with the other teams, and then check out the mall." Walker paused, shaking his head. "Jeez, did I just say 'check out the mall?' I sound like my daughter."

Munoz smiled for the first time all day. He waited a moment and then asked, "What should we say to Mr. Allen?"

Walker grew serious. "I don't want to lie to him, but I don't want to start dashing his hopes, either. Why don't we tell him that one of the witnesses confirmed that Eric went into the school? He can draw the inference himself that we know for sure that he was telling the truth about dropping off his son. That may comfort him somewhat. Then we can tell him that the re-canvass of the neighborhood is not quite complete, and we're hoping to get some leads from that. Let's not mention the Sex Offender Registry unless he brings it up."

They agreed that Munoz should take the lead, because he already knew Jonathan Allen. They discussed putting him on TV, but Walker said, "I think we should wait until we can hold a press conference and make him part of it. Right now we don't have much that we can comment on. But if nothing breaks by tonight, we'll set something up tomorrow, regardless."

They spent the next half hour with Jonathan. Munoz kept to the script, never lying, but never quite telling the whole truth, either. He reconciled his actions by reminding himself that offering the unvarnished truth would be more cruel than anything else. Munoz didn't explore whether that was merely a rationalization on his part.

Jonathan posed a number of questions to Walker, which the FBI agent answered cautiously. At the end of the visit, Jonathan asked, "Are you going to get my son back?"

This time, Walker was totally honest. "I just don't know, Mr. Allen."

Once they returned to the car and started heading for the Stateline Mall, Walker phoned the other three teams, none of whom reported any real progress. The only piece of relatively good news was that the team working with the probation officers had been able to cut the list of eighty-eight down to forty-nine. But forty-nine would still require a lot of man hours.

They arrived at the mall ten minutes later and parked near the main entrance. As they exited the car and headed inside, a quick survey of the parking lot found two security cameras mounted high on the light poles. Neither Walker nor Munoz said anything; they just pointed to their location.

The directory inside the mall entrance indicated that the security office was on the second floor. They found it easily and knocked on the door. A man who looked to be approaching sixty opened up and said, "Yes, can I help you?"

The badges came out. "I'm Special Agent Walker, with the FBI, and this is Detective Munoz. We'd like to speak with someone about your surveillance cameras."

The security guard looked concerned. "Is there a problem?"

"No, nothing to do with the mall. We're hoping your cameras may have picked up something that will help us with a case we're working on."

"Is this about the little boy who's missing?" the man asked.

Walker considered being evasive, but then decided that telling the truth would move things along more rapidly. "Yes it is, as a matter of fact. And time is critical, so …"

"Of course. Actually, I think you're in luck. The guy who knows the most about our security system happens to be here this morning. I saw him about ten minutes ago by the food court across from the photo place." The security guard could see that Walker wanted him to speed things up, so he said, "Sorry, let me go inside and get his number."

He came out less than a minute later and started punching in numbers on his cell phone. He continued talking while he waited for the call to connect. "The guy is actually the night watchman, but he's a whiz with computers and electronic stuff. His name's Tony Sarno."

"Hello, Tony? It's Jack Carven from security. Yeah, hi. Listen, are you still here in the mall?" A pause. "Okay, good. Can you come back to the office? There are two policemen—well, actually one of them is an FBI agent. They want copies of some security tapes." A longer pause. "Tony, are you still there? Did I lose you? Tony … Oh, there you are. Can you come to the office? Okay, I'll tell them."

The security guard disconnected the call and spoke to Walker. "He says he'll be here in five minutes."

"Thank you."

The guard pointed to a nearby door. "You can wait in the office if you'd like."

Walker nodded his thanks. "Yeah, that would be good, thanks."

Tony made it in less than five minutes, although for a fleeting moment, a wave of panic overtook him, and he considered taking off. But then he was able to calm himself. He realized the surveillance camera story had to be legitimate. He knocked on the security office door and walked in. Of course the knock was unnecessary, but Tony calculated that it would make him appear respectful and somewhat meek, just what he wanted anybody investigating the case to think.

Once Tony was inside, Walker and Munoz stood up, and they all shook hands. Tony fought to keep his nerves in check. "Hi, I'm Tony."

"I'm Special Agent Walker and this is Detective Munoz. We were hoping you could help us out."

"Sure, if I can," Tony said.

Walker decided to be straightforward again. "We're investigating the disappearance of a young boy, Eric Allen. Maybe you saw it on TV?"

Tony tried to sound sympathetic. "Yeah, I did. Terrible thing. But what's it got to do with the mall?"

"We're hoping that something might show up on one of your surveillance cameras," Walker told him.

Hearing that, Tony was finally able to relax slightly. He asked, "You really think whoever took him brought him to the mall?"

Munoz answered the question. "The mall probably wasn't even open yet. But maybe they went through one of the parking lots, or used the back road to get to I-95."

Tony didn't say anything for a moment, and then he offered, "I don't think the cameras cover the back road, but I can get you videos for the parking areas. What date and times do you need?"

Walker said, "Yesterday, from nine o'clock until noon."

"Okay," Tony calculated aloud. "There are five parking lot cameras, three hours each. That's fifteen hours of video. That's a lot to go through."

Walker silently agreed, but the only thing he said was "How soon can you have that for us?"

"It's going to take a while to burn five DVD's."

At this point Munoz spoke up again. "What if you transferred the video to a thumb drive, wouldn't that be quicker?"

Tony would have preferred to delay things as much as possible; the longer the authorities were focused in the wrong direction, the better it was for him. But he couldn't come up with a plausible excuse for not doing what the cop had asked. It appeared that he knew what he was talking about. And if Tony threw out some lame excuse, it might raise some suspicion. "Yeah, that'll work."

Munoz said, "Can you do that as soon as possible? We can wait."

This time Tony did have a legitimate reason to delay. "We're in the process of upgrading the system. I have to shut some things down and then back them up. It'll be faster than burning the DVD's, but it'll still take a while."

Munoz glanced at his watch. "What time should we come back?"

Tony wanted to appear cooperative. "I know you guys are busy. As soon as I'm done, I'll drop it off."

Walker said, "We'd appreciate that."

"No problem."

After Walker and Munoz left, Tony started to access the parking lot surveillance videos. A few minutes into it, he spoke to the other security guard. "I need to get something out of my car to finish this. I'll be right back."

Of course, Tony's statement was a total fabrication. He might not have been able to fool the detective, thought Tony, but Jack was another story.

Tony left the security office and walked toward the food court. He stopped in front of First Class Photo, as he had done earlier. But this time he was able to catch Josh Raybeck's eye, and he signaled for him to come to the food court.

Tony got a couple of cups of coffee, found a small table tucked in the corner, and waited. A few minutes later Josh showed up and sat down. He looked at Tony with contempt, and then spoke to him more aggressively than he had ever dared to before. But that was because he was more frightened than he had ever been in his life. "What happened?! I was supposed to hear from you last night. I tried calling, but your secure number was blocked. What the hell is going on? I'm …"

Tony spit out the words. "Shut the hell up! Don't you dare question me."

It was Josh's fear that had forced him to ask the questions in the first place; now it was a different kind of fear that made him back down. "I'm sorry," the photographer said nervously. "But I didn't sign up for this. I can't eat. I can't sleep."

Tony glanced around to make sure nobody was listening. "Tough shit. And what do you mean, you didn't sign up for this? You knew exactly what you were doing. I don't remember hearing any complaints when you were making all that extra cash."

"I'm not talking about that." Just as Tony had done, Josh looked around before he finished his statement. "I'm talking about what's happening now."

Tony sneered. "Yeah well, that wasn't your call, was it? You work for me, so suck it up."

Josh remained quiet. He knew it wouldn't do any good to continue arguing. He just wanted this over with.

Tony spoke again. "Nothing else to say, Josh?"

Josh shook his head.

"Good. Now, listen carefully. There's been a change of plans."

Concern entered Josh's voice. "What?"

"We're going to leave things the way they are for the time being."

Josh looked panicked. "You can't do that! Why?"

"Mainly, because I said so," Tony retorted. "But also, because I just had a conversation with an FBI agent and a detective."

Panic spread across Josh's face, and all the color drained from it. When Tony saw this, the corners of his mouth turned up slightly. "You look like you just shit your pants. What a pussy. Why the hell did I get mixed up with you, anyway? I should have picked somebody with some balls."

Josh struggled to speak. "What happened … with the FBI agent?"

Tony spoke with a superior tone. "It's not that big a deal. He wanted some security videos. If that's the best lead they've got, they're screwed. Just the same, I don't want to take any chances. So we're not going to do anything for the time being." Tony paused. "Did you at least take the … take care of what you're getting paid for?"

Josh was afraid to tell the truth. So he didn't. "Yeah, all done," he said.

"Good. Maybe you're not as big a fuck-up as I thought. Now we just sit and wait until things calm down. I don't want you contacting me. And don't do anything else unless you hear from me. Do you think you can handle that?"

Josh wanted to protest, but the fight had left him. He was devoid of both energy and emotion. "Yeah."

Tony reached across the table and patted Josh's cheek. "That's my boy." Then he threw two dollars on the table. "Have another coffee; it's on me."

On the walk back to the security office, Tony had more confidence in his step. Part of the reason for that was the exchange with Josh. He always felt better when he showed people who was in charge, although in Tony's world, showing people who was boss was more about berating and belittling them. That was what truly raised his spirits. And it didn't matter who it was—Gleeson, Josh, or the prostitutes he was back to frequenting. It simply made him feel good.

Tony was also buoyed by the information the FBI agent had given him. Once Tony had gotten over the initial shock of meeting with the agent, it became obvious that the FBI was clueless. Tony would gladly provide the videos from the parking lot cameras. They could have the ones from inside the mall too, if they wanted. Eric Allen had been nowhere near the mall yesterday, at least not between nine and noon. Of that he was absolutely certain.

CHAPTER TWELVE

On the way back to the police station, Walker and Munoz discussed the game plan for the rest of the day.

Walker started the conversation. "I don't know how long it's going to take for us to get those videos, but in the meantime, we should check in with the other teams to see how they're doing, and also check the hotline." A pause. "Any other ideas on possible camera locations?"

Munoz shook his head. "I know there aren't any at intersections, like Boston has," he began. "I guess it's possible that some stores or businesses might have some, but those cameras would most likely be inside. They wouldn't be pointed toward the street. Other than that, there are only two places I know that definitely have them: Town Hall and the nature preserve."

Walker turned toward Munoz. "The nature preserve?"

"I know," replied Munoz. "Ordinarily that would sound promising, but I already had it checked out; it's a dead end."

Walker frowned. "Why do you say that?"

"When we first canvassed the neighborhood yesterday, I had one of the teams touch base with the guard on duty."

"There's a guard at the preserve? Why?"

Munoz had only recently learned the details himself. "Evidently, for years the town was having trouble with teenagers drinking in there. There were a couple of proposals to limit access, but nothing came of them. Then after Cindy Allen was killed, they decided something had to be done. So about four or five months ago, they built a combination comfort station and guardhouse. They put up a gate in front of the parking lot entrance. It's the only way in and out.

"The rest of the preserve is surrounded by marshland. It costs two bucks to park there unless you're a town resident; then it's free. Anyway, it's open eight to eight, and the guard monitors all the traffic. The town added the security cameras to make sure the teenagers weren't sneaking in on foot after hours. The guard told our guys that there was only one car there yesterday morning, and that was two women birders— you know, bird watchers. I can still get a hold of the video, but I'm sure there won't be anything on it. The Town Hall cameras might be a better bet. I'll call over as soon as we get back."

Once inside the station house, Walker spoke to the officer manning the hotline while Munoz phoned Town Hall. They met back in Munoz's office. "Anything on the hotline?"

"Nine calls, nothing promising. What about you?"

"They're going to send over a copy of the video. But the guy I spoke with claims all the cameras are inside except one, and that's directed at the front steps and the sidewalk. He's pretty sure it doesn't cover the street."

Walker looked defeated. "I feel like we're spinning our wheels. What's making this especially tough is there's no real crime scene. In most abductions, the child is taken from a house or someplace where we can get plenty of forensics. And that invariably leads to suspects, but we don't have that here." He paused. "I think maybe we should shake things up a bit. Let's call a press conference and have the father speak."

Munoz looked up, surprised. "I thought you wanted to wait on that."

"I did. As I said, I'd prefer to have something positive to report. But at this point, I'm running out of ideas, and sometimes a plea from a parent brings people out of the woodwork."

Munoz said, "Okay. What time?"

Walker glanced at his watch. "Let's say two o'clock. That'll give us a chance to prep Mr. Allen."

Munoz reached for the phone. "I'll call Jonathan and make sure he's up for it, and then I'll contact the media and set it up."

"That's good, thanks," Walker stood up. "While you're doing that, I'm going to check in with the other teams. I was going to suggest to you that after the press conference, we should go help them. You know, break up the sex offender list." He paused. "And then I thought, since we really can't do much of anything else tonight, we could look at the video from the mall. Are you up for that?"

Munoz nodded. "Yeah, absolutely."

Walker took the lead at the press conference. He made an initial statement, answered a few questions, and then turned it over to Jonathan, who made an impassioned plea for the return of his son. His remarks were so gut-wrenching that even the media representatives and the law enforcement personnel were seen wiping their eyes.

While the news conference was under way, Josh Raybeck was still at work, trying to act as normal as possible after his confrontation with Tony. Finally, at around three o'clock he told his boss he wasn't feeling well and left for home.

Ironically, if he had gone home only an hour earlier and watched the press conference, especially Jonathan Allen, Josh probably would have ignored everything Tony had told him to do. And the next few days would have played out much differently.

By contrast, Tony Sarno had watched the press conference in its entirety. He scoffed at Walker's image on the TV screen as he spoke about the "progress" that was being made. He even shouted at the TV when one of the reporters editorialized and referred to the individual responsible as "sick."

But when Jonathan Allen spoke, Tony watched without reaction. And as soon as it was over, he clicked the remote and went into his bedroom. *I probably should take a nap;* he thought. *I have to work tonight.*

Following the press conference, Walker and Munoz ushered Jonathan back inside the police station. Walker was the first to speak. "I know that must have been difficult, but you did very well, Mr. Allen."

Jonathan looked at Walker. "Other than burying my wife, that's the hardest thing I've ever had to do in my life." He paused. "Do you think it'll do any good?"

Walker met his gaze. "Obviously I hope so, but there's just no way to know."

Jonathan's voice broke. "All I can think of is how scared he must be." At that point, the emotions he had somehow kept below the surface during the press conference exploded. He found a chair next to Munoz's desk and collapsed into it, sobbing.

Munoz located a box of Kleenex and handed it to Jonathan. He then started to say something but realized the words he was about to offer were empty. After a few minutes, Jonathan composed himself and said, "I'm sorry. I'm not sure how I held it together when I was speaking, but ..."

Munoz patted Jonathan on the shoulder. "There's nothing to apologize for. We're going to do everything we can to bring him home."

"I know," Jonathan responded shakily. A pause. "Can you tell me, do you really have any leads?"

Walker took that one. "Detective Munoz and I will be heading out in a few minutes to check out some possibilities."

Jonathan glanced at the open file on Munoz's desk. "Sex offenders?" he asked grimly.

"We don't have any specific information that points in that direction, but it's standard procedure to look at individuals with that in their history," the FBI agent replied.

Jonathan sighed wearily. "I know. I appreciate you being up front with me."

Walker nodded. "I'm going to have the agent who brought you here drive you home."

Jonathan nodded. "Okay."

Shortly after Jonathan left, Walker and Munoz got in the car and drove to Providence. There was a concentration of eight Level Threes within a four-block radius. Only two of them were home. And while neither had an alibi that could be easily corroborated, the men cooperated fully. Walker and Munoz both agreed that it was very unlikely either man was involved.

In order to interview the other six parolees, Walker and Munoz had to visit work sites, relatives' homes, and local hangouts, none of which produced anything resembling a lead or a suspect.

It was nearly seven o'clock when they returned to the station house. Nobody working the case there had any good news, either, although Tony Sarno had dropped off the thumb drive.

Walker and Munoz went into the conference room, sat down and remained quiet. But both of them were thinking the same thing: they were no closer to finding Eric than they had been when he first disappeared.

Before viewing the video from the mall security cameras, they decided to order some Chinese takeout. In between bites of beef teriyaki, Munoz said, "I'm not exactly sure how it helps us, but I still think a lot of planning went into this. It just doesn't feel like it was random."

"You're thinking the Allen boy was targeted?" Walker asked.

Munoz nodded. "Maybe not him specifically, but probably whoever did this planned to take somebody from the school. I mean, either the guy was incredibly lucky, or he scouted things out ahead of time. Think about it—no surveillance cameras, a fire alarm box in an out-of-the-way corridor, no fingerprints, not to mention the rain."

"He couldn't control the weather, Dave."

"No," acknowledged Munoz. "But the forecast was pretty solid—rain for forty-eight hours straight."

Walker leaned forward thoughtfully. "Let me play Devil's advocate. If this was planned, then whoever's responsible had to be watching the school, which means he probably would have had to go inside at some point. How come nobody noticed him hanging around?"

"I don't know," the detective mused. "Maybe he's one of those guys that just blends in. Or maybe he found the school's floor plan online."

Walker didn't respond immediately. "That's a possibility. But no matter how he pulled it off, I tend to agree with you. It wasn't random. But unfortunately, just like you said, I'm not sure how that helps us, at least not that I can see." Walker paused. "So, you want to get started on the videos?"

Munoz began to pack up the cartons of food. "Yeah, let's do it."

"Could be a long night."

Immediately after Walker said those words, he and Munoz had exactly the same thought—*nothing compared to what Eric Allen is going through, assuming he's still alive.*

The first half hour of each video—nine o'clock through nine thirty—was relatively easy to analyze. The mall didn't open until ten, so the few cars that showed up during that time were mostly employees or delivery personnel. So what easily could have taken over two hours, took about an hour and fifteen minutes.

Still, it was very tedious. Shortly before eight thirty, Walker suggested they take a break. He leaned back in his chair, closed his eyes, and sighed. After a moment he mumbled under his breath. "I was hoping this was going to be the one."

Munoz heard what Walker said, but wasn't sure whether he was meant to. He responded anyway. "What do you mean?"

Walker sat forward again. "I was just thinking out loud."

"Sorry. I thought you were talking to me."

"Maybe I was," the agent replied. "I don't know."

There was an awkward silence for a few moments, and then Walker said, "I've been thinking about retiring for about six months now."

Munoz didn't respond, although the surprise was evident on his face.

Walker noticed it and said, "Yeah, I just turned fifty and I have enough years in. I've been telling myself that I'm going to go out on the next one that ends right. The last four have been horrendous. And I probably don't have to tell you that the bad ones stay with you. If I'm going to retire, I want my last case to overshadow all that other baggage."

He let out a breath. "Pretty naïve for an FBI guy, huh? Don't misunderstand; I'm not giving up on this case yet. It's just that the odds are starting to pile up against us, the longer it goes without any suspects." Walker paused. "Sorry. It's probably just the frustration talking."

Munoz felt as if he should say something, but nothing appropriate came to mind.

The silence was brief as Walker continued. "You know, it's funny. Over the years I've gotten a lot of satisfaction from what I do. But if someone asked me whether I love my job, I'd say no. How can you love doing something that half the time ends up with some kid being scarred for life, or worse? So why did I keep doing it?" A pause. "Well, at the risk of sounding like a self-serving jerk, I'm good at it. And just maybe a few more kids are alive because of that. But as great as the successful ones make you feel, somehow they don't make up for the other ones." Another pause. "Does that make any sense?"

Munoz nodded. "I haven't been on the job as long as you, but I get what you're saying."

Walker kept watching Munoz. "Do you mind if I ask you something?"

"No, go ahead."

"Why'd you leave Boston? I mean, no offense to Stanfield, but you're an excellent detective. I could see that right away. You should be working someplace else—maybe even with the FBI."

Munoz smiled. "Yeah, I just heard a ringing endorsement for that career path."

Walker returned the smile. "No, that was about me, not the Bureau. But you still didn't answer my question about Boston."

The detective's smile faded. "It's a long story."

"Sorry, I didn't mean to pry."

"No, it's okay." Munoz took in a breath before continuing. "A year ago I got engaged. Although my fiancée and I had a lot of conversations about what I did for a living, it was never a deal breaker. But then one day it was. She said that she couldn't spend her life worrying each night whether I was going to come home or not; at least, that's what she told me. So I offered to make a change. I'd still be a cop, just not in a big city. I applied to Stanfield and got the job. I knew I was going to be the only detective on the force, because we're so small. But I was all right with that, especially because in a place like this, you don't figure there's going to be a lot of serious crime. Little did I know. Anyway, it didn't matter; two months later, she dumped me."

Walker winced. "Wow! I'm sorry."

Munoz shrugged. "No need. The truth is, she probably just pushed me before I jumped. I'm sure that if I had stayed in Boston, I would have been assigned permanently to the abduction cases. I don't think I could have handled that. This is the first one I've done in almost a year, and just like you, it's eating me up."

They decided to start viewing the video again, pledging to stick with it until either they finished, or their eyes gave out.

~

A few miles away, Eric Allen was about to be visited again.

~

Although the man's face was covered, just as it had been the last time he came, Eric knew it was the same man. And just like the last time, he had brought something for Eric to eat—some chicken nuggets, French fries, applesauce, and a juice box.

In nearly every other context, offering food to a child is the most normal thing in the world. But even as young as he was, Eric understood that what was happening to him was anything but normal. Still, somewhere deep inside, his fear began to diminish ever so slightly, probably because the man had not harmed him. But individuals in the throes of terror, especially children, are incapable of feeling that distinction. Terror is terror; there are no degrees.

Eric began shaking as the man came closer and put the food down. He started to look at the man, but for some reason turned away. And in a voice made scratchy and raw from crying, he said, "I want to go home. I want my daddy." The man stared at Eric through slits in the mask he was wearing, but didn't say a word.

Eric spoke again between sobs. "Why can't I go home?"

The man remained silent. When Eric's crying had subsided somewhat, the man picked up the opened plastic cup of applesauce, and as he had done the last time, spooned out a small portion and offered it to Eric.

Initially, Eric didn't want to take it. He could feed himself; he wasn't a baby. But he was hungry, and the man kept pushing the spoon against Eric's lips. Finally, he opened his mouth just enough for the applesauce to make its way inside. After the third spoonful, Eric felt a small piece of something hard mixed in with the apple sauce. But it was tiny enough that he could swallow it without any trouble.

Once the man finished feeding Eric, he walked over to the place where he had indicated Eric could go to the bathroom. It wasn't like the bathroom at his house, or even at school. Eric could still sit on it though, and even push the handle down when he was done. But it looked funny.

The man reached up above his head to one of the shelves and took down a box. He then sprinkled something into the place where Eric had gone to the bathroom and flushed. Watching the man had briefly calmed Eric by taking his mind off how frightened he was. His fear quickly returned, however, as the man turned around and headed back to where Eric was sitting.

As the man got closer, Eric saw him take something out of his pocket. At first he couldn't tell what it was, but then he recognized it; it was a camera. The man held the camera in his left hand and with his right hand pointed to the rest of the food. And although the man hadn't spoken, Eric knew what he meant—He wanted Eric to eat. Eric tried to be brave. He said, "I don't want to eat. I'm not supposed to have French fries anyway. I just want to go home." And then his tears came again.

For the next five minutes, as Eric continued to cry, the man stood over him and simply watched. Eric could feel himself beginning to get sleepy. He tried to stay awake, but his eyelids became heavier and heavier.

Despite not getting home until after two o'clock in the morning, Munoz was back up by six. And while there wouldn't be much to do at the station this early, sitting at home wasn't going to accomplish anything, either.

Munoz decided that reviewing the last hour of video from the mall parking lot wouldn't be a bad idea. Both he and Walker had been pretty tired when they had viewed it five hours earlier.

Munoz arrived at the police station before seven. The first thing he did was to check on the hotline. And while the number of calls had increased, most of them consisted of an outpouring of sympathy and praise for Jonathan Allen after his emotional plea at the press conference. People meant well, thought Munoz, but that wasn't what the hotline was for, and their comments didn't provide any assistance. Still, he understood why they felt the need to reach out.

A few minutes later he set up the video, and had another look at it. But the second time around was no more helpful than the first. And neither was a quick scan of the video from the Town Hall. Day three of Eric's disappearance was starting off as unproductive as days one and two.

Walker showed up around eight. Munoz filled him in on his review of the two videos, as well as the hotline calls. They talked for several more minutes and then Walker called everyone working on the case into the conference room. He asked each of the combined FBI and Stanfield teams to give an update.

The teams interviewing the Level Threes reported that they were now down to twelve sex offenders who had not been contacted, and another eight that they wanted to re-interview. The fact that there were only twelve more parolees to visit was both good news and bad news.

After the teams finished their recap, Walker spoke again. "I've held off as long as I could, but I think it's time to bring in the state police, as well as some volunteers. We need to start searching the lakes and ponds in the area. Those of you who know me know that unless I'm reasonably sure that the child has already met with foul play, I'm hesitant to go this route. And while there's nothing to suggest that that's what's happened to Eric, at this point there's nothing to suggest it didn't. One of the reasons I don't like beginning these searches without more to go on is that it sends the wrong message. If the public thinks the boy has been killed, they stop paying attention to things. But if they think he's just missing, they continue to keep their eyes open." Walker hesitated, appearing reluctant to finish his remarks. "But I'm not sure we can wait any longer. If Eric's been killed, we had better find ... his body or some other evidence as soon as possible, otherwise it might deteriorate to the point that it's of no value."

No one spoke for a full minute. And although Walker had tried to make it clear that he wasn't giving up on finding Eric alive, it didn't feel that way to anybody in the room. And if it didn't feel that way to *them*, it was going to be a lot worse when the general public heard the news.

Munoz thought of Jonathan and broke the silence. "Before this hits the TV, I think we should call Mr. Allen and let him know. No matter what, it's going to be devastating, but it would be better coming from us."

Walker responded. "I was going to suggest that we do that as soon as we finish up here. If you don't mind, I think you should talk to him, Dave."

"Not a problem."

When the meeting ended, Munoz made the call; Walker contacted the state police, and the other teams headed out to continue their interviews with the sex offenders. Shortly after that, Walker joined Munoz in his office. "How'd you make out with Jonathan Allen?"

"Not great," the detective reported. "One of your guys answered the phone and told me that Jonathan was having a real tough time today. And after he got on the line, I could sense it in his voice. My news didn't help. I told him we would stop by later. How'd you make out with the state police?"

Walker responded, "They'll be here in less than an hour, with twenty officers and five search dogs."

"Cadaver dogs?" Munoz asked.

Walker nodded. "At least two of them, yeah."

Munoz grimaced. "Maybe we shouldn't mention that to Jonathan."
Walker agreed.

"What about volunteers?"

"The state police said they have a list of people from Southeastern
Mass. that are on some sort of permanent volunteer list. I've never heard
of that before."

"I think it's fairly new," Munoz told him. "How many on the list?"

"Around fifty, they said. Of course, who knows how many are
available today. But it's a good starting point. Let's see how many show
up, and if we need more, we can broadcast an appeal. The commander I
spoke with indicated that he wanted to start with the lakes and ponds in
the area, which was exactly what I was thinking."

"Do you want the two of us out there also?"

Walker shook his head. "Not right away. I'd like to finish up the
interviews this morning if possible. I took the information on three more
of the parolees. Let's check them out first."

The first two Level Threes on their list were both home. Walker
and Munoz spent fifteen minutes with each, but didn't discover anything
that raised their suspicions.

On the way to the third parolee's house, Walker got a phone call.
"Craig, it's Bob Hastings. We went to interview one of the guys on our
list, and the guy's P.O. was already there. He made a surprise visit this
morning and evidently found a laptop that the parolee was trying to hide
under his couch. Normally, that wouldn't be a big deal, except one of the
conditions of this guy's parole is no computers in his house. Again, not a
big deal, except that when the P.O. opened the laptop, he found child
pornography on it."

"What's the address? We're on our way."

Walker and Munoz arrived ten minutes later. Agent Hastings filled
them in on some additional details, and then they spoke directly to the
parolee. While he was undoubtedly headed back to jail on new charges,
they wouldn't involve Eric Allen's disappearance; he had an alibi for the
time Eric was abducted.

Walker had the laptop confiscated and called the Boston office to have someone pick it up and bring it back to the FBI lab. The IT personnel there would scour it for images of missing children, including Eric Allen. And while the face recognition software had improved dramatically over the last several years, sometimes the computer images were just too small to provide a usable means of comparison. But Walker believed it was worth a try.

After they finished up with the parolee and his laptop, Walker and Munoz went to see the last sex offender on their list, but he wasn't home. They checked the data sheet they had on him and discovered that he worked less than a mile away.

At his workplace, they pulled him aside without drawing too much attention. The parolee seemed to appreciate that and was very forthcoming. The one piece of information that seemed to disqualify him as a suspect was the fact that he didn't have a car. The odds on him borrowing someone else's car or taking public transportation to kidnap someone in Stanfield were through the roof. It appeared that the Level Three sex offender list was a non-starter.

Feeling more lost than they had at almost any other time in the investigation, Walker and Munoz drove back to Stanfield and checked in with the state police at a few of the search areas. To a large degree, they were pleased that nothing had turned up, especially a body. Even a significant piece of evidence near a lake or in a wooded area rarely led to a happy ending.

By the time they finished talking to the state police at the various sites, it was past noon. They decided it was time to go see Jonathan Allen. But before Munoz started up the car, he sat back and turned toward Walker. "Something's been gnawing at me about the guy with the laptop."

"You don't think his alibi's going to hold up?" the agent asked.

Munoz shook his head. "No, it's not that. I haven't been able to put my finger on what was bothering me. But now I'm wondering if this could be about what was on his computer."

"I'm not following."

"The child pornography," Munoz said. "Is it possible that's why Eric was taken? I mean, we know children get abducted for stuff like that. And he's such a good-looking kid. It would also explain why it didn't feel like it was random, because maybe it wasn't."

Walker jumped in. "That would make some sense. If Eric was the specific target, then whoever did this could have been watching him for quite a while, figured out patterns, and knew the father's drop-off routines at the school. It would also explain the lack of forensics. If the guy planned this out, he certainly knew what he was doing." Walker paused. "I know it doesn't sound like it, but if you're right, this is actually good news."

"Why?" Munoz asked.

"Because it means that Eric Allen is probably still alive."

CHAPTER THIRTEEN

For the first time since the investigation began, both Walker and Munoz felt as if things might be moving in the right direction. While they understood that the child pornography idea was still just a theory, it all seemed to fit together, like a giant jigsaw puzzle.

Shortly after Munoz started the car and drove toward Jonathan Allen's house, Walker voiced his feelings. "I really think you may be on to something. And if that's true, we need to shift focus slightly. Why don't you swing by the station and drop me off? We need to generate a new list from the Sex Offender Registry. It's just as likely that guys who are into child porn are Level Twos as Level Threes. We need to get going on those interviews as soon as possible. That means you'll have to go talk to Mr. Allen on your own."

"That's okay. I don't mind," Munoz said. "What do you want to do about the searches?"

"I don't want to call them off yet," Walker replied. "If we get something more concrete on the child pornography angle, then we can pull back."

"When I'm talking with Jonathan Allen, should I mention anything about child pornography?" Munoz asked.

Walker hesitated. "That's a tough call. I guess I'd play it by ear. If you feel like he needs something more positive to hold on to, then yeah, I'd tell him. Use your judgment."

Munoz dropped Walker off at the police station and then continued on to the Allen house. He tried to rehearse some of the things he might say, but then recognized that there were too many variables. He would have to play it by ear, just as Walker had suggested.

As soon as the FBI agent on duty opened the front door and Munoz entered, he could feel a sense of hopelessness pervading the entire space. The agent spoke quietly. "I'm glad you're here. He's in lying down. I've worked about twenty of these cases. And at this stage, three days in, this is as bad as I've ever seen any one of the parents."

"Really?"

"Yeah. Obviously, I'm not a doctor, but I think he might be suicidal. I check on him every ten minutes. We've talked some, and he said he was a basket case after his wife was killed, but he felt like he was just starting to pull himself together - and now this."

"It's probably a good idea we posted someone here twenty-four/seven."

"No question. I was even thinking that you should consider taking him into protective custody—although I know Craig doesn't like to go that route, except as a last resort, because even protective custody makes him look guilty of something, at least in the public's mind."

Munoz nodded. "I think I'll go knock on his door and see if he wants to talk."

"Yeah, go ahead. I was just about to check on him anyway."

Munoz tapped lightly on the master bedroom door. The quickness with which Jonathan responded made it obvious that he hadn't been sleeping. "Yes?"

"It's Detective Munoz, Mr. Allen."

Jonathan spoke very softly. "All right, I'll be out in a minute."

"I'll wait for you in the other room."

When Munoz returned to the living room, the agent asked, "Any luck?"

"He says he'll be out in a minute."

"That's good. I'm going to go outside and let you two talk. If you need me, just holler."

Three minutes went by before Jonathan came into the living room. He looked as if he had aged five years since Munoz had seen him the day before. "Hello, detective, please sit down."

Munoz searched for some way to open the conversation. Finally, he settled on something that at least acknowledged Jonathan's pain. "As I told you before, I can't imagine what you're going through. If it will help in any way, you can ask me whatever you want, and I'll be as honest as I can."

"I appreciate that, detective." Jonathan forced a smile and invoked some gallows humor. "I don't suppose you know where my son is."

Munoz didn't respond, knowing that Jonathan wasn't expecting him to.

Jonathan shook his head. "I'm sorry. I know you're doing everything you can."

Munoz decided to get right to it. "Is there somebody you can call to talk to, a friend, a minister, a clergyman, somebody like that?"

"After Cindy died, I kind of pushed our friends away. They were mainly Cindy's friends, anyway. And as far as a clergyman goes, that was Cindy's territory also. I was never a very religious person to begin with, and then after she died, any remnants of faith I might have had went by the boards."

"I could try to find out if there's somebody that the FBI or the state police might recommend."

Jonathan shook his head. "No. That's okay." He paused. "If you don't mind, I'd just as soon talk to you."

"Of course," the detective said. "It's just that I don't have very much experience in situations like this."

"Neither do I."

"I didn't mean ..." Munoz began.

Jonathan shook his head. "I know. I shouldn't have said that. I didn't mean to sound so flip. I'm sorry."

Munoz decided to leave it alone. "Is there anything else you'd like to ask me?"

"I don't know. It feels like I keep asking the same questions over and over."

"It's okay," the detective reassured him. "Ask whatever you want, as many times as you need to."

Jonathan didn't say anything; he just stared straight ahead. Finally he turned toward Munoz, but instead of asking a question, he said, "The only thing that's keeping me going is the possibility that Eric's still alive. If it turns out that he's not, then ..."

Munoz didn't need clarification as to what Jonathan meant, nor did he have any idea what to say. He felt so far out of his element that he wanted to run in the other direction. But then he surprised himself. "I'm not going to tell you that you shouldn't feel that way. Anyone who hasn't been through something as horrible as this shouldn't make that kind of a judgment."

"That's not what I expected you to say."

"I told you, I don't know what I'm doing when it comes to this. But I do know that I don't like other people telling me how I should feel."

Jonathan actually formed a smile. "Maybe you're better at this than you think."

"I'm not so sure about that. I'm just trying to be honest with you."

They were both quiet for a moment and then Jonathan said, "When you asked me about a clergyman before, and I mentioned that Cindy was the religious one, it reminded me of something, something I've never told anyone—A few days after Cindy was killed, I was sitting here in the living room, in this very chair as a matter of fact. Eric came over and stood next to me. I'd already explained to him that his mother was up in heaven with God. He had seemed to accept that, but Eric has always been a child that thinks like an adult or at least sees other possibilities in most situations. That was Cindy's doing as well. Anyway, as he was standing next to me he said, 'Do you think God would let me visit Mommy in heaven? I'll come right back; I promise. I just want to see her again.' "

There might have been more to the story, but Jonathan had lost all control and couldn't continue. Munoz was not much better.

After several minutes, once Jonathan was able to compose himself, he asked, "I guess I'd like to know if you have anything new?"

Munoz decided that, after the story Jonathan had just told him, he had to offer some hope, regardless of how premature it might be. "Maybe. We think it's possible that Eric could have been the specific target."

"But why?" Jonathan asked. "There was no ransom demand."

"It's still just a theory, but we think someone may have wanted him for …" Munoz hesitated. "… pornographic pictures."

"Pornographic pictures? Child pornography?"

"As horrible as that may seem, when children are taken for that reason, they're very rarely … killed," Munoz offered.

Jonathan took a moment to process what he had just heard. "And you really think that's what happened?"

"It seems to fit with everything we know." Munoz was aware that he was building this new theory up more than he should. But one look at Jonathan's face made him push it even further. "If we're right, then there's a good chance you're going to get your son back. He's probably going to need counseling." A pause. "And he'll certainly need you. But you'll have him back."

Jonathan put his face in his hands and started to sob. Whether his tears were tears of sadness or hopefulness, Munoz couldn't tell. And neither could Jonathan.

~

Eric awoke with a start. He had been having a bad dream about being in a closet. For a brief moment, when he opened his eyes, he felt relief that he had only been dreaming. But then as he looked around, he remembered where he was. And other than the size of the space, what was happening to him was the same as the dream.

He had no idea what time it was, what day it was, how long he had been in this room, or even how long it had been since the man had been there. His mind shifted back to the last time he had seen the man. He remembered eating applesauce, and he remembered the camera the man had. But he didn't remember the man taking any pictures; maybe he had been asleep. It seemed like all he wanted to do was sleep.

It was another few moments before he was fully awake, and then his fear and sadness returned. He didn't understand why the man wouldn't let him go home. And where was his daddy? He buried his head in the pillow and started to cry. He lay there for ten minutes before he heard someone outside the door.

Six-year-olds still believe in superheroes, so somewhere in Eric's brain he thought one of them was coming to take him home. But that notion didn't last long, as the same man wearing the same mask pushed open the door and entered the room. He carried the same food items he had before. But Eric sensed that there was something different about him. It was definitely the same man, but he seemed upset. The man then dropped the juice box he was holding, and for the first time since Eric had been in the room, he heard the man speak. "God damn it."

Even though his daddy said that sometimes, Eric knew that you weren't supposed to. He sensed that the man was angry, so Eric curled himself into a ball. The man came closer, stood over him, and signaled for Eric to get up. But he didn't move; he was too afraid. The man stared at him, and then in a hushed voice said, "Get up."

The sound of the man's voice surprised Eric, so he didn't respond immediately. The man spoke again. "I said, get up." This time Eric began to stand. As he did, the man reached into his pocket and took out a camera, the same one that Eric had seen the last time.

As Eric stood up to his full height, he was shaking and crying uncontrollably. The man waited a moment and then said, "Now I want you to take..." He stopped abruptly and turned away. He walked to the other side of the room and stayed there for a few minutes with his back to Eric.

Finally, he turned around and walked back. The man returned the camera to his pocket, and made his way over to the food he had brought in. He signaled for Eric to sit back down. The man picked up a spoon and the container of applesauce and began to feed it to Eric.

Eric tried to calm himself so he could swallow the applesauce. After he took the first spoonful, he glanced at the man's face. Only his mouth and eyes were visible through the mask. But when Eric looked into the man's eyes, he could see tears.

On the drive back to the police station Munoz couldn't help but reflect on the emotional scene he had just been part of. Jonathan Allen was barely holding himself together. Munoz was reasonably sure that Jonathan wouldn't harm himself while there was still hope that his son might come home. But if this ended any other way, all bets were off.

As soon as Munoz entered the station, Walker caught his eye and said, "I'll meet you in your office in a couple of minutes; I'm just finishing up something here."

A couple of minutes turned into ten. Walker had a folder in his hand as he came into Munoz's office, closed the door behind him, and sat down. Munoz pointed to the folder. "Is that the list of Level Twos?"

"Yeah. There were four more added since just the other day, so we're up to seventy-three. I thought we should follow the same plan we used with the Level Threes—contact their P.O.'s and have them eliminate the ones who were at work when the Allen boy was taken. I've already got three teams working on it. I think we should be able to reduce the list quite a bit by late this afternoon. Then we should probably start the interviewing right away after that. I don't care if we have to knock on doors until ten o'clock tonight."

Munoz agreed.

"What happened with Mr. Allen?" Walker asked.

"I'm not sure how to answer that. The agent you posted there was right on target; Jonathan's a mess. But he did want to talk, and it seemed like when we finished, he was somewhat better. I was thinking about it on the ride back. I don't believe he's suicidal at this point, but if this ends badly, I think we're going to have to protect him from himself."

Munoz debated for a moment whether to tell Walker about the story Jonathan had related to him, but decided against it. For one thing, he didn't know how Jonathan would feel about that. And secondly, Munoz didn't think he could get through it without getting emotional himself.

Walker sensed some hesitation. "Is there something else?"

"It's just that he's hurting so badly. I did tell him about the possible child pornography angle. I felt like I had to. He was begging me with his eyes to give him something."

"I think telling him was a good call." Walker paused. "Maybe interviewing the Level Twos will give us the break we need."

Munoz sighed. "I hope you're right. The thought of having to tell him that his son is … gone … I'm not sure I could do that."

"Let's hope we don't have to," Walker replied.

Three hours later the list of seventy-three was down to forty. Walker decided that he and Munoz should join with the other three teams if they were going to have any chance of getting through the list by the end of the day. A few minutes before they were scheduled to head out on the interviews, Walker phoned the state police search teams for an update—nothing. He indicated to each of the troopers in charge that they should wait until they heard from him in the morning before resuming the searches. Walker also checked in with the Stanfield cop monitoring the hotline. Obviously, Walker knew that if there had been anything significant to report, the cop would have already done so. But Walker also wanted to know whether they were still getting a fairly steady stream of callers. That might influence his decision as to whether to continue the searches or not.

And while there were no calls to the hotline that warranted more than a cursory follow-up, the volume of calls had increased, much to Walker's surprise. Searches almost always cut down on hotline call volume. But then he realized why this might have been an exception. The media in two large markets—Boston and Providence—had been broadcasting excerpts from the press conference during every teaser and lead-up to the evening news for hours. You'd have to be living in a cave not to have seen or heard about the missing boy.

CHAPTER FOURTEEN

Around the same time the four teams were heading out to start interviewing the Level Twos, Tony Sarno received a text message from Runner—*midnite*. He stared at the screen. It was only one word, but Tony knew exactly what it meant, and it wasn't good. If Runner wanted to see him, something was wrong. He waited another minute before he responded—*ok*.

As he put down his phone, he tried to convince himself that the requested meeting had nothing to do with his recent activities, but he knew better. Even if that were the case, he thought, why would Runner necessarily think he was involved? The only thing he could come up with was that Josh Raybeck might have disobeyed him and done something stupid.

To try to put his mind at ease, Tony broke his own rule about no contact, and sent a text message to Josh. The phone Tony was using was secure and untraceable, but he still was cautious with the words he used—*again, r u sure everything's done that u were told to do.*

Ten minutes later came the one word reply—*yes.*

Tony debated whether to follow up with another text, to make sure Josh was telling him the truth, but decided it wouldn't accomplish anything. It was very difficult to intimidate someone with a text message, especially with a limit of a hundred and forty characters.

Maybe he should pay Josh a visit. But he acknowledged that that was probably too risky. Ultimately, he gave up on the idea, convincing himself that Josh wouldn't dare lie to him. Still, Tony's paranoia stayed with him, less because of anything Josh may or may not have done, but more because of why Runner wanted to see him.

He spent the next several hours contemplating all the possibilities. Only two plausible explanations came to mind: Either one of the workers at the auto repair shop where he used to work had shot off his mouth and told Runner about the earlier incident with the kid's mother. Or, the guy who wanted the new pictures had complained to Runner that he hadn't gotten them yet.

In terms of how the meeting was going to turn out, Tony thought if Runner already knew that he was involved, it really didn't matter how he figured it out. Even if he had a good reason for everything he did, Runner would find something wrong with it and try to humiliate him.

Tony waited until the last possible minute to go to work, hoping to avoid meaningless chitchat with any of the employees staying late at the mall. He wasn't in the mood.

It turned out that only a few people had remained, and they were all gone by ten thirty. He made an announcement over the P.A. indicating that he was going to activate the exit alarm system, just to be certain. Then he headed for the computer store.

He logged in to one of the demo computers and opened up his accounts, scanning them for any activity. There was nothing. Everything appeared to be on hold just as it was supposed to be. Still, he felt a sense of relief wash over him. Next he checked each of the demo computers' history. And although there was nothing to connect him to the histories, he wiped them clean anyway. Might as well keep the computer store manager happy, he thought.

By then it was eleven fifteen. He still had forty-five minutes to kill. His nerves hadn't settled down very much, and the waiting didn't help. After a few minutes, he logged in to some mindless game on the Internet. It didn't calm his nerves, but it did make the time go more quickly.

At eleven forty-five he went upstairs to the security office, turned the cameras back on in the computer store, and turned off the ones in the back parking area. Doing that made him think about the FBI agent and the detective who had come to see him. For a brief moment, his ego pushed away the fear he was experiencing as he recalled his interaction with the two cops. The respite was short-lived, however, as the realization that Runner would soon be arriving kicked back in.

Runner showed up a few minutes before midnight. Tony was waiting in the usual spot, next to the rear door. When Runner got within ten feet of Tony he said, "Inside."

Tony obliged, and Runner followed. As the door closed behind Runner, Tony turned to face him. Without any warning, Runner pushed Tony before he could square himself. If the chair Tony had put in place hadn't been there, he would have gone straight down on his back. As it was, he barely caught himself before he toppled over.

"What the hell are you doing?" Tony asked.

"Was that you?" Runner demanded.

"What do you mean?"

This time it was an accusation rather than a question. "The missing kid, that's you."

Tony answered with some bravado. "What's the problem?"

"What's the problem?! You're a fucking idiot, that's what the problem is. Now answer me. Did you take that kid?"

"Yeah, but …"

Runner was now shouting. "Damn it! I ought to break your fucking neck!"

"What else was I supposed to do?"

"You're shitting me, right? After we arranged to save your sorry ass, you were supposed to stay under the radar. That was the deal, and then you do this." He paused, and then with a sickening smirk on his face said, "So you're into little boys now? Is that it? You gave up on the skanky prostitutes?"

Tony was as angry as he had ever been in his life, but he knew better than to lose it with Runner. He held back enough to say, "I was trying to do what the local guy wanted."

"What local guy? What the hell are you talking about?"

"You know, the local guy who pays so much for the pictures."

"What about him?" Runner demanded.

"You don't know?"

"Assume I don't. So tell me, and it better be good."

"A few weeks ago, he sent me a text message," Tony began.

"He contacted you directly?" Runner asked, disbelieving

"Yeah. You really didn't know that? I mean, that's how I figured he got my number, from you."

"He didn't get it from me."

"Then how did he get it?"

Runner was starting to get angry again, but then realized how the guy must have gotten Tony's number. He would have had access to all of

Tony's personal information. Runner backed off slightly. "Start from the beginning, and you better not lie to me."

Tony still couldn't comprehend what he should have done differently. The local guy was the best customer they had. All Tony was trying to do was keep him happy. Runner spoke again. "Are you going to stand there like a fucking moron, or are you going to tell me?"

Runner had said to start from the beginning, but Tony wasn't sure he meant it. He decided not to take any chances. "After the mistrial I came up with that new plan, remember?" Runner nodded, as Tony continued. "For months I just Photoshopped regular pictures, and made them look like they were the real thing."

"I know all that," Runner snapped. "Keep going."

"A few weeks ago, the guy I was talking about sent me a text and said that he could tell the pictures were fake. He wanted real ones. And he wanted new pictures of … this one specific kid. He sent me back a copy of the Photoshopped picture, so I'd know who he was talking about."

"You didn't know who the kid was?" Runner quizzed him.

In reality, as soon as he saw the photo, Tony knew exactly who the little boy was; he had the same platinum blond hair as his mother. But Tony wasn't about to answer truthfully. It was still possible that Runner didn't know about the incident with Cindy Allen. And things might go easier on Tony if Runner didn't find out. He tried to answer with as much confidence as possible. "No."

Runner looked at him skeptically. "Then how did you find out his name?"

Tony thought quickly. "From the photographer."

Runner was pretty sure that Tony was lying, but he decided not to confront him. It might not be necessary, if he got the information he needed. "Then what?"

"Once I found out the kid's name, I used the computer to find out where he lived, and where he went to school. But there was no way to get more pictures of him."

"So then what? You decided to kidnap him?! That was your solution? The last thing you were told after we got you out of that other mess was to just stick to the fucking plan. The Photoshopping wasn't a problem, but this is a disaster." Runner shook his head. "And what's the end game here? Have you thought of that?"

Tony took some pride in his answer. "Yeah. After I get a bunch of new pictures, I'm going to take the kid down South. I know some guys from the Internet. They'll pay a lot for a kid like this."

"Are you crazy? It's all over the news every minute. And what do you think, the FBI is just going to forget about it, like it didn't happen?"

Tony thought he was doing himself a favor by offering the next piece of information. "The FBI doesn't have a clue. That Agent Walker was already here."

Runner couldn't believe his ears. "What?" he practically shrieked. "The FBI was here? They talked to you?"

"Yeah, but they have no idea what's going on," Tony insisted. "Did you see the press conference?"

Something changed in Runner's demeanor after the mention of the FBI visit. Tony noticed, but wasn't sure what to make of it. He was just glad that Runner seemed less angry.

Runner took a few moments before he spoke again. He was thinking about earlier in the day when he had watched the news clips. In fact, that's what had raised his suspicions about Tony. He had no hard evidence, but he knew Tony inside and out, and this was exactly the kind of screwed-up stunt he would pull. At least that's what his gut told him.

Runner had taken his concerns to the boss, and told him what he was planning to do, assuming that his suspicions about Tony were correct. The information about the local guy contacting Tony directly had caused Runner to waver slightly. But this new revelation about the FBI visit put the original plan back on track.

Runner knew he had to keep his cool in order to make sure the boss was protected. He spoke more calmly than he had since he showed up. "Listen, Tony. We can't undo what happened, but the main thing is we can't have this traced back to the boss."

"It won't," Tony said quickly. "There's no way."

Runner again fought to keep himself under control. "I need to make sure. First of all, did you take any new pictures of the kid?"

Tony answered literally. "No, *I* didn't."

Runner heard the nuance, and raised his voice more than he intended. "Don't play word games with me! So who took them then, that

Raybeck kid you were using?"

Even though Tony had told Runner Josh's name, he was surprised that he remembered it. Tony was not sure how to play this. Eventually, he decided that saying the pictures hadn't been taken provided some cover. If Runner got pissed off either way, he could blame Josh. "No, he didn't take them yet."

Always wanting to appear as if he knew what he was doing, Tony added, "I figured there was too much heat, and it was better not to do anything."

Runner eyed Tony suspiciously, not sure he believed him. "After we finish here, we're going to go to the computer store and check your e-mail accounts to make sure Raybeck didn't decide to take them on his own."

Even though Tony knew the accounts were clear, he responded with some trepidation in his voice. "Sure, if that's what you want."

Runner moved on. "Where's the kid?"

"He's stashed someplace," Tony evaded. "Why?"

Runner hated being questioned; the calm façade started to crack. "Because I'm going to have to clean up this mess, and I want to know everything I need to."

Tony began to get angry again, but he knew better than to push back against Runner. "I can take care of this. I'll get the pictures done, even if I have to take them myself. And then I'll move the kid in the next couple of days."

"You won't do anything of the kind. Now listen to me. No pictures!" He eyed Tony's reaction as he added, "Assuming they're not already on the computer."

Tony tried to grasp at anything he could to retain some semblance of control. "But what about the guy who asked for the pictures? He's going to be pissed."

"Why the hell are you worried about that? I'll handle him. Now where have you got the kid?"

Tony still wanted to take care of the situation his way; he didn't need Runner stepping in. So he convinced himself that as long as he made it right, Runner wouldn't care if he had been lied to. "The place where we used to take the pictures."

"That old storefront?"

The lies came a little easier now. "Yeah, it's got a small room in the back," Tony said. "But the building is empty, so nobody goes near it."

"I thought the other photographer, the one who took off, that was his place."

Tony was relieved that he could go back to the truth. "It was. He's still paid up for a couple of more months. But he's long gone. There's nothing to connect it to me."

Runner was still skeptical, so he tested Tony. "I'm pretty sure I know where it is—on Palmer Street, right?"

"No, Rogers, the next one over."

Runner kept pushing. "How often do you check on the kid?"

Tony delivered the next few sentences as if they were the Gospel. "Twice a day. I bring him something to eat. I put pills in the food to make sure he sleeps most of the time. I used chloroform when I first took him, but the pills work better now."

"And there's no way the kid can get out of the room?" Runner pressed.

"No, there's a bolt on the outside of the door."

Tony had given a masterful performance. So much so, that any doubts Runner had about Tony's story had all but disappeared. "Okay, let's go to the computer store and look at your e-mail accounts."

"I've got to turn off the security cameras first. You want to wait here?"

Although Runner believed Tony, he still didn't trust him. So he wasn't about to give him the opportunity to be alone. "No, I'm coming with you. You can erase the five minutes of video it'll take for us to get up to the second level, and then you can turn the cameras off."

For a brief moment, Tony had forgotten how much Runner knew about technology. It wasn't as much as Tony, but Runner had been the one to recruit Tony out of the auto repair shop, and he had asked him some fairly sophisticated questions. Given Runner's level of expertise, Tony was glad that there would be nothing to be found in the accounts they were going to examine.

They made their way to the security office in silence. Tony erased what he needed to, and shut off the rest of the surveillance cameras both inside and outside, just in case. The walk to the computer store was also made in silence. Finally, when they were in front of one of the demo computers, Runner said, "I want to see all three accounts."

"Only two are encrypted."

"I know, but isn't the other account the one that screwed you up last time?"

"Yeah, but ..."

Runner interrupted him. "Just show me all the accounts."

Tony opened them one by one. To his relief, there had been no activity since he had last checked on them an hour ago. Runner said, "All right, they look clean." He paused. "I want you to come out with me. Once I've left, you can turn the cameras back on."

"What are you going to do?" Tony asked nervously.

"I told you, I'm going to fix this."

Tony couldn't leave it alone. "Now? Tonight?"

"Why the hell do you care, as long as it gets done?"

Tony was scrambling. He needed to buy some time to fix this himself. If Runner found out he had lied to him before Tony had been able to take care of everything, he knew he was screwed. He was trying to think of something to say when Runner added, "No, not tonight. I need to talk to the boss first." That was a lie, but Runner didn't want to listen to Tony whine anymore.

Tony was relieved, but he shouldn't have been.

This time Eric didn't awake with a start. Instead, he slowly came to, opening and closing his eyes periodically. Eventually, the fog cleared, and he took in his surroundings. It didn't take long for the fear to envelop him again.

For some reason, he was sure it was very late. He didn't think the man came when it was late, but he didn't know for sure. He looked over to where the man usually put the food to see if he had been there while Eric had been asleep. But there was nothing there except a leftover juice box.

Eric wasn't particularly thirsty, but he went over and picked up the drink. He could tell that there was some juice still inside by the weight. He finished what remained, and started to go back to lie down.

After a few steps, he started to shake. At first he thought it might be because he was cold, but it felt different than that. He then thought it was because he was afraid. But he was afraid all the time, and it hadn't felt like this. Something was going to happen, he could sense it.

And then he heard noises on the other side of the door.

Munoz woke up at four thirty in the morning. Although he had gone to bed around one, he hadn't been able to get to sleep right away, and he hadn't come close to sleeping straight through. If he was lucky, maybe he had accumulated an hour. But how was he supposed to sleep when every inch of his brain was consumed with the case?

Everyone, including Munoz, had thought that the break was going to come sometime last night. But the Level Two interviews had been a bust. The investigation was right back where it started, and Eric Allen was still missing.

Munoz rolled over, trying to find a more comfortable position, or at least one that would allow his mind to shut down. But he acknowledged that no amount of tossing and turning was going to accomplish that.

As he laid there, he thought about the story Jonathan had told him about Eric wanting to visit heaven. He thought about the sadness and defeat he had seen in Jonathan's eyes. He thought about what he perceived as his own shortcomings, and whether he was really meant to do this job.

Eventually his mind did shut down briefly, and when he glanced over at the clock, it read 5:45. It was probably too early to get up, he thought. But lying in bed, dwelling on all the emotionally charged dead ends that made up this case, seemed self-destructive.

He sat on the side of the bed, put his head in his hands and rubbed his face. Then the phone rang.

It startled Munoz. As he picked up the receiver, he felt equal parts of anticipation and dread course through him.

"Hello."

"Detective, it's Zach Donovan from the night shift. We've got a dead body."

CHAPTER FIFTEEN

Munoz could feel his stomach clench, as he forced himself to ask the question he was afraid to ask. "Is it a child?"

"No. It's an adult male, Caucasian."

Munoz closed his eyes and breathed a sigh of relief. "Are you at the scene, Zach? Where is it?"

"In back of the mall," the officer reported. "I just got here."

"Any I.D.?" Munoz asked.

"I didn't want to touch anything until someone from the county coroner's office got here. I called them just before I called you."

"Okay, good. What else can you tell me?"

"A garbage truck driver called it in. Evidently, he showed up a little after five o'clock this morning to empty the dumpsters. It was still dark out, and the parking lot lights don't shine that far, so he didn't notice anything. But when he backed up his truck, he couldn't get it close enough. He got out to check, and that's when he saw the body. It looks like two gunshot wounds, one to the stomach and one to the forehead."

"All right. Secure the scene as best you can. I'm on my way."

After Munoz ended the call, he remained seated on the edge of the bed, allowing everything to sink in. Somebody was dead, and that was awful. But thank God it wasn't Eric Allen. And so much for Stanfield being a sleepy little town where nothing much happened.

Munoz dialed Walker. The FBI agent picked up after the second ring. He saw Munoz's name on the screen and said, "Hey, Dave. What's going on?"

"I just got a call," the detective said. "We've got a dead body in back of the mall." He quickly added. "It's not Eric Allen; it's an adult. I'm heading over there right now. I may be at the scene for a while, so I'm not sure when I'll get back to the station. I'll call you when I know more."

"Any idea who it is?"

"Not yet."

"This isn't exactly what you signed up for when you came to Stanfield, is it?"

Munoz gave a short laugh. "You read my mind."

"I'm going to go in shortly and take another look at the Level Two interviews," Walker told him. "I'll see you when you get back. Good luck."

Munoz arrived at the mall twenty minutes later. After he located Zach Donovan, they ducked under the yellow tape and went over to the body. The sun had risen enough so that the crime scene was now clearly visible. The victim was lying on his back with his eyes wide open. Munoz took a quick glance at the body and said, "No coroner yet, Zach?"

"No," the officer reported. "They said between six-thirty and seven."

Munoz was about to respond, but instead knelt down next to the body. "Wait a minute. I know this guy." He leaned closer to be sure. "He's the night watchman here. I forget his name ... Tony something, I think. We asked him for some video in the Eric Allen case. Jeez, I just talked to him a couple of days ago." Munoz shook his head. "He didn't seem like the kind of guy who'd end up with two bullet holes in him."

Zach Donovan remained silent as Munoz stood up and asked, "Where's the truck driver?"

"He's giving a formal statement to one of our guys."

"All right. I'm going to head over there." Munoz looked toward the back entrance of the mall. "Do me a favor—check next to the door and see if there's a number for mall security. If not, call the station; we must have something on file. I'll be over talking to the truck driver."

As he headed across the parking lot, Munoz began to organize his thoughts. *I better wait until we're allowed to examine the body for a wallet or something. I'm pretty sure it's the night watchman, but I don't want to try to locate someone to make a positive I.D. until we have more. Once security gets here, I'll have them get me a copy of the surveillance video for the back of the mall. Hopefully, that'll show us something.*

In his subconscious, for a fleeting moment, Munoz wondered if the death of the night watchman was somehow connected to Eric Allen's disappearance. But before that thought became fully formed, his mind dismissed it.

Munoz spent less than ten minutes with the truck driver. It appeared that he had nothing additional to offer beyond what he already had told them. Munoz then glanced toward the mall and saw Zach Donovan approaching. "Anything?"

The officer held out a piece of paper. "Yeah, I found a number."

"Thanks. Hang in here a minute while I make this call." After Munoz finished, he was about to say something when Zach Donovan pointed over Munoz's shoulder and said, "I think that's the coroner coming."

For the next half hour, the coroner and his assistants provided some helpful information to Munoz; unfortunately the victim's full name and address weren't part of that. After taking pictures of the scene, one of the assistants checked the victim's pockets. All he found was a comb and some breath mints—no wallet, no phone, no car keys, in fact, no keys of any kind.

Munoz briefly considered the possibility that this had been a robbery, but it didn't feel like that. Then he considered that Tony might have simply left those items inside. But that didn't make any sense. Why would he leave without his phone, and more importantly, without his keys? How did he expect to get back into the mall?

Munoz briefly put all those thoughts on hold as he listened to the coroner offer some preliminary findings. He suggested that the victim had died from the gunshot wound to the head; the one to his stomach probably wouldn't have been fatal. Not that it mattered, but Munoz figured the stomach shot came first in order to incapacitate the victim, and the head shot followed. The coroner also believed that the victim had been killed several hours earlier—rigor mortis was already setting in.

Munoz acknowledged that he would probably have to hold off doing much more until he had a positive I.D. But then the name came to him. He spoke it out loud. "Sarno. His name's Tony Sarno."

It didn't amount to a positive I.D, but having a probable first and last name would at least allow him to take some additional steps forward. He took his phone out of his pocket and called the police station. "Hi, it's Detective Munoz. I've got a possible I.D. on the body we found. His name's Tony Sarno, probably Anthony Sarno. See what you can find out.

Thanks."

Munoz was about to place another call when he noticed a car heading in his direction. It stopped about twenty feet away. As the driver exited the car and came closer, Munoz recognized him as the security guard that he and Walker had first spoken to about the surveillance videos.

The man offered his hand. "Hello, Detective. It's Jack Carven; we met the other day."

"Yes. Sorry to have to make you come out here so early, especially under these circumstances."

Carven looked puzzled. "I'm not sure what's going on. Was there a break-in or something? The answering service just told me to come to the mall; the police wanted to talk to someone from security. Why isn't Tony here?"

Munoz had no idea what kind of relationship Jack Carven had with Tony Sarno, but regardless, he was certain the next words he spoke were going to come as a huge shock. "We think that Tony's been killed."

Carven gasped. "What? Oh my God, how?"

"We think he was murdered."

The guard shook his head in disbelief. "That can't be possible. What happened?"

"We don't know yet." Munoz pointed to the crime scene tape. "He was found over there by a truck driver who came to empty the dumpsters."

"Oh my God, I can't believe this."

"I know this is difficult, but right now I could use your help. Could you possibly take a look at the body, and confirm that it's Tony? I only met him the one time, so I'm not positive."

Jack Carven went pale. "I don't think I can do that. I'm very squeamish about things like that. I'm sorry."

Munoz wanted to push it, but another look at Carven's face told him it wouldn't do any good. "It's okay; I understand." Munoz paused. "Do you know if Tony has any family in the area?"

Carven shrugged. "Not that I know of. He never talked very much about his personal life."

"Do you know where he lived?"

The older man thought a moment. "Rhode Island, I think. Maybe Cranston."

"Okay." Munoz paused. "Also, I'd like to look at the surveillance video from last night to see if there's anything on it that might help us."

Carven shook his head. "That's ironic, huh? Normally when we need to check out video, Tony's the one to put it together." Carven was able to gather himself enough to focus on Munoz's request. "We can go in that door over there. I just need to punch in the security code to shut off the alarm."

As they walked toward the rear entrance, Carven asked again, "Do you have any idea what happened?"

Munoz debated whether to mention that Tony was shot, but decided not to. Instead, he gave the standard police response. "Not at this point; it's too early."

"This is unbelievable." Carven took out a ring full of keys, found the one he wanted and inserted it into the lock on the security box. He opened the box and started to press numbers on the touch pad, but stopped abruptly. "It's not on."

"What do you mean?" Munoz responded.

Carven gestured to the security panel. "The alarm system's not on. See the green light? If the system were activated, that light would be red."

"Can you think of any reason that Tony would have turned the alarm off?" Munoz asked him.

"No, absolutely not."

"Okay," Munoz replied. "I'd still like to go up to the security office to look at the surveillance video."

"Of course." Carven got his key ring out again, fumbled through four or five possibilities until he found the one he wanted.

On the walk up to the second level, Carven continued to express his disbelief at what had happened, and to ask Munoz additional questions, most of which Munoz couldn't answer.

Once inside the security office, the first thing Munoz did was look around for a set of keys or a phone that might have belonged to Tony

Sarno. There was nothing. He had just finished the cursory search when Carven said, "This doesn't make any sense; they're turned off."

Munoz joined him in front of the surveillance monitors. "What?"

Carven pointed. "Look, the cameras aren't on."

Munoz stared at the blank screens. "Can you tell what time they were turned off?"

"Yeah. It'll take a couple of minutes though; I'm not as good as Tony." Carven shook his head.

A few minutes later Carven said, "It looks like they were shut off around eleven forty-five last night. The running time is in the corner of the screen."

"And what time does the mall close?"

"Ten o'clock."

"Can you get me the video from ten until eleven forty-five? I don't think it's going to show us anything, but I want to cover all the bases."

"Sure." Carven paused. "Do you know if anyone's contacted the manager of the mall?"

"I don't think so," Munoz told him.

"I better do that. And I'm sure he's going to want to know whether we can open up today."

"I don't see why not. We'll probably be gone in the next hour or so." Munoz paused, remembering something. "I only saw one car in the parking area in the back. It's a black Lexus. Do you know if that was Tony's?"

Carven nodded. "Yeah, he drives a Lexus, but I'm pretty sure it's silver. Oh wait, that's right, he traded the silver one in. Yeah, I think the black one's his. "

Munoz thought to himself that a Lexus was a pretty expensive car for a night watchman. But before he could explore that notion any further, his phone buzzed.

He glanced at the screen; it was Walker. "Hi, Craig, I was just about …"

Walker interrupted. "We got a call on the hotline; the caller gave us an address where he claims we can find Eric Allen."

On the man's last visit, Eric had pretended to be asleep. He used to do that sometimes with his mommy, and especially now with his daddy. But his mommy and daddy always seemed to know that he wasn't really sleeping. Eric had wondered if the man could tell. He had hoped not. He hadn't wanted the man to talk to him. He was less afraid when the man didn't talk. And it was even better when the man wasn't there at all.

After the man had gone, Eric had sat up and looked over to the shelf that still held his jacket. There appeared to be something else there. He had gotten up and walked over to get a closer look. The man had left some applesauce, some bottles of water, and a Walmart bag. Eric had opened up the bag and found a coloring book and some crayons.

Eric had been very hungry, so he quickly ate the applesauce. He then had colored a few pictures until he became tired again. For those ten minutes, he had been less frightened than at any time since he had been in the room.

On this visit, the man didn't bring applesauce. Instead, he brought oatmeal from McDonald's. As soon as Eric saw it, he began to cry; he didn't like oatmeal, and sometimes he and his mommy would argue about whether he had to eat it.

But even Eric knew that his tears had little to do with oatmeal; his fear had simply shot to the surface as soon as he saw the man again. Between his sobs Eric said, "I don't like oatmeal."

The man adjusted the mask he was wearing so that his mouth wasn't covered. "Well, that's all there is."

Even though the man had said it with a stern voice, Eric could tell that the man didn't mean it. Then Eric's six-year-old mind thought of something—"If I eat the oatmeal all up, can I go home?"

The man stood there for a moment and then said, "I'll go get you something else to eat."

"But I want to go home."

The man turned to leave and mumbled to himself. "I know."

As the man exited the room, he decided that he had to do something. This just couldn't go on any longer.

CHAPTER SIXTEEN

Once the words about the hotline call registered with Munoz, he had to force himself not to overreact. "Do you think it's credible?"

"The guy must have used some sort of voice alteration device," Walker informed him. "If this was just somebody looking for attention, I'm not sure he'd go through all that trouble." "Okay," Munoz took a deep breath. "What do you want me to do?"

"I should have our team assembled in the next ten minutes. Two guys are already here, and the other two are on their way. I'd like you to meet us there. But park a distance away." Walker paused. "Our team needs to take the lead on this, Dave. As I said, I want you there, but primarily as backup. Every one of our guys has been through this before. We need to go in there with weapons drawn. We have no idea what we're going to find."

"I understand," Munoz replied. "That's not a problem. What's the address?"

"One eighty-six Rogers. It looks like a commercial building, from what I could see on Google Earth."

Munoz thought a moment. "I think you're right," he said. "There are a couple of abandoned stores in that area. From what I understand, a bunch of local businesses went belly up when the mall came in about five years ago."

"Are you sure it's okay for you to leave the crime scene you're working?" Walker asked.

"Yeah, there's nothing else I can do right now," Munoz told him. "I've made some phone calls; I'm just waiting to hear back."

"All right. We're heading out in a couple of minutes. I'll see you there."

Munoz was so wrapped up in his conversation with Walker that he almost forgot that Jack Carven was in the office with him. As he ended the call, he looked toward Carven. "Sorry, I'm going to have to take off for a little while. Give me your phone number. I'll call you and let you know when I'll be back." Munoz reached into his pocket. "Here's my card; my number's on there, in case you need to reach me."

With that, the detective excused himself and went back outside. He caught up with Zach Donovan, explained the situation, hopped in his car, and drove the two miles to the Rogers Street address.

Less than ten minutes later, Munoz was parked down the block from the abandoned store. A few minutes after that, three cars with the FBI agents inside pulled up next to the detective's unmarked car.

Walker got out of one of the cars and went to talk to Munoz. "I'm going to have one of our agents block the street right about here. I'd like you to drive past the address and block the street from the other direction. As soon as both of you are in place, we're going in. If you hear gunshots, call for backup. If we're not out in ten minutes, call for backup. I don't want you coming in, understood?"

Munoz nodded. "Yeah. I understand."

Walker's parting words were, "Keep a good thought."

Once Munoz was in place, he watched as two vehicles with the agents in them sped up to the storefront. They parked at a forty-five degree angle to the curb and quickly exited the cars. It appeared that they were all wearing bulletproof vests underneath their FBI-emblazoned jackets. They all had their guns drawn. One of the agents went around back, and the other three, including Walker, moved to within twenty feet of the front door.

Walker raised the bull horn he was carrying. "FBI, FBI. We have agents surrounding the building; come out with your hands up."

There was no response. Walker repeated his instructions. Still no response. He waited another minute, and then motioned the other two agents to move forward. When the lead agent reached the door, he stood to the side, and tried the handle. Initially, the door didn't move. But after another tug, the rotted wood surrounding the door jamb gave way.

The agent looked toward Walker, who nodded. The agent then pushed the door wide open while he remained off to the side. He waited another fifteen seconds and then raised the shield he was holding up to his face. He peered through the bulletproof Plexiglas window embedded in the shield and entered the store. Walker and the other agent followed.

Munoz glanced at his watch. It was 7:22. At 7:27 Walker came out and waved Munoz over, announcing, "All clear."

Munoz ran to the storefront. "Nothing?"

Walker shook his head. "Nothing. I doubt anyone's been inside there in months. There's dust everywhere." He paused. "When we get back to the station, let's try to find out who owns this place, although I don't think it's going to help us. Still, we've got to let him know about the broken door."

Walker shook his head again. "I'm still puzzled about the call to the hotline. If it was just a hoax, why did the guy alter his voice? There was no need. He didn't stay on long enough for a trace. He must have known that ..." Walker answered his own question. "Unless he believed what he was telling us was the truth." He paused. "But that doesn't necessarily make any sense, either."

He turned to face Munoz more directly. "When we get back, I'd like to have another brainstorming session. And I'd like you to be there, if you can free yourself up from the other case."

"I already called the chief on my way over here. He told me that he'd step in and help out with the other investigation, and that I should stay with you on this one. I think his exact words were 'we can't do anything for the murder victim, but Eric Allen's still out there.' "

At the brainstorming session, Walker announced that he had decided to resume the search of the lakes and ponds in the area. That piece of news, while understandable, escalated everyone's frustration level, especially the FBI agents. This investigation had been conducted by the book—canvassing, Sex Offender Registry interviews, follow-up interviews, surveillance videos, a press conference, and a hotline—and they had no clues, no witnesses, and no suspects.

It was now after 9:00 a.m.; they had been brainstorming for over an hour, and still nobody had any idea what to do next.

Walker rarely displayed any sign of defeatism, especially in a public meeting, but he couldn't help himself. "It's not only that we haven't been able to get a break in the case; I don't even have a sense of what direction we should be going in. The Allen boy disappeared on Monday, and here it is Friday. And basically, we have nothing."

The brainstorming session broke up five minutes later.

Shortly before 10:00, Munoz was sitting in his office with both the Eric Allen case folder and the Tony Sarno case folder open on his desk. One of the Stanfield officers poked his head in. "Detective, I just got a hold of the owner of the building on Rogers. Here's the phone number and address, if you want it." The officer handed a piece of paper to Munoz.

"Thanks," he replied.

Pursuing this was probably not worth the effort, thought Munoz, but it was better than sitting here staring at the case files, so he went to find Walker. A few minutes later, they were in the car heading to the offices of Beacon Realty to talk to Fred Pendel, the owner.

It was obvious from the outside of Beacon Realty that business was far from booming. In fact, thought Munoz, the storefront on Rogers was probably in better shape than this building. Nevertheless, Mr. Pendel greeted both Walker and Munoz with a smile on his face. After the introductions he said, "I told the officer who called me that I'd send somebody out to secure the Rogers Street property as soon as I could. I just haven't had a chance."

Walker responded. "No, it's not about that, Mr. Pendel. We're doing some follow-up. When was the last time that property was leased out?"

"Actually, it's still leased out," Fred Pendel informed them.

Walker looked at Munoz, obviously surprised. "Can you get us that information?"

"Sure." Pendel went over to a battered gray filing cabinet, shuffled through some folders, and pulled one out. He turned back toward Walker and Munoz, as he opened it up. "It's leased to an Edward Gleeson until … let me see … June thirtieth."

Pendel looked more closely at the folder. "Oh yeah, I remember this now. I've been trying to contact him for a few months to see if he wanted to renew the lease, but I haven't been able to get in touch with him. He must have moved. I sent him a couple of letters, but they were returned. It said on the envelope that the addressee was unknown, and there was no forwarding address. Same with his phone—out of service."

Walker pointed to the folder. "Can we have copies of that?"

The Realtor nodded. "Yeah, although I'm not sure what good it's going to do you."

Walker was thinking the exact same thing.

Munoz spoke up for the first time. "Do you know what this Gleeson was using the property for?"

"Storage mostly, I think," Mr. Pendel told them. "Although, come to think of it, when he first rented the place he said something about a photography studio."

This time Walker raised his eyebrows as he looked over at Munoz.

Back in the car, Walker said, "Not exactly a major break. In fact, it might be the definition of grasping at straws. But doesn't it seem awfully coincidental that the guy's a photographer, and we're looking at the child pornography angle? On the other hand, he's probably not our guy if he disappeared months ago. When we get back to the station, let's do some more digging on this, and see if we can locate him."

As it turned out, when they arrived back at the police station, they put the idea of locating Edward Gleeson on hold. There was something more interesting to pursue. Zach Donovan showed up outside Munoz's office shortly after he and Walker had sat down.

Munoz saw him first. "Hey Zach, What are you still doing here?"

"The chief asked me to continue to help out with the murder investigation so that you could stay on the abduction case."

"I appreciate that." Munoz eyed the folder Donovan was holding. "What's that you've got?"

"The information on Tony Sarno that you wanted. It doesn't appear that he's got any next of kin, at least that I could find. His parents are deceased, and he has no siblings. I have an address in Cranston, and as you already know, he worked at the mall."

"Anything else stand out?" Munoz asked.

Donovan nodded. "Yeah, one thing. He had no arrests for a number of years, and then last July there were two charges filed against him."

"What were they for?"

The officer examined the rap sheet. "Solicitation and possession of child pornography."

Munoz leaped to his feet. "What? Let me see that!"

Donovan handed it over.

Munoz glanced through the folder, and then turned his gaze toward Walker. "Are you thinking what I'm thinking?"

"Yeah, too many coincidences."

Munoz expressed his thoughts out loud. "Why wasn't he in the Sex Offender Registry?"

Zach Donovan responded. "The solicitation charges were dropped, and there was a mistrial in the child porn case. He was never convicted of anything."

The news about Tony Sarno's past charges was all Walker needed to become re-energized. He immediately called the FBI's Boston office to begin the application process for a federal warrant to search Tony Sarno's apartment. If they had a positive I.D. on the body, they probably wouldn't even need a warrant to go in. But without the I.D., getting the search warrant was far from a slam-dunk. It was also problematic because Walker couldn't show a definitive connection between Tony Sarno and the disappearance of Eric Allen. But his gut told him there was one. Unfortunately, judges needed something more substantial than what a cop's gut told him.

While Walker started the ball rolling on the search warrant, Munoz called the Cranston police and asked them to be on standby. If the search warrant was executed, Walker wanted the local police to assist.

The Boston office faxed over the application a half hour later. Walker started calling federal judges as soon as he removed the papers from the fax machine. The first few calls produced the same result— "The judge's calendar is full for the rest of the day"—which Walker interpreted to mean that the judge was long gone.

Finally, Walker found a judge who was willing to at least see them. Walker and Munoz drove to the Providence Federal Court Building, and as they made their way up to the third floor, they rehearsed what they were going to say.

Walker handed the papers to the judge and outlined his argument. He opened his remarks by emphasizing that a search of Tony Sarno's apartment might lead them to the missing boy.

The judge countered with the fact that there was nothing to link Tony Sarno to the suspected abduction, and more to the point, they didn't have a positive I.D.

Munoz jumped in to indicate that he had seen the body and was reasonably sure that it was Tony Sarno, but the judge wasn't convinced.

Walker went for half a loaf—a search limited to any computers found on the property, and anything else in plain sight.

The judge looked at him with skepticism, and wanted to know—while the FBI agents were searching for computers in closets, for instance, would the closets then be considered in plain sight?

Walker didn't bother to answer.

The judge then indicated that, while he was sympathetic, without a positive I.D., his hands were tied. "I can't throw the Fourth Amendment out the window because you think you know who this person is. If you bring me something more conclusive, then I'd be happy to sign it."

Walker wanted to keep the conversation going, even though he knew it was futile. He struggled to find something to say.

The judge saw the expression on his face and asked, "Is the property a private home or an apartment?"

"It's an apartment."

The judge sat back in his chair, never taking his eyes off Walker. "You know, this reminds me of a hypothetical case I read about in one of my law magazines many years ago. It seems the police wanted to enter a man's apartment because they suspected that there was something inside that would help them solve a crime. However, the man who was renting the apartment was missing, and had been for quite a while. Anyway, in that situation, the police contacted the apartment building manager, who legally has control over those apartments, and asked him to let them in. He agreed; the police went in and found what they were looking for." The judge paused. "It's interesting, don't you think, that the manager was even willing to open the apartment for the *local* police? I mean. It wasn't as if the *FBI* made the request."

Walker smiled. "Thank you for your time, Your Honor. You've been very helpful."

"As you can probably tell, Agent Walker, I believe very strongly in the rule of law. And I won't compromise on that. But every once in a while, I subscribe to the notion that sometimes it's better to ask for forgiveness after the fact, rather than permission before it. Good luck."

He and Munoz were barely out of the building when Walker called one of his agents to contact the building manager of Tony Sarno's apartment complex and let him know they were coming. Munoz called the Cranston Police and alerted them to what was happening.

They met the manager at three fifteen. At the sight of Walker's badge, he was more than willing to cooperate. The search took forty-five minutes and yielded very little—no desk computer, no laptop, nothing to connect Tony Sarno to Eric Allen. They did find a set of car keys for a Lexus, and assumed it was a spare set. So on the way back to the station, they stopped by the mall, parked next to what they believed was Tony's car and opened it up.

If Tony's apartment was incredibly clean, especially for someone who lived alone, his car could be described as immaculate. They checked the glove compartment, the trunk, and under the seats—not even dust.

The disappointment was evident on Walker's face. But he had one more idea—Since Tony Sarno had been arrested for possession of child pornography, maybe his computer had been seized. It took a series of phone calls, but Walker finally was put in touch with someone who might be able to answer his questions. "Yes, Agent Walker, his computer was taken from his apartment last July, shortly after he was arrested."

"Do you still have it?" the agent asked

"No."

"So it was returned to him?" Walker persisted.

"No." A pause. "I remember what happened, though, because I was on duty when he called. We had sent out a letter telling him he could pick up his computer. This was probably a month or two ago. Anyway, he calls and asks if I'm the person he should talk to about arranging to get his computer back. I said 'yes,' and he says, 'I don't want the fucking computer; throw it out.' So we did."

It was almost five o'clock on a Friday afternoon. And while most people were looking forward to a nice spring weekend, Walker and Munoz felt as if they were in a maze, one with ten-foot-high steel walls that kept them constantly retracing their steps.

CHAPTER SEVENTEEN

A s had been the case for the past several nights, Josh Raybeck had hardly slept. It was now a little after nine on Friday morning, and he had been awake for more than four hours, nearly every moment of which had been spent trying to decide what to do.

He really wanted to speak to Tony, but Tony had made it clear that there should be no contact between the two of them. Of course, Tony had already broken that rule. But Tony broke rules all the time when it suited him. Josh had little doubt, however, that if he broke the rules, there'd be hell to pay.

Every time Josh thought about what he was involved in, a wave of panic threatened to overwhelm him. And there was no respite. More than once, his emotions had begun to take charge of his reason, and he had nearly done something that he knew he'd regret. But he almost didn't care; he just wanted this to be over.

Josh had avoided looking at a newspaper, or watching TV, or even turning on the car radio earlier when he had gone out to McDonalds. He was sure that the disappearance of Eric Allen was still dominating the local news, and if he heard any mention of it, he was convinced it would put him over the edge.

He had even called in sick for the past two days, fearful that the boy's disappearance would be the primary topic of conversation among his co-workers. But he couldn't afford to lose another day's pay; he had to go into work today. And maybe that wasn't all bad, he thought—there might be a chance that Tony would show up, as he sometimes did. And if he ran into Tony at the food court, it wouldn't be breaking the rules. Josh felt good about having made a decision, however small it was.

Since he didn't have to be to work until noon, Josh turned on the TV, immediately hit the On Demand button, and searched for a movie that might distract him for the next couple of hours.

He left his house at eleven thirty and arrived at the mall fifteen minutes later. He parked where he always did, near the front entrance. Once inside, he took the escalator to the second level, all the time fighting to keep his nerves in check. He got in line at the Dunkin' Donuts in the food court, and scoured the area for any sign of Tony. No luck.

A man and a woman, both a few years younger than Josh, were directly in front of him in the coffee line. They were both wearing name tags indicating that they worked at The Computer Supermarket. Josh was lost in his own thoughts, until he heard part of their conversation.

The young man said, "Did you hear what happened?"

"No, what?" the woman asked.

"They found a dead body in back of the mall this morning."

The woman gasped. "For real?"

"Yeah, and I heard the dead guy worked here at the mall."

"No way."

"Yeah, he was the night watchman. I think his name was Tony something. He used to come into the store sometimes."

Josh could feel the color drain from his face, as his breath caught, and his knees started to buckle. He addressed the young man. "Who told you that?"

The young man turned to him. "I overheard my boss talking to one of the security guards."

Josh brought his hand up to his mouth. "God, no! This can't be happening."

The man was apologetic. "Sorry, man. Was he a friend of yours?"

Josh didn't hear the last question; he had already turned his back and left the line. His first thought was that it must be a mistake. But then he acknowledged to himself that everything the young man had said rang true. Still, it was hard to believe.

He started to go into First Class Photo to ask his co-workers if they had heard what happened. But then Josh realized—if they confirmed that the dead man really was Tony—there was no way he'd be able to function at work.

He turned away from the photo studio and walked in the other direction, still trying to wrap his head around what he had heard. After a few moments he came upon the mall security office. Without even thinking about it, he went over and knocked on the door. Jack Carven opened up. "Yes?"

Josh figured it was better to pretend that he already knew most of the facts. "I just heard about Tony. Do you know what happened?"

Jack Carven looked as if he were weighing how much he should say, but he recognized Josh, so after a few seconds he offered, "The police told me he was murdered. It might have been a robbery; they took his wallet."

Although the security guard's statement convinced Josh that Tony was definitely dead, he was able to hold himself together long enough to appear concerned, but not in a panic. But it didn't take long for the panic to set in. And as he walked away from the security office, the stark realization hit him that this was no robbery. This was related to what Tony had gotten him mixed up in, and now he was in danger.

Josh drove back to his house in a total daze, still having difficulty accepting that any of this was real. But by the time he pulled into the driveway, a number of questions had pushed their way to the front of his mind – *Was Tony definitely killed because of the kidnapping? Does the person who killed him know about me? Does anyone else know where Eric Allen is?*

Shortly after he entered his house, Josh turned on the TV, trying to find any news about Tony's murder. He only had to wait about ten minutes before the story appeared on the screen underneath the caption "Breaking News."

The reporter said that the police had not released the name of the victim, but that sources had told him that his name was Anthony Sarno of Cranston, Rhode Island, the night watchman at the Stateline Mall. He had been shot twice, but there were no other details.

If Josh had thought he was in panic mode before, it was nothing compared to the fear he was feeling now; the news report had seen to that.

His next thought was that he should go to the police and tell them the whole story. But he questioned why they would believe him. He had no proof of anything. Wouldn't they just as easily suspect that he was responsible for the kidnapping? Plus, if he went to the police, he'd have to tell them about some of the other illegal things he had done. And again, there was no way to prove that Tony had intimidated and threatened him.

Josh also considered just taking off. But to where? And how would he survive, always looking over his shoulder, and with no house and no job? He broke down in tears three different times. Hours passed with no solution in sight.

At least once, the unthinkable entered Josh's mind. The only thing linking him to Tony and the people who probably killed him was the boy. If he were not around ... Josh was never able to finish the thought.

Just when mental exhaustion threatened to shut down Josh's brain, a realization came to him—with the exception of the people responsible for Tony's murder - everyone was focused on Eric Allen's disappearance. That meant he had information everybody wanted, information he could use to bargain with.

Of course, while that was true in theory, Josh realized, the reality was much different. He still wasn't about to go to the police and try to negotiate a deal, at least not by himself. That last thought triggered a memory—somebody Tony had told him about. The only person Tony had never bad-mouthed.

Josh rushed to the computer and started searching. One link led to another link, and then to a third and a fourth. But since he didn't know a lot of the specific details, it took much longer than he anticipated.

Eventually, Josh found what he had been searching for. He printed it off the screen, took the paper from the tray, and stared at it for a moment. For the first time since this ordeal had begun, he actually believed that things might turn out all right.

He wanted to place the call immediately, but he forced himself to pull back. He needed to rehearse what he was going to say, to make sure that he didn't divulge too much. He took a piece of paper from the printer tray and made an outline. He even wrote down some key phrases to use in case he froze in the middle of the conversation.

When Josh finally thought he was ready, he went into his bedroom, rummaged through one of his bureau drawers and found the untraceable phone that Tony had given him. He decided that after he placed this call he would get rid of the phone, hoping he would never have to use it again. Josh took a deep breath and punched in the number.

After two rings, he heard a man's voice say, "Jerry Hanson."

Josh hesitated. "Uh ... Mr. Hanson, you don't know me, but it's very important that I speak with you."

"Can you tell me your name?"

Another hesitation. "Josh."

"No last name?" Jerry inquired.

"Just Josh for now."

"Okay, Josh. What's this in reference to?"

"A few months ago you were Tony Sarno's lawyer, right?"

Jerry knew that Tony had been killed earlier in the day, so his antennae went up. "That's public information. But why do you want to know?"

"I need to talk to you about some things having to do with Tony," said Josh.

Jerry was still suspicious. "Like what?"

"I really need to do this in person."

The attorney sighed. "You're not giving me very much here, Josh."

"I know, but I don't want to talk about certain things until I know I can trust you. You know, if you represent me."

"You want to hire me?" Jerry asked.

"Probably."

Jerry decided to cut to the chase. "Are you suggesting that you know something about Tony's death?"

Josh remained evasive. "Maybe."

"Well, unless you're the one who shot him, you should go to the police. And if you are the one who shot him, I'm not your guy anyway; I don't defend murderers."

Josh felt as if he were losing Jerry, so he went further than he had intended. "I didn't kill anybody, and I do have some information about Tony." He paused. "But I also have some information about that boy who disappeared."

Jerry felt his stomach drop, but he kept his cool. "And you won't go to the police?"

Josh threw out the next line almost as a challenge. "Not unless that's what you advise me to do."

Jerry didn't get the sense that the person he was speaking with was dangerous, although the thought of him being connected to Tony Sarno in any way still made him wary. But in the end he said, "It's nearly four o'clock. When can you be here?"

"Twenty minutes."

"Okay, I'll see you then." Jerry paused. "And Josh, no promises, understand?"

"I understand. Thank you, Mr. Hanson." Josh was about to disconnect the call when he added. "I know sometimes people exaggerate and say that something is a matter of life and death, but this really is."

Jerry didn't doubt that for a second.

At four thirty, Josh arrived at Jerry Hanson's office, which was actually a small Cape Cod house in a predominantly residential area. He rang the doorbell, and a moment later Jerry greeted him and invited him inside. They shook hands, as Josh announced, "I'm Josh, Josh Raybeck."

"I'm Jerry Hanson. Come on in and sit down. How do you spell your last name?"

"R-a-y-b-e-c-k."

As soon as Jerry got behind his desk, he wrote the name on a legal pad. "So how do you want to do this, Mr. Raybeck?"

"Please call me Josh."

"Okay, Josh." the attorney replied.

Jerry was about to say something else when Josh interrupted. "I think I could be in a lot of trouble. But I have some information that I know the police would be interested in, so I want to make some sort of deal ... and protection. I think I may need protection."

"From whom?"

Josh shifted in his chair. "The people who killed Tony."

"Why would they be after you?" Jerry asked.

"They might think I know more than I really do," Josh replied.

Jerry decided not to pursue that for the time being. He wanted to move into the area that was more pressing. "On the phone you said something about the boy who's missing."

"Yeah, I have information about him too. It's all connected."

Jerry was obviously surprised. "How?"

Josh appeared even more nervous than he had when he first walked in. "No offense, Mr. Hanson, but I don't want to say anything else until we have an agreement."

Jerry felt as if he were too far down the road to back away now. Plus, he couldn't help but think about the missing boy. He reached into the bottom drawer of his desk and extracted some papers. "This is a standard representation form. Once we both sign it, I'm officially your attorney, and all the rules of confidentiality apply."

Jerry could see a sense of relief spread across Josh's face. "I don't have much money," the young man confessed.

"Let's not worry about that now."

After Jerry filled in the necessary blanks on the form and they both signed it, Josh took a deep breath and said, "If it's okay with you, I'd like to start at the beginning when I first met Tony."

"Whatever you want."

And so Josh began.

"I'm a photographer at First Class Photo in the mall. Sometime last August, when I was on my break in the food court, this guy introduced himself and started talking to me. He showed up like three days in a row. We were just shooting the breeze, so I didn't think anything of it. The guy was Tony Sarno.

"At the end of our conversation on the third day, he told me that he needed a favor. Actually, he said it was for a friend of his. He claimed that his friend had just gotten divorced, and his ex-wife had taken off with the two kids, a boy and a girl. And this friend of his thought that his ex-wife might have come to this area, since she has family here."

Josh went quiet for a moment, so Jerry prompted him. "What was the favor?"

Josh let out a long breath. "Tony told me that the ex-wife was big on having the kids' pictures taken, so he wanted me to make copies of all the photos we had taken over the past few months with little kids in them—from ages three to ten. I told him I couldn't do that. Those pictures were private property; I could get fired.

"He said he understood that I'd be taking a chance, so his friend was willing to pay me five dollars for each picture; it would be worth it to him. I told Tony that there were probably hundreds of pictures taken during the summer alone. But he said that was okay, and it was an easy way for me to make five hundred dollars. He said it was 'win, win.' "

Josh looked sheepish. "Obviously, I knew it was wrong, and I'm not sure that I totally believed him. But I agreed to do it anyway. A couple of weeks later, Tony arranged for me to meet him at the back entrance to the mall at, like, two o'clock in the morning. Since he was the night watchman, he had access to all the stores. He unlocked the pull-down gate and let me in to the photo studio. I printed out about a hundred and twenty pictures. But I was so nervous that I printed them out by families. I didn't even check to see if it was just kids, or even the right ages. When I finished, I gave Tony the pictures, and he handed me five hundred dollars in cash. I remember driving home, feeling really lousy, but just happy that it was over.

"Then about two weeks after that, Tony showed up at my house. I still don't know how he found out where I lived. He wasn't fall-down drunk, but he had been drinking. I didn't even want to let him in, but I didn't feel like I had a choice. Almost as soon as we were inside, he handed me one of the pictures I had printed out. This one had a little boy sitting on his mother's lap. I thought maybe Tony was pissed off because the picture wasn't just of a kid. I apologized, and offered to give him some of the money back. But he told me not to worry about it. He wanted to know who the woman was. So then I thought maybe Tony's friend had recognized her, and I asked him that."

Josh paused. "I'll never forget the way he looked at me. And then he said, 'There was never any guy looking for his kids. Don't pretend that you didn't know that. Just find out who that woman is, or I might have to pay a visit to your boss."

Jerry started to feel some sympathy for Josh; Jerry had seen that same look on Tony's face that Josh had described.

Josh continued. "I didn't know it at the time, but the two people in the photo were Eric Allen and his mother."

Jerry, who had been taking notes, stopped abruptly. "And when was this?"

"Sometime last September, about eight months ago."

Jerry put his pen down. "Why was Tony interested in the Allen boy way back then?"

"That's just it. He wasn't. That would come later. It was the mom he was interested in."

"What?"

"Yeah, he kept talking about how hot she was. How he was sick of the whores he went to. I just listened. I wanted him out of my house as quickly as possible, so I told him I'd find out who she was the next day when I went to work. It actually took me a few days, because I had to go through hundreds of pictures and try to match them up with their order numbers. But it didn't matter, because Tony didn't contact me for another few days. Then he showed up at my house again, even more drunk than he was the last time. He wanted the woman's name, so I gave it to him. Then he said something like 'This is good. I think maybe I should go see her.' He was quiet for a minute, and then he told me to meet him in back of the mall again that night. He had another job for me.

"I told him I couldn't get any more pictures because it was the beginning of the school year and business was slow. Most parents just wait and have their kids' pictures taken at school, rather than at the mall. He told me it wasn't about that; it was something different."

Josh shut down for a minute, obviously struggling with a memory. Jerry asked, "Are you all right?"

"No, not really. But I need to get through this." He gathered himself. "When I went to the mall that night, Tony let me in, and we went up to the second level. I asked him what he wanted from me, and he said, 'You'll see.'

"He stopped in front of First Class Photo; the gate was already up. I was scared out of my mind, but I still challenged him. I said, 'You told me I wasn't going to have to print out any more pictures.' He said, 'You're not. You're going to take some new ones.' And then he pointed to a couch in the corner."

Josh paused, nearly in tears. He took a moment to pull himself together, and then continued. "There were two little kids asleep, a little boy around four and a little girl around three. I asked Tony who they were, and what they were doing here. It was one o'clock in the morning. He didn't like it that I had questioned him. I thought he was going to take a swing at me, but all he did was push me. Then he told me not to ever raise my voice to him again. I don't think I've ever been so scared in my life. And then it got worse.

"Tony told me they belonged to one of the prostitutes he went to." Josh paused. "And they weren't just asleep; he had used chloroform on them."

Now it was Jerry's turn to shut down. He knew it was important, but a large part of him didn't want to hear any more. However, after another minute he asked, "Then what happened?"

"Tony told me that the kids would wake up in about fifteen minutes, and then I was supposed to take their pictures." Josh could only whisper the next few words. "He was going to take their clothes off."

Jerry threw his pen down. "Shit! That sick bastard! I should have known even before the trial that he was playing me. He was guilty as sin."

Josh's face took on an expression of resolve. "It's still bad, but it's not what you think. Let me finish this part and then I'll tell you what he told me about the trial."

Jerry's curiosity was piqued, but he took Josh at his word and encouraged him to keep going.

The young man continued. "I'm not sure why; maybe because Tony was always trying to impress me with what a big shot he was. But while we were waiting for the kids to wake up, he told me all about the business he was in.

"He had Photoshopped the pictures I gave him, and turned them into pornography. That's what I meant before. The pictures of Eric Allen weren't for him. He worked for some guy who made tons of money distributing child pornography. Evidently, Tony would send the pictures halfway around the world, and they'd wind up on some Web site. Tony told me that there were thousands of subscribers who paid $19.95 a month."

Jerry shook his head, and almost to himself said, "It's hard to believe how many sick people there are out there."

Josh didn't reply. He waited another moment, and then went on with the story. "I was getting more and more frantic about what Tony wanted me to do when the kids woke up, so I tried something else. I offered to print out some more pictures. Of course that was the wrong thing to say. Tony stared at me for a minute, and then said, 'I thought there weren't any more pictures. You were lying to me? The last photographer I used lied to me too, and then he disappeared.' I wasn't sure what he meant. I'm still not. But I honestly thought he might kill me if I didn't do what he wanted.

"The kids still hadn't woken up, so Tony kept talking. He knew I was petrified, so I guess he felt like he could say anything, and I wouldn't dare cross him. Next, he told me that even if I had more photos, he wanted me to take these new ones. He claimed that it was easier to add real pictures to existing ones rather than to Photoshop the whole thing. It was like he was taking pride in what he was doing. He also told me that he never used to have to resort to Photoshopping at all. But that the last photographer, the one who disappeared, he had screwed up and sent pictures to his unprotected e-mail account."

Jerry's mouth flew open. "That's what he was arrested for!"

"I know. He told me that he had to keep a low profile after he got off. That's when he came up with the Photoshop idea. I remember that he got quiet after that, like he was remembering something. Then he started talking about you."

Jerry's eyebrows raised. "About me?" he repeated.

"Yeah. He probably told me your name at the time, but I didn't remember it. I had to find you on the Internet. Anyway, he told me that you had treated him with respect; that you had done right by him."

"So that's why you contacted me, because of what Tony said?" Jerry asked.

"No, not at all. I just figured that if anyone knew what Tony was really like, it might be you. And that would give me a better chance of being believed. You'd probably know that Tony was capable of doing all the things I told you."

"You're right about that. But to be honest, at the time of the trial, I wasn't sure whether he was guilty or not."

"Tony told me he thought you weren't sure. But in the end, it wasn't going to matter anyway," Josh stated.

"You mean because he got off?"

The young man shook his head. "No, because he said that the trial was in the bag. He knew that he was never going to be convicted; at least that's what he told me."

CHAPTER EIGHTEEN

Jerry looked intently at Josh. "What did he mean by that? Did he say anything else?"

"No. I think he was going to, but then the kids woke up."

Jerry decided not to push any further; he suspected that the next few minutes were going to be very difficult for Josh, as he described what had happened.

Josh continued. "I tried to get out of taking the pictures by trying to reason with Tony. I pointed out that both kids had seen our faces, and could tell someone what we'd done. But Tony said, 'Who are they going to tell, their mother? Besides, they've had pictures like this taken before. It's nothing new for them.'"

Josh broke eye contact, as he tried to finish this part of the story without breaking down. "I took ten pictures, five of each. I printed them out, and gave them to Tony. After I finished, I couldn't even look at the kids."

Josh struggled to keep going. "Then Tony told me he wanted me to drive the kids home. I felt like I was going to pass out. Then he started laughing, telling me that I should have seen the look on my face, but that he was only kidding; I didn't really have to drive them home. Then he reached into a bag he had, and took out two cups of apple sauce, and gave one to each of the kids. He whispered to me that it had something in it to make them sleep."

Josh made eye contact again. "I think that was the worst night of my life, although there have been a couple more just as bad since then. I really wanted to go to the police, but I was too scared. What if the police didn't believe me and Tony ended up back on the street? I'd be a dead man. I just kept hoping that maybe I'd never see him again. But, obviously, that didn't happen."

Josh closed his eyes for a moment. When he reopened them he asked, "Do you have any water?"

"Sure, in the mini-fridge over there."

Josh got up and grabbed a bottle. When he returned and sat down, he said, "I wish I were done with this. But there's still a lot more I have to tell you."

"It's okay," Jerry encouraged. "You're doing fine."

Josh grunted. "Maybe from where you're sitting."

"I just meant that there's nothing you've told me so far that would preclude me from making a deal," Jerry elaborated.

"You're sure?"

"As I said—so far. But I need to hear the rest of it."

"I know." Josh took another sip of water and began again.

"Last October, I came home early from work. I can't even remember why. As I pulled into my driveway, I pushed the button on my mirror to open the garage door, but nothing happened. I've got a two-car garage, so I tried the button for the other side. But again, nothing happened. I figured maybe the electricity was out. I usually go into the house through the garage, but obviously I couldn't, so I had to use the front door. I put in my key and turned it, but it was already open. I didn't think that much of it; sometimes I forget to lock it.

"Anyway, I hit the light switch next to the door, and the hall light came on, so I knew I hadn't lost power. I decided to go into the garage to see why the doors wouldn't open. I have to go through the kitchen to get there. As I entered the kitchen, there's Tony sitting at a table. He had a couple of empty beer bottles in front of him and one in his hand. I almost passed out. I asked him how he had gotten into my house. When he answered, his words were a little slurred. 'It wasn't that tough, Josh. You really should get an alarm system.'

"I felt like the nightmare was starting all over again. I asked him what he wanted, and he said something about me being almost out of beer. I asked again, and he told me that he needed a ride home. I asked him where his car was; he pointed to the garage and said it was in there. I went over to the door leading to the garage, opened it up, and sure enough, there it was. I think once he got into my house, he opened the garage door from the inside, pulled his car in, and then put on the locks. That's why I couldn't get the doors to open."

Josh stopped for a moment and took another drink of water. When he spoke again, he shifted away from the story he was telling. "You know, for the past few months I've asked myself why I didn't stop this thing in the beginning, when I had the chance; why I didn't do something before this? Yeah, I was scared. But I'm even more scared now." Josh started to fill up. "Maybe if I had done something earlier, then nobody would have been killed."

Jerry showed panic on his face. "I thought you told me that Eric Allen was all right."

"He is. I wasn't talking about him. I was talking about his mother."

Jerry was confused. "His mother?"

"Yeah." It took Josh another few moments to regain his composure. And then he picked up the story from where he had left off. "Obviously, I wanted Tony out of my house. Hell, I wanted him out of my life. So I said to him, 'Okay, I'll take you home.' We got into my car, and he told me to drive toward Cranston.

"When I started the car, the radio was already on. I decided to leave it, hoping that the music would prevent Tony from talking to me. After a few minutes, an announcer cut in with a news bulletin. A woman's body had been found in the nature preserve in Stanfield, and it had been identified as Cindy Allen. The name didn't register at first, but then I remembered the photograph. I looked over at Tony, and he returned my stare. Then he said, 'Turn off the radio; I don't want to hear that.' I had the feeling from his reaction that he was involved somehow. And then he confirmed it.

"Neither one of us spoke for a minute, and then Tony said, 'The bitch deserved it. I just wanted to talk to her. Maybe something would have come of it, maybe not. But she looked at me like I was a piece of shit. Who the hell does she think she is, anyway? I started to force her, but, I don't need to rape anyone. But she started to hit me, and then she tried to run. I caught up with her and gave her a couple of shots, and threw her down on the ground. She must have hit her head. There was a lot of blood. But she got up again and staggered for a few steps. I got in my car and finished it. There's a little damage to the car; not too much. But what could I do? I wasn't about to let her get away and tell someone I had done something I really didn't.' "

Josh looked up toward the ceiling. "It was almost like I wasn't there, like he was talking to himself. He never even looked in my direction. And then he said, 'You know whose fault this really is? It's that fucking loser …' "Josh paused. " I'm not sure what he said next. It sounded like 'Gunner,' but I was so shook up, I don't know if I heard it correctly."

Jerry had stopped taking notes. "You're telling me that he admitted killing Cindy Allen?"

Josh nodded. "Yes."

"This complicates things, Josh. Whoever we talk to about making a deal, probably a prosecutor, is going to ask why you didn't go to the police at that point."

"I know. And I really had made up my mind that I was going to. But Tony was two steps ahead of me, and obviously nowhere near as drunk as I thought."

Jerry eyed him. "What do you mean?"

"For another minute or so, Tony continued ranting about this guy, Gunner, or whatever his name is; about how he wouldn't let him go to the best prostitutes. And that he was sure that was all Gunner's doing, that the big boss wouldn't care about stuff like that.

"Then, almost like he just remembered that I was there, he said, 'And don't go getting any ideas, Josh.' I wasn't about to ask him what he meant, but I didn't have to; he filled in the blanks. ' I guess I should let you know that after my little encounter with that Allen bitch, your house wasn't my first stop. I dropped by our place of employment, long before it opened. And you know that car that's parked in your garage? Well congratulations, it's now registered in your name.'

"I remember that he looked over at me and smiled. ' Being the night watchman at the mall has so many perks. I mean, it allows such easy access to the computers in the RMV, not to mention the security camera system. In fact, I was recently looking at the video from the night we were in the photo studio with the kids. The clarity is amazing. It showed you taking their picture. But you know it's funny; I'm totally out of view. I made a DVD of it, if you'd like to see it sometime.'"

～✍

Jerry sat back and shook his head. "That's unbelievable. I suspected he was good with computers, but ..." His voice trailed off. A moment passed and then Jerry asked, "Is the car still registered in your name?"

"I don't think so, but it doesn't matter. Tony saw to that, too. A week after Cindy Allen was killed, he came to the food court and signaled for me to join him. After I did, he told me to pick him up in back of the mall at midnight and drive him back to my house. He said that he was going to take the car off my hands; he had a place that was going to repair the front-end damage, some place he used to work. Then, once it was fixed, he was going to get rid of it and get a new one."

Josh paused. "He warned me again not to get any ideas, because the title history of the old Lexus would still show me as the owner at the time of Cindy Allen's death.

"He kept talking to me like I was his best friend. I think in some twisted way, maybe he thought that, or like I said before, he was trying to impress me with how smart he was."

Jerry leaned forward. "Is there anything else about your conversations with Tony, or the circumstances surrounding Cindy Allen's death, that he might have mentioned that you haven't told me?"

Josh shook his head. "No. I don't think so."

Jerry was about to bring up something that had been bothering him, but decided to wait until he heard the rest of what Josh had to say. "All right." Jerry glanced at his watch. "It's getting late; we need to move this along if we want to get a deal negotiated tonight. Tell me about Eric Allen."

"Okay, I'm almost there."

Josh took another drink of water and then started in again. "From October until April, I only saw Tony a few times. Twice, he wanted me to give him more pictures from the studio, which I did. And the third time, probably in March, he wanted me to take some more live photos.

"I told him I wasn't going to do it. But he said if I didn't meet him at the mall like the last time, he'd bring the kids to my house. I decided I'd better do what he asked. But just before I was about to leave for the mall that night, he showed up at my house with the kids anyway. I took the pictures as fast as I could, just to get him out of there. These kids weren't the same ones I had photographed before, but they were about the same ages."

Josh took a deep breath, and looked away. When he turned back he said, "The next time I saw Tony was at the food court again a few weeks ago. He told me he wanted every picture I had of Eric Allen. I remember him smiling when he said, 'You know, the kid whose mother was killed by the car that was registered to you.' I told him that there weren't any more, at least none that I had taken. But he said to check again. And I did find a couple, but they were from two years ago, before I worked there. When I gave them to Tony the next day, he said something like 'I might have been able to satisfy the guy with something current, but not this shit. It's going to have to be the real thing.' I was pretty sure I knew what he meant, but he didn't elaborate, so I left it alone.

"Then, last Monday morning, he called me and said he had a special job. And that he was coming over to my house to talk about it. I tried to make up some excuse, but he said he'd be there in ten minutes, and I'd better be home. He also said to open up the garage doors.

"I honestly considered just leaving, but I knew he'd find me, and I'd be worse off. He pulled into the driveway less than ten minutes later. I was waiting in the kitchen when I heard the garage door go down. And then a minute after that, Tony came into the house. I had my back turned when he first came in so I didn't see that he was carrying something. And then I realized it was a child. A moment later I realized it was Eric Allen. He had kidnapped Eric Allen."

Jerry dropped his pen and stood up. "You can't be serious."

Josh watched Jerry for a moment and then said, "I started to flip out, and then I screamed at him. ' What's wrong with you?' He didn't say anything; he just took Eric into the living room and put him on the couch. He appeared to be sound asleep like the other kids, so I assumed Tony had used chloroform."

"When Tony came back into the kitchen, I knew he was pissed at me. He grabbed my shirt and said, 'Shut the fuck up, and do what you're told. As soon as the kid wakes up, take off his clothes, and then take plenty of pictures. I'll be back in half an hour to pick him up. I'll take him someplace, and then if I need more pictures, I'll bring you there to take them.' When he came back, I told him I took the pictures, but I really didn't. And then he left with Eric."

"Where did he take him?" Jerry asked.

Josh hesitated. "He didn't tell me, but I'm pretty sure I know."

"Only pretty sure?"

"Well, yeah, because Tony never contacted me again."

For the first time, Jerry had some serious doubts about Josh's story, at least the last part. The vocabulary he used, the lack of eye contact, and the clipped way he spoke, all suggested he was being deceptive.

Jerry decided he had to confront him. "Josh, up until now, I've believed everything you've told me, but this last part doesn't make sense. Why would Tony take off for a half hour? Why wouldn't he check to make sure you took the pictures? And he confided in you that he had killed someone; why wouldn't he tell you where he was taking Eric Allen?"

Jerry paused to allow all the points he had just made to register. Then he spoke calmly. "Josh, everything you tell me is privileged."

Josh barely made eye contact. "I know. And I do trust you. It's just that … I'm so scared, and …"

Jerry pressed him. "Are you telling me that some of this isn't the truth?"

Josh didn't answer right away. "All the important things are."

Jerry raised his voice. "That's not good enough."

"I know what you're saying. But I feel like the fact that I know where Eric is, that's my only way out of this." A pause. "And I do know where he is. Isn't that the most important thing? Whoever you have to make a deal with is going to be more willing to do that if I can produce Eric, right?"

"I think you're looking at this all wrong, Josh." Jerry paused. "I'm going to ask you a question and you may not like it, but it's probably the same question an ADA or a prosecutor is going to ask you."

Josh took a deep breath. "It's okay, go ahead."

"Do you have an alibi for the time of Cindy Allen's death, or Tony's, or Eric Allen's disappearance?"

Josh didn't appear necessarily surprised by the question. "No. But I told you, that's exactly why I came to you. You're the only one who knows what Tony was capable of."

"Josh, you're being naïve. Even if I believe every word that you said, you've got to see how this looks—Cindy Allen's dead; the car that ran her over was registered in your name, at least at the time; there may be a DVD showing you taking naked photos of little kids; Eric Allen is missing, and you say you know where he is. But the person who you claim is responsible for all of this is dead."

"I know how it looks. But that's why I need you. I didn't do any of those things."

"And I believe that's true. But the fact that you're not telling me everything is a problem. When we go to try to make a deal, if the ADA catches you in a lie, all bets are off."

Josh paled. "You mean they could arrest me?"

"It all depends on what you lied about," Jerry told him.

"Then I'm not going with you."

"You have to," Jerry argued.

"Why?"

"For one thing, it'll look suspicious. And secondly the district attorney is not going to make a deal until they've heard the whole story."

Josh sounded a lot tougher than he felt. "You were taking notes; you tell them."

"I don't know the whole story," Jerry retorted. "That's my point."

"You know enough. I'm not willing to take the chance of going there and getting arrested. Plus, if I'm not there, I can't possibly be caught in a lie, can I?"

Jerry spent the next several minutes trying to persuade Josh to come with him, but to no avail.

Eventually, Jerry gave up, and instead outlined what he was going to do next in an attempt to secure a plea agreement. "It seems to me that there are a number of things that you could be charged with; the most serious of which would be aiding and abetting in a kidnapping after the fact."

Josh looked horrified, but Jerry continued. "The next most serious charge would be taking lewd photographs. And the least serious, although still something to be concerned about, would be the theft of the pictures from your employer. Even though some of the offenses took place in Massachusetts, potentially the most serious offense took place in Rhode Island. So I'm going to contact the DA's office in Providence to try to strike a deal.

"Ironically, I was up against one of the ADA's in that office when I represented Tony. Her name is Maria Lopez. I'm going to see if I can go through her. I think she'd be willing to listen to what I have to say."

Josh had some questions. "If you make a deal with an ADA in Rhode Island, could I still face charges in Massachusetts?"

"Yes. And you could also be charged by the Feds. But honestly, as long as you lead them to Eric Allen and you weren't involved in his abduction, they're not going to do anything; they'll honor whatever deal is negotiated."

"So what does that mean exactly, in terms of what could happen to me?"

"It's very hard to imagine that they'd push for jail time, especially if I can convince them that the crimes you committed were a result of coercion, because you were in fear for your life."

"Well, that's true," Josh interrupted.

"And I believe you," Jerry assured him. "But that's why you should be there. Hearing it from you will be much more convincing than hearing it from me."

"I'm sorry. I'm just not willing to do that."

"Okay," sighed Jerry. "I figured I'd give it another shot."

"So if I can get out of serving jail time, then what?"

"At the most, I'd say probation, and possibly community service."

"Does First Class Photo have to find out about me copying the pictures?"

"I don't know. We'll have to see," Jerry said.

"And what about protection?"

"I'm sure that won't be an issue, once a deal is in place." Jerry paused. "You will have to come to the DA's office and sign the plea agreement, you know."

"I don't have a problem doing that after it's all worked out."

"Good." A pause. "I'm going to ask one more time. Will you tell me where Eric Allen is?"

"I'm sorry, I can't. I feel like I need to do this my way. But I promise you, he's okay."

"I sincerely hope so, for both your sakes."

Jerry stood up, as did Josh. They shook hands, and then Jerry said, "Keep your cell phone on, and I'll call as soon as I have any news."

Immediately after Josh left, Jerry went over to the cabinet that held all the files of his previous cases. He found the folder for Tony Sarno and began flipping through it. He skipped over copies of the motions he had filed, the unopened DVD of the trial, and hard copies of the pictures that had been found on Tony's phone. He hesitated momentarily, once again repulsed by the photos.

Finally, he came across the contact information for Maria Lopez. He looked at his watch; it was nearly five-thirty. He asked himself - *What are the chances of finding her still at work at this hour, and on a Friday to boot? And if she isn't there, how am I going to get a hold of her?*

But he was in luck; she answered on the second ring. "ADA Lopez."

"Hello, Ms. Lopez. This is Jerry Hanson. I don't know if you remember me. We were involved in a case together several months ago – Tony Sarno."

"Yes, of course. Actually, when I saw the news today, that he had been killed, I couldn't help but think of the trial, or should I say the mistrial. Not exactly my finest hour. What can I do for you, Mr. Hanson?"

"Jerry, please."

"Okay, Jerry. And you can call me Maria."

"Thanks. Actually, the reason for my call is related to Tony Sarno."

"Really?"

"Yes. It's a rather long story, but there's some urgency here. So I'd like to give you some of the particulars in a nutshell, and then I hope we can get together to discuss it further."

For the next ten minutes Jerry launched into Josh's story, emphasizing the likelihood that a plea agreement would lead to discovering Eric Allen's whereabouts. As soon as he was done, Maria said, "Come on over. Let's see what we can work out. I've had a pretty crappy couple of weeks; finding that little boy would more than make up for it."

"I'm on my way."

As Jerry put down the phone, he began to wonder if Josh may have been right. Maybe his idea of letting Jerry carry the ball had been the way to go. Maria Lopez was a tough ADA; he knew that from firsthand experience. But as soon as he had mentioned Eric Allen, he sensed a willingness on her part that he hadn't necessarily expected.

Jerry decided to call Josh and share a little good news. "Hey, Josh."

"Hi, Mr. Hanson. Is there a problem?"

"Just the opposite," Jerry told him. "I talked to the ADA, and she sounded very receptive. I'm on my way over there now."

Josh sounded relieved. "That's terrific."

"I figured you'd like to know. I'll call back when I have something more definitive."

"Thanks," said Josh. "I appreciate everything you're doing."

Maria Lopez was waiting in the lobby of the building that housed the DA's office. It was now officially after hours, and the doors were all locked. As soon as she spotted Jerry approaching, she pushed open the door and let him in.

"Hello, counselor."

"Jerry, remember?"

Maria Lopez extended her hand. "Right. Let's go back to my office."

The next half hour involved a substantial amount of give and take, but most of it was procedural. Maria never threw up any roadblocks.

In essence, she agreed to every one of Jerry's suggestions, keeping the main focus on the safe return of Eric Allen. When the plea bargain outline was completed, she said, "I don't usually work this way in regard to plea agreements, but obviously these are unusual circumstances. Still, I need to ask a few more questions. If I'm satisfied with the answers, then we have a deal, okay?"

"Okay, shoot," Jerry replied.

"Tell me again why you're so convinced that Josh Raybeck is telling the truth—that Tony Sarno was behind all of this."

Jerry suspected that a question like this was coming, so he was very prepared. The fact that everything he was about to say, he also believed, made it even easier. "I know it's not hard evidence, but his demeanor, for one thing. He was clearly very frightened. And he was uncomfortable when he talked about taking the pictures of the little kids. Secondly, he described things about Tony that I've also witnessed." He paused. "Can I say with a hundred percent certainty that Josh wasn't more involved than he's saying? No. But I also asked myself, if that were the case, why come forward at all?"

"Maybe, because with Tony out of the way, there's no one to contradict him," Maria offered.

"I thought of that too. But he doesn't strike me as being anywhere near that manipulative. Also, why would he even tell me about things that happened months ago? There's no way anybody would have found out about those. He would have been free and clear." Jerry paused and looked directly at Maria. "And honestly, the more he opened up, it almost seemed like he thought he was in confession."

For the first time, Maria smiled. "And you played Father Hanson?"

Jerry smiled back. "Hardly. I'm not in a position to absolve anybody of anything."

Maria let her smile linger for a moment longer, and then said, "What about the fact that he doesn't have an alibi for either of the deaths, or for the abduction? Does that bother you?"

Jerry shook his head. "No. All three of those events occurred either early in the morning or after midnight. I don't have an alibi for any of them either."

"Okay, one last question—why do you think he won't tell you where Eric Allen is?"

"I'm not sure. I know what he told me. He said he thought that the information was like his ace in the hole. Those are my words, not his. He said he thought it was more likely he'd get a deal if he was the only one who knew."

Jerry debated whether to say any more. All his professional training told him not to, but his gut told him differently. He went with his gut. "Maybe I shouldn't be telling you this, but I think he is hiding something. I don't believe it's a deal breaker, because I warned him about that. I don't even think it's crucial to the plea agreement. But for whatever reason, there's something he wants to keep to himself."

"I appreciate you being up front about that," Maria said. "And, strange as it may seem, from my perspective, it actually makes his story more believable. I've seen it a lot. When people are scared, they often hold something back. It's as if it gives them some semblance of control over their situation." Maria paused. "Or maybe he just didn't want to lie to Father Hanson."

This time Jerry smiled more broadly.

Maria waited a moment, and then continued. "I could ask a few more questions, but I think I've heard enough; I'm satisfied. Let's get this moving. We need to get that little boy back home."

"Thanks. I agree. So what do we do next?" Jerry asked.

"First we need to get a judge to approve the agreement in principle. Then we'll draw up the formal document and have your client sign it. As soon as that's done, we should contact the FBI agents who are working the case, and get them over here."

Jerry nodded. "Okay, that sounds good." A pause. "I know it's a long way from being over, but I want to let you know how much I appreciate what you've been willing to do."

"We're not always the enemy, you know."

He smiled. "I guess I'm finding that out."

Maria smiled back, and then said, "Here's some irony for you. All the judges are long gone for the day. But I happen to know that my dear friend Judge Lancaster, from Tony's trial, lives close by. If he's willing to come in and approve this, it would probably speed things up. I can live with that, if you can."

"Yeah, absolutely. We need to get this done."

"I also think Judge Lancaster may be more willing to sign off on the deal when he realizes that he helped put the kidnapper back on the street." She added.

A few minutes later, Maria placed the call to the judge, apologizing profusely for disturbing him at home. Initially, he seemed quite put out by the intrusion. But after hearing the details, he agreed to come in and review the plea bargain. "I have a few things to attend to first, but I'll be there as soon as possible."

"Thank you, Your Honor."

Immediately after the judge ended the call, he went into his study, unlocked the bottom drawer of his desk, extracted a cell phone, and punched in a number.

CHAPTER NINETEEN

M aria had barely put the phone down when Jerry observed, "It sounded like he's willing to come in."

She nodded. "He is."

"That's great. Did you get any sense of what he's thinking?"

"It's always hard to tell with him," Maria said. "When he first answered the phone, it was pretty clear that he was less than thrilled to get the call. But after I started explaining things, he calmed down, and seemed quite interested. Hopefully, that's a good sign."

Maria glanced at the papers in front of her. "And honestly, I don't know why he'd have a problem with what we've drawn up. But as I said, I've given up trying to figure out judges."

Her last remark made Jerry think back to Tony Sarno's trial. "Does that apply to all judges, or just Lancaster?"

Maria gave a small smile. "Mainly him."

Jerry hesitated for a moment, and then said, "What's the story behind that, if you don't mind me asking. I mean, it was obvious at the trial that the two of you don't like each other very much."

"I guess it was, wasn't it?" Maria hesitated, apparently trying to decide exactly how to phrase what she was going to say. And then, "I don't take it personally anymore. He just dislikes women."

Jerry couldn't hide his surprise. "Really?"

"Yeah, that's my take, anyway. I've observed him in court a number of times with female attorneys, and it doesn't matter if you're arguing for the prosecution or the defense. If you're a woman, he's going to give you a rough time."

"Has anyone reported him?" Jerry asked.

"It's nothing you could prove," Maria said. "Most of us have come to accept it as an occupational hazard."

"Then I guess I owe you an even bigger thank you for being

willing to get him involved."

She gave a wry smile. "Well, first of all, don't thank me yet; let's see what happens. But also, he may very well be more accommodating toward me since we're not in open court. But if need be, I'll pretend to have second thoughts about the deal. That way, he'll have the opportunity to put me in my place. I suspect he'll be more willing to sign off on the agreement after that."

Jerry looked at her, surprised. "That's pretty cynical."

Maria smiled again. "Sometimes that's the only way for me to get through my day." The smile left her face. "But I meant what I said before. I'll do whatever it takes to get that little boy back."

They spent the next ten minutes looking over the plea bargain again and then went out to the lobby to wait for Judge Lancaster. He finally arrived at seven thirty, more than an hour after Maria had called him. He didn't offer an apology or an explanation for the delay.

Maria spoke first. "Thank you for doing this, Your Honor."

"It's fine." The judge turned toward Jerry. "Good to see you again, Mr. Hanson." He turned back to Maria. "Is there a conference room we can use?"

"Yes," she replied. "On the second floor."

"Let's go, then."

They settled in five minutes later, and the judge opened up the discussion. "I'd like to hear from you first, Mr. Hanson, from the beginning."

Jerry looked over at Maria, who seemed as surprised as he was. Retelling the whole story was going to take a lot of unnecessary time. But it didn't appear to Jerry that he was in a position to question the judge. He attempted to shorten and summarize as many events and conversations as possible, but Judge Lancaster kept asking questions and encouraging him to elaborate. So, what should have taken fifteen minutes ended up taking more than half an hour.

When Jerry finally thought he was finished, the judge followed up with some new questions and several more that he had already asked.

After Jerry and Maria responded to what they thought was the end of the judge's interrogation, he said, "There are still a number of things troubling me. Assuming everything this Josh Raybeck has told you is true, Mr. Hanson, then he's still admitted to taking lewd photographs. There should be more of a consequence for that than simply a slap on the wrist and some community service."

The judge looked over at Maria. "And frankly, Ms. Lopez, I'm surprised that you're willing to go along with that."

Jerry jumped in. "We both feel that the only reason my client did what he did was because he was threatened by Tony Sarno."

The judge eyed Jerry. "You mean the same Tony Sarno whom you defended in my courtroom? The very same person you described as an innocent bystander who had no knowledge of how the photos on his phone got there? So which is it, Mr. Hanson? Is Tony Sarno the Devil incarnate? Or is it possible that your new client is trying to blame someone else for his own criminal behavior?"

Jerry sat there, speechless. Maria tried to diffuse the situation. "Your Honor, you know that under most circumstances, I'd be arguing the same points that you just raised. But in this case, I believe it's in everyone's best interest, especially Eric Allen's, that we finalize the approval of this agreement as it's drawn up."

"That's a nice sentiment, Ms. Lopez. But it begs the question— why should Mr. Hanson's client get a free pass after he's admitted to committing these crimes?"

"Because Tony Sarno forced him to commit them."

"Well, at least you're consistent in your assessment of Mr. Sarno, which is more than I can say for you, Mr. Hanson."

Jerry started to respond, but the judge held up his hand. "Save it for a minute. I want to ask you something else. What if, as part of the plea agreement, your client is required to give us all the information he has on Tony Sarno's boss? Would you have an objection to that?"

"According to my client, Tony Sarno didn't share that information with him." Jerry thought about Josh mentioning someone named Gunner, but Josh had made it clear that he didn't think this Gunner was the one in charge. Jerry felt certain that if he brought up Gunner's name, it would just prolong things even further.

The judge looked at Jerry, evidently expecting him to say more. When he didn't, the judge said, "Really? Nothing at all?"

"No, Your Honor."

Just at that moment, a phone buzzed. Both Maria and Jerry fished in their pockets, but the ring tone had come from the judge's phone; the same one he had removed from his bottom desk drawer an hour and a half earlier. As the judge took the phone out of his suit coat, he didn't even look at the screen. He simply stood up and said, "I have to take this."

After the judge left the conference room, Maria and Jerry looked at each other and shook their heads. Jerry broke the silence. "What was that?"

Maria shook her head. "I have no idea. He seems to have a hair across his ass about something."

"It's like, no matter what I say to him, he turns it against me."

"Welcome to my world. Although you seem to be getting it even worse than I usually do. I really thought that since it was just the three of us, he'd act differently."

"So what do we do?" Jerry asked.

"I wish I could tell you."

A few minutes later the judge returned. "All right, where were we?"

Jerry began to say something, but the judge answered his own question. "Oh, yes, I was asking about your client's willingness to give us additional information about Mr. Sarno's boss. And you said that you were sure he doesn't know any more about that. Correct, Mr. Hanson?"

"Not that he told me, no," Jerry replied.

"All right. And you believe that to be true as well, Ms. Lopez?"

Maria looked at Jerry and then back at the judge. "Uh ... yes, sir."

The judge then focused on Jerry again, as he asked expectantly, "Okay. Let's go back to the issue of your client taking the photographs. What about that, Mr. Hanson?"

Jerry had no idea what was going on, why things had shifted the way they had. So all he could do was repeat what he had already said. "I don't believe my client had a choice. He was in fear for his life."

Lancaster turned to Maria. "And you also accept that, Ms. Lopez?"

Maria was just as surprised as Jerry was by the change in the judge's demeanor, but she was able to pull back on her response. "There's no way to know for sure, Your Honor, but it seems to fit with everything else Mr. Hanson's client told him, otherwise I wouldn't have agreed to the plea bargain we worked out."

The judge spoke coldly. "You do know, Ms. Lopez, that if anything goes wrong here, it's on you."

Typical, thought Maria. Place the blame on somebody else. She gritted her teeth and said, "Getting this little boy back is the number one priority, and I think this plea bargain will accomplish that."

"Just for the record, I want you both to understand that I have some real reservations about this," Lancaster said. "But I'll sign off on it, if that's what you want."

Maria didn't trust herself to speak. Jerry recognized that and offered, "We appreciate that, Your Honor."

It took another five minutes for the judge to sign the necessary papers. As soon as he did, he was out the door.

Immediately after he left, Maria turned to Jerry and said, "How bizarre was that?"

"I have no idea what just happened. He was like a light switch—first he was off, and then a second later he was on. You're right; that was bizarre." Jerry shifted his attention. "Do you mind filling in the rest of the formal agreement while I give Josh a call to come in?"

"Not at all," she agreed.

Jerry left the conference room, took out his phone, found Josh's number, and pressed send. After five rings, it went to voice mail.

Josh Raybeck wasn't answering.

Jerry went back into the conference room where Maria was finishing up with the formal plea agreement. "He's not picking up."

Maria showed concern on her face. "What?"

"I tried once, then waited a few minutes and tried again. Both calls went to voice mail. I don't have a good feeling about this."

"Is there any chance that he's someplace that doesn't get a signal?"

"I doubt it," Jerry returned. "I spoke to him on my way over here."

"But that was well over two hours ago," she reasoned.

"I know, but I told him I'd call as soon as I had any news. He sounded pretty upbeat."

Maria put down her pen and turned to face Jerry. "Is it possible that he's having second thoughts?"

"I guess it's possible," he considered. "But as I said, he sounded upbeat, like he knew this was going to be over soon; he could see the light at the end of the tunnel."

"But from everything you've told me, he was still really scared. And scared people don't always think straight."

Jerry was only half listening; he was lost in his own thoughts. "I'm going to go to his house."

"You really think he's going to be there?" she asked

Jerry made a helpless gesture. "I don't know, but I wouldn't know where else to look."

"Do you want me to come with you? Maybe I could help persuade him."

"I appreciate that," Jerry said. "But if he is having second thoughts, especially if it's because of whatever he's been hiding, I don't think he'll open up with you there."

His words made sense, but his body language suggested to Maria that attorney-client confidentiality had little to do with it. And she was right.

From the first instant that his call to Josh had gone to voice mail, Jerry had known something was wrong. He had entertained all the benign reasons that Maria had offered up. But Josh was in trouble; he could feel it in his bones.

He tried not to convey his fear to Maria. "Give me your cell phone number, and I'll call you as soon as I've talked to him."

Maria wanted to ask some more questions, but didn't. "Sure."

Josh's address was about eight miles away in an older section of East Providence. Most of the homes there had been built in the early 1950s to accommodate soldiers who had come back after World War II and were ready to start a family.

It took Jerry nearly fifteen minutes to drive there. The entire time in the car, he could feel his heart rate racing and his blood pressure skyrocketing. He found himself trying to come up with a simple, innocuous explanation for all this, but there was none.

As he approached Josh's house, Jerry noted that there was no car in the driveway. He decided to pull in and park in front of the garage door closest to the house. It was more likely that if Josh's car was in the garage, it was on that side. And if Josh wanted to leave, for whatever reason, it would give Jerry some additional time to try to talk him out of it.

Jerry sat in the driver's seat for a few moments, trying to gather himself. He had never been a person who liked confrontation—a somewhat odd trait for a lawyer, he readily admitted—but he would more than welcome a confrontation with Josh right now.

He exited his car and walked to the front door. There were no lights on in the house that he could see. He tried to convince himself that that didn't necessarily mean anything, even though it was almost eight thirty.

He rang the doorbell, waited a moment and then knocked. Thirty seconds went by, and he heard nothing. He repeated his actions twice more, but still there was no response. Finally, he tried the door handle, but it was locked.

A part of him was relieved that Josh appeared not to be home. Maybe because he didn't want to entertain the notion that Josh had chickened out, or that whatever Josh had been hiding was more serious than he had let on. But a larger part of Jerry was frightened, fearful that something much more sinister was going on.

As he stepped away from the front door, Jerry decided to try to call Josh again. He pressed the button for his contact list, scrolled down to the "R's," found Raybeck, and pushed the send button.

It took a moment to connect, and then he heard the first ring and then the second. Before the third ring, however, he heard what he thought was an echo. But then he realized it was a delayed ring, and the sound wasn't directly in his ear; it was more muffled. Then just before the next ring, he realized the sound was coming from inside the house.

Jerry quickly ended the call and hit redial. As he did so, he moved away from the front door toward the large picture window a few feet away. After another moment, the first ring came through the phone clearly. He then removed the phone from his ear, and listened intently. There was little doubt; the second ring had come from inside, and not far from where he was standing.

He took a deep breath and tried to peer through the window. He couldn't see much, but then he heard the next ring, and his eyes moved to the pulsing light coming from the phone. It appeared to be on the floor under the couch.

Next to it, Jerry could see the silhouette of a body.

He cupped his right hand over his eyes, attempting to see more clearly. But in reality, there was no need to. It was definitely a body; and he was sure it was Josh Raybeck's.

Somehow he found the wherewithal to do what he needed to. He pushed the end button on his phone, waited for the screen to change, and then pressed 9-1-1.

Jerry gave all the required information to the dispatcher as calmly as he could. But he didn't implore her to tell the police to hurry. Jerry knew in his heart that it wouldn't make any difference how quickly they got there.

As soon as the call ended, ten different thoughts began to cascade in Jerry's brain, as he struggled to accept what had happened, and what it meant for Eric Allen. Despite his relative certainty that the body lying on the floor inside the house was his client's, Jerry opted not to call Maria yet; he'd wait until after the police arrived.

A cruiser with lights flashing pulled up to Josh's house within ten minutes of the 9-1-1 call. The first officer who exited the car spotted Jerry, came over, and asked for identification. After he scrutinized Jerry's license and confirmed that Jerry was the person who had placed the original call, he told him to wait on the sidewalk next to the police car.

Two other cruisers came on the scene less than three minutes later. All of the policemen conferred briefly. And then two of them went around back, one stayed with Jerry, and two began to approach the front door. They announced their presence, and after hearing no response, forced the door open.

Jerry heard some yelling, but was sure it emanated from the policemen inside, letting their counterparts in the back know that the house was clear. After several more minutes, the officer who had been first on the scene came out of the house and approached Jerry. "You said you were his lawyer?"

Jerry ignored the question. "Is it definitely Josh Raybeck?"

"That's what his driver's license says," the officer confirmed.

"Yes. I ... was his lawyer."

"What were you doing here?"

"I was checking up on him," Jerry explained. "He wasn't answering his phone, and he was supposed to meet me to take care of some business."

"Okay. One of the detectives should be here soon. He'll take your statement, but he may also want you to go to the police station to answer some additional questions."

Jerry knew he couldn't allow himself to be tied up for half the night at the police station, given what was at stake. But he didn't want to appear uncooperative, so he simply said, "Sure." He figured it wasn't going to come to that anyway.

Jerry pointed toward the driveway. "Is it okay to wait by my car?"

"Not a problem; just don't go anywhere."

The policeman then signaled to the other officer who had been babysitting Jerry to leave him be, and go inside to help out.

As soon as they were out of earshot, Jerry took out his phone and punched in Maria's number. She answered right away. "Hello."

"Maria, it's Jerry. I've got some horrible news. Josh Raybeck is dead."

"What?" she gasped. "Oh, my God! How?"

"I'm not sure. I rang his doorbell, and when he didn't answer, I looked through the window. That's when I saw a body on the floor. The police are telling me it's Josh."

Maria started to speak, but Jerry barged ahead. "Listen, I need you to call the FBI hotline, and let them know everything. They need to get here as soon as possible. Right now, the local cops don't know anything about Josh's connection to Eric Allen's disappearance. They look like they know what they're doing, but they're not focused on looking for clues about that. It would be easy to miss something. And Maria, you should come too. I think it's better if we talk to the FBI together."

There was silence for a moment.

"Maria, are you there?"

"Sorry," she stammered. "I … This is just so unreal."

"I know."

"Are you all right?" Maria asked.

Jerry gave a shaky sigh. "I'm shook up, but I'm okay."

"What's the address?"

"One oh seven Barton Street in East Providence," he told her.

"I'll call the FBI, and then I'll come right over." She paused. "If Josh is really dead, how are we going to find Eric Allen?"

"I wish I knew."

CHAPTER TWENTY

Over the past several hours, Walker and Munoz had been reviewing everything they had on Tony Sarno, but nothing was jumping out at them. They both felt strongly that Tony Sarno was involved, but that was more of a hunch, borne of their collective experience, than anything more definitive.

If they had had Tony's computer, or cell phone, or some surveillance video, it might have been a different story. But with none of those things available to them, they were forced to treat their hunch as if it were rock solid DNA evidence.

A few minutes before nine thirty, one of the Stanfield policemen rushed into Munoz' office. "Agent Walker, there's a woman on the hotline who says she has to speak with the agent in charge. She says it's urgent."

Walker jumped up and ran toward the desk where the hotline was located. The Stanfield officer who was manning the phone said, "Line two."

Walker pushed the blinking button. "Agent Walker."

"Hello, Agent Walker. My name is Maria Lopez, and I'm an assistant district attorney in Providence, Rhode Island. Earlier tonight, a defense attorney named Jerry Hanson contacted me. He wanted to work out a plea deal for one of his clients, a man by the name of Josh Raybeck. Later, I found out that this Josh Raybeck claimed to have information concerning the whereabouts of the missing boy, Eric Allen."

Walker interrupted. "Where is this Josh Raybeck now?"

"That's just it. Evidently, he's been killed."

"What? When?" demanded the FBI agent.

"Probably a couple of hours ago. The East Providence police are at the scene now. And so is Jerry Hanson, the attorney I mentioned. He's the one who asked me to call you."

"What's the address?" Walker asked.

Before Maria gave him the address, she said, "Something else you should know. Besides being Josh Raybeck's attorney, Jerry Hanson also represented Tony Sarno—the night watchman who was killed this morning. It looks like he was involved in this, too."

After Walker got the address and hung up, he went back to Munoz' office, gave him the short version of the phone call, and prepared to head out to East Providence. "I'd like you to come with me, Dave."

"I don't have any jurisdiction there."

"It doesn't matter. I'll take the lead; you can assist."

Munoz nodded.

Just as they were leaving, Munoz asked, "What was that guy's name again?"

Walker checked his notes. "Josh Raybeck."

Munoz opened the case file he had grabbed off his desk. It took him less than fifteen seconds to find what he was looking for. He turned over the photo and checked the back. His memory hadn't failed him.

Munoz handed the photo of Eric Allen to Walker. "Take a look at this."

There on the back in bold ink from the rubber stamp was the name Josh Raybeck. Walker shook his head, as Munoz offered, "It can't possibly be a coincidence that this guy Raybeck just happens to be the same one who took this picture."

"Maybe this is the break we've been waiting for."

Walker and Munoz drove together, followed by the other FBI agents. On the ride over to East Providence, Walker outlined what he intended to do once they arrived. Munoz was impressed with how quickly he had pulled the plan together. And once they were all at the address, his command presence was even more in evidence.

Walker spoke with one of the other agents, telling him to find Maria Lopez and Jerry Hanson and have them sit tight until he returned. He then signaled for the other agents to remain on the sidewalk. Then he and Munoz approached the front of the house and spoke to the local detective in charge.

Walker exhibited the same degree of respect toward the East Providence detective that he had shown when he first met Munoz. "Hello, Detective. I'm Agent Walker with the FBI." As he said it, he flashed his badge. "And this is Detective Munoz from Stanfield. He's assisting us in the Eric Allen case, the boy who disappeared last Monday."

The local detective nodded. "The reason we're here is that we believe your homicide victim may have a connection to the missing boy."

The detective looked surprised. "Really?"

"Yes. Let me say upfront that we have no intention of compromising your crime scene, but I would like to suggest a way in which we can both go about our business."

Munoz could tell that the local detective appreciated the tone of Walker's remarks. "Certainly. What did you have in mind?"

"I'd like to have our agents search the entire house. But they'll avoid the room where the body was found. Of course, they'll be sure to point out anything they find that may help you in solving the homicide. But their first priority is to look for anything pertaining to the missing boy."

"I understand" replied the detective. "I have no problem with that."

"Excellent."

As Walker turned back toward the sidewalk and the other agents, he saw that Munoz was staring at him. "What?"

"That was nicely done."

"I told you, that's how I operate," Walker reminded him.

"I know, and I've seen it firsthand," Munoz reflected. "It's just that it's not what any of us are used to."

Walker didn't respond as he walked over to the other agents and addressed them. "Okay, I've cleared everything with the local detective. You all know what you're looking for—anything that will help us find Eric Allen. I want you to start with the house, but don't go near the living room. Make sure you check the garage and any cars that might be in there. It looks like the house was built on a slab foundation, so it probably doesn't have a basement. But double check anyway. Detective

Munoz and I will take the yard, but since it's pretty dark outside, I want at least two of you to go over it after we're finished. Any questions?" He didn't wait for an answer. "Okay, let's get to it."

Out of the corner of his eye, Walker spotted a man and a woman to his left, obviously waiting for him. Introductions were exchanged, and then Walker said, "I appreciate the phone call. So, do either of you have any idea where the boy might be?"

They both answered simultaneously. "No."

Then Jerry continued, "As I think Ms. Lopez told you, my client wanted a plea agreement in place before he would give out that information."

Walker eyed Jerry. "I'm sure I don't have to tell you, Mr. Hanson, that confidentiality doesn't usually apply when your client is dead."

Jerry didn't take offense, although under different circumstances he might have. "I know; and if I knew where that little boy was, I would tell you."

Walker believed him. "Is there anything at all that your client said that would at least point us in the right direction?"

"Not really, no," Jerry replied sadly.

"All right." He paused. "I'd like you to remain here on site for a few minutes while I take care of some other things, then I need to ask you some additional questions. Okay?"

"Of course. It's just that I was in such a hurry to get here, I left all my notes at Ms. Lopez's office."

Maria spoke up for the first time. "I can drive you back, if you want." She turned toward Walker. "Or we could just use my office when you're finished here. It's only a few miles away."

Munoz looked over at Walker and said, "I've got the case file with me. It might be faster to do that, if it's okay with you."

"That's fine." He turned back to Maria. "Give us about twenty minutes." And then back to Munoz. "I'm going to get a flashlight, then let's take a walk around the backyard."

The house sat on about a quarter of an acre of land, so there wasn't a whole lot of property to survey. And as much as they could tell in the dark, there was no area that had been recently dug up—a huge relief to both of them.

The outside of the house appeared reasonably well maintained. And like most of the homes in the neighborhood, the basic structure had had some amenities added on in the sixty years since it had been built. But in the case of the Raybeck house, the only major addition was a two-car garage.

As Walker and Munoz checked out the back yard, they noted two air conditioning condensers, a small brick patio, some lawn chairs, and a somewhat strange metal sculpture that resembled a Minuteman. Aside from the Minuteman, there was nothing to distinguish the property from that of its neighbors.

The medical examiner had arrived while Walker and Munoz were in the back yard. Walker spotted the insignia on the car door as they came around the side of the house, and pointed it out to Munoz. He then moved toward the front door, where a uniformed officer was positioned. Walker spoke to him. "Officer, could you ask the medical examiner if he could come out and speak with me for a moment? Please tell him I'm with the FBI."

The medical examiner appeared less than three minutes later, introduced himself, and then asked, "How can I help you?"

Walker responded. "I know you just got here, but is there anything at all you can tell us?"

The coroner responded, "You have to understand that this is very preliminary. But I know there's a lot at stake, so I'll tell you whatever I can." A pause. "There's a single gunshot wound to the temple. My guess would be that the victim was on his knees when he was shot. That's consistent with the blood spatter. Also, there are signs of torture—burns—and a lot of them. It's not my area of expertise, but I'd say whoever did this wanted something from the victim. And from the number of distinct burn marks, I'd say the victim didn't give it up very easily, if at all."

The medical examiner went back inside, and Walker was left to consider what he had just been told. It didn't take him long to conclude that the medical examiner's assessment was probably right on target. Unfortunately, there was no way to know what information Josh Raybeck's killer had been looking for. If it were the whereabouts of Eric Allen, and Josh Raybeck had given it up—Walker didn't want to think about that.

He turned toward Munoz. "Before we leave, I'm going to touch base with my agents. Would you speak to the local detective and see if his people have come up with anything?"

"Okay."

They headed off in different directions and were gone for about ten minutes. When they met up again, neither of them had any positive news. "Nothing's standing out to any of my guys," said Walker.

"The same for the local police. The detective did say that even though it's late, he's going to have his officers canvass the neighborhood. Maybe somebody saw or heard something. He said he'd call if there was anything to report."

"Good." Walker took out his phone. "There's one more thing we can do before we talk to the attorney and the ADA." He punched in a special number for the FBI office in Boston. Before the call connected, he asked Munoz, "Did you have anyone check to see if Tony Sarno owned property anywhere?"

"Not specifically. At that point we were just trying to find out his address."

Walker nodded, as a voice came on the other end of the line. Walker waited for the standard protocol phone check to be completed, and then said, "This is Special Agent Craig Walker. I'm working the abduction case out of Stanfield, Mass. I need you to find out if either of these individuals owns property in Rhode Island or Massachusetts— Anthony Sarno and Josh Raybeck. That last name is spelled R-a-y-b-e-c-k. Get back to me as soon as possible."

When Walker ended the call, he motioned to Munoz to follow him over to Jerry and Maria. Walker spoke first. "Before we head out to your office, is there anything else either of you can think of that might help us?"

Jerry answered. "Josh gave me a lot of information, almost all of which implicates Tony Sarno in a number of crimes, including Eric Allen's disappearance. But he never told me, even indirectly, where the boy was, at least not that I'm aware of."

He paused. "There is one thing though, that I just remembered, although it doesn't have anything to do with what you were just asking me—Josh's phone."

"What do you mean?"

"That's how I knew Josh was inside his house. I heard his phone ringing, and then when I looked through the window, I saw it."

"Where?"

"Under the couch, right near the body."

"Did you tell the local police?" Walker asked.

"No, I didn't think of it until just now."

Walker looked at Munoz. "I'll go let them know. I'd love to get my hands on that phone to see who Raybeck has been talking to."

Jerry spoke again. "Well, I spoke to him, a bunch of times."

Walker looked surprised. "You have his number?"

Jerry took out his phone, scrolled through some contacts, found Josh's number, and held the phone up for Walker to see.

"Well, that's all we need. We don't have to have the phone itself."

For the second time in the last few minutes, Walker called the FBI's Boston office. This time he asked for all the phone records for Josh's number.

It was probably another long shot, thought Walker. But long shots seemed to be all they had at this point.

Maria and Jerry each took their own cars back to the district attorney's office; Walker and Munoz followed in Munoz's car a few minutes later, after Walker had alerted the local detective about Josh's phone.

They had driven about a block when Walker said, "It seems like every time we get some sort of a break, we come right up against a dead end. Although, I think there's little doubt that either Sarno or Raybeck, probably Sarno, took the Allen boy. But even if we knew that for certain, it doesn't get us any closer to finding him."

Walker continued to think out loud. "If the same guy who killed Sarno also killed Raybeck, why didn't he take the phone, like he did with Sarno?"

Munoz wasn't sure Walker was addressing him, but he answered anyway. "Maybe he didn't know it was there. The attorney said it was under the couch. Or maybe the killer knew there was nothing on it to implicate him."

"I think the second one is more likely."

They were quiet for another moment, and then Walker said, "I think I'm going to call off the search of the ponds and lakes."

"You're that sure that Raybeck was telling the truth about Eric Allen still being alive?" Munoz asked.

"Yeah, I am. It's really the only thing that makes sense. I just hope it's more than wishful thinking."

Munoz looked over at Walker. "What about Jonathan Allen? I called him earlier just to see how he was holding up. Do you think we should tell him anything about these new developments?"

The FBI agent shook his head. "Not yet. I want to hear everything else the attorney has to say first; then we can decide."

Maria and Jerry met Walker and Munoz at the front entrance to the DA's office building. They all proceeded up to the second-floor conference room, where Jerry opened up the conversation. "My notes are in chronological order, just like Josh related the story. Is that okay?"

Walker answered, "That's fine. Unless, as I said, there's something you can think of that will lead us to the boy's location."

"I've been racking my brain, but I can't come up with anything. Maybe once I'm into it, something will click."

"Okay then, go ahead."

For the next twenty minutes Jerry related the story Josh Raybeck had told him, beginning with the seemingly chance encounter with Tony Sarno in the food court, all the way to Tony showing up at Josh's house with a chloroformed Eric Allen.

Munoz initially pressed Jerry for additional details about Cindy Allen's death, but then backed off. There would be time for that once they found Eric Allen.

Maria periodically interjected with an idea or opinion when she believed it might be helpful, or if she thought Walker was skeptical of Jerry's response.

For the most part, Jerry did very little editing of Josh's story, hoping that some minor detail that he thought was irrelevant might resonate with Walker or Munoz.

As Jerry was winding down, Walker began to ask more pointed questions. "Tell me again why you think Josh was lying about something, and why he wouldn't tell you where the boy was."

Jerry answered the second part first. "He kept saying that he wanted the deal in place first. He never used the words 'ace in the hole,' but it was clear that's what he meant. He kept insisting that he trusted me, but he wouldn't budge on that.

"As far as the other thing is concerned, Josh's version didn't make sense. Tony Sarno was not about to kidnap someone, and then take off for a half hour, not unless he had covered himself some way, or something happened to force his hand. Plus, Josh all but admitted that he wasn't telling the truth about that part of his story."

"So, what do you think happened?"

"I don't know. I guess it's possible that Tony took the boy someplace after he brought him to Josh's house. And then maybe he was going to bring Josh there later to take pictures. But then why go to Josh's house at all?"

"Are you sure that he did?" the agent asked.

"Not completely, no."

"Do you think Eric Allen is still alive?"

Jerry didn't hesitate. "Yes. Josh never showed any signs of lying about that. And if he knew or even suspected that the boy was dead, why would he come forward to try to make a deal? I made it clear to him that getting Eric Allen back safely was his only way out of this mess."

Walker spoke more to himself than to Jerry. "If that's true, then he must have known where the boy was."

Jerry answered as if it were a question directed at him. "He seemed a little uncertain at first, but I'm convinced that he knew."

Walker changed direction. "Tell me again what Josh said Tony was going to do with the boy afterwards."

Jerry looked away briefly. "Sell him to somebody down South."

"So there was never any mention of physically harming the boy?"

"No. I got the impression that this was all about the child pornography business."

Walker got up out of his chair and started to pace. "And Josh had no idea who wanted the pictures taken?"

"No. As I said, Josh told me that Tony made a reference to someone named Gunner, but Josh was sure that he wasn't the boss or even the one who wanted the pictures taken."

"All right. I'll have the name Gunner run through the system just in case."

Nobody said anything for a minute as Walker continued to pace. And then his phone buzzed. He withdrew it from his pocket, put it to his ear, and said, "Walker."

The voice on the other end didn't bother to identify himself; he simply started to speak. "I ran a check on both Anthony Sarno and Josh Raybeck. Anthony Sarno doesn't own any property in either state. And as far as I can tell, other than his apartment, he didn't lease any property, not even a storage unit. Josh Raybeck owned the house in East Providence. He inherited it from his father after he passed away seven years ago. But there's nothing to indicate that Raybeck leased any other property either."

Walker cut in. "Anything on the phone records?"

"That news is a little better, but not much. Josh Raybeck received five calls today, all from the same number. The first one was received at 5:47 p.m. and lasted less than two minutes. The cell phone company can't give us an exact location, but Raybeck was probably about five miles from his house when he got the call. I'll send the street names in that area to your phone. Two other calls were received at 8:50 and 8:54, and the last two came in at 9:04 and 9:05. None of the last four calls lasted more than a few seconds; they must have gone to voice mail. But all four of them were received at Raybeck's home address."

Walker thanked the agent, and then related the information to Munoz and the two attorneys. As Walker had suspected was the case, Jerry confirmed that the five calls had been from him. Once again, thought Walker, nothing seems to be coming together.

The four of them talked for a few more minutes, and then Walker decided it was time to head back to Josh Raybeck's house. He asked Maria and Jerry to hang around for a few minutes and review everything with each other. "And call me no matter what time it is, if you think of anything."

Five minutes later Walker and Munoz left the conference room, exited the building, and got into Munoz' car. They drove to the area where Josh had received the first call from Jerry, hoping that something would present itself. But it didn't. The surface streets they were on were exactly the ones Josh would have used if he were headed home.

Shortly after that, they arrived back at Josh Raybeck's house. The local detective indicated that the initial canvass by his officers hadn't turned up anything of significance.

Walker thanked him for his cooperation, and he and Munoz went in search of the other FBI agents. Only one of them had anything to report, and it didn't appear to amount to much. "I was looking around in the kitchen, and right there in plain sight was a ski mask. It just seemed so out of place; there was no other ski clothing or equipment anywhere around. It probably doesn't mean anything, but it was just strange."

"Where is it now?" Walker asked.

"I left it there," the agent replied. "I can bag it for analysis if you want."

"Let me take a look first."

Walker and Munoz went into the kitchen and spotted the ski mask immediately. It certainly looked out of place, thought Walker. But what relevance it might have to the case escaped him.

Fifteen minutes later, he and Munoz went back to the station house in Stanfield, and tried to come up with anything that might lead them to Eric Allen. They decided not to call his father; there was nothing definitive to tell him.

Finally, well past two AM, they opted to call it a night. They hoped that grabbing a few hours of sleep before they came back at six the next morning might make a difference. But the frustration they were feeling was starting to take its toll.

Both Walker and Munoz knew that in every investigation the five "W's" were critical—who, what, where, why, and when. They were reasonably certain that they knew the "who" and the "why"—usually the most difficult 'W's' to determine. But in this instance, it was the "where" that continued to elude them. And the two people who knew the most about the "where" were both dead.

Chapter Twenty-One

*E*ric was very hungry. It had been a long time since the man had been there. Eric wondered if he had dreamt what he remembered, or if it really happened. He thought it probably really happened, but he wasn't positive. He hoped it had.

The man had come into the room with no mask on. Eric had been crying, so his tears prevented him from seeing the man's face clearly at first. But then he did. The man looked familiar, but Eric wasn't sure.

After a few moments, the man asked Eric if he knew who he was. Eric started to say "no," but then he remembered. "You took my picture and my mommy's picture, too."

"You're right, I did."

"I thought you were a nice man." Eric thought back to the schoolyard and the fire alarm. "You put something over my mouth."

"No, I didn't. That wasn't me."

Eric was confused. "Who was it?"

"You don't know him."

"Why did he take me away from the school and away from my daddy?"

The man didn't answer right away. Eventually, he said, "I don't know."

"Is he your friend?"

"No."

"Will you take me home? I want to see my daddy."

Again, the man didn't answer immediately. And then, "Soon."

Eric's six-year-old mind needed more. "Do you promise?"

"I promise. I have to go now, but I promise I'll be back soon."

And the man left.

Eric had never been sure what "soon" meant. Sometimes his daddy said that word, and it seemed like a long time. And his mommy used to say it too, and it seemed like a long time. But the man had been gone much longer than anytime his mommy or daddy had said that word.

He started to cry again. The man had promised he would come back. And he had promised that Eric could go home. But the man hadn't come back. And now Eric was scared again, and hungry. The only thing he wasn't was sleepy.

As the minutes turned into hours, being wide awake made him even more frightened. And still the man didn't come back.

～

For the fifth night in a row -ever since Eric Allen had gone missing—any kind of meaningful sleep for Munoz was out of the question. But on this night, something was slightly different. He could sense the presence of something unsettled in the back of his brain. There was something that he had seen or heard, or had subconsciously figured out, that was struggling to become a coherent thought. But it wasn't there yet.

He had experienced this same sensation three or four times in the past while working in Boston. But unfortunately, he had never discovered a way to speed up the process. He knew that eventually this germ of an idea would grow and move to the front of his brain. He just prayed it would happen before time ran out for Eric Allen.

Around three thirty Munoz got out of bed and went into the living room. He opened up the case file, which was now nearly an inch thick, and began to review it for the twentieth time. He knew it was a futile gesture, but he did it anyway.

An hour later, the only thing he had accomplished was to make himself more tired. He closed the file, went into the kitchen and got a glass of water, and then headed back to bed. He closed his eyes and tried to sleep. He realized that his body must have shut down for a little while, because when he looked over at the nightstand clock, the green digits read 5:15.

It was almost time to get up, but he decided to give himself a few more minutes. He kept his eyes closed and tried to relax every part of his body, as if he were in a meditative state. And then, just as he was about to throw off the covers, the unexpected happened. The niggling idea in the back of his brain started to grow. It was still far from being fully formed, but it now had enough substance to allow Munoz' mind to grab hold of it. And it did.

There was nothing he had to decipher or piece together; it was simply a fact that he now knew. Something he had seen or heard in the last several hours was the key to locating the missing boy. He now felt certain that he wasn't going to find it in the case file; and it wasn't going to require exhaustive police work. It was right there for the taking, if he could just figure out what it was.

Munoz decided that he wouldn't try to explain any of this to Walker, although he was fairly sure that Walker had experienced something similar. But just in case he hadn't, Munoz decided to simply suggest that they review the notes from the interview with the attorneys, and pay another visit to Josh Raybeck's house. There was little doubt in Munoz' mind that Walker would indulge his suggestion After all, he thought, at this point they were chasing their tails anyway.

Munoz arrived at the station house at five-fifty; Walker showed up several minutes later. Munoz decided not to wait; he launched into his first request immediately. And as he had hoped and suspected, Walker went along with him.

As the other agents trickled in over the next few minutes, Walker informed them that he wanted everyone in the conference room for a brainstorming session at six-fifteen to review the statements given by Jerry Hanson and Maria Lopez.

The session lasted forty-five minutes, but nothing had come into focus for Munoz. Under most circumstances, he would have been extremely disappointed. But in this case, he simply accepted the fact that the information he needed wasn't part of the interviews; so it had to be at Josh Raybeck's house.

As the session broke up and Walker began assigning tasks for the next few hours, Munoz pushed the second part of his plan. "I think we should go back to the Raybeck house." He decided that he had to offer Walker more. "I know it might sound crazy, but something's not sitting right with me about what we saw there yesterday."

"Anything specific?" the FBI agent queried.

"Not that I can identify yet. I'm just hoping that when I see it again, I'll know it."

Walker looked at Munoz more closely. "Okay. That's good enough for me." He paused. "Why don't you phone the East Providence police and give them a heads-up that we're coming? I'm going to contact the state police and have them call off the searches."

A few minutes later, they were in Munoz' unmarked car, heading for the Rhode Island border. Walker started the conversation. "You've got something gnawing at you, huh?"

"Yeah. Thanks for indulging me, especially since I can't even call it a hunch; it's not even that concrete."

Walker smiled. "I know exactly what you mean. My first commander used to have a name for it. He called it 'making a pearl.' I can still remember him asking us during our brainstorming sessions if anybody was 'making a pearl.' "

Munoz glanced over at Walker. "I don't follow."

"I didn't either, when I first heard it. But evidently, pearls are formed when a tiny grain of sand or dirt finds its way inside an oyster. And it irritates the oyster so much that the oyster secretes a substance to surround the sand particle. It keeps doing that over and over again, until eventually it produces a pearl." Walker paused. "So my commander thought that when something was bothering any of us about a case, it was like we were trying to make a pearl."

"I've never thought about it like that, but actually it's a good analogy." Munoz paused. "Sometimes I think to myself that it's like an itch that I can't scratch. I suppose that's almost the same idea."

Walker looked over again. "Over the years, I've just come to call it a 'cop's instinct.' Although, I doubt that there's anything in any law enforcement manual that refers to a 'cop's instinct,' every cop I've ever worked with would know what that meant. On the other hand, I don't think the same could be said for 'making pearls' or 'scratching an itch.'" Walker smiled. "No offense."

For the first time in days, Munoz allowed himself to laugh. "None taken."

～

An East Providence police car was parked in front of Josh Raybeck's house, which was cordoned off with crime scene tape. The officer sitting behind the wheel got out as Walker and Munoz pulled in behind him.

190

Walker took out his badge as he exited the car and showed it to the officer, and after introductions, they all shook hands. The officer said, "Everything's open. My chief said to give you full access."

Walker responded. "Thanks. And pass along my appreciation to your chief as well."

He turned his attention back to Munoz. "Where do you want to start?"

"Let's do it the same way we did last night—the back yard first."

"Okay."

Now, in the morning light, they saw everything more clearly. But Munoz didn't feel that that was going to matter. Whatever had initiated his cop's instinct must have been readily visible, even in the dark.

They gave a quick once-over to the lawn furniture and the metal sculpture, but looked more closely at the patio and the air conditioning condensers. "Anything?" asked Walker.

"No, not yet. Although that Minuteman sculpture looks even stranger in the daylight."

"Yeah, I agree. I'm still not sure what to make of that." Walker paused. "Do you want to go inside?"

"I'll just take a look in the kitchen. That was the only room I was in last night. Oh, and maybe the garage. I poked my head in there, too."

Fifteen minutes later they were back out at the curb. Munoz said, "I'm sorry. I really thought for sure something was going to jump out at me, but nothing did."

"Maybe it's going to take you a little time to process everything. For whatever reason, I don't think you can rush these things." Walker put his hand on Munoz' shoulder. "It'll come. As my commander used to say, 'It takes time to make a pearl.' "

Munoz smiled and was about to say something when he noticed an elderly woman crossing the street toward them. When she got within a few feet, she said, "Excuse me; are you police officers?"

Munoz was sure that Walker wouldn't object to the generic terminology. "Yes we are."

"Well, I'm Elmira Saunders, and I was wondering if you could tell me what happened."

Walker spoke next. "What did you want to know, Ms. Saunders?"

"Please call me Elmira. Growing up, I didn't much care for the name, so I went by Ellie. But then I got used to it. My parents named me after the place I was born, you know, Elmira, New York. I used to tell everyone that I was thankful I hadn't been born in Poughkeepsie or Schenectady." She offered a smile and a twinkle in her eye as she spoke the last sentence.

Walker returned the smile. "Do you live nearby, Elmira?"

She pointed across the street to a green ranch-style house—the only one on the block that didn't have an addition. "Right there. My late husband Ed and I bought it new in 1951, shortly after we were married. So, can you tell me what happened?"

Walker again. "You weren't here last night?"

"No. I was at my sister's. I came home early this morning. It was still dark, so I didn't see the police tape until I looked out the window a few minutes ago."

"Do you know Josh Raybeck?"

"Of course. I knew his father and grandfather too. The Raybecks have lived here as long as I have. Don't tell me something's happened to Josh."

"I'm afraid so."

"Oh, no. That's awful. Was he in an accident or something? Is he going to be all right?"

"No, Elmira. I'm sorry. He was found dead last night inside his house."

The elderly lady was visibly shaken. "Dead? Oh, that can't be. What happened?"

"He was shot."

"Shot?" she repeated. "Why would anyone want to shoot Josh?"

Walker ignored the question. "Did you know him well?"

"Not real well, although he was much more outgoing than his father or grandfather. They always kept to themselves—not very neighborly. Josh was different. He'd always wave hello, and sometimes in the winter, he'd shovel my walk, and wouldn't accept any money for it."

Walker put on his investigator hat. "I know you weren't here last night, but did you see anything unusual in the neighborhood in the last week or two?"

"I don't think so." She looked toward the Raybeck house. "Oh, I feel so badly about Josh."

"I know." Walker faced Munoz. "Dave, do you have one of your cards to give Elmira?"

Munoz didn't answer immediately, appearing to be distracted about something. Walker repeated himself. "Dave, I wanted to give Elmira one of your cards with the local number on it."

Munoz reached into his pocket, found one and handed it to Walker. But he still didn't say anything.

Walker addressed Elmira, as he gave her the card. "Please call the number listed there if you think of anything that might be helpful."

"Certainly."

Walker was about to thank her. But before he could, Munoz asked, "Ms. Saunders ... uh, Elmira, do you know how big your house is—how many square feet?"

Although Walker looked surprised by the question, Elmira appeared to take it in stride. "Around eight hundred and eighty. I know that's small by today's standards, but that's all we needed. We only had the one child, a daughter. She lives out in California. The two bedrooms were plenty for us."

Munoz barely heard anything Elmira said after the square footage number. His brain had started to respond to the irritant grain of sand, and the pearl had begun to take shape.

Munoz pulled himself back into the moment. "I'm sorry, Elmira, I didn't mean to be rude. I was just thinking about something, and it distracted me. Thank you so much for your help."

"You're welcome," she replied shakily. "I hope you find out who did this to Josh."

"We'll do our best."

Elmira was barely a few strides into crossing the street when Munoz said, "We have to go into the back yard again."

As they started heading there, Walker said, "What was with the square footage business?"

"I think that's what was bothering me," Munoz responded, still musing. "Why would you need two air conditioning condensers for a house this size? Of course, it's a lot more than eight hundred and eighty square feet now, with the two-car garage. But nobody air conditions their garage."

Neither of them spoke until they reached the back yard. Munoz knelt down next to the condensers. "This one seems to be running. I don't think it was before, although I'm not sure we would have noticed; it's pretty quiet."

"It's probably on automatic, and just kicks in when the temperature inside gets too high," Walker said.

Munoz wasn't buying that. "I didn't look at the thermostat setting, but it didn't seem that warm inside. Did it to you?"

"No. And why would the air conditioning be on at all? It hasn't been above sixty degrees all week."

Munoz didn't answer, as he shifted his attention to the other condenser. "Even if the air conditioning was on for some reason, there's no need for two of them."

"Couldn't one just be a backup?"

"I doubt it. People don't have backup condensers; it's too expensive. The only thing you have as a backup around here is a generator, in case you lose electricity."

As he spoke the last sentence, Munoz glanced back to the first condenser. "Wait a minute." Then he looked more closely at both units. "These covers are the same, but I don't think they're both condensers." He cupped his hands around his eyes and looked through the vent cover on the first condenser. "This isn't for air conditioning; I think it is a generator."

"It's awfully quiet for a generator, isn't it? And why would it be on?"

"I know," Munoz pondered. "It doesn't make any sense."

They didn't say anything for a moment, and then Munoz offered, "I wonder why they made it look like a condenser. It's almost as if they didn't want anyone to know what it was."

Munoz knew that he was on to something, but couldn't quite pull it together. He continued to survey the back yard, not sure what he was looking for. After a minute or two, he spotted what appeared to be a clothes dryer vent. Again, he knelt down to get a closer look. It was much larger than any dryer vent he had seen before, and it was divided into two sections. But other than that, it was ordinary.

Munoz shook his head. "I don't know what to make of any of this. Let's go back inside and take a look at the thermostat."

As they walked around to the front of the house, Walker asked, "How do you know so much about this stuff, Dave?"

"My father. He had his own plumbing business. He also did heating and air conditioning. He wanted me to join him, but it wasn't for me. I worked a few summers during high school and college, but that was it. He still works part time at the condo complex where he and my mother live in Florida. It keeps him busy."

They entered the house again, and Munoz located the thermostat on the wall in the living room. He lifted the cover and squinted, trying to read the small print. As it came into focus, he said, "The air conditioning's not on, not even on automatic. I wish I could figure out what the hell is going on."

"Could there be anything in the garage that needs a generator?" Walker asked.

"Not that I noticed, but we should take another look."

They left the living room and entered the kitchen on the way to the garage. Munoz was about to open the door when he stopped and turned around. He walked across the kitchen to the other side and opened a pair of louvered doors. Inside were a washer and dryer. "This doesn't make any sense, either."

"What's the matter?"

"The dryer vent I saw outside. It's got to be fifteen or twenty feet away from the dryer. Nobody would do that. Plus, there wasn't any lint around the dryer vent. You always see that. I don't care how clean it is. I want to look at that again."

This time, when they went outside, they went around back in the opposite direction. And there, on the side of the house, Munoz spotted what appeared to be another dryer vent. And on the ground below it were a few pieces of lint. As he reached inside, he came away with some more. "This is the dryer vent."

"Then what's the other vent for?"

Munoz shook his head. "I don't know. Let's take another look."

They went to the rear of the house, and Munoz again squatted next to the larger vent. He put his hand on one side and then the other. On the second side he felt some suction.

And then things started to tumble into place.

"I think I know what this is," he said excitedly. "It's an air exchanger."

"A what?" Walker asked blankly.

"An air exchanger." Munoz tilted his head to the side, obviously considering something. And then he stood up and faced Walker. "I think maybe I know what's going on. The only reason you'd need an air exchanger is if there's someplace in your house that doesn't have access to outside air."

Walker thought for a moment. "You're not talking about an attic or a basement? You mean something more like a panic room, or a safe room?"

"Yeah, or maybe just a room that you want to keep hidden."

CHAPTER TWENTY-TWO

W alker didn't say anything for a moment as a number of thoughts flooded his brain. And then, "If there is a hidden room, and that's where Eric Allen is, then where is it? There's no attic in the house, and no basement. It would have to be under the patio or the garage. But then how would you get inside?"

"I don't know. Maybe I'm wrong. Maybe the air exchanger is for the garage. I guess it's possible that if someone worked on cars in there, they might have an air exchanger. But I didn't see any evidence of that when I looked in there before."

Walker still thought Munoz' original idea was correct. "I know the local police were all over the property twice, not to mention my guys. But that's exactly the point of a hidden room. You're not supposed to be able to find it easily. Let's try the garage again."

Without another word, they went back inside through the kitchen and into the garage. The first thing they did was open both garage doors. Munoz peeked into Josh's car, saw that the keys were in the ignition, and backed it out into the driveway. They spent the next fifteen minutes knocking on walls and stomping on cement floors, hoping to hear a hollow sound that might suggest a hidden space underneath. But there was nothing.

Josh did have a workbench area with a raised steel platform to stand on, but nothing that would indicate he worked on cars. At the end of their search, Walker said, "The only thing that seems odd is that Raybeck parked his car on the side of the garage farthest from the house. Why would he do that?"

"I thought of that also, but I don't have a clue."

Walker stared at Munoz for a moment. "So, what's your best guess?"

"It might be a stretch, but I still like the hidden room idea. Like you said, that's the whole purpose of it. I'm just not sure how we find it."

"I agree with you. And it certainly would fit with everything the attorney told us last night. Although it might mean Raybeck was more involved than he let on."

"Unless Tony Sarno just left the boy here and took off. That's kind of what Josh originally told his attorney happened, right?"

It was Walker's turn to be distracted. "Yeah, something like that."

"What's the matter?"

"I just thought of something," the agent murmured. With that, he took out his phone and punched in the number for the Boston FBI office. After he identified himself and was cleared, he said to the agent on the other end of the line, "I want you to get hold of whoever handles building permits in East Providence. I know it's Saturday morning, but get them out of bed if you have to. I want them at City Hall as soon as possible. I'll meet them there."

As soon as they were in the car, Munoz typed the East Providence City Hall destination into his GPS, and they were on their way. Walker thought out loud. "You have to have a building permit to add on a garage. And if there was anything else done, it would have to be in the plans as well."

Munoz didn't respond, as Walker continued. "I hope to God there's something to this; otherwise I'm out of ideas."

They sat outside City Hall for nearly twenty minutes before someone showed up. "Hi, I'm Steven Andrews, the building inspector. Sorry I didn't get here sooner; I was at my son's soccer game. They said something about an emergency."

Walker took out his badge and showed it to Andrews. "Hello, I'm Special Agent Walker, and this is Detective Munoz. And you're right; this is urgent. We need you to check on a building permit."

Andrews hesitated for a moment, and Walker was sure he was about to ask what this was all about, but evidently he thought better of it. "Okay. We can go in through the side entrance. I have the alarm key." As he walked toward the door, Andrews continued talking. "Do you know what year the permit was issued?"

Walker answered. "No. Is that a problem?"

"Not necessarily. It'd just be faster."

Once they were inside the office, Andrews went over to a large filing cabinet. "It'll be great once all this is transferred to computers, but right now, we have to do it the old-fashioned way. What's the homeowner's name and address?"

Munoz pulled out his notebook and read the information to Andrews.

"Can you narrow down the time frame?"

Munoz answered. "No more than fifteen years ago; probably less."

"Okay. I'll start there, to be on the safe side. It shouldn't take that long. The permits are filed by year, and then alphabetically by the homeowner's name. We need the address because some people own more than one piece of property. So, the address confirms where the work was done."

Andrews was right; it didn't take long. Within ten minutes he had checked and double-checked the last name Raybeck going back fifteen years. There had been no building permits issued.

"Let me go back another five years, just in case," said Andrews.

He did. And there was still nothing.

Walker asked, "Are you legally required to get a building permit for every kind of construction?"

"Absolutely. Of course, I can't say for sure that everybody does. And unless the construction causes a problem, we wouldn't necessarily know."

A few minutes later Walker and Munoz were outside standing next to Munoz' car. "Every time I think we're catching a break, we get stymied again. Any ideas, Dave?"

Munoz was thoughtful. "Maybe."

"What?" Walker asked.

"It's probably a long shot, but what about Elmira? She seemed like she'd know everything that happened in that neighborhood. Maybe she'd remember who built the garage for the Raybecks."

The FBI agent nodded approvingly. "Good call. I'll bet she would."

Walker knocked on Elmira's door; she opened it twenty seconds later. "Oh, hello again, officers."

"Hello, Elmira. We were wondering if we could tax your memory," said Walker.

She smiled. "Well, it isn't what it used to be, but it's still pretty good, if I do say so myself. Would you like to come in?"

"That's very kind, but we're in a bit of a hurry."

"Is this about Josh?" she asked anxiously.

Walker shaded the truth. "Yes, partially. What we wanted to know is if you remember who built the add-on to Josh's house. You know, the two-car garage."

"Well first of all, Josh didn't have that done; he was barely out of high school. That was his father, Henry. Now, there was a piece of work. Of course, he was just like his father, Samuel. The apple doesn't fall far from the tree and all."

Walker was about to try to move Elmira along, when she must have realized herself what she had been doing. "But that's for another time. Yes, I remember. They built the garage nine or ten years ago, somewhere around then, and it was Cannon Construction. They've been around a long time. I think the grandfather started the business back in 1940s. Anyway, the reason I remember who did the garage is because of the owner's name. On the side of all their trucks it says 'Grant Cannon Construction—three generations.' All I could think of every time I saw it was the Grand Canyon. That's how I remembered. Also, I remembered that the grandfather did work for Samuel Raybeck back in the fifties." Elmira shook her head. "The damn fool put in a bomb shelter. Can you imagine?"

With some encouragement from Walker, Elmira elaborated about the bomb shelter. "I think it's possible that my husband Ed was the only person Samuel Raybeck told about it. Of course, Ed told me, but I don't think anyone else knew. There was a lot of controversy back then about bomb shelters. People who built them kept guns inside to keep their neighbors out in case the Russians bombed us. Bunch of foolish nonsense, if you ask me."

She paused. "I hadn't thought about that bomb shelter in forever. And then that Grant Cannon Construction truck showed up. I'm pretty sure they built the garage right on top of where the bomb shelter was."

Walker and Munoz cut short their conversation with Elmira. The additional information about the bomb shelter had all but confirmed their suspicions about a hidden room. But more importantly, she had provided them with the name of the contractor, and they needed to move on it.

As soon as they left Elmira, Walker took out his phone, pressed the app for Google, and typed in Cannon Construction. Within fifteen seconds, he had a phone number. He tried it immediately, but there was no answer. The options he listened to, however, provided an emergency number. When Walker tried that, someone answered on the second ring. "Grant Cannon."

"Mr. Cannon, this is Special Agent Craig Walker with the FBI. It's urgent that I speak with you in person. You're not in any trouble, but we have reason to believe that you have information that's critical to an investigation we're conducting."

Initially, there was no response, and then, "The FBI? What's this about?"

"I'll give you more details when I talk with you," Walker assured him.

The contractor hesitated. "This isn't a joke?"

"No, Mr. Cannon, it's not. Please, where are you?"

"I'm on a job in Providence," he said.

"What's the address?"

Cannon gave it to Walker, who in turn passed it along to Munoz to plug into the GPS. Walker spoke again to Cannon. "We should be there in about ten minutes."

It was obvious from the tone of his voice that Cannon was having trouble processing what was happening. But he managed to say, "All right. I'll be here."

As Walker and Munoz got into the car, Munoz placed the portable flashing light on the roof of the unmarked car, and they sped away. Eleven minutes later they were at the Cannon Construction work site.

While Walker was exiting the car, he took out his badge and headed toward a man who was pacing on the sidewalk. The man appeared to be in his forties. He had his hands in his pockets and looked nervous. Walker said, "Mr. Cannon?"

The man took his hands out of his pockets. "Yes."

Walker displayed his badge. "I'm Agent Walker, and this is Detective Munoz."

"So, what's this about?"

"Do you remember doing some work for the Raybecks in East Providence—a two-car garage—about eight or nine years ago?"

Cannon appeared wary. "That's a long time ago."

Walker decided to take a chance. "There was probably more to the job than just the garage, maybe something underneath the garage."

Walker could tell from Cannon's expression that he had struck a nerve. But Cannon recovered quickly, "I'd have to check my records."

Walker threw out his trump card. "Mr. Cannon, you know that little boy who went missing nearly a week ago?"

"Yeah," he replied slowly.

"Well, we think he might be on the Raybeck property somewhere." Walker watched as all the color drained from Cannon's face, and then he continued. "Listen. We know that there weren't any permits filed for that construction, and we couldn't care less; it's not about that. But if you have information that could help us find that little boy, and you're holding back, I'm going to nail you to the wall. Now, what's it going to be?"

"Do I need a lawyer?" the man asked warily.

Walker was getting frustrated. "I told you. You're not in trouble. But you will be, if we don't get some cooperation soon."

Cannon continued to hesitate, so Walker tried another tack. "Have you got kids, Mr. Cannon?"

The contractor nodded. "A girl ten and a boy seven."

"And you're not going to help us?"

That did the trick. Cannon's shoulders slumped, and he looked away for a moment before he spoke. "Henry Raybeck said he was going to get the permits, but he never did. He didn't trust the government, not even the local one. And he sure didn't want anyone knowing about what was under the garage. He paid me an extra two grand to keep my mouth shut, and not say anything about the permits or the room."

Walker interrupted. "So, there's definitely a room down there? How do you get into it?"

"It's tricky. There was an old bomb shelter under there. Actually, my grandfather put it in. Anyway, I had to gut the whole thing and reinforce the walls. Henry was one of those survivalists. You've seen that Minuteman statue, right?"

Walker had no patience left. "Tell us how to get into the room."

"It's through the garage, near the workbench. But it's really complicated to get inside, unless you know what you're doing. I think it'd be faster if I showed you."

Walker didn't hesitate. "All right. Let's go."

Cannon called out to one of his workers to let him know that he was leaving, and then hopped in the back seat of Munoz' car. As they sped away, Walker took out his phone and called one of the agents back at the Stanfield Police Station. "Hi, it's Craig. We've got a very strong lead on the whereabouts of Eric Allen. I want all agents out to the Raybeck house immediately. Also, I want you to contact the local EMTs in East Providence and have an ambulance there as well."

Walker didn't wait for a response. He hit "end" on his phone, and punched in the number for the agent staying with Jonathan Allen. "Hello, it's Craig. Listen, don't say anything to Mr. Allen directly, but we've got an excellent lead on his son's location. Make sure he's good to go, if something comes of this."

Munoz looked over at Walker, again impressed with his ability to be in command of the situation. He was about to say something when Cannon spoke up from the back seat. "So, you really think the missing kid could be in that room?"

Walker responded. "It's a strong possibility."

"How did he end up there? I remember seeing in the paper a few years ago that Henry Raybeck had died. I think the son owns the house now. He contacted me awhile back, wanting to find out how much it would cost to turn that room into a regular basement. I think he called it a bunker. He seemed like a good kid. He's not involved in this, is he?"

Walker ignored the question. "You're sure you can get us into that room?"

"Yeah. There's a series of switches in the circuit breaker box next to the workbench. Once you put them in the right sequence and press a button, it opens a trap door under the platform on the floor. Henry insisted that I make it so he could change the sequence whenever he wanted. But I also put in a backup sequence, you know, like a PIN number, just in case there was a problem. Henry would have had a fit if he knew I did that. He was as paranoid as they come, especially after 9/11. He was convinced the federal government was in on the attack. I told you that he was one of those survivalists, didn't I? When I first talked to him about the job, he said that if he were younger, he would move to Montana or someplace like that."

When they pulled up to the curb in front of the Raybeck house, the local police officer they had spoken with before was out of his cruiser, standing next to the ambulance Walker had requested. The other FBI agents had yet to arrive.

Munoz asked, "What do you want to do, Craig?"

"We can go in together. I don't anticipate anything dangerous; if Eric's in there, I'm sure he's by himself. But I don't want to scare him, so no guns."

Cannon said, "There's not enough room for both of you to go in at the same time; the stairs are too narrow."

"Then I'll take the lead and you follow," Walker said. "All right, Dave?"

Munoz nodded. "Okay."

Walker went over to the local police officer. "I'm going to open up the garage doors. When the other FBI agents get here, have them come up to the house."

Walker leaned into the ambulance window. "Back into the driveway, and be ready."

Walker, Munoz and Cannon headed into the house. A moment later, one of the garage doors started moving upward. Even before it was fully open, Walker spoke to Cannon. "Get me into that room."

Cannon went over to the circuit breaker box, opened it up, and started moving some of the switches on the right side. There were three possible positions for each switch. Cannon maneuvered the first four so that they were in a 1-2-1-2 sequence. "I used the police phone number as the backup sequence so I wouldn't forget it," said Cannon. "Now I just have to push the button under the top switch on the left side, and that should activate the hydraulic lift."

Initially, when Cannon pushed the button, nothing happened. But a moment later, there was a "whooshing" sound and the platform in front of the workbench began to rise. "It should get up to about five feet. Once it stops, you can duck under and go down the steps. It's dark now, but as soon as you put your foot on the first step, a light will go on. At the bottom of the stairs, there's a reinforced door. Unless there's somebody inside who knows how to set the locks, you should be able to open it."

The platform stopped its upward movement at the five-foot mark. Walker did as Cannon had suggested—He ducked his head and put his foot on the first step. As soon as the light went on, he began his descent. Munoz asked, "Do you want me to follow you?"

"No." Walker called back. "It's too narrow. I'll call up to you once I get inside and know what's going on."

As Walker reached the bottom of the stairs, he saw a handle on the steel door that resembled the type he'd see on old bank vaults. He pushed down, heard something click, and then pulled the door toward himself.

CHAPTER TWENTY-THREE

I n the first split second after Walker entered the room, his brain took in the stacks and stacks of shelving around the perimeter. In the next split second, he concluded that, because the shelves were empty except for a few bottles of water, Josh Raybeck probably hadn't shared his father's survivalist views.

Within the next few seconds, Walker had taken in the whole rest of the room. His eyes came to focus on what looked like a pile of blankets on the floor about fifteen feet away. But as he took another step forward, he could see that there was a sleeping bag there as well.

Walker started to rush toward it. But then something moved, and he saw a shock of blond hair emerge from underneath the covers. He stopped in his tracks as the little boy sat up and let out a low cry that was laced with fear. The boy pushed himself back against the far shelving.

Walker stayed where he was, but in a quiet voice said, "It's okay, Eric. I'm not going to hurt you; I'm here to take you home."

Eric started shaking, and his eyes threatened to overflow. "The other man told me he was going to take me home, but he never came back." Walker began to say something, but Eric continued. "Are you the man who brought me here?"

"No, Eric. I'm a policeman. Would it be all right if I came closer and showed you my badge?"

With the mention of the word "policeman," Eric's whole posture changed. "Are you really a policeman?"

"Yes."

Eric stood up. Walker took that as a sign that it was okay to move forward. As he did, he looked more closely at Eric. From Walker's perspective, he didn't appear to be hurt. He was disheveled, and obviously traumatized, but a quick assessment suggested that he was physically unharmed.

Walker slowly took out his badge as Eric started to move toward him. He then tilted his head to see the badge more clearly. It seemed to

Walker that Eric's expression had become one of curiosity rather than skepticism.

And then Walker's feelings were confirmed. "It says FBI; that's different from a regular policeman. Can you still take me home?"

Walker smiled. "Yes, I can. Are you all right?"

Eric appeared to think about that for a moment. "I was really scared. The other man said I could go home, but he didn't come back." Eric waited a moment and then added, "I want to see my daddy and I'm kind of hungry."

This time Walker let out a little laugh. "I think we can take care of both of those things."

Walker moved within a few feet of Eric. "I can take you to your daddy right now. Would you like me to carry you?"

"No, I'm six years old;" the boy announced. "I can walk by myself."

Walker smiled again. "Would it be okay if I held your hand, just while we climb the stairs?"

"Yeah, that would be okay," Eric replied.

As they left the room and began the trip up to the garage, Walker called out "He's all right. I've got him; we're coming up."

Once they reached the top of the stairs, Walker ducked under the raised platform and knelt beside Eric. "I know you told me that you're all right, but we have to be sure. So you're going to have to take a ride in the ambulance. But I'll ride with you in the back." Walker looked over toward one of the EMTs, who nodded. "And your daddy will meet us at the hospital."

Eric didn't say anything for a moment, and then, "Okay." And he quickly added, "But you're coming with me, right?"

"Absolutely."

As the EMTs put Eric on the gurney, Walker spoke to Munoz. "Call Jonathan Allen's house and give him the good news. And have the agent who's with him drive him to the hospital. Check with the EMTs to find out where we're going."

"Got it." Munoz glanced over toward Eric. "He seems okay. Did he say anything about what happened?"

"Not a whole lot. He did mention that another man had promised to bring him home, but hadn't returned. He also asked me if I was the man who had brought him here. That was about it."

At that moment, two cars pulled up with the other FBI agents inside. Walker turned his attention back to Eric. "I have to go over there and talk with some of the other FBI agents, but I'll be right back."

As Walker headed down the driveway, the other agents got out of their cars and rushed to meet him. "The boy seems fine, but we're taking him to the nearest hospital," he told them. "I'm going to ride with him. You guys work with the local police here and help them secure the scene. Believe it or not, there's a hidden room under the garage. That's where he was."

Walker shook his head. "I don't want to even think about how this could have turned out." A pause. "After you help the local police, head back to the Stanfield station. I'll meet you there after I'm finished at the hospital."

Walker then went over to Munoz. "Follow us to the hospital, okay?"

"Sure."

Less than fifteen minutes later, the ambulance pulled up to the emergency room entrance. As soon as it came to a stop, the hospital personnel waiting outside opened the rear doors. Walker jumped out to let the EMTs do their work. Eric was wheeled down a corridor, and as they reached the final set of doors leading into the emergency room, Walker leaned over. "Eric, I'm going out front to wait for your daddy. I'll bring him to you as soon as he gets here."

Eric didn't respond, but tears began to flow freely from the corner of his eyes.

Munoz was already in the lobby when Walker got there. "Any sign of him?"

"Not yet, but it shouldn't be long," the detective replied.

They were quiet for a moment, each lost in his own thoughts. Munoz was about to share his when the car carrying Jonathan Allen arrived at the front door. Jonathan sprinted out of the car, navigated the revolving door, and spotted Walker and Munoz. "Where is he? Is he all right?"

Walker said, "Come on, we'll take you to him. And he seems fine,

Mr. Allen."

At the sound of those words, Jonathan lost all control of his emotions, and Munoz had to step in to help support him. "Do you want to sit for a minute?"

"No," Jonathan replied shakily. "I just want to see my son."

Munoz continued to hold onto Jonathan's elbow as they moved toward the back of the hospital. Once they arrived at the ER, they got directions at the nurses' station and headed for the intensive care room where Eric had been brought. Walker ran interference so that the doctors allowed Jonathan to see his son before they continued the examination.

Ten minutes later, Jonathan emerged from the room, wiping his eyes. But as soon as he saw Walker and Munoz, the tears started in again. He extended his hand to Munoz and said, "I don't know how you properly thank someone who saves your child's life ..." He and Munoz shook hands, and then Jonathan offered his hand to Walker and added, "... and saves yours as well."

Several hours later, once Walker was satisfied that he had gathered as much solid information as possible concerning Eric Allen's abduction, he called a press conference. And while Walker usually attempted to avoid the spotlight, he recognized that the positive media exposure for the FBI resulting from this story made it necessary.

As Walker looked out from behind the podium, he saw at least a hundred reporters and onlookers, as well as a dozen media vans and satellite trucks. The abduction of Eric Allen, and more importantly, his safe return, had become national news. And the reporters' thirst for additional facts had become unquenchable after someone leaked the presence of the hidden room under the garage, not to mention that Josh Raybeck's body had been found in the same house.

"Thank you all for coming. I'm Special Agent Craig Walker of the FBI's Child Abduction Rapid Deployment team. I'd like to make a brief statement, and then I'll answer some questions.

"Many times in the past, I've had to stand up in front of a gathering similar to this and deliver the most heartbreaking and unthinkable news any parent could possibly hear. Thank God, today is not one of those days. Six-year-old Eric Allen was reunited with his father, Jonathan, several hours ago. The preliminary examination of the boy showed no signs of any physical harm. The doctors are planning to keep Eric overnight for observation, however. Arrangements have been made for Mr. Allen to stay in the hospital room with his son.

"First of all, I would like to thank the rest of our team …" Walker went on to name each member, and then turned his attention to the local police. "Without question, this case would not have ended successfully without the cooperative efforts of the Stanfield, Massachusetts and the East Providence, Rhode Island Police Departments." Walker paused and turned slightly. "However, if there is one individual who deserves the lion's share of the credit for the safe return of Eric Allen, it's Detective David Munoz of the Stanfield Police Department. Detective Munoz' hard work, perseverance, and tremendous instinct literally solved this case."

Walker continued praising Munoz for a few more minutes and then opened up the press conference to questions. But before he did, he issued a caveat to the reporters. "While finding Eric Allen was always our top priority, discovering who abducted him, and why, is still under investigation. In view of that, it may be necessary to keep certain aspects of the case out of the public domain for the time being. Please bear that in mind when you ask your questions."

Despite his warning, the reporters kept pressing Walker to reveal specific details about the hidden room, about Josh Raybeck's suspected involvement, and about the motive. But Walker held his ground.

Once the press conference concluded, there was some milling around for a few minutes, and then Munoz went over to Walker. "Nice job. But you were a bit overly generous with the praise, don't you think?"

"No, I don't think so at all."

Munoz was about to protest, but his cell phone rang. He glanced at the screen and saw that the call had been forwarded from the station house. "This is Detective Munoz."

"Hello Detective Munoz. This is Jerry Hanson, Josh Raybeck's attorney."

"Of course, Mr. Hanson. What can I do for you?"

"First of all, congratulations," Jerry said. "I was just watching the press conference in my office."

"Well, you should save some of those congratulations for yourself," Munoz responded. "If you hadn't come forward when you did, I'm not sure what would have happened."

"Thank you. That's nice of you to say." He paused. "The reason I called is that after the press conference, I finally had a chance to take a look at my mail ... and there was a letter from Josh Raybeck."

"What?"

"Yeah, it's postmarked yesterday afternoon. He must have sent it out right after he talked to me. It may not mean anything now that you found the boy, but I thought you should know what it said." Jerry paused. "I'll read it to you, if you'd like."

"Go ahead," Munoz said.

Dear Mr. Hanson,

I wanted you to know that everything I told you was the truth, except about where the boy is. After Tony took him, he brought him to my house and just took off, like he did with some of those other kids. Only this time, he never came back. I have a secret room in my house and that's where the boy is now. In case anything happens, I wanted you to know how to find him. The room is under the garage. You can get in by ...

The rest of the letter described the same procedure that Grant Cannon had followed to get into the room, except for the circuit-breaker sequence.

When Jerry finished, he said, "It sounds like Josh wanted to make sure somebody knew where the boy was, in case something happened to him. Is that how you found out about the room? Did he send you a letter, too?"

"No," replied Munoz. "Uh ... we figured it out another way."

Jerry was about to ask how, but decided not to. "Anyway, I'm just glad the boy is all right. And for what it's worth, I believe Josh was telling the truth about everything else. I don't know if it will help in finding out who killed him, but ..." Jerry's voice trailed off.

"I don't know either, at this point. But can you bring the letter in? I'd like to take a look at it. And then I'll turn it over to the East Providence Police. It's their case now."

After he hung up, Munoz filled Walker in on everything Jerry Hanson had told him.

At the end, Munoz added, "Despite the fact that Josh Raybeck had Eric hidden in his house, I think it's likely that he was telling the truth. It was probably Tony Sarno who did the actual kidnapping. Of course, now that they're both dead, there's no way to know for sure, unless we find out who's behind this whole thing."

They were quiet for a moment, and then Munoz asked, "So, is this it for you? You said you wanted to go out on a good one."

Walker smiled. "I did, didn't I?" He paused. "I think so, probably, but I'm going to give myself a few days to think about it. I'll send the rest of the team home, clean up some odds and ends, finish the paperwork, and then decide."

"So, you're sticking around for a few more days?" Munoz asked.

"At least until Monday." A pause. "There's a part of me that would like to see this thing through. This is the first case I've ever been involved in where we didn't know who was behind the abduction. I mean, I agree with you. Tony Sarno probably took Eric from the schoolyard, but someone else had to be pulling the strings. And somebody had to have ordered Tony Sarno and Josh Raybeck dead." Another pause. "The Bureau may want to send another agent out here to follow up, somebody who has more experience with murder investigations."

"If you're definitely leaving, then I hope they do; I don't have a whole lot of experience with murder investigations, either. Plus, I've got to try to coordinate everything with the East Providence Police."

Walker kept his gaze on Munoz. "If you want, while the Bureau decides whether to send somebody, I could probably get permission to stick around, maybe through Tuesday. At least that way, if you or East Providence develops a lead, I might be able to get the FBI to provide some technical assistance."

"I'll take all the help I can get," Munoz told him. "Even if it's only for a few days."

"Okay. I'm going to be in and out of the station house tomorrow, but I'll make it a point to be there on Monday at noon, so we can talk."

"That'd be great," Munoz responded. "I'm going to use tomorrow to get up to speed on the investigation into Tony Sarno's murder, and then I'll see you on Monday."

~

For the first time in a week, Munoz had an uninterrupted seven hours of sleep. And even though Sunday was his day off, he went into the station house around ten o'clock. He got a copy of the case file on

Tony Sarno's murder, read through it, and made some notes. There was nothing in the file, however, that gave him a sense of what his next step should be.

He went home around one o'clock, turned on the Red Sox game and looked through the file for the second time. Shortly after the game ended, he took a ride over to the mall to view the crime scene again. But still, nothing stood out.

The rest of his day was spent answering e-mail and reading the Sunday paper, which was filled with stories about the safe return of Eric Allen. Munoz was mentioned at least ten times.

He also received a call from the officer on duty at the station, who had fielded half a dozen phone requests from various media outlets that wanted to schedule an interview with "the detective who had found the missing boy."

Munoz told the officer to tell them he was on vacation for two weeks. He figured that would allow enough time for the news cycle to shift to something or someone else.

On Monday morning, Munoz came into work around nine, did some follow-up with his chief, contacted the East Providence police about setting up a coordination meeting, and then re-read the Tony Sarno case file.

Walker showed up an hour earlier than he said he was going to. He knocked on the door jamb of Munoz' office. "Hey, Dave. Anything new?"

The detective shook his head. "No. I'm afraid not."

"Is there anything at all that I can help with?"

"Not that I can see," Munoz replied. "I'm meeting with the East Providence police this afternoon. Maybe they'll have something."

"Why don't you give me a call after the meeting and let me know? As of now, I'm planning on heading out tomorrow morning. I'm going to take the next few days to figure out whether I want to retire or not."

Munoz started to respond when his phone rang.

Walker's decision was about to get more difficult.

CHAPTER TWENTY-FOUR

Munoz stared at the phone for a moment before he picked it up. "This is Detective Munoz."

"Hello, Detective. It's Jerry Hanson again."

"Hi, Mr. Hanson. I'm sorry I wasn't here the other day when you dropped off the letter, but thanks for bringing it in. So, what's on your mind?"

"Well, it's kind of related to what was in the letter. When I got back to my office after dropping it off, I started thinking about what Josh had written. He seemed pretty emphatic that what he had told me was the truth. So, I decided to read through my notes again, and that led me to do some more digging. And I found a few things that are troubling me."

"Having to do with Josh's murder?"

"Maybe, but it seems more directly connected to Tony Sarno."

"What is it that you found?" Munoz asked.

"It has to do with Tony's trial ..." Jerry began.

"But that was months ago, wasn't it?"

"I know, but it feels like that's when everything started. Would it be okay if I came by and showed you what I'm talking about? I think it would be easier than trying to explain it over the phone."

Munoz hesitated for a moment, remembering the meeting with the East Providence police in a few hours. "Yeah, that would be fine."

"I'll see you in about twenty minutes. Oh, and I'll need a DVD player."

Jerry's last comment put a curious expression on Munoz' face as he hung up. Walker saw it, and said, "What was that all about?"

"That was Jerry Hanson. He said that he came across something that's bothering him. He said it's connected to Tony Sarno."

"Any idea what it is?" Walker inquired.

"He's coming to show us."

"Us?" Walker repeated.

"You said you weren't leaving until tomorrow." Munoz paused. "I'd like to get the full benefit of your expertise before you take off."

"You want *my* expertise … or is it really the Bureau's resources you're looking for?"

Munoz smiled. "Well, there is that, yeah."

Walker smiled back. "Okay. I did say I'd be here until Tuesday." He paused. "Did you get any sense about what Hanson might have found?"

"I'm not sure. He did say it had more to do with Tony Sarno than Josh Raybeck, although he also indicated that he thought it was probably connected to both of them somehow."

Walker was quiet for a moment, and then he shifted topics slightly. "You didn't say anything to Jonathan Allen about the possibility that Tony Sarno was responsible for his wife's death, did you?"

"No, not yet. I wanted to see if I could come up with some more evidence before I sprung that on him. It might help him if he knew the truth. But it also might freak him out, knowing that Tony Sarno was probably involved in both his son's kidnapping and his wife's murder."

"I agree." Walker paused. "I talked to him last night, by the way. It looks like Eric's getting released tomorrow, probably around two o'clock in the morning. Mr. Allen wanted to avoid a media circus, and the hospital's going to go along with it. He's got a sister in upstate New York. He's taking Eric there for a while."

"Good for them." Munoz was about to continue when his phone rang again. "Detective Munoz."

"Hi, Detective. It's Detective Pierce from East Providence."

"You're not thinking of canceling on me, are you?"

"No," replied the other man. "But I think things just got more complicated for the both of us. Your victim, Tony Sarno—what caliber gun was he shot with?"

"Thirty-eight."

"That's what I thought," Pierce said. "Josh Raybeck was killed with a nine millimeter, probably a Glock."

"What?" Munoz said in surprise.

"Yeah, I know. We were all assuming that they were killed by the same person. And I guess that's still possible, although why would the guy switch guns?"

"It certainly doesn't fit with what you'd expect." Munoz paused. "Okay, thanks for the heads up. I'll see you in a couple of hours and we can try to sort it out then."

Munoz was shaking his head as he put the receiver in its cradle. "Sarno and Raybeck were shot with different caliber guns."

"What?" Walker responded.

"A thirty-eight and a nine millimeter."

Walker waited a moment, and then said, "It could still be the same guy. Maybe he's just trying to throw us off."

"I suppose. I'm just going to add that to the list of things about this case that don't make sense."

They talked for another ten minutes, and then Jerry Hanson showed up. As he entered the office, Munoz pointed to one of the chairs opposite his desk. "Come on in, Mr. Hanson. You remember Agent Walker."

"Of course. I didn't realize the FBI was still involved."

Walker responded. "I'm finishing up a few things. The Bureau may assign someone else to assist with the murder investigations, but that hasn't been determined yet. In the meantime, I'm here to help out if I can. Detective Munoz tells me you've found something that you want us to take a look at."

Jerry nodded. "Yeah, I've gone back and forth on this. I even called Maria Lopez yesterday to get her perspective. For what it's worth, she agrees with me. Maria's still at work, but she's checking out some of the things we talked about yesterday. She's going to call me when she knows more."

Munoz spoke up as he motioned toward the corner of the office. "I've got the DVD player you asked for."

"Thanks," acknowledged the attorney. "Let me give you some of the background first, before we look at it, all right?"

"Sure."

Jerry appeared to gather himself as if he were about to deliver a summation in front of a jury. "The first time I met Tony Sarno was almost a year ago. I was assigned to be his public defender. Initially, he was charged with solicitation, but that was dropped. Then he was charged with possession of child pornography. I don't know, maybe you knew all that already. Anyway, his trial was held last August, and Maria Lopez was the ADA prosecuting the case. The original judge presiding over the trial was Judge Titus, but he was replaced with Judge Lancaster."

"Why was that?" asked Munoz.

"We were told that there was some sort of robbery at Judge Titus' house the night before, and he ended up in the hospital," Jerry explained. "So a new judge had to be assigned."

Walker and Munoz both nodded as Jerry continued.

"Neither Ms. Lopez nor I objected. I think we both figured that we didn't want to alienate the new judge. Besides, it was a jury trial, so the jury was going to decide the case, not the judge. But it didn't turn out that way. Less than an hour into the proceedings, Judge Lancaster declared a mistrial. It was primarily because of what *he* said in open court in front of the jury. Although, as Ms. Lopez readily admits, she lost her cool, too. But anybody who was there would certainly agree that it was the judge's fault."

Jerry took a deep breath and then continued. "Defending Tony Sarno wasn't exactly my favorite thing to do. But I got through it. Then I just tried to put the case out of my head. And I did, until Josh Raybeck came to see me a few days ago.

"When I first spoke with you about what Josh had told me, I didn't say much about the trial, because it didn't seem to have anything to do with Eric Allen's disappearance. And maybe it still doesn't. But according to Josh, Tony Sarno told him the trial had been in the bag; that there was no way he was going to be convicted.

"When I first heard that, I figured that it was just Tony's bravado talking. And then I was so wrapped up in getting the plea deal for Josh, I didn't give it another thought. But when I received Josh's letter about everything he told me being the truth, it started me thinking, and I decided to take a look at the trial folder." Jerry held it up as he continued.

"After the trial was over, I was sent a copy of the trial on a DVD. I had never looked at it before; there was no reason to. But as I watched it yesterday, there were a couple of things that didn't seem right. I had to watch it a few more times before I figured it out. As I said, maybe it doesn't mean anything, but I wanted to show it to you, and let you decide."

Jerry took the DVD out of its case and moved toward the TV in the corner. "I have the critical section bookmarked." He inserted the DVD and pressed the fast-forward button before he paused it.

"As I mentioned before, Tony Sarno was being tried for possession of child pornography. The pictures were in an e-mail on his phone. For the purposes of the trial, the court had hard copies made. I argued that they were prejudicial and shouldn't be shown to the jury. Ms. Lopez argued that they should, and that's when the hullaballoo started. I'm going to show you two minutes' worth. On some of it the audio is faint, but I think you can still make it out."

Munoz asked, "What exactly are we looking for?"

"I'd prefer not to tell you ahead of time," Jerry responded. "I think it's better if you just look at it cold."

If Jerry Hanson hadn't been so incredibly helpful in providing information that eventually brought Eric Allen home, both Walker and Munoz might have been inclined to cut this exercise short. But he had; so they let him continue.

Jerry pushed the play button.

The screen showed Jerry Hanson and Maria Lopez heading up to the judge's bench for a side bar. Much of the audio was undecipherable, except when the participants raised their voices.

Walker and Munoz watched in silence for just under two minutes, and then Jerry paused the DVD again. "Obviously, this is the part that eventually led the judge to declare a mistrial. But there are a couple of things that seem curious to me. I'll play it again, so you can see what I mean."

Jerry pressed rewind and went back to the original starting point. "Okay, here's the first thing: Notice that the judge has his hand over the microphone every time that he's speaking to Ms. Lopez or me." Jerry waited another thirty seconds, and then said, "Except now, when he lets loose with his diatribe at Ms. Lopez. It's like he wanted the jury to hear what he was saying."

Jerry increased the volume, and Judge Lancaster's voice filled

Munoz' office. "*That's exactly the point that Mr. Hanson was trying to make. Viewing those photos could easily prejudice the jury. You want it in legal terms, Ms. Lopez? The photos have no probative value. You're just looking to sensationalize this. Some people would find that disgusting.*"

Walker and Munoz looked at each other and had the same thought. Walker expressed it out loud. "I know what you're saying, Mr. Hanson. And obviously, the judge shouldn't have allowed his comments to be heard by the jury. But don't you think that the judge taking his hand off the microphone was just an accident?"

"Of course it could be, but there's more."

"All right. Let's see what else you've got."

"The next thing actually occurs a few seconds before the judge's outburst. He has the microphone covered, but I think you can still make out what he says."

Jerry manipulated the DVD to the appropriate spot, and pushed play. And while he was correct – the audio was difficult to hear – it was relatively easy to read the judge's lips.

Jerry paused the DVD and asked, "Could you make out what the judge was saying?"

Both Walker and Munoz nodded, and then Munoz responded. "He said, 'and yes, I told you. I saw them last night.'" Munoz appeared puzzled. "What's the significance of that?"

"He was talking about the photos. But Judge Lancaster wasn't assigned to the case until the next morning. How would he have seen the photos the night before?"

This time Walker answered. "Couldn't that have just been an expression, like a slip of the tongue?"

"Honestly, that doesn't seem likely to me. Supposedly, he just got the case an hour or so before he was in court. I don't think he would have made that kind of mistake," Jerry paused. "I realize that all of this is very circumstantial, but ..." he didn't finish the sentence.

Walker avoided directly addressing Jerry's remark. "So, even if what you're suggesting is true, then what? You think that Judge Lancaster purposefully caused the mistrial?"

Jerry perked up. "It does seem like he wanted Tony Sarno to get off. Was he paid to make that happen? I have no idea. But I believe Josh Raybeck was telling the truth. Tony Sarno is mixed up in all of this, and Judge Lancaster made sure he was back on the street. I'm convinced that was no accident." He paused. "There's also something else. Judge Lancaster was the one who approved the plea agreement for Josh."

Walker appeared more intrigued. "How did that come about?"

"Well to be honest, that was just by chance. It was late last Friday night, and he lives close by the courthouse."

"So, you're not suggesting that he manipulated that situation?" Walker asked.

"No. But he did show up over an hour after we called him, and then, once he was there, he kept stalling. Then he got a phone call, and when he came back, he was like a different person. We wrapped up the agreement in a few minutes after that. And then less than a half hour later, Josh Raybeck was dead."

Walker maintained a sympathetic expression. "I certainly don't want to dismiss what you're saying out of hand, Mr. Hanson. But it does seem as if it's primarily based on supposition and coincidence. I wish it were more than that, because, frankly, we don't have any leads. Someone had to be behind this; I don't believe for one minute that Tony Sarno did this on his own." He paused. "And while Judge Lancaster didn't acquit himself very well, I'm not sure there's anything more to it."

Jerry smiled. "As I said when I first came in, I kept going back and forth on whether to bring this to you. It was like I was on the other side of the courtroom, like a prosecutor trying to prove his case. But you know, you're right; this is all conjecture." Another smile formed on his lips. "There's a ton of reasonable doubt. Even I could drive a truck through those arguments."

Walker returned the smile. "Don't be so hard on yourself. I told you before, we would have never found Eric Allen if you hadn't come forward."

"I appreciate you saying that," Jerry told him. "Thanks. I wish I could have been more helpful with this part of it."

They all shook hands, and then Jerry packed up and left.

A moment passed, and Munoz turned toward Walker. "I know it might be a stretch, but is it possible that there's something to what he showed us?"

"I guess it's possible. But you're talking about a sitting judge involved in fixing cases and God knows what else. You'd have to have a lot more than we just saw to go down that road."

They talked for several more minutes, and then Munoz looked up and saw Jerry Hanson rushing back toward the office. A moment later he barged in. "I just got a call from Maria Lopez. She's on her way over here. She convinced a friend of hers at the courthouse to do some checking. Judge Lancaster did sign out the case file for Tony Sarno's trial the night before he was assigned to it."

A pause. "And get this: Those hard copies of the child pornography photos? They're missing from the file. And Judge Lancaster was the last one to have it."

Walker raised his eyebrows. "Really? Well, that could put a different light on things, certainly as far as the trial folder goes. I'm not sure what to make of the fact that the photos are missing. And you said that Ms. Lopez is on her way here?"

Jerry glanced at his watch. "Yeah, shouldn't be more than ten or fifteen minutes."

"Well, assuming that she confirms what she told you on the phone, I'd be willing to take a closer look at this. There still could be a reasonable explanation for signing out the case file the night before, but it certainly raises some questions."

Walker began to take charge. He turned to Munoz. "I think you should postpone your meeting with East Providence. Make up some excuse. But I don't want too many other people knowing that we're looking into a judge. Information like that has a way of getting leaked."

"Okay." Munoz paused. "I take it this means you're sticking around?"

"Yeah," Walker said. "I'll have to clear it with the Bureau, but I don't see why that would be a problem."

Walker then addressed Jerry. "Mr. Hanson, once we talk with Ms. Lopez, I'm going to suggest that the two of you step away from this. I don't know where it's headed. But if it turns out to be nothing, it wouldn't be good for your careers if the judge discovered that you were the ones who brought this to our attention."

"I appreciate that," Jerry replied.

"Also, it goes without saying that you shouldn't mention any of this to anybody else," Walker added.

"That's not a problem."

Walker gave him a half smile. "I didn't think it would be." Walker paused. "And thanks for being so persistent. It appears that your instincts may have been better than mine."

Jerry didn't know how to respond, so he simply nodded.

Maria arrived fifteen minutes later. Walker offered the same caution he had given to Jerry about not telling anyone. Maria indicated that she understood completely. She then spent the next several minutes outlining what she had discovered at the courthouse.

"One of the clerks there is a good friend of mine. I told him that I had been the prosecutor in the Tony Sarno trial last August, and that Tony Sarno had just been murdered. I wanted to review the file in case the police had questions about what he was involved in, but that I was having trouble locating the file in the DA's office. And I wondered, since it had been a mistrial, if it were possible that both copies had been filed with the court by mistake. I asked if I could come to the courthouse and look at their copy.

"He said to give him about twenty minutes. When I got there, he told me that there was only one folder on file, and he had pulled it for me. As the prosecutor, I'm allowed to view the file, but I can't remove it from the premises. On the inside of the folder there's a sign-out sheet to record everyone that has accessed it. I added my name and my court I.D. number. Above my name, Judge Titus had signed in a few times, and so had Judge Lancaster. But interestingly, there was a notation on the night before Tony Sarno's trial that the file was to be delivered to Judge Titus' chambers. But the I.D. number of the person making that request was Judge Lancaster's.

"I think what probably happened is that, after Judge Titus left for the day, Judge Lancaster asked to have the file delivered to Judge Titus' chambers, which wouldn't be unusual. After all, Judge Titus was the presiding judge. But I think Judge Lancaster made a mistake and wrote down his own I.D. number. And that raises the question—how did Judge Lancaster know he'd be given the case the next day? And if there were some other innocent reason for him to want to see the trial folder, why didn't he have it delivered to his own chambers?"

Walker looked impressed. "Those are excellent questions. I think that we need to take a closer look at the judge's behavior. What about the photos that are missing? How do they enter into this?"

"I don't know. After I discovered the discrepancy with the sign-up sheet, I decided to look more closely at the trial folder. In the front, there's an inventory sheet that lists all the contents. I glanced at it, and then started to thumb through the file. Of course, when Jerry asked me to come over to his office yesterday to look at the DVD, I looked at his copy of the file as well. I didn't expect to see anything different in the one at the court, so it didn't hit me right away. But then I realized that the hard copies of the photos that I had seen in Jerry's folder were missing from the court folder. I double-checked the inventory sheet, and sure enough, they were listed. Again, I have no idea what it means. But I've worked as an ADA for five years, and I've never heard of evidence going missing from a trial folder. Those are pretty secure."

Walker said, "As Detective Munoz will tell you, I don't like coincidences. And there are too many of them starting to build up here. We're going to pursue this."

"Good," Maria replied. "I've never been a fan of Judge Lancaster. I think he's a misogynist, but it's not just that. In the last year or so he's seemed preoccupied all the time; something's been "off" with him. And then there was his behavior at the trial, and the way he acted during the plea agreement ... Don't get the wrong idea; this isn't a personal vendetta. I just think somebody needs to find out what's going on, especially if it's criminal."

Walker broke in. "Obviously at this point, we don't know any more than you do about what's going on, but we intend to find out." He paused. "You and Mr. Hanson have been extremely helpful, both with getting Eric Allen back, and now with this. But at the risk of seeming ungrateful, we need to take it from here."

"I understand. That's fine," Maria paused. "Do you mind if I ask you something?"

"Not at all," Walker responded.

"If you're considering getting a search warrant for Judge Lancaster's home or office, I could help with that. I've had a lot of experience, and it might save you some time."

Walker smiled. "You're certainly not like any ADA I've ever met, Ms. Lopez."

"Please call me Maria. And I'm going to take that as a compliment."

"Well, you should; that's exactly how I meant it … Maria."

Walker looked toward Munoz and Jerry, as he appeared to be contemplating something. "I'll tell you what. Again, this is a bit unusual, but why don't you and Mr. Hanson—Jerry—join Detective Munoz and me for a brainstorming session? If we think that the search warrant idea is the best way to go, then I'll take you up on your offer, but only in terms of the paperwork. I want someone else to sign the application. As I told Jerry, you need to distance yourself from this."

"Okay," Maria agreed.

"How about you, Jerry? Can you stick around?"

The attorney shrugged. "Yeah, I've got nowhere I've got to be."

"Excellent. Is the conference room available, Dave?"

"I'm sure it is."

Despite the fact that Jerry and Maria were new to the law enforcement version of brainstorming, they both took to it easily, and made a number of significant contributions. Toward the end of the session, it was decided that they would try for the search warrant, but limit it to putting a tap on the judge's home and office phones.

Walker reasoned that they needed to know who the judge was talking to if they were going to make any headway. Plus, in Walker's estimation, the likelihood that the judge would have anything on his computer at work, or even at home for that matter, was questionable. In addition, seizing his computers would let him know that he was under suspicion, which would probably cause him to avoid communication with anyone else involved.

Maria asked, "Do you want me to draw up the warrants?"

"If you don't mind," Walker agreed.

"Glad to do it. I did have one more thought, though. I prosecuted a case last year where the police couldn't get a search warrant for a drug dealer's residence, but the judge did allow them to use parabolic microphones—you know, like the ones that you see on the sidelines of football games. They can pick up sounds from a long distance. Would you consider adding that to the application? I could just tack it on. Even if the judge is unwilling to approve the phone taps, he might be willing to go along with the microphones."

"I've never used them before, but all right, sure. We've got nothing to lose." Walker continued. "Is Judge Lancaster at the courthouse today, do you know?"

"He was when I left. He just started a trial. Up until this past year, you never would have seen him leave before four o'clock if he was on the bench. But as I said, he's different now."

"Okay. Once you finish writing up the warrant application, we'll take it to a federal judge. At its core, this is still a kidnapping case, and that's a federal crime. Besides, I'm not about to take the warrant to one of Lancaster's colleagues." Walker looked over at Munoz. "But no matter what the federal judge says about the warrant, I think we should start to tail Lancaster as soon as possible." Then Walker thought out loud. "I'll contact the Bureau and have somebody get the information on the judge's car."

Maria spoke up. "No need. I've parked next to him a few times in the court parking garage. He owns a black Mercedes, fairly new. It has Rhode Island plates—WAL dash LAW—his initials forwards and backwards."

CHAPTER TWENTY-FIVE

While Maria was writing up the warrant application with some assistance from Jerry, Walker phoned the FBI field office in Boston and got clearance to stay on the case in Stanfield. He also alerted them to the fact that he might have need for a parabolic mike. When he returned to Munoz' office, Munoz was hanging up the phone.

"I was just talking to East Providence. I told them something came up and we'd have to reschedule. I got the distinct impression that the detective in charge isn't convinced that the two murders are connected, now that he knows different guns were used."

"He may be right, but I doubt it," replied Walker. "It doesn't matter at this point. We can pull them in after we see where this thing with the judge is going. Speaking of judges, I was considering bringing the warrant application to the same federal judge we went to before. What do you think?"

"Well, he didn't give us exactly what we wanted, but he did steer us in the right direction," Munoz reasoned.

"That was my thought."

"Then I'd say, yeah," the detective concluded.

Walker placed the call five minutes later, and got the go-ahead from the judge's clerk to bring the application to the federal courthouse. True to her word, Maria finished the warrant in less than fifteen minutes. Walker arranged for it to be signed electronically by someone in the Boston field office. Then he and Munoz drove to Providence.

The judge was waiting for them when they arrived, and invited them into his chambers. "Before I take a look at the application, I wanted to congratulate the two of you for finding that little boy. I watched the press conference. That was very impressive work."

Walker said, "Thank you, Your Honor."

And Munoz, "Thank you."

"Does this warrant have anything to do with the kidnapping?" the judge asked.

"We believe so," Walker confirmed. "But we're not exactly sure how. That's why we're requesting the phone taps."

"All right, let me have a look." The judge spent five minutes reviewing the paperwork, and then peered over his glasses. "I'm afraid I'm going to have to disappoint you again, Agent Walker. I'd be hard pressed to sign off on this for a private citizen. But in view of the fact that we're talking about a sitting judge, it's much more problematic. If this Lancaster is anything like me ..."

Walker interrupted. "Trust me; he's not anything like you."

The judge smiled. "At my age, I'm immune to flattery, but I appreciate the implied compliment nevertheless. As I was saying, if the judge is anything like me, he'd be on the phone discussing five different cases in the course of a day, both at work and at home. I can't allow you to listen in on private conversations involving cases unrelated to what you're investigating." A pause. "I'm curious. Although I probably would have ruled against it, why didn't you request to confiscate the judge's computers?"

"I doubt that he'd be careless enough to leave anything incriminating on them, certainly not at work," Walker explained. "And also, we didn't want to tip him off that he's under investigation. That's why we thought the phone taps might get us what we need. He'd have no idea anyone was listening."

"I think your reasoning is sound, but your argument is not compelling enough for me to allow them. I'm sorry." The judge paused. "I know it's not everything that you were looking for, but I will sign off on the use of the parabolic mikes. But only when your subject is in a public place; his home and office are off limits."

The judge removed his pen from its holder and signed the appropriate section of the warrant. "Five years ago, I would have never allowed the use of these microphones. But because of the proliferation of surveillance cameras, cell phones, and Wi-Fi, if you're outside, there's no way you should have an expectation of privacy, no matter where you are. In reality, someone could be watching you or listening in on your conversation, even if you're just walking down the street, or sitting on a park bench." The judge shook his head.

Walker appeared to be considering something, and then he asked,

"Can I assume that that would also apply to phone conversations the subject held outside … or even in his car?"

The judge smiled. "By the standard I just described, absolutely." A pause. "I think you're getting the hang of this, Agent Walker."

Walker and Munoz exited the federal courthouse, got into Munoz' unmarked car, and sat there for a moment digesting what had just happened. Walker spoke first, acknowledging the judge's ability to walk a fine line. "He's something else, isn't he? He finds a way to stick to the letter of the law, while still allowing us to do our jobs."

"I suspect there aren't too many like him," Munoz observed.

"Not that I've seen." Walker eyed his watch. "I know it might be too early for Lancaster to leave for the day, but I don't want to take a chance that we might miss him. Let's head over to East Providence."

On the drive to Rhode Island, the topic of conversation shifted to the parabolic microphones. Walker said, "From my understanding, they're only effective from fifty to a hundred yards, and then only with an unobstructed path. Sometimes you can get decent audio through walls if they're relatively thin, but that's a crapshoot. I think our best bet might be any phone calls Lancaster makes from his car. But there are issues with that, too. There's no guarantee he's going to make any calls while he's in his car. And even if he does, he probably won't be stationary, and we're only going to hear one side of the conversation."

"I haven't ever seen them used. But they're pretty big, aren't they?"

"Yeah, they're a little bit bigger than the satellite dishes people have on their houses. The FBI has two of them in the Boston area. One is freestanding, and the other one is mounted on the top of a fake media van. The Bureau's sending that one tomorrow. The agents will have to follow Lancaster at a distance. And it wouldn't make sense for them to tail him for two or three days with the van; that would be too obvious. So we may only get one shot at this."

Munoz was about to respond when he noticed a black Mercedes speeding out of the parking garage. The plates read WAL-LAW. "It looks like the judge is leaving early, and he's in a hurry."

"I'm glad we showed up when we did."

Munoz kept the unmarked car about five car lengths back, but fortunately made every light that Lancaster made.

The judge had been driving for about ten minutes when he took a right turn down a side street.

Munoz slowed down and did the same. It was a quiet residential area, and there were no cars between their car and the Mercedes, so Munoz slowed down even further.

After three blocks, the zoning changed to commercial. The judge pulled over across the street from a couple of abandoned stores and parked. Munoz didn't have a choice but to keep going and pass the judge. Anything else would have looked suspicious. About fifty yards after he passed Lancaster's car, Munoz came to a major cross street. He asked Walker, "What do you want me to do?"

"I think he's just stopping temporarily. See if you can find a spot to park where we can watch to see if he starts moving again."

Munoz had to double back once, but he found a parking spot almost directly across from the street where they had left Lancaster.

Less than five minutes later, the judge showed up on foot. As he rounded the corner, he glanced up and down the street, and appeared to check out the cars parked close by. He then walked a few more strides and headed down a dead-end side street.

He was gone a few minutes, and when he emerged he had a cell phone in his hand. He appeared to punch in some numbers and then put the phone to his ear. After ten seconds he became very animated, but Walker got the impression from the judge's body language that he was leaving a voice mail, not speaking to anyone directly.

"I wish we had that long distance mike here now," Walker lamented. "That could have been our only chance."

Munoz didn't respond. He just kept watching the judge, who looked back over his shoulder, and then took a few steps back toward the dead-end street. But then he appeared to change his mind and began walking with more purpose in the direction of his car.

Walker asked rhetorically, "I wonder what that was all about."

"I don't know. But it's going to take him a few minutes to get to his car. Why don't we take a look down the dead-end street?"

There was no traffic coming, so Munoz was able to cross both lanes right away. On the right side of the dead end street was a small parking lot. The sign on the chain link fence enclosing it read—For Elite Auto Body Customers Only.

Across from the parking lot was an older brick building housing three garage bays with the doors open. Above the garage doors was another sign—Elite Auto Body, Luxury Cars Are Our Specialty.

Walker said, "An auto body shop? Not exactly on the beaten path, is it?"

"I think there's a front entrance on the main street. This is probably just the access road for the repair area."

Munoz turned the car around, and as they exited the dead-end street and came out to the main drag, he glanced to his left. As he had suspected, there was a front entrance. And above the door was the same Elite Auto Body sign he had seen on the side of the building.

Munoz said to Walker, "So what do you think he was doing here? He didn't even go inside. And why park half a block away?"

"I have no idea. But his car looks brand new. So the only thing I'm certain of is that he didn't come here to get his Mercedes fixed."

Munoz continued past the street where the judge had parked his car, took the next right, went down three more blocks, took another right, and then pulled over. From that vantage point, both he and Walker could see Lancaster just about to get back into his car.

They watched as he did a U-turn and drove past them. Munoz waited a few moments and then fell in behind him as he took the same route in reverse back to the courthouse. Both Walker and Munoz assumed he was heading back to work. But Lancaster drove past the courthouse, got on I-95 for a couple of exits, and ended up at an upscale condo complex five miles outside of the Providence city limits. Although Walker and Munoz hadn't taken particular note of the judge's home address, it seemed obvious that that's where he had gone.

While they were staked out in front of Lancaster's condo, Walker placed a call to the FBI field office. After a couple of transfers, he got to the person he was looking for. "Hi, Peter. It's Craig Walker. Listen, I need you to find out everything you can about Elite Auto Body in Providence, Rhode Island—who owns it, any code violations, any suspected criminal activity—whatever you can find out. And as usual, I need it yesterday." Walker smiled at whatever the person on the other end of the line had said to him.

He was still smiling when he spoke to Munoz. "That was Peter Stansky. He works out of the financial fraud division. We came to the Bureau at the same time; I've known him for over twenty years. He helps me out sometimes, even when it's not related to financial fraud. Let me tell you, I'm glad the guy's on our side. He can find out anything about anybody. I don't know how he does it, but I guess everything in Cyberspace is fair game. Anyway, if there's something going on at Elite Auto Body that's not kosher, he'll find it."

They waited another fifteen minutes, and then decided that watching the outside of the judge's condo building was not going to result in anything productive. And even though it was only a little after four o'clock in the afternoon, it was possible that Lancaster was in for the night. So they headed back to the station house in Stanfield.

Once they were back in Munoz' office, they exchanged ideas and theories about the case. But that's all they were—theories. Neither of them had a strong sense of how anything fit together. And while they had never had qualms about putting in long hours, this phase of the investigation didn't have the urgency that trying to find Eric Allen had posed.

They were about to call it a day around six o'clock when Walker's phone buzzed. He glanced at the screen and saw Peter Stansky's name. "Hey, Peter. That was pretty quick, even for you. I'm going to put you on speaker mode, so the detective I'm working with can hear what you're saying."

Walker touched the screen on his phone, scrolled through a page of apps, found the one he wanted, and a moment later Peter Stansky's voice was clearly audible. "First the easy stuff. There were no violations for Elite Auto Body going back at least ten years, which in and of itself isn't necessarily that strange for an auto body shop. It would appear at first glance that it's a legitimate business. However, somebody's trying to hide something. The ownership is really convoluted. You know, I'm pretty good at this stuff. But everything was buried in trust holdings, dummy partnerships, and shell companies."

"So, no luck at all?" Walker concluded.

"I didn't say that," his friend replied. "It just took me longer than it should have."

Walker smiled again. "I knew you'd come through."

"Thanks for the vote of confidence. But in all honesty, I got lucky. The only reason I found anything is because there was a recent transfer of ownership. I came across a court filing that someone went to a lot of trouble to try to bury. But all those kinds of transfers have to be published somewhere; it's part of the public record. Anyway, the bottom line is that someone by the name of Michael Corwin was the owner of Elite Auto Body until a few months ago, when the ownership was transferred to a Nicholas Runnels.

"Actually, what happened was that this Nicholas Runnels was granted power of attorney for Michael Corwin, and he signed the property over to himself. Once I found out the names, some other things started to fall into place. I'm not done looking, but I figured I'd call and tell you what I had at this point."

Walker chimed in. "So, who are these guys?"

"Michael Corwin is sixty years old, lives in a huge house in Barrington, Rhode Island. I checked it out on Google Earth and a real estate Web site. It's about fifty-two hundred square feet, gated, with a swimming pool and tennis courts. Notice I said courts. So far, I haven't been able to find any other source of income besides the auto body shop. Either repairing automobiles has become substantially more lucrative than I imagined, or he's got to be into something else that I haven't found yet. He's never been convicted of a crime, but that just may mean that he's careful."

"What's his relationship to this Nicholas Runnels?"

Stansky's tone was lively. "Now this gets very interesting. Runnels is Michael Corwin's nephew, although it appears that shortly before the power of attorney was granted, Michael Corwin petitioned to adopt Nicholas Runnels."

"What? How old is this Runnels?"

"He's thirty-five. Adult adoptions are somewhat unusual, but not unheard of. But they can have the same degree of confidentiality that the adoption of a child has. But from what I can see, it doesn't appear that they followed up on the adoption idea."

"What happened to Runnels' real parents?"

"That's what makes this even stranger. Runnels' parents were killed in a car accident when Runnels was five. And get this. Runnels' mother was Corwin's sister. It appears that Corwin raised his nephew after the kid's parents were killed, but never even tried to adopt him until a few months ago. How's that for bizarre?"

Walker looked over at Munoz and shook his head. Munoz did the same. Walker addressed Stansky again. "There isn't anything about this case that's making very much sense right now. Is there anything else about Runnels that you found out?"

"He had a couple of run-ins with the local police as a juvenile, but not serious enough to have a sealed record. As an adult, he had a DUI and was charged with leaving the scene of an accident, but nothing came of either one. I'm sure he's no choirboy. But if he's involved in something illegal, like maybe helping out his uncle Mike, he's gotten away with it. As I said, I'm going to keep digging. Give me your fax number there, and I'll fax all this over to you."

Munoz recited the fax number, and then said, "Do you have an address for Runnels?"

"He's now living in the Barrington house with his uncle," Stansky reported.

Walker spoke up next. "Thanks for everything, Peter." Walker paused. "Can I ask one more favor?"

"Of course, what do you need?"

"See if you can find any kind of a link between a judge by the name of William Lancaster and the two names you just gave us—Corwin and Runnels."

"A judge, huh?" Stansky sounded intrigued.

"Yeah, I think he may be right in the middle of this, but I feel like I'm light years away from figuring out how."

"That's what you've got me for." Stansky paused. "If this judge is dirty, maybe that's why Corwin and Runnels have been able to stay beneath the legal radar."

~

Munoz got in to work shortly before eight o'clock on Tuesday morning. Once inside his office, he opened the case file he had been looking at before he left home. He had made a few notes last night and a few more this morning. He transferred those to the white board on the wall next to his desk. He had just finished when Walker came through the door.

"Something new?" the agent inquired.

"Not really," Munoz said. "I just wanted to make sure that everything we know, or think we know, is up on the board."

"Makes sense. So, do you want to run through it? We've probably got about a half hour before the agents show up with the van and the parabolic mike."

"Have you decided what you're going to do with that?" Munoz asked.

"I think I'm going to have them set up outside the auto body shop. Who knows if the judge will show up there again, but it's the only place we've seen him away from the courthouse or his condo."

They spent the next forty minutes continuing to theorize about the murders of Tony Sarno and Josh Raybeck and how Lancaster, Corwin, and Runnels might be involved.

Munoz had included Cindy Allen's name on the white board. Both he and Walker felt as if Tony Sarno was the one who had killed her, although they had no hard evidence to prove that. They also believed that if what Josh Raybeck had told Jerry Hanson were true, Cindy Allen's death was not directly related to the other two murders, anyway.

As they were wrapping up the mini brainstorming session, Walker's phone buzzed. As he glanced at the screen, he smiled and said to Munoz, "It's Peter Stansky. I don't think the guy ever sleeps." Walker then spoke into the phone. "Well, good morning, Peter. I'm going to put you on speaker again. Should I assume you've got some more information for me?"

"I do, two things actually," Stansky announced.

"Great. What have you got?"

"I found another property transfer—a place called the Regal Hotel and Apartments in Providence. The reason I didn't see it before is that after the initial transfer to Nicholas Runnels, he sold it again, a couple of months ago. The new owner is some big-time developer in the area. I'll include his name when I fax this over to you. The guy paid nearly two million for the property."

While Stansky was speaking, Munoz went back behind his desk and opened up the case file. He started thumbing through it as Stansky continued. "The second thing I found was a connection between two of the names you gave me—William Lancaster and Michael Corwin. It's from fifteen years ago. There's a picture of Lancaster and Corwin together at a charity event. They were being honored for their financial support of a foster children's program. The article that went along with the picture indicated that they were both foster kids. I took it one step

234

further and found out that they graduated together from the same high school. There's a good chance that they've known each other for over forty years."

"That's great work, Peter."

"I love the Internet," Stansky quipped.

Walker laughed. "When you get results like that, so do I. Listen, don't go crazy looking, but if you come across anything else, give me a call."

"Will do."

"Thanks again; this was really helpful."

Walker turned the phone off and looked toward Munoz. "Well, we've got our connection."

Munoz continued to flip pages in the case file. "And maybe something else."

"What are you doing?" Walker asked.

"The first thing Peter said, about the property… give me a second …" the detective absently replied.

Half a minute later Munoz tapped his finger on one of the pages in the file. "Here it is."

Walker moved around behind the desk to join Munoz. "What?"

"The Regal Hotel that was sold—that's where Tony Sarno was arrested."

Walker read silently from the case file page outlining the information about Tony Sarno. "We're getting into that 'too many coincidences mode' again."

"I agree. I was thinking that I'd like to give Jerry Hanson a call and feed him all this information. He might be in a better position to figure out how this ties together."

"Okay, good idea. I'm going to get Peter's fax."

Munoz was able to reach Jerry immediately, but he indicated that he was about to go into court in Providence. Munoz gave him the quick version of what he and Walker had just found out, and Jerry confirmed that Tony Sarno was arrested at the Regal.

"I'm probably going to be tied up until about noon, but I'll swing by my office, pick up my notes, and come to Stanfield after that," the attorney proposed.

Munoz took him up on the offer.

A few minutes later, Munoz was sharing that information with Walker when the two agents who had brought the parabolic mike showed up. After introductions, Walker gave them the address for Elite Auto Body. "I think your best bet is to park on the street. There is a parking lot around the corner, but you'd be too conspicuous there. The main street is probably the way to go, although I have my doubts he's going to show up, especially this early in the day. You're equipped to get video as well, right?"

The older of the agents replied. "Usually, unless there's some sort of obstruction."

"Okay, good luck. Keep me posted."

After the agents left, Munoz wrote some additional notes on the white board, and then said, "I hate to just sit around here and wait, but I'm not sure we have much choice."

"We could take a ride over to the Regal, maybe ask a few questions. It's better than sitting here. Why don't we do that?"

When they arrived, it was obvious that the Regal was not open for business, and wouldn't be again. It was being prepped for demolition. Walker asked around and was directed to a foreman, who seemed surprised when he saw Walker's badge.

Walker tried to put him at ease. "This has nothing to do with the demolition. We're investigating something that happened months ago, before the hotel was sold."

The foreman seemed relieved. "I wouldn't know anything about that."

"Is there anybody here who might?" Walker asked.

"I don't think so. These guys are all my crew. We were hired to tear the place down. There's a developer coming in—as my boss told me—'to gentrify the area.' " The foreman raised his eyebrows.

Walker offered a small smile in response, as the foreman continued. "I guess you could try Lucky's. I was told it's been here for years. Maybe somebody in there might know something. You better hurry, though. As you can see, it's part of the building we're tearing down. It'll be rubble by Friday."

Walker looked over. It was still fairly early in the day, and the bar was closed. As they headed back to the car, Walker said, "That was a bust. Although I'm not sure what I expected to find, anyway."

For a few minutes they rode in silence. Then it was interrupted by a ringtone. Walker recognized it as his, and fished the phone out of his pocket. As he looked at the screen, he said, "That's a surprise." He pushed a button, and then said, "This is Walker … You're kidding. All right, send it to me as soon as you can."

Walker closed his phone and spoke to Munoz. "That was one of the agents at the auto body shop. They've got something—video and audio. I should have it any minute."

As soon as he and Munoz were back in Munoz' office, Walker opened up the account that contained the newly sent transmission from the agents. Munoz, who was standing behind him, moved in closer to get a better look.

A man who appeared to be in his mid-thirties came out of the front door of Elite Auto Body. His face wasn't easily seen because he wasn't facing the cameras in the van, and the video lacked some clarity because of the distance. But that was not true of the audio.

The ringing of a phone could be easily heard as the man on the screen reached into his pocket, pulled it out, and said, "Hi, it's Runner. What's going on?" There was a fairly long silence, and then the man spoke again. "What? Let me talk to him." Another twenty seconds passed, and then, "Hi, Uncle Mike. Remember I told you I'd be gone for a while? … Okay… All right, soon. Good bye." With that the man appeared to shake his head as he returned the phone to his pocket, got into a silver SUV parked at the curb, and left.

Walker played the piece twice more before he asked Munoz, "What did you get from that?"

"I'd say that was Nicholas Runnels, although it seemed like he said 'Runner' not 'Runnels.' "

"That's what I heard too. Could be a nickname. It also sounded like he was talking to his uncle. We have to assume that's Michael Corwin. Although I don't think he was talking to him at the beginning. At the beginning, it sounded like he was talking to somebody else."

"That's what I thought." Munoz paused. "Did the last part of the conversation seem strange to you?"

"Yeah, almost like he was talking to a child—'Remember, I told you.' "

Munoz nodded in agreement. "Exactly."

Another thought about what he had just heard entered Walker's brain, but before he could articulate it, the phone on Munoz desk rang. "Detective Munoz... Hi, Jerry. I'm going to put you on speaker."

A moment passed, and then Jerry Hanson said, "We just got a short recess from the trial. I've only got a few minutes. I should be done between noon and twelve thirty. I can be out to Stanfield around one."

Munoz answered, "That's fine."

"Also, I ran into Maria. She's stuck in court, but she asked me to call and let you know that there's a prostitute that's been in lockup for the past few days. She had a bunch of priors, and the judge decided to make an example of her. Anyway, evidently she just found out about Tony Sarno being killed. The prostitute told her public defender that she knew Tony Sarno very well, and that she has some information that she wants to trade for a lighter sentence. Maria wasn't sure there was anything to it, but she asked me to call and let you know. Maria won't be able to check it out until this afternoon."

Walker was skeptical, but felt like there was nothing to lose. "I think we'll take a ride and talk to her. Where's she being held?"

"In East Providence, for the time being. Maria called and let them know that you might be showing up, just in case."

"That's great, thanks."

Shortly after Walker and Munoz arrived at the East Providence jail, they were shown into a conference room. Less than five minutes later, one of the guards ushered in a woman who appeared to be part Caucasian and part Asian. According to the arrest report, her name was Ming Choi, age thirty-three, although she looked closer to forty. As she sat down opposite Walker and Munoz, Ming said, "My public defender can't be here until this afternoon. Can I still make a deal with you guys?"

Walker said, "We can work something out, if you have information we can use." A pause. "This is Detective Munoz, and I'm Agent Walker."

"I'm Ming." She looked more intently at Walker. "Did you say Agent Walker?"

Walker nodded. "Yes, I'm with the FBI."

"The FBI? Why does the FBI care about Tony Sarno? If this is an important case, does that mean I can get the charges dropped?"

"We need to hear what you have to say before we can discuss anything like that," Walker replied. "Tell us how you knew Tony Sarno."

Ming hesitated, not totally convinced that she was doing herself any favors. Finally, she said, "He was a customer. But not when I was at the Regal; after that."

Walker looked over at Munoz, before looking back at Ming. "Tell us about the Regal."

Ming's face brightened. "That was one sweet deal. I think Big Mike Corwin was the one who set that up. He had the apartments done up real nice, and brought in big guys from out of state—well, rich guys—trust me, they weren't always big." Ming laughed at her own joke. "Some of the girls said Big Mike was around a lot in the beginning, but I only saw him once; Runner pretty much ran things."

Another look passed between Walker and Munoz, as Ming continued. "I never liked Runner. He was the one who made me leave the Regal—me and two other girls."

Munoz spoke for the first time. "What does this have to do with Tony Sarno?"

"Like I said, Tony was a customer, but not at the Regal. I don't think Runner would allow it, and Runner was like Tony's boss. Tony complained about him all the time, and he said that Runner wasn't his real boss. But I think he was."

Munoz again, "So, there's no doubt that this Runner and Tony Sarno knew each other."

Ming got a strange look on her face. "Yeah, of course."

"Do you know Runner's real name?" Munoz pressed.

She shook her head. "No, he was just Runner."

"Did you see Runner and Tony Sarno together a lot?"

"No, especially after Tony started in with that other shit."

"What other … shit?"

"The pictures."

"Tell us about that."

For the first time, Ming appeared uncomfortable. "Some of the girls have little kids. Tony would take them for a couple of hours, and someone would take pictures of them, you know, without their clothes on." Ming shook her head, obviously disgusted. "Hey, I know. I spread my legs for a living; I've got no right to judge. But getting off by looking at pictures of little kids … that's just plain sick."

Walker asked, "How do you know all this?"

"The girls told me," she said. "They got paid each time their kids were used."

"Do you have their names?"

She shook her head firmly. "I may not have liked what they did – letting someone take those pictures of their kids. But I'm not going to get them in trouble. Plus, I heard it stopped after Tony was arrested. I was out of the Regal by then. I did hear that it might have started up again. But that might have been with different kids."

"Just give us the names, and we'll figure it out," Walker said.

"If I give you those names, I want all the charges dropped," she demanded.

Walker hesitated a moment, but mainly for show. "I think we can arrange that. But only if everything you've told us is the truth, including the names."

Ming sat back in her chair. "It's all true. I'm a lot of things, but a liar's not one of them."

CHAPTER TWENTY-SIX

I n the car, driving back to the station house, Walker called in the names Ming had given them, and then he and Munoz tried to piece together the new information.

Munoz observed, "Everything she said fits with what Josh Raybeck claimed Tony Sarno told him."

"It seems like it," Walker agreed. "Plus, we now have a link between Tony Sarno and this Runner. And that's the same name we heard on the tape earlier. That's got to be Nicholas Runnels, right? Also, she mentioned Michael Corwin. That's Runnels' uncle."

"The only thing she didn't help us with was Lancaster. We still don't have anything substantial to tie him to any of this."

"Not yet, no."

But that was about to change.

Once they were back at the police station, Munoz added some notes about the new information they had received from Ming to the white board. Shortly after that was completed, Walker's phone alerted him to the fact that he had a text message.

He read it, and then said to Munoz, "It's from the agents outside the body shop. They're sending me something else. Let's take a look."

They both went behind the desk to view the video on Munoz' computer screen; Walker opened up his FBI account and some frozen images appeared. He clicked the play function and the video began.

A man, whom they both recognized as Judge Lancaster, could be seen coming around the corner and heading toward Elite Auto Body. He then started moving toward another man, whom they were able to identify from the earlier video as Nicholas Runnels—Runner. Runner was about to get into the same silver SUV that they had seen him enter in the other video.

Lancaster appeared to speak first. "Where the hell are the pictures, and where's Richie?"

Runner said, "I told you, there are no pictures. And how the hell should I know where Richie is?"

"Because I know you went to see him after … things were taken care of, and now he's gone missing. I called his brother; he hasn't seen him, either."

"Well, I don't keep tabs on Richie. He's your flunky."

There was a brief silence, and then Lancaster said, "I want those pictures. And I want to talk to Big Mike; it's been months. I swear, Runner, if you're holding out on me … I don't care if he is your uncle; he'll back me up on this."

It appeared that the man Lancaster had called Runner was about to come around the car, as he took a few steps in that direction, but then he stopped. "For the last time, there are no pictures. And my uncle doesn't want to talk to you. And if you think he'd back you over me, you're a bigger idiot than I thought. You're the reason we're in this mess. You shouldn't have come here. I told you to let things die down."

"What was I supposed to do?" Lancaster fumed. "You won't answer my phone calls."

"There's a good reason for that. I didn't want to hear your pathetic voice."

"I'm going to the house to see Big Mike. I don't care what you say. This is bullshit."

"Don't you go anywhere near that house. And don't come here again. Go back to your … fucking courtroom and pretend to be a judge. If I need to talk to you, I'll call. But I wouldn't sit by the phone waiting; it could be a long time."

With that, Nicholas Runnels, aka Runner, got into his SUV and drove off.

Walker played the video once more without commenting. As he and Munoz were about to start a discussion, Jerry Hanson arrived. Walker asked him to wait outside for a moment. Then he said to Munoz, "It's not exactly by the book, but I'm inclined to let him see what we've got."

"I agree," Munoz answered. "He's already been a huge help. And what can it hurt? There's no question we can trust the guy."

Jerry was invited back into the office. They told him about their conversation with Ming and showed him the two video clips. He recognized Judge Lancaster immediately, but had no idea who Runner was. As Jerry started to refer to his notes, he asked, "Who's Big Mike, and who's Richie?"

Walker explained who Big Mike was, and his relationship to Runner and Lancaster. "But we have no idea who this Richie is. We were hoping that maybe you could tell us."

The attorney shook his head. "Sorry, I've never heard that name before connected to any of this."

"That's okay."

"Is there some other way I can help?" Jerry offered.

Walker responded. "Can you confirm some of the things that the prostitute told us?"

"A lot of it's the same as what Josh told me."

"Like what, for example?"

"Like the little kids being taken by Tony to be photographed," Jerry elaborated.

"Anything else?"

"Let me check my notes again, to refresh my memory."

"What might also help is for you to try to connect the people you just heard about with the people in the story Josh Raybeck told you," Walker suggested.

"All right. I can do that."

Walker excused himself to see how the attempt to locate the other prostitutes Ming had identified was going. Unfortunately however, every inquiry thus far had resulted in the same response—moved, no forwarding address.

When Walker returned, he and Munoz gently pushed and prodded Jerry into making as many connections as possible. After nearly an hour, a number of reasonable theories emerged.—Runner was most likely the "Gunner" Josh had heard Tony mention, and he was probably Tony's immediate contact.

It also seemed reasonable to assume that since most of this initially took place at the Regal, and Michael Corwin owned it at that time, he was probably Big Mike, and also the big boss that Tony had spoken of.

And although they were generally pleased with how far they'd come, Walker pointed out that, even if all their speculation were true, it still left Judge Lancaster's role undefined.

Jerry thought out loud. "On the video, Lancaster asks about the pictures. And we know that there are pictures missing from Tony Sarno's trial folder. Could that be the connection? Could he be the one who wanted the pictures taken?"

Munoz answered. "I think it's possible that Lancaster took the photos out of the trial folder. And it's also possible that he was the one who ordered the other pictures to be taken. But we don't know why, and we can't prove any of it. At least with some of the other stuff, we've got people who can testify as to what they saw, assuming they're willing to. But none of that gets us any closer to solving the murders. We still have no idea why Tony Sarno and Josh Raybeck were killed."

Several minutes passed in silence, and then Walker said, "I'm somewhat out of my element here, but as they say on the cop shows on TV—follow the money." He addressed Jerry. "Didn't Josh Raybeck say that Tony told him the photos were being put up on a child pornography Web site? So who was getting rich off of that?"

Jerry was about to respond when Munoz jumped in. "If I had to guess, I'd say that was Michael Corwin. He's obviously got a lot of money, and no discernible income stream. To take it one step further, if somehow Tony and Josh threatened that money source, that'd be a pretty strong motive to get rid of them. Of course, he'd have to come up with a new middleman and a new photographer. But that might have been the least of his concerns."

Walker responded. "I think what you're saying makes sense. But again, that doesn't really explain Lancaster's involvement."

Jerry offered a comment. "You said that Michael Corwin and Judge Lancaster have known each other since they were kids. Could Corwin have asked Lancaster to fix Tony's case so Tony could go back to work for him?"

Walker nodded. "That's certainly possible. But if that's all it was, why is Lancaster continuing to confront this Runner character? And why is he still asking about pictures?" Walker paused. "Unless it's personal, and not about the money."

No one spoke for nearly a minute, and then Walker said, "Jerry, we really appreciate you coming in; you've been a great help. I think Detective Munoz and I are going to take a little ride. We'll be in touch, okay? And give us a call if you think of anything else."

Jerry wanted to ask what was going to happen next, but he recognized that it wasn't his place. "Sure. No problem."

Once Jerry left, Munoz asked, "So what are you thinking?"

"There's no way to know for sure, but at least from the money angle, it seems more likely that Corwin and his nephew are at the center of this, rather than the judge. I think we need to put some pressure on them. They both live in the same house. Let's go pay them a visit. Maybe we'll get lucky and they'll both be home."

"You really think there's any way that they'll talk to us?" the detective wondered.

"Probably not, but there's only one way to find out."

The trip to Barrington took twenty-five minutes. The house that Michael Corwin and his nephew shared was much more impressive up close than the picture Walker had viewed on Google Earth. There was an ornamental gate in front of the house, but it was open, so they just drove straight in, up the quarter-mile driveway.

Fifteen seconds after Walker rang the bell, a tall man wearing khaki slacks, a blazer, and a buttoned-down shirt opened the door. "Did you forget your key ..." he broke off. "Who the hell are you?"

Walker answered, "We'd like to speak with Michael Corwin and Nicholas Runnels."

The man's expression was cold. "That doesn't answer my question. Who the hell are you?"

Walker took out his badge, and Munoz did the same. "I'm Special Agent Walker, and this is Detective Munoz."

The man was momentarily surprised, but recovered quickly. "I'm not sure whether they're here or not, but I am sure that neither one of them wants to talk to you."

Before Walker could respond, a voice came from inside the house. "Who is it, Frankie? Is Runner back?"

The man who had opened the door closed it slightly and turned toward the inside of the house. "No, it's not Runner."

"Well, who is it then?" the unseen man inquired.

"Just some people looking for Runner. They're about to leave."

The voice continued to move closer. "Are they friends of his? Why don't you let them in?"

"I don't think that's a good idea, Big Mike."

The man behind the voice finally arrived at the door, and opened it wider. Big Mike had earned his nickname honestly. He was at least six foot four and weighed in at about two hundred and sixty pounds. "You want to talk to Runner?"

Walker wasn't sure exactly what was happening, so he kept it simple. "Yes."

"I'm his uncle, Mike Corwin, or Big Mike, as they call me. Are you friends of Runner's?"

"We just want to talk to him about something," Walker said.

"Well, he's not here. But maybe I can help." Corwin headed back into the house. "Come on in."

The man whom Corwin had called Frankie stepped in front of Walker and Munoz before they could enter, and called over his shoulder. "Runner's not going to like this, Big Mike. Why don't you wait until he gets home?"

"It's all right, Frankie. It'll be fine."

Walker and Munoz exchanged looks, neither of them having any clue as to what was going on. As they moved to follow Corwin inside, Frankie took out his phone and placed a call, presumably to Runner. As he was waiting for the call to connect, he spoke to Walker and Munoz. "You shouldn't be here. You should leave."

Walker spoke quietly. "We were invited in; we're staying."

Corwin led them into a large living room where he suggested that they take a seat. Walker wasn't sure how much time they had; he was confident that once Runner showed up, they'd be kicked out. Even so, he felt as if he had to ease into things. "This is a beautiful house, Mr. Corwin."

"Thanks. But please call me Mike or Big Mike."

"Okay, Mike," Walker corrected himself.

"What did you want to talk to Runner about?"

Walker decided not to waste another second. "He was having an argument with Judge Lancaster earlier today. We were wondering if everything was … all right."

Corwin perked up. "You know Billy? We grew up together. I never got used to calling him judge." Corwin didn't say anything for a moment, and got a confused expression on his face. And then he said, "So what did you want to talk to Runner about?"

"About an argument he had with … Billy."

Corwin appeared to be lucid again. "It was probably about Billy's pictures."

Walker didn't even take the time to look at Munoz. "What about them?"

The old man reflected. "Billy never used to be like that, wanting to look at that stuff."

Walker had to prompt Corwin again. "When did that start?"

"A couple of years ago. You can make a lot of money, but I still don't think it's right. But I grew up with Billy; we were foster kids together, my sister, too. Billy's like a brother to me. Other than Runner, he's the only family I've got."

Walker probed some more. "So what exactly was Billy doing that you didn't like?"

"Having those pictures taken. I went along with it because it was Billy. But Runner said we should stop. He never liked it. And then all that stuff with Tony Sarno made it worse."

Walker was about to follow up when Runner burst into the room. "Get the hell out of this house!" Then he turned and spoke more calmly. "Uncle Mike, don't say another word."

Walker and Munoz stood up, but didn't make any effort to leave. Walker said, "Your uncle invited us in."

"I don't care," retorted Runner. "I want you out of here right now."

Walker decided not to escalate the situation any further and headed for the front door.

Runner followed behind them. "I don't know what he told you, but you won't be able to use any of it."

Walker maintained his cool. "I'm not sure that's true. I think it's probably enough to get us a search warrant."

Runner seemed less sure of himself when he spoke. "You won't find anything."

Walker stopped just before he reached the front door and turned to face Runner. "We'll see. But your uncle's not the only source we have, you know." Walker paused. "Were you telling Lancaster the truth earlier today when you said there were no pictures? Just curious."

Runner didn't respond, but it was obvious from his body language that Walker's comments had shaken him.

Walker and Munoz didn't say a word to each other as they got in the unmarked car and exited the property. Munoz found a small strip mall close by, parked, and turned to Walker. "What the hell do you make of that?"

"Which part?" the agent asked.

"Pretty much all of it."

"Yeah," Walker said. "I certainly didn't expect what happened. Obviously, Michael Corwin's got some mental health issues. When Peter Stansky told us about Corwin petitioning to adopt his nephew, and also that the nephew had been granted power of attorney, I wondered if something like this might be going on. But then I figured it was all some legal maneuver to shield money. Of course, that may still be part of it, but I've got to believe that's the least of the nephew's problems right now."

"How much of what Corwin said do you think we can use?"

"Probably not much, at least directly," Walker calculated. "Even if everything he told us is true, it's not as if we can call him as a witness. There'd be no telling what you'd get. And I don't think it's worth trying to get a formal statement; the nephew would just block it. But at least it appears we've got some confirmation on the judge's dirty little secret. And it looks like his involvement is probably less about money and more about his personal gratification. Although at this point, we can't prove either one. I wish Lancaster had been more explicit when he asked Runner about the existence of the pictures."

""Speaking of that, I was wondering why you let Runner know that we knew about the conversation he had with Lancaster."

"I wish I could tell you that it was part of some master plan I had, but the truth is, the guy was really starting to piss me off. There's an arrogance about him that I was having trouble stomaching. Usually, I don't lose it like that. But you know, as I think about it, it was probably a good thing. He's got to wonder whether we've talked to Lancaster, or whether Lancaster was wearing a wire, or even whether we're recording all of his conversations. Any one of those scenarios has to make him nervous as hell. You saw what he looked like after I repeated the question Lancaster had asked him."

"So what do you want to do now?"

"Let's go back to the station house," Walker suggested. "Let Runner stew for a while. He doesn't know what his uncle told us, and he might think that Lancaster's cooperating with us. That could send him into a bit of a panic. People in that situation often make mistakes. The other thing I want to do is to see if we have enough to get a search warrant for the house we just left, as well as Lancaster's condo."

Runner watched Walker and Munoz drive away. He then went into the living room to see his uncle. Runner hid any anger or anxiety he was feeling when he spoke. "I'm going to stay home for a while, Uncle Mike. Why don't you go upstairs and take a nap or something?"

"Okay, Runner. Were those guys friends of yours? Because I heard yelling."

Runner kept his tone light. "We were just kidding around; nothing to concern yourself with." Runner called out. "Frankie, come and take Big Mike upstairs, will you?"

A few minutes later, Runner was sitting by himself in the living room, thinking. He had already taken some preliminary steps to protect his uncle, but there was no way he could have anticipated what the last few days had brought, never mind the last few minutes. *And now they know about the conversation I had with the judge. But how? And what else do they know? There's no way of telling*, he thought.

He tried to figure out what he should do next. He wasn't worried about them getting a search warrant; they wouldn't find anything, at least not at the house or at the body shop. But the judge's condo might be a different story.

Runner slammed his fist on the coffee table in front of him. "Shit!"

It took a full two minutes for his anger to subside to the point where he could think straight. And then an idea began to form. It started slowly, began to accelerate, and then within a few minutes took on a life of its own. Runner knew he'd have to get busy; he had a lot to do. But he also knew that this was probably his best shot.

Walker and Munoz had spent the better part of two hours discussing strategy, search warrants, and theories. Finally, they decided it was time to call the federal judge and ask him for a preliminary sense of whether he would approve the search warrants, given the new information that they had uncovered. They both knew that judges didn't usually like to offer an opinion on something over the phone, even something preliminary; they wanted to have it in their hands. But Walker thought it was worth a try. "It's better than spending an hour or more on something that has no prayer of being approved."

Walker looked at his watch; it read 3:45. He was about to reach over Munoz' desk to use the phone, when it rang. He pulled his hand back, as Munoz picked up the receiver. "Detective Munoz ... Yeah, he's right here. It's for you."

Munoz handed the phone to Walker, who listened for a moment, and then said, "Speaking."

Another full minute went by before Walker said anything else, and then, "If this is about our visit to see Michael Corwin, save it." Walker continued to listen, raised his eyebrows a few times, and finally said, "When? ... All right, we'll see you then."

Walker returned the receiver to its cradle, and spoke to Munoz. "You're not going to believe this. That was a lawyer representing Nicholas Runnels—Runner. He's bringing his client in. He says he has some information we might be interested in."

CHAPTER TWENTY-SEVEN

Martin Tedesco, Esquire, arrived at the Stanfield police station at five o'clock. Anyone observing him walking in would have easily surmised that he was a lawyer. He was right out of central casting—early fifties, six feet tall, graying at the temples, and wearing a $1,500 suit.

But his client was nowhere in sight.

After introductions outside of Munoz' office, Walker asked, "Where's your client?"

"He'll be along shortly," Tedesco explained. "He wanted me to come in first and lay the groundwork."

"For what?"

"Hopefully, something beneficial to both parties," the attorney replied.

"You're going to have to be more specific than that," Walker retorted.

"I intend to be," Tedesco paused. "Is there someplace more private that we can talk?"

Munoz responded. "We can use the conference room. Follow me."

When they were seated, Tedesco said, "I assume that there are no recording devices in this room."

"None that are turned on," said Munoz.

Tedesco smiled. "Sorry, Detective. I'm just naturally suspicious." Munoz didn't say anything. Tedesco continued. "Although, depending on how things go, we may actually request that the proceedings be recorded, in order to protect both parties' interests."

Walker glanced over at Munoz, and then said, "We certainly appreciate your concern for our interests, Mr. Tedesco. But what is it that you wanted to discuss?"

Tedesco seemed to gather himself like some movie actor about to deliver a critical piece of dialogue. "My client, Mr. Runnels, has information that would be extremely helpful to your investigation."

"You do realize that Mr. Runnels is one of the subjects of our investigation?"

"I understand that. But he's really not the one you're after, is he?" Walker didn't answer. Tedesco continued. "If he is, then your investigation is way off track."

Walker leaned forward. "Well, by all means, enlighten us."

"Mr. Runnels can do that, but he's going to need some things in return," the lawyer declared.

"Such as?"

"Let me backtrack for a moment. You saw my client's uncle earlier today. Obviously, Mr. Corwin is not in good health; he's suffering from a neurological disorder. In the spirit of candor, I can tell you that it's a rare condition related to Alzheimer's. As you no doubt witnessed, the affliction renders the person unable to ... filter ... what they're saying. They're unable to competently assess the appropriateness of their comments, especially in terms of who they're speaking with."

"Are you suggesting that Mr. Corwin didn't know what he was saying when he spoke to us?"

Tedesco shrugged. "I don't know. He may have, or he may not have."

"That's a convenient answer," Walker interjected.

"It may appear that way, but it happens to be the truth. Mr. Corwin's neurologist would tell you the same thing."

"So, your client would give us permission to talk to him?"

"He might. But I doubt that will be necessary. I can tell you that Mr. Corwin's problems started seven or eight months ago. My client took him to the best doctors in Boston, and they came up with a diagnosis of this Alzheimer's-like illness. I can't recall the specific name. Just like Alzheimer's, there's no cure. But there are ways to hold off the progression, and more importantly, Mr. Corwin has been accepted into a clinical trial in New York for an experimental drug that has the potential to reverse the symptoms."

Walker was getting impatient. "With all due respect, counselor, what does this have to do with our investigation, other than to suggest that we should ignore everything Mr. Corwin told us because he's sick?"

Tedesco waited a moment, and then said, "That's the price for my client's information."

"What's the price?" Walker demanded.

"You drop any investigation involving Michael Corwin for past or present criminal activity."

Walker sat back in his chair and stared at Tedesco. "You're kidding, right? For all we know, he may have ordered at least two murders. And he was, or still is, very likely involved in an enterprise that makes its profits from child pornography. And we're just supposed to look the other way?"

"He didn't kill anybody. He didn't order anybody to be killed. And he's not behind any child pornography business."

"And we just take your word for that?"

"No, of course not. My client has some information concerning the murders you're investigating, and he's willing to tell you everything he knows." Tedesco leaned forward. "And he can serve up Judge Lancaster to you on a silver platter."

"What exactly does that mean?"

Tedesco said cooly, "For that, you'll have to talk directly to my client. He didn't share all the details with me."

"So, in exchange for this information, he wants immunity for his uncle."

"Technically, it's not immunity," the lawyer corrected him. "It would only be immunity if Mr. Corwin were in line to be charged with something. My client doesn't want it to get that far. As I said, he wants your assurance that there won't even be an investigation."

"And what does your client want for himself?" Walker asked.

"Nothing, as far as I know. But you'll have to ask him."

"Well, where is he?" Walker asked. "We're not going to even give this a second glance unless there's something substantial in what he has to offer."

The attorney looked at his watch. "I understand. He should be here any minute."

Walker didn't say anything for a few moments, and then,

"Detective Munoz and I are going to leave you alone to wait for your client. We'll be back when he shows up."

As soon as they returned to his office, Munoz asked, "What do you think?"

"I think we may have scared him a little. My gut is telling me that everything we've heard so far, and everything we're going to hear from this Runner character is designed to protect the uncle."

"I agree. But isn't it also possible that there's some truth to it?"

"I don't doubt that the uncle is sick. But if he really is scheduled to be part of that clinical trial, that's all the more reason for the nephew to lie. He wouldn't want anything interfering with that." Walker paused. "The part about Judge Lancaster is pretty intriguing, though. I wonder if the nephew has hard evidence, or is just willing to testify against him. That could make a big difference as to how this plays out. I'm curious, but the nephew's going to have to give us a hell of a lot more before I'd be willing to give him what he wants."

"What do you make of the fact that he's not asking for anything for himself?" Munoz asked.

"It'll be interesting to see if that continues. Of course, on the other hand, it could simply be his arrogance coming through. You know—'I'm better and smarter than you guys, so I don't need to make a deal.' We already saw a glimpse of that attitude at the house."

They remained quiet for a brief time, each lost in his own thoughts. Several more minutes went by, and then a uniformed cop came back to Munoz' office, followed by another man.

Munoz was glancing at the open file on his desk and didn't notice them initially. When the detective finally did look up and saw who it was, he said to the officer, "We're in the conference room; bring Mr. Runnels back there."

Runner didn't say anything, but as he turned around, he happened to notice the white board in Munoz' office. He stared at it for a few seconds, smiled to himself, and then followed the officer to the conference room.

Runner and Tedesco were seated when Walker and Munoz entered. Tedesco made the formal introductions. Nobody offered to shake hands. Walker thought that Runner looked calmer than when he and Munoz had last seen him—but not much.

Tedesco opened up the discussion by asking, "Would you like me to recap where we are?"

"I don't think that's necessary," said Walker. "It's pretty clear. Mr. Runnels doesn't want us investigating his uncle. But I guess I have to ask, why is that, Mr. Runnels? Are you afraid of what we might find out?"

Runner visibly bristled, but held himself together. "He's sick. He doesn't need to be hassled right now."

Walker pressed him further. "And it has nothing to do with what he might have told us, or what a search of your house might turn up?"

"No, it doesn't. But if you make us stick around here, he'll miss his treatment, and they'd probably kick him out of the study."

Walker changed gears. "Why did you seek power of attorney?"

Again, Runner bristled. "What does that have to do with anything?"

"I was under the impression that you were willing to answer all our questions in exchange for dropping our investigation," Walker declared.

"Only the questions having to do with the murders and Judge Lancaster."

"What do you have on him that we would be interested in?" the agent inquired.

Runner shook his head. "No. I'm saving that for the end. Even if you don't believe anything else I tell you, you'll believe that."

"Is there any reason why we wouldn't believe you?" countered Walker.

Runner made a smirk. "Other than because you're cops?" Tedesco put his hand on his client's arm and shook his head.

Walker ignored Runner's comment. "So, where do we begin, then?"

The smirk returned to Runner's face. "How about Cindy Allen's murder? That was the first thing listed on your little board, wasn't it?"

Munoz thought Walker was about to lose his cool, so he jumped in. "Do you know who did it?"

"Tony Sarno."

"How do you know that?" Munoz asked.

"I figured it out" Runner said smugly.

"How?"

"A couple of weeks after she was killed, he brought his car in to Elite to have the front end fixed. I put two and two together."

"He never told you he did it?" Munoz asked.

"It's not something he would have shared with me. We weren't that close."

Walker stepped in. "That's not what we heard. We heard that you were his boss at the Regal."

"You heard wrong."

"So then how did you know him?" the agent wanted to know.

"He worked at Elite for a while."

"You never saw him outside of the body shop?"

Runner shrugged. "I guess it's possible. I don't remember."

"We have a number of people who saw the two of you together at the Regal," Walker informed him.

"So what?"

"It was pretty well known that there were prostitutes working out of there, and your uncle owned it. The same people who saw you and Tony Sarno together indicated that both of you were working for your uncle."

Runner responded, "I can't control what other people think. And as far as the Regal is concerned, I'm sure you know that my uncle no longer owns it. I think it's possible that he found out about the prostitution and whatever else was going on there, and decided he didn't want any part of it."

"Would the 'whatever else' include taking pornographic pictures of little kids?"

Runner stared directly at Walker. "I guess it could. But as I said, my uncle doesn't own the Regal anymore."

Walker heard Runner's hidden message loud and clear—*Whatever my uncle was involved in, he isn't anymore. And you can't prove it anyway, so leave him alone.*

Walker didn't like it, but he realized that he might have to do just that. Still, he had trouble dropping it. "So, we're supposed to believe that neither you nor Tony Sarno knew anything about the pictures that were being taken." Walker waited a moment, and then added, "That's not what your uncle indicated."

At the mention of his uncle, and what he might have said to Walker, Runner's body tensed. It looked as if he had to hold himself back from speaking right away. Eventually, he said, "My uncle may have been confused. Although he did know that Tony was arrested for something like that, so maybe that was what he was thinking of."

Walker wanted to follow up about Tony Sarno's arrest and trial, but decided to wait. Instead he asked, "Why did Tony Sarno kidnap Eric Allen?"

Runner was obviously surprised by the question. "I thought you already solved that case. Well, partially solved it, at least."

"You didn't answer my question."

"How should I know?" retorted Runner.

"We believe it's related to why Tony Sarno was killed."

Runner became visibly angry. "Tony was killed because ..." Runner caught himself. "He was probably killed because he started doing things he wasn't supposed to be doing."

"And how would you know that?"

"Just a guess."

"What would you guess were the things he wasn't supposed to be doing—abducting a child and taking pornographic pictures of him?"

"That's possible," Runner conceded.

Walker decided to try to rattle Runner some more. "Is that why you killed him?"

Runner didn't take the bait. "I don't know what you're talking about."

"Of course you don't."

Runner was quiet for a moment, and then offered, "You know, hypothetically, if someone wanted to scare Tony, but wasn't aware that Tony had a gun, it could easily have been self-defense. But I read in the paper that there were no witnesses and no surveillance video, so I guess we'll never know."

"People who kill other people in self-defense don't usually try to cover up what happened," Walker pointed out.

"Evidently, sometimes they do." Runner couldn't help himself, as he added, "Even if they can't come forward, sometimes people try to do the right thing. Didn't you get a call on the hotline telling you where the boy was? I know it turned out not to be correct. But it was the thought that counts, don't you think? I listen to my police scanner all the time."

Walker stood up. "Let's take a break."

Munoz got up also, and followed Walker out of the conference room. They headed for Munoz' office. As soon as they were seated, Walker said, "Jesus, he's infuriating. But he's covered himself well. He all but admitted that he killed Tony Sarno. And I'm not buying that self-defense bullshit. I think he killed him because of exactly what he said— Tony Sarno had started doing things he wasn't supposed to. But there's no way to link Runnels or his uncle to any of it."

"What about the phone call? That information wasn't released to the public, and I don't think it was on the scanner."

"I think you're probably right. But what are we going to arrest him for—giving us the incorrect location of an abducted child? That's not a crime." Walker paused. "When we go back inside, I'm going to try to move it along to find out what he's got on the judge. That's the most important thing, as far as I'm concerned. But you jump in whenever you want."

"It's okay. I'll just follow your lead."

Once they returned to the conference room, Walker decided to ask one more question before moving on to Lancaster. "Do you know who killed Josh Raybeck?"

Runner nodded. "I think so."

Walker leaned forward. "Who?"

"Richie Cardarelli."

"Who's he?" the agent asked.

"He works for Lancaster."

"Doing what?"

Runner evaded. "Odds and ends."

"What does that mean?"

"It means that he's not employed by Lancaster in his capacity as a judge. It's more for personal services."

"Where can we find this Cardarelli?"

"I heard that he disappeared."

At that moment, Walker remembered something from the recording he and Munoz had watched earlier. "Is that the same Richie the judge asked you about during your conversation?"

Runner didn't answer immediately. He knew that he had to be careful. This was rapidly becoming a cat and mouse game, and he had no intention of becoming the mouse. He had come to the conclusion that the FBI had probably recorded his conversation with Lancaster somehow. He didn't believe that the judge could have been wearing a wire, because he wouldn't have asked the questions he did, if that had been the case.

Before Runner had come to the police station, he had tried to remember if he had said anything incriminating during his conversation with Lancaster. He couldn't come up with anything, so he continued to play the game. "Yeah, that's the same Richie whose name you heard on the recording you made."

Once he heard the word 'recording,' Tedesco spoke up. "What recording? You shouldn't have been recording my client unless you had a warrant."

Walker wasn't sure how to respond, but he figured the truth might prevent the discussion from being sidetracked. "It was on a public street."

Tedesco started to say something, but Runner stopped him. "It doesn't matter. It's okay."

Walker was a little surprised, but he didn't let it show. "And you said that this Cardarelli disappeared?"

"That's what I heard."

"And what does all this have to do with the pictures Lancaster asked about?" he followed up.

"Pretty much everything."

"Are you finally ready to tell us about what you have on the judge, or are we going to continue to play twenty questions?"

"Do we have a deal about my uncle?"

Walker hesitated. But he realized that he had to take what he could get. "Assuming that your information is as ironclad as you suggested, and there are no loopholes."

"There aren't," Runner assured him. "It's rock solid. You won't have any doubts, once you hear it."

"If that's true, then we have a deal," replied Walker.

Runner began his narrative, one he had rehearsed ten times before he had come here.

"The judge is a pervert. He's into child pornography big time. He got Tony Sarno to hire some photographer to take pictures. But then Tony got arrested. The judge needed to make sure Tony didn't get convicted; otherwise the pictures would stop. So he had Richie beat up the judge that was supposed to preside over Tony's trial. Lancaster took over, and Tony got off."

Munoz spoke up. "First of all, how do you know all this, if you and your uncle weren't involved?"

Runner had anticipated the question. He answered with the partial truth. "Lancaster and my uncle have been friends ever since they were little. Lancaster wanted my uncle to go into the child pornography business with him, but my uncle refused. Then, when Tony got arrested, Lancaster asked my uncle to fix the case by bribing one of the jurors. When my uncle wouldn't do it, that's when Richie Cardarelli stepped in."

Walker spoke next. "And you're willing to testify to all of this?"

"Yeah," said Runner. "But I don't think that's going to be necessary."

Walker had major doubts that Runner was telling the whole truth, but he didn't interrupt him.

Runner continued. "After Tony got off, the judge enlisted him to set up the child pornography Web sites. Tony was real good with computers. Eventually, whatever Tony was doing with the pictures didn't satisfy the judge, so he told Tony he wanted new ones taken. That's when the Allen kid got snatched."

Runner looked at Munoz with a half-smile on his face. "In case you're wondering how I know all this, Tony told me."

"I thought you two weren't that close," Munoz reminded him.

Runner continued to smile. "What can I tell you? People trust me; I'm a good listener."

Munoz appeared disgusted. "Just tell us the rest."

"Somehow the judge found out that this Josh Raybeck was the one who had supposedly taken the new pictures. The judge wanted to know where they were, and where the kid was. So, I'm guessing he must have sent Richie to find out. I heard that there were cigarette burns. That would be Richie's style."

"Why would this Richie kill Josh Raybeck?" the detective challenged.

"If he didn't get the answers he wanted, he would have been pissed off enough to kill him. And if he did get the answers he wanted, he would have eliminated any witnesses. Either way, this Raybeck didn't have a chance."

Walker appeared skeptical. "Why did Lancaster ask you where the pictures were earlier today?"

"He probably thought Tony had told me. But you heard what I said. There are no pictures."

"But you don't know that?"

"Not for sure, no," admitted Runner.

"Why did you tell Lancaster that this was all his fault?"

As difficult as it was, Runner maintained eye contact with Walker. "Because it was, and what he did was bringing heat on my uncle, even though my uncle didn't do anything wrong."

"Why do you think Richie Cardarelli disappeared?"

"Probably because he didn't get the judge what he wanted, and he figured the judge would be upset."

"The judge seemed more concerned than upset."

"I don't know what to tell you. I'm not really tuned into the judge's feelings."

Walker was sure that Runner knew a lot more than he was letting on, but he couldn't see a clear way to trip him up. "All right. Tell me what else you have on Judge Lancaster."

Runner reached into his pocket and extracted a couple of sheets of paper. "This."

"What's that?"

"Something Tony Sarno gave me. He kept it to protect himself, although obviously, it didn't work. I assume you have somebody who's good with computers. Give him these."

Runner handed over the pages. "There's a list of encrypted child pornography Web sites with the passwords. But better yet, there's a list of five offshore accounts that the judge has been funneling money into from the monthly fees from the subscribers."

Walker took the papers from Runner. Although he still thought this was all too pat, if Peter Stansky could confirm that the accounts could be traced back to the judge, they had him dead to rights.

After a few minutes passed, Tedesco said, "I'm assuming that if all this checks out, we have a deal, and there'll be no need for my client to testify."

Walker spoke without enthusiasm. "It appears that way."

Tedesco and Runner stayed in the conference room while Walker and Munoz returned to his office. Walker sent the information to Peter Stansky, and thirty minutes later he called back.

"There's no question that these accounts have Lancaster's fingerprints all over them," he told Walker. "This will definitely hold up in court. They're solid. Although I have to tell you, without the passwords, it would have been next to impossible to find the links. Whoever did this knew what he was doing."

"Okay, thanks, Peter," Walker said quietly.

"You don't sound very excited," Stansky observed.

"I feel like I've been sold a bill of goods," sighed the agent. "But if you tell me it's the real thing, then so be it."

"Do you want me to keep digging?" Stansky asked.

"No," Walker responded. "Maybe it is time for me to retire. Evidently, my gut's not working the way it used to."

Walker went into the conference room by himself to deliver the news that they had a deal. Tedesco thanked him. Runner didn't.

Walker and Munoz spent the next half hour formulating a plan to execute the arrest warrant on Lancaster. They decided that they'd take it to the federal prosecutor in the morning. Judge William A. Lancaster would be charged with multiple counts of trafficking in child pornography.

On the ride back to Barrington, Runner readily acknowledged to himself that Tony Sarno was much better with computers than he was. And then he smiled, and said out loud, "But I'm still pretty good."

Runner maintained a self-satisfied expression on his face as he thought about how the last half hour had gone. He was so wrapped up in mentally patting himself on the back that he failed to notice the car that had been following him for the past several miles.

Judge Lancaster was arrested the following afternoon. Walker wasn't part of the arrest team, but word had come back to him that a preliminary search of the judge's computer had found child pornography, including what was suspected to be altered images of Eric Allen.

The judge had immediately wanted to make some sort of deal. He was willing to cop to possession of child pornography, but not to the more serious trafficking charges. He maintained that he knew nothing about the offshore accounts. Unfortunately for the judge, there was a lot of evidence to the contrary. And as far as making a deal was concerned, anything he had to offer in terms of Runner or Michael Corwin was old news.

Walker shared all this information with Munoz, and then added, "It looks like the judge is going away for a long time, and he should. But I wish I was totally convinced that Runner and his uncle weren't more involved. I guess I should just let it go." He paused. "I think I'll need one more day to finish up the paperwork, and then I'll be on my way. It appears that retirement beckons."

Munoz looked skeptical. "That didn't sound particularly convincing."

Walker sighed. "I don't know. We'll see. I'm going to go work in the conference room. I need to spread out these files."

"Okay."

A half hour went by and Walker rushed back into Munoz' office. "You won't believe what just happened. I got a call from Peter Stansky. He took another look at the stuff Runner gave us, and he found something he hadn't seen when he first looked at it. I don't understand how it works, but he was able to determine that those offshore accounts were only switched over to Lancaster two days ago. Somebody else owned them before that. And we both know who that is."

"Is there any way to prove it?" asked the detective.

"Peter says it's all circumstantial, but the fact that Runner had all the passwords is pretty incriminating. It's true that he could have gotten them from Tony Sarno, but Tony couldn't have linked them to the judge, Tony was already dead." A pause. "Runner's arrogance may have done him in this time. He pushed for the deal to protect his uncle, but he didn't ask for anything for himself; he's fair game."

"Do you think we can move on him yet?"

"Not today, maybe tomorrow. I need to get more details from Peter."

"When was the uncle scheduled for his treatment in New York? Runner might not be around."

"Good point," Walker acknowledged. "I've got Tedesco's card in the conference room. I'll call him on some pretext and find out when they're leaving."

Walker was gone for twenty minutes. When he returned, Munoz could tell something was wrong. "What's the matter?"

"This has got to be the most bizarre case I've ever worked. I just talked to Tedesco. The police in Barrington called him early this morning. Are you ready? Runner and his uncle were found murdered."

"What?" shouted Munoz.

"He didn't have all the details, but that's what he told me."

"You can't be serious!" the detective exclaimed. "Let me call over to Barrington and see what I can find out."

"Okay," agreed Walker. "I'm going to call Peter and tell him to hold off doing anything else until we know more."

Fifteen minutes later, Walker and Munoz were back in Munoz' office. Walker asked, "Anything?"

"Yeah. They've already made an arrest; his name's Gino Cardarelli. Ring any bells? He's *Richie* Cardarelli's brother. You remember, the guy the judge asked about, and Runner told us had disappeared. Well evidently, his brother found out that Runner was the one who made Richie disappear *permanently,* and he figured he'd return the favor. They think the uncle was just collateral damage."

Walker shook his head. "This case … it's hard to believe. And now we'll never know exactly who was guilty of what."

"You're probably right." Munoz paused. "So, how did you make out with Peter?"

"Actually, he has to continue investigating the offshore accounts. Anything he finds, he has to pass along to the federal prosecutor, which probably means the trafficking charges against the judge will be dropped. But he's still facing serious jail time, even if we can't pin anything else on him."

Walker and Munoz sat in silence for several minutes, and then Walker said, "I feel badly about Josh Raybeck; he certainly did some questionable things, but he didn't deserve what happened to him. All the other people involved were a lot more guilty than he was."

Walker paused. "Remember when I told you about my first commander, the one who talked about 'making a pearl?' "

"Yeah."

"Well actually, he had a lot of sayings. There's another one I remember that fits this case perfectly. Obviously, it didn't happen very often, but when a case somehow got 'resolved,' although not in the way you expected, or even the way you wanted, he called it 'a dead heat on a merry-go-round.' "

Munoz smiled.

"There was a movie with that title that came out in the sixties. I think that's where he got it from. I watched the movie once; it was pretty good." Another pause. "It's funny, I haven't thought about that saying in years –a dead heat on a merry-go-round. But that kind of sums it up, doesn't it?"

EPILOGUE

Three Months Later

Munoz was about to leave his office when the phone rang. "Detective Munoz."

"Hey, Dave. It's Craig Walker."

"Craig, how're you doing?"

"Can't complain. How about you?"

"The same," the detective replied. "So, to what do I owe this call from a distinguished former FBI agent?"

"Pretty formal, aren't we?"

"Just trying to raise the status of the law enforcement community."

"Oh, so you're going to retire also?" Walker joked.

Munoz laughed. "Speaking of that, how's retirement treating you?"

"It was great for the first month or so, like an extended vacation. But now ... I mean ... I'm glad I retired when I did; it was time. But I feel like I should still be doing something. Actually, that's one of the reasons I called. I don't know if you remember Peter Stansky, but he retired shortly after I did. We've kept in touch, and ... well, we've got a proposition that we'd like to run by you."

THE END

ABOUT THOMAS HALL

Thomas Hall is a former English teacher and middle school and high school principal. Two of the schools where he was the principal received national recognition for their academic excellence. He and his wife Marcia live in Central Massachusetts. They have three adult children.

Mr. Hall was born on Long Island, New York and lived there for the first seventeen years of his life before his family moved to Massachusetts. After graduating from high school he received a full athletic scholarship to Northeastern University for track. He received his Bachelor's and Master's degrees from Northeastern.

Although writing has always been a passion, he limited his efforts to short stories and non-fiction articles until after he retired and had sufficient time to tackle a novel.

When Mr. Hall is not writing, he enjoys reading, going to the movies, jogging, and playing softball. Over the past several years he has participated in numerous Senior Softball tournaments throughout the United States and Canada.

He is currently working on his next novel. You can contact him at tomhallauthor@aol.com.

CPSIA information can be obtained at www.ICGtesting.com
Printed in the USA
LVOW13s1032091113

360570LV00001B/155/P